his eleventh hour

A HAMMOND FAMILY FARM NOVEL

IVORY PEAKS ROMANCE
BOOK 11

LIZ ISAACSON

Tarr Olson adjusted the collar of his button-down shirt, checked his reflection in the mirror above the sink, and tried not to wonder for the eighth time whether he looked like a man going to Thanksgiving dinner with his friends, or a man chasing a woman who'd made it very clear she didn't want him.

He sighed as he pulled his sleeves down over his forearms and buttoned the cuffs slowly, methodically. His knuckles were still a little scraped from trying to fix the busted heater in the RV —something he had yet to mention to Tuck, because he wasn't in the mood to be razzed for *still* living in the RV, two months after the wedding.

He didn't want to live with newlyweds. It wasn't that hard to understand, was it?

So he'd bought an RV, and he parked it at the site where his house had been under construction for the past nine weeks. He appreciated that Tuck and Bobbie Jo let him shower in the mansion, and he actually liked the coziness of the RV.

He'd never needed a huge house; Tarr much preferred a wide open space, a big yard, a huge pasture with as many horses as he could put on the land. So the RV wasn't a bad place to live—if he was still living in Tennessee.

Colorado had a much different winter season, and Tarr obsessively checked the weather every day to make sure he had the supplies and energy he needed to survive.

Honestly, survival was so hard these days.

He exhaled and rolled his shoulders, loosening the tension that sat across the back of his neck rent-free. From his work around the facility, to keeping himself fed and warm in a shelter that didn't have electricity or running water, to making sure Briar Prescott was taken care of—all of it had combined in the past three months to show Tarr he only had to sleep a few hours each night.

For a moment, he considered texting Hunter, Deacon, and Tucker and telling them he wasn't feeling well and wouldn't make it to the farm for turkey and cranberry sauce.

But if he did that, Tucker would show up on his doorstep.

Maybe he should take a leaf out of Tuck's game plan when it came to Briar. Tarr had watched his best friend flirt shamelessly with his now-wife. His feelings for Bobbie Jo had never been a secret to anyone, but Tarr felt smothered by his hidden, repressed feelings for Briar.

"Thanksgiving," he said to himself as he crossed to the small closet and pulled out a jacket. "Time for food, family...and finally drawing the line."

He'd asked Briar Prescott out a couple of times since her encounter with the coyote. She'd turned him down both times. So he'd retreated again—but only when it came to trying to get her to go out with him.

He showed up at her cabin every single day, whether she told him to leave her alone or not. He wouldn't. He couldn't.

She'd healed really well from the attack, to be honest. Her leg only bore a scar now, not that she ever let Tarr see it. He'd seen it when the doctor had removed the stitches, and he could still see the marks all along her abdomen, whether his eyes were open or closed.

That side wound hadn't been as bad as he'd originally thought, though Briar had gotten seventeen stitches to get her skin sealed back together again. He'd sat with her while she slept, ordered or made food so she could keep her strength up, and set timers to make sure she took her medicines on time. Then she wouldn't wake up in a massive amount of pain.

He'd seen her cry, and listened to her yell at him to get out and never come back, and held her in his arms while he soothed her and his feelings for her deepened and deepened and deepened.

"So not fair," he muttered—what he usually did when telling the Lord he wasn't satisfied with how things were going in his life.

And when it came to Briar Prescott, Tarr was absolutely dissatisfied. He wanted so much more than she'd allowed, and he swiped his phone up from the top of the slim bureau he'd crammed in beside his bed.

He'd texted her a few hours ago, before he'd gone out to do the morning feeding, about the Thanksgiving luncheon out at the Hammond Family Farm.

I'm good, she'd said. *But thanks.*

He growled, because he *hated* it when she told him *I'm good.*

Ab—so—lute—ly—hate—d—it.

He looked up, his mind sparking at him, situations between Tucker and Bobbie Jo firing through his memory.

Maybe he really did need to be more explicit with Briar.

At the very least, he was done following her rules. He was done waiting for permission to care. Done waiting for her to recognize how good they could be together—if only she'd let him in.

"I just want a chance, Lord," he whispered. "Is that too much to ask? A real opportunity?" He closed his eyes and forced his mind to go blank, quiet, still. "Not a single date with hardly any conversation, and not me forcing myself on her to make sure she heals up good."

He opened his eyes, seeing the narrow interior of his RV in a whole new way. "A real try."

He felt like he'd thrown out everything he had, but deep down, he knew he hadn't. It only felt like the eleventh hour, because of the miserable way he laid awake at night, dreaming of holding Briar when they were both happy and laughing, instead of when she sobbed into his arms after a painful physical therapy appointment, or wept into his chest, frustrated about the slow speed at which she'd healed.

But healed she had. Almost all the way now, though Tarr caught her limping for a couple of steps sometimes, when she first got up from a table or couch.

His alarm went off, because Tarr did everything by alarms. Then he wasn't late, and he didn't have to think about anything further out than the moment he lived in.

After silencing it, he grabbed his cowboy hat from the hook by the door and walked out into the chilly November air, boots thudding softly on the steps of the RV. The sun had turned weak as they moved into winter, and just because Tarr had lived through a Colorado winter before didn't mean he enjoyed it.

He slid into his truck, started the engine, and turned the heat on full blast. The RV hadn't held heat worth a darn since the first snowstorm, and while he could make do, he didn't particularly enjoy wearing a beanie to bed, pulling on down puffy pants, and layering a feathery sleeping bag over the one he slept in.

"I need a more permanent solution to my shelter problem," he said as he glanced over to the construction site currently covered in white, opaque plastic sheeting. The bad weather the past week or so had stalled the progress on his cabin build completely, and it hadn't been going well before that.

Sighing, he drove away, putting those problems in his rearview mirror for now. Nothing to do about them on Thanksgiving, though he did consider calling a nearby hotel and getting a room there for the next month.

Then, he'd have access to a hot shower any time he wanted, and Tarr could admit he'd already scoped out the hotel options close to the farm where Tuck worked with rodeo stars and Tarr trained animals for them to use.

He turned onto the gravel road that led to the far edge of the property, where Briar's cabin sat tucked back against a patch of pines. It wasn't much, but it was homey—one of the original structures on the ranch from way back when—and Briar had made it her own in the time she'd lived there.

He'd been inside that house more times in the past few months than he'd expected. Starting the night of the coyote attack, when he'd dropped everything and sprinted to the barn because she'd called him.

Him.

Not Tuck. Not Bobbie Jo. Not anyone else who worked with them at the facility.

Him.

And from that moment on, it had been *him*, whether she liked it or not.

He'd shown up at the hospital and sat outside her room until they let him in. He'd brought Wiggins in to visit when she was missing her dog so bad it broke his heart. He'd run to the pharmacy for her meds, brought groceries when she couldn't stand upright, and helped her into her bed when the pain flared so bad it left her shaking.

He'd been there when she couldn't sleep.

When the nightmares came.

When her hand trembled too hard to hold a coffee cup, and when she finally—*finally*—walked across the barn without needing to lean on a wall or brace herself against a railing.

And through all of it, she kept trying to keep him on the outside of the walls she'd so clearly built around herself.

But he wasn't going anywhere.

Not tonight.

It was Thanksgiving, for crying out loud. No one should be alone on Thanksgiving.

Tarr pulled into her driveway, eyed the front windows, and killed the engine. The porch light was on, and smoke curled lazily from the chimney. He took a breath, climbed out, and walked slowly toward the front porch.

Wiggins would know he'd arrived, so he wasn't surprised to hear the hound barking inside. He couldn't hear Briar's correction, but he knew she'd hiss at the dog to be quiet.

He climbed the steps—the second one from the top sagging under his weight; that needed to be fixed—and moved right into the door to knock.

Tap, tap.

He tucked his hands into his jacket pockets, stepped back, and waited.

Beyond the door, claws scrambled on wood, and that made him smile. When Wiggins appeared in the window beside the door, tail wagging wildly, he chuckled. Oh, how he loved that dog.

And the nights when Briar let him bring Wiggins home with him? Heaven, because the dog slept cuddled up next to him and kept him *so* warm.

He'd really like a good woman for that, and of course, Briar was the image in his head whenever he thought about who he'd like to get to know better.

Despite his constant attention to her for the past few months, she'd revealed very little about herself. Tarr hadn't pushed her either, because God had told him to focus on her physical healing. She'd had a lot of that to do, and Tarr simply prayed that the Lord would give him more time with Briar.

Wiggins barked happily and disappeared, only to reappear a couple of seconds later. Briar wouldn't be happy about that, but Tarr had already knocked.

It took a good ten seconds for Briar to pull open the door, and Wiggins came wagging out to greet him.

"Hey, buddy." Tarr crouched down and scrubbed Wiggins's head and jowls, stroking his hands along his neck and down his back.

"I said I wasn't coming."

Tarr looked up at Briar, her blue eyes captivating him the moment his met hers. "It's Thanksgiving."

"I don't even like cranberry sauce."

"Good thing there are dozens of other things to eat, then." He straightened and took in her bright purple pajamas, this pair one he'd seen before. Yellow and blue stars covered them, but none of their shine had spread to Briar's expression.

Tarr leaned a shoulder against the frame and smiled. "Happy Thanksgiving to you too."

She'd left her hair down today, her curls loose and wild

around her face, like she'd just pulled it out of a bun and hadn't planned on seeing anyone. His chest tightened, and not just because of how good she looked like that.

"I'm not going," she said again, softer this time.

Tarr didn't move. "Yeah, you are."

"No, I'm—"

"Briar." He straightened, folding his arms. "You're not staying home alone on Thanksgiving. That's ridiculous. So you can go change and get ready yourself." He pulled his phone out of his pocket, his heartbeat positively pounding at him as he casually checked the time. "We have about ten minutes before we need to leave."

He only moved his eyes as he looked at her again. He swallowed, about to throw gasoline on a live flame, what with her glare kicking up a notch like that.

"So you can go get ready, or I'm going to carry you to my truck wearing those pajamas. Your choice."

She blinked, clearly stunned. So maybe being more like Tuck would play in Tarr's favor. Or maybe Tarr just hadn't spoken to Briar like this since she'd been injured, and she didn't know what to do with it.

Wiggins sat at his feet, both of them facing Briar as they waited for her answer. He panted, closing his eyes halfway as if that would keep Briar's irritation at a minimum.

Oh, to be a dog.

Tarr's nerves ran freely through his body, especially when Briar opened her mouth.

Closed it.

Glared.

But he didn't flinch. In fact, he found himself smoothly folding his arms. "I'll wait right here."

two

Briar Prescott stared at the cowboy standing on her front porch, waves of shock cascading through her. Tarr Olson had rendered her mute like this several times in the past couple of months, but not for the same reason.

Right now, she'd label him belligerent.

No, that's you, she thought.

Tarr glared back at her, unyielding—and that wasn't usually a word she used when thinking about him. Which, honestly, Briar couldn't get this man out of her head on the best of days, and now she'd have to see his dark-haired, dark-eyed good-looks glaring at her as she tried to fall asleep.

He stood there, all calm confidence and quiet steel, like he hadn't just threatened to bodily carry her—*in her pajamas*—to his truck.

And, oh, she believed he would.

He'd told her several times that he wouldn't leave her alone while she needed him, and he'd come back over and over, even after she'd treated him badly. After she'd told him to leave her alone. After she'd rejected his offer to take her to dinner.

Wiggins sat at his feet, tongue hanging out in a dumb, happy pant, as if he was also just thrilled about the idea of her getting dragged to Thanksgiving dinner in flannel and stars.

She blinked, her brain still trying to catch up. Of all the nerve.

"You can't just show up and boss me around," she managed to say, clutching the doorframe like it could anchor her.

"I'm not leaving you home on Thanksgiving. I just can't do it."

"I'm fine."

"I don't think you are—and I just don't care to let *you* boss *me* around anymore." Electricity zipped between them, the energy striking her straight in the heart even as her jaw dropped open.

Tarr deflated, those broad shoulders holding up that sexy black leather jacket sinking. "Briar, sweetheart," he murmured. "It's *Thanksgiving*. No one should be alone today, and I just...God wouldn't let me drive away while you were still here." He reached out and brushed the tips of his fingers along hers. "Please, go change your clothes and brush your teeth. We're down to eight minutes."

Him and his timers.

"I don't want you to be alone."

She hated how those words hit her right in the soft and quiet parts of her heart, which sat far too close to the place she didn't let anyone touch. Not anymore, at least.

But if there was someone she wanted to let in, it was Tarr.

"I like being alone," she lied.

Tarr arched one eyebrow and waited, steady as a fence post,

the kind of cowboy who wasn't going to budge until something gave.

And for once, it wasn't going to be him.

Briar exhaled hard through her nose, turned, and stalked back into the house. "Come in and close the door, then. It's not warm out there, cowboy."

She stormed down the hall and slammed her bedroom door behind her. Not because she was mad—well, she *was* mad—but mostly because she needed to breathe without the heady scent of Tarr's cologne infecting her rational brain cells. If she looked at him for one more second, she might do something foolish, like let him see her vulnerability. Or that it meant a lot to her that he cared, that he wouldn't give up on her, that he *saw* her.

In her bedroom, Briar turned in a full circle, trying to get her bearings. She really just wanted to go across the hall to her painting studio and use the good light coming in the west windows to create something amazing.

After that, she'd planned to bake off the homemade mac and cheese she'd gotten from Shelley, a woman Briar bought food from all year. She was a good cook and was trying to support a daughter on a highly competitive dance team.

Briar liked lemon zucchini bread she didn't have to make, and chicken tamales, and Shelley's mac and cheese couldn't be beat.

"I was going to watch that romance with the sled dogs," she grumped as she pulled off her pajama top and reached for a dark purple sweater. She sniffed it first, found it fresh enough, and pulled it over her head.

She wanted to leave her teeth unbrushed just to show Tarr that she didn't have to do everything he said. But in the end, Briar hated leaving the house with dirty teeth, and she scrubbed as fast as she could before sitting down on the bench beside her bedroom door and pulling on a pair of cowgirl boots.

She sighed as she stood up, her anger blown out. She now wore real clothes, and her very-near future held sitting at a table full of people who actually liked each other. People who had *families.*

People who weren't broken.

Because she still felt broken, though she looked pretty normal on the outside.

It had been almost three months since the coyote attack. Twelve weeks since she'd woken up in a hospital bed with Tarr Olson sitting in the corner, watching her like she was something fragile and precious at the same time.

He'd never left, not really. He was there the next day. And the next. And every day after that.

He brought all the foods she liked. Medicine. Wiggins. Movies. Her favorite soda pop.

Himself.

And Briar, who had lived so long with no one to rely on but herself, had let him in. Not all the way, but more than she'd ever meant to.

She'd cried in front of him. Clung to him when the pain got too sharp. Let him lift her into her own bed, help her with zippers, bring her ice packs, and distract her with dumb, cowboy-dad jokes and dog stories when she couldn't sleep.

Tarr Olson had become her *person*—and she hated how easily it had happened. How much she wanted to reach for him sometimes, even when she didn't need the help. How, when something happened, he was the first person she wanted to call and tell.

She joined him out in the living room, where he barely glanced up from his phone. "Ready?"

"Yes." She watched him as he stood, his demeanor much calmer and slower than she'd expected for him demanding she spend the holiday with him.

Because he didn't want her to be alone.

Because he cared, even though he'd literally said he didn't care what she thought or wanted.

"Let's go, sweetheart." The smirk on Tarr's face—half-satisfied, half-something else entirely—made her want to punch him and kiss him in equal measure.

She had no idea what to do with that, so she simply said, "Okay," dumbly, and let him put his hand on the small of her back and guide her out of her own home with pure magic sparkling down her spine from his touch.

* * *

The Hammond Family Farm looked like something from a greeting card. Soft white lights hung along the wraparound porch. A festive wooden turkey welcomed everyone to the farmhouse. Laughter spilled out the front door as they approached, because someone had already opened it.

Tucker, of course. Briar would recognize his loud laugh anywhere.

Briar hesitated at the bottom step, and Tarr automatically slowed with her, though Tuck said, "Hey, you guys made it," with his smile as wide as a mile.

Tarr took her hand and dang near pulled her up the steps, laughing as he did. "Hey, brother." He released her to hug Tuck, and Briar put a smile on her face and did the same.

Wiggins bounded into the house like he belonged there, but Briar let the two cowboys go ahead of her before she followed.

Inside, the warmth hit her like a hug. So did Bobbie Jo,

immediately wrapping Briar in an embrace that nearly knocked her sideways. "I'm so glad you came," Bobbie Jo said, grinning. "We're just putting out the place cards right now."

She led her down a hallway, past a formal living room, and into the back of the house. An ornate table had been set with candles, autumn leaves, and more soft lights. Two of Molly's teenagers squabbled over who should sit where while Molly and Hunter bustled around in the kitchen together.

Things this busy and loud usually overwhelmed her, but today, it didn't. Deacon nodded at her with a warm smile, and Jane and Cord waved from the couch where they were trying to wrangle their son into a bib. But oh, Clint wasn't having any of it, which made Briar smile at the adorable baby.

A table positioned against the wall groaned under the weight of the food. Turkey. Rolls. Three kinds of potatoes. Even as she watched, Molly set down a bowl of salad on the end and turned to ask, "Baby, where's that butter?"

"It's on the table, Momma," Lisa said. "The turkeys? Daddy said to put them on the table."

"They're on the table," Hunter said, his grin infectious. He trained it on Briar, wiped his hands on his apron and came toward her. "Howdy, Briar."

"Hey," she said, almost cowed by his height and presence. "Thank you so much for having me."

"I'm glad Tarr convinced you to come." Hunter shook her hand and turned as his younger kids started to argue over where their older siblings had placed them at the table.

Tarr came to her side and nodded to another woman in the living room. "That's Alaska Whitby," he said, his voice low enough to be meant just for her. "She's a riding instructor here at the farm and didn't have anywhere else to go."

Another stray, Briar thought, but it comforted her that she wasn't the only one there. She also noted how Tarr had found out who she was and come to tell her, knowing that she wouldn't like sitting down to a meal with someone she didn't know.

She remained on the sidelines, Tarr's steadiness at her side. She'd forgotten what this felt like. People passing plates. Joking. Teasing. Talking over each other. The scrape of chairs, the clink of silverware, the scent of hot, baked bread.

"We're ready!" Hunter yelled as he pulled a tray out of the oven. "Molly's finishing up with the gravy, so it's time to sit down."

"Everyone has a place card with their name on it at their spot," Ryder, Hunter's oldest, said. "You can trade places if the other person is cool with it." He exchanged a look with his daddy, who smiled at him like Ryder was made of gold.

What would that feel like?

Briar hadn't had anyone look at her like that in so long.

Wrong, shouted in her mind, and her eyes migrated to Tarr as he once again took her hand and led her over to the table. Tarr didn't look at her right now, but he'd definitely looked at her with that soft, loving edge in his eyes that only confused her more than anything.

"You're here, sweetheart," he said, pulling out her seat. "I'm right next to you."

Bobbie Jo sat on her other side, with Tucker next to her. Across from Briar sat Alaska, with Cord and Jane down on this end of the table too, and Deacon and the kids flowing down and around the end of the table where Molly and Hunter sat.

She blinked fast and sat very still, letting the glorious, familial energy wash over her.

"Let's pray," Molly said into the settling silence at the table, and everyone seemed to know what to do. They joined hands, and Briar quickly latched onto Bobbie Jo's on her right and sighed silently as Tarr once again secured her smaller hand in his much larger one.

"Ryder, buddy, you're up," Hunter said.

"Please remember it's Thanksgiving," Molly said. "It's not a race to see how fast you can say the prayer, okay?"

Her son grinned at her, and Briar bowed her head as everyone else did. These movements, this thing they all knew, it grounded her. She found herself exhaling as Ryder started with, "Dear Lord, we are so grateful for Thy bounteous blessing in our lives."

He spoke at a normal speed, and he went through his gratitude for the farm, the horses, the cattle, and their friends and family before he asked for a single thing.

Like a lightning bolt to her mind, Briar knew she needed to be more grateful. Even the little things needed to be recognized, and she lifted her head after Ryder had said, "Amen," properly chastened.

Tarr took her plate as he stood. "Be right back."

She stared after him as others queued up to get food too. Tuck and Bobbie Jo remained at the table, and only Cord went with Clint to get something to eat, leaving Jane behind as well.

"You look amazing in purple," Jane said kindly, and it took Briar a moment to realize she was talking to her.

"Thank you," she blurted out. "This is one of my favorite sweaters."

Jane smiled and nodded. "So, are you and Tarr seeing each other?"

Briar reached for her glass of ice, and then the sparkling apple-grape cider. "Uh, no," she said. "He's just persistent and irritating and wouldn't let me stay home today."

Jane's smile faltered completely, and she glanced over to

Bobbie Jo. "And I thought you were salty," she said good-naturedly.

Bobbie Jo turned toward them. "Is Briar being thorny?"

"It's Tarr," she said by way of explanation.

Bobbie Jo grinned and nodded. "He rubs her the wrong way." She got to her feet as Tucker did, and she squeezed Briar's shoulder as she passed. Bobbie Jo was a bit salty from time to time, but she and Tucker were also the cutest couple in the whole world.

He treated her like royalty, and she respected him like a king.

Tarr returned with their plates, and he set a fully loaded one in front of her with the words, "I'm going to go snag the strawberry jam."

Jane got up as Alaska returned, and Briar wasn't sure if she could pick up her fork and start eating or not. Despite her reservations about coming, the turkey steamed in front of her, looking juicy and delicious with the gravy and mashed potatoes alongside it.

No cranberry sauce, she noted, but plenty of bread and butter. Tarr really knew how to earn gold stars, that was for dang sure.

"How long have you and Tarr been dating?" Alaska asked as he returned with his coveted jam.

Briar stared at her now, wondering what everyone else saw when they looked at her with him. "I'm sorry, what?"

Alaska sighed. "He knew exactly what to get you—and not to get you. He's so sweet, the way he took care of you." She beamed over to Tarr as he tuned into the conversation. "I so need a boyfriend like him." She grinned, her blue eyes brightening. "Do you have any brothers?"

Tarr, to his eternal credit, blinked at her in apparent surprise. Briar sat frozen, throat tight.

"So, how long have you been together?" Alaska finally put a bite of cooked carrot in her mouth, and Briar almost wished she'd choke on it.

Briar's heart beat so loud she could barely hear the noise from the rest of the Thanksgiving crowd, most of them returning to the table now, the chatter increasing into a dull roar that made zero sense to her.

Tarr turned to look at her, brows drawn down slightly. "How long have we known each other?" His eyes searched her face, and horror washed through her, because she didn't know what to say. She didn't *have* words for the way he made her feel sometimes. The way he made her *want* to feel.

Tarr smiled, gentle and sure. "We'll have to work it out tomorrow, while we're on our breakfast date." He scooped up a bite of creamed peas and put them in his mouth.

Briar stared at him. "Breakfast? Tomorrow?"

Together? screamed silently through her mind.

"Just say yes," he said quietly, tapping her fork with the tines of his. "We're eating now, sweetheart."

She wanted to argue against a breakfast date tomorrow morning. And snap at him that she knew how to pick up her fork and start eating. She couldn't, not with so many people around.

Oh, this Tarr Olson. Smart and handsome, he'd brought her to a Thanksgiving meal to show her that some families were normal, and then asked her out in an environment where she couldn't say no.

She put her hand on his knee, satisfied that he flinched and that his gaze flew to hers. "Yes, I can't wait for breakfast tomorrow. Should be a real *scream*."

She gave Alaska a tight smile she hoped didn't come across as too manic, then she picked up her fork and cut a piece of turkey. Laughter rose up from the other end of the table, leaving Briar to stew as she put that first juicy bite of turkey and gravy in her mouth.

Thoughts flew from one side of her mind to the other, things like, *Why does Tarr make me feel like I'm on fire?* to *What do other people see when they look at us?* to *How did he know to get me double mashed potatoes, no peas, and extra bread?*

In short, when had Tarr Olson snuck into her life, and why couldn't she seem to kick him back out?

Worse, why didn't she want to?

Yes, she had a lot to talk about at breakfast tomorrow—assuming she didn't cancel between now and then.

Even if you do, she thought as the salted butter melted over her tongue. *Tarr will just stand on your front porch until you agree to go with him.*

She glanced over to him, and blast him all the way to the moon, he gifted her with a small smile, the kind meant only for her.

He knew he'd won, and she knew she'd be dining with him tomorrow morning whether she wanted to or not.

three

arr drew a card, getting the exact thing he needed to go out. His heartbeat skipped at the six of spades he deftly slid between two other cards. He looked up, his gaze automatically meeting Tucker's.

"Tarr," his best friend warned. "Don't you dare go out."

Tarr couldn't stop the grin as it spread across his face. "I can't help it," he said. "The cards are just being lucky tonight."

"You have got to be kidding me." Jane groaned as she threw her hand down. "How do you win *every* time?"

"It's not every time." Tarr's eyes switched to Briar, who now sat at his side. She wore the cutest little frown between her eyes as she tried to peek over his forearm to see his hand. He automatically recoiled his cards into his chest.

"Are you cheatin'?" he asked.

"You're gonna go out anyway," Tuck said, and he threw his cards down too. "Just do it."

Tarr chuckled as he laid out his hand, which ended the

round. Technically, everyone had one more turn, all the way around to him again, but Tuck pushed his chair back and stood.

"You don't want to finish?" Deacon asked.

"I'm not going to be able to go out," Tuck said. "One card's not going to make a difference." He strode into the kitchen, where he opened the freezer and pulled out a container of ice cream.

They'd had a delicious turkey dinner followed by a movie, where Tarr had sat next to Briar on Hunter and Molly's enormous couch, trying to formulate a way to hold her hand. For two solid hours, he'd thought about it. He'd shifted left, then right, hoping she'd somehow sink into his body.

He hadn't been able to come up with anything, which was simply ridiculous. He'd had girlfriends before. Plenty of them. He'd never struggled to get a woman's attention, but something about Briar had him walking, breathing, and living on eggshells.

When the movie ended, the party had come upstairs for the pie bar, where Hunt and his kids had served key lime pie, coconut cream, banana cream, and chocolate banana cream, in addition to the classic Thanksgiving pumpkin pie.

Now, they'd been playing card games for about an hour. And fine, Tarr had won every round, even the two where he hadn't gone out first.

A yawn pulled through his chest, and Tarr looked over to Briar while Deacon took his turn. He leaned down, a preposterous amount of excitement parading through him when she migrated toward him too. "You almost ready to go, sweetheart?"

She kept her attention on her cards, studying them as if she'd never seen them before, but she nodded and looked up as Deacon played.

"That's the best I can do," he said grumpily. "You go out so fast, man."

The game continued, with Ryder playing for Tuck, who ate mint chocolate chip ice cream right out of the container, and people playing as many cards as they could. Finally, Jane added up the scores.

"Tarr's the winner, of course," she said, and she grinned at him before turning to find her husband. "I think we're gonna head out, Molly. We've got to get Clint home and in bed."

"We're gonna go too," Tarr said, seizing onto Jane's words. "I've got to get myself to bed."

Molly stayed on the couch, but Hunter rose to come say goodbye to them as Deacon and Ryder started cleaning up the card game.

Tarr and Briar stayed at the table and helped too, and once he wouldn't be leaving a mess for Hunter and Molly, Tarr got up from the table too.

"Leftovers, Tarr?" Jane picked up a ready-made container. "Briar? It's turkey, mashed potatoes and gravy, and green beans." She nodded to a series of brown paper bags. "Bread in there."

"Yeah, I'll take one," Tarr said, keeping the fact that he couldn't reheat it in the RV to himself. He could go over to the barn and use the microwave and break room there. He and Tuck weren't working again outside of keeping the animals fed until Monday, when Rosie Young would actually arrive in town.

Tarr had met her a few times, but Tuck had mostly been training with her down in Texas. But with the National Professional Rodeo finals in only another week and a half, they'd train at the Deerfield facility before heading to Vegas.

Tuck had gone over everything with Tarr at least five thousand times. Where Rosie would stay. Which horses she could practice with before they brought out her professional horse. They'd been cleaning up the barns and stables, revamping the facilities, and making sure everything was set for when Rosie walked through the door.

Tarr, followed by Briar, moved into the living room and leaned over to hug Molly, who remained on the couch. "Thanks so much for having us."

She lifted up her eye mask at the sound of his voice. "I'm sorry I'm not the best hostess," she said, and she looked utterly exhausted. "Thank you so much for coming."

"You're fine," Tarr said, a slip of guilt for making her work so hard today. She'd suffered a concussion over the summer, and big events, loud noises, and go-go-going all the time caught up to her quickly. "We had a great time."

He moved back, and Briar took his place, leaning down to hug Molly. "Thank you," she said. "You're a great cook, and I had an amazing time."

"It's so good to see you again, Briar," Molly said, her voice filled with warmth. "You two drive safe now. It's a long way across the city."

It sure was, and Tarr got reminded that winter had definitely arrived in Colorado the moment he stepped outside. Full darkness consumed the sky, and one breath in told him not to do that too deeply, lest his lung walls might freeze together.

"Come on, honey." He reached for Briar's hand then, the movement natural, and hurried her along to the truck. The way his blood foamed in his veins had become his new normal whenever he got close to Briar, and with her slender fingers enveloped in his, Tarr definitely needed to hold her hand again.

Soon.

Once he'd helped her up into his big beast of a vehicle, and he'd catapulted himself behind the wheel, he glanced over to her. "I should've come out and started the truck. We're gonna freeze for ten minutes."

Briar gave him a half-smile and simply tucked her hands between her legs to keep them warm. "I doubt that," she said. "This truck is so nice. I bet the heater doesn't take long to get hot at all."

"Yeah." Tarr got them off the Hammond Family Farm and onto the two-lane highway that led away from Ivory Peaks and into the city. He'd skirt north up toward Boulder and go around the top edge of Denver, a route he and Tuck had mapped as the shortest and quickest way back to their rodeo training facilities, which sat just northwest of the city.

"You seemed like you had a good time," he said, hoping Briar would pick up the conversation from there.

"Yeah," she said. "It was nice."

He swallowed, pure fantasy running through his mind. Making a quick decision, he reached over and took Briar's hand in his. He pulled it over to his chest as he leaned down, and he placed a tender kiss just on the inside of her wrist. "Thank you for coming with me."

He dropped their hands to his thigh, and to his great surprise, she didn't immediately pull away. In fact, she didn't pull away at all.

Maybe Tarr didn't need a huge elaborate plan in order to hold Briar's hand and have her in his life. Maybe he just needed a little more courage to do what he wanted to do and take control of the situation.

He'd felt so out of control in his life since his injury, but as the radio warbled at a low volume, and Briar kept her hand in his, Tarr finally felt like he was back on top of the world.

Coming home with Tucker after the pause in his rodeo career had saved Tarr. Literally. He still had the fondest memories of living in a simple cowboy cabin on Tuck's family farm, and he'd fallen in love with the Rocky Mountains, the way the trees turned shades of fire in the autumn, went blank in the winter, and revived every spring.

He hadn't wanted to go back on the rodeo circuit, but Tuck wasn't one to sit still and do nothing. He still had plenty of spunk and spark left inside him, and he loved the rodeo with his whole heart. Fine, Bobbie Jo had taken all of that, and she cared for the goats and lambs Tuck had bought for her.

They'd only been on the farm for one season, and Bobbie Jo had met with Keith Whettstein and Deacon to get a plan ready for next year's planting season. Tarr was sure she'd be able to get the farm right back to its former glory, and he glanced over to Briar.

She'd come with the farm for a year, and that meant they'd only have her for another month. Tarr didn't involve himself in the business side of things, because he hadn't bought the farm. Tucker had, and he'd sold four acres to Tarr for his cabin and land.

No matter what, Tarr didn't get to decide to keep Briar on as their vet once the new year started. He wanted to ask her if she'd met with Tuck about renewing her contract or whatever she needed to do to stay in her house and on the farm.

But he didn't want to complicate anything by starting a conversation, especially since he could never predict how it would turn out. The question of a breakfast date with her teemed beneath his tongue, but Tarr had had so much practice holding back what he really wanted to say to Briar that he didn't let it out.

They made the eighty-minute drive back to the Deerfield farm in silence, and Tarr finally cleared his throat as he walked Briar up her steps to the front door.

"So, I was thinking Yolks Up for breakfast," he said. "I can do an online reservation and let you know what time I'll be here to get you."

He wasn't *asking* about breakfast, but pure fear shot through him when Briar turned toward him, those gorgeous eyes—which could be so sharp—sinking into him. He swallowed, but otherwise didn't move and managed to remain silent.

Enough time went by for Wiggins to circle at her feet and lay down, and Tarr definitely felt like the dog, as they were both at Briar's mercy. Tarr was just about to say, "Please," again when everything that Briar kept boxed tight inside her fell.

She put one palm on Tarr's chest, smoothing down something imaginary there. If she had any idea what her touch did to him....

"All right, cowboy," she said, and she looked up at him again. "But nothing too early, okay? I'm still kind of in a food coma from all that pie."

Tarr chuckled and ducked his head, catching Briar's hand as she let it fall from his chest. "Nothing too early," he promised. "And you know, you didn't have to try the coconut cream, the key lime, *and* the pumpkin."

"Yes, I did," Briar said, her smile wide and glorious. It painted light and joy through Tarr, and he wondered if she could feel herself smiling so beautifully. He hoped so, because he didn't think Briar experienced much happiness in her life, and he yearned to give that to her.

With that, she squeezed his hand and then released it, moving the few steps to her door. She opened it and said, "Let's go, Wiggy."

Wiggins didn't look at Tarr for permission. He simply trotted inside. Briar nodded at him again, and Tarr did the same, lifting his hand to tip his hat at her before she disappeared into the cabin and brought the door closed between them.

Tarr practically floated back to his truck, and he couldn't remember the drive back to his RV at all. He whistled as he rotated his keys around his fingers and went up the steps and into his temporary dwelling.

The fact that it didn't get any warmer now that he stood inside brought Tarr harshly back to reality. He quickly moved over to the wood-burning stove that he'd installed last week, and though his hands shook, he couldn't stop smiling as he built a fire that would hopefully keep him from freezing to death overnight.

"Please, dear God," he begged. "I've got to make it through one more night, because I finally have a date with Briar in the morning."

four

Briar brushed smoky eyeshadow over her eyelids, the same way the woman in the "get ready with me" video did. No, she'd never look like the women online, because she wasn't a size zero and blonde. But she thought her makeup came out just fine for a Black Friday breakfast at a yuppy place in the Highland Square area of the city.

Tarr had texted only a half-hour after dropping her off, telling her Yolks Up had a nine-fifteen and a ten o'clock reservation. She'd opted for the ten AM one, because they'd have to drive thirty-fives minutes just to get there, and she didn't want to have to be ready before nine o'clock.

She got up from her vanity and reached for the dark brown sweater she'd laid out on her bed. She'd paired it with a pair of black jeans, and she pulled on her ankle boots about the time Wiggins started barking.

He ran down the hall toward her, his claws skidding on the hardwood floor as he went "Bark! Bark! Bark-bark!" He looked at her, barked again, and took off out of the bedroom and down the hall again.

At least Briar knew no one could get into the cabin without her knowing. Still. "Wiggins," she complained as the dog came back toward her. "I hear you. It's just Tarr."

Just Tarr.

More false words had never been spoken. Nothing about Tarr was "just" anything. The man exuded power from his broad shoulders, and he moved with fluidity and grace. She'd never seen him try something he couldn't do perfectly, and she somehow fit exactly against his chest and could fall asleep in his arms in less than ten seconds flat.

Wiggins jumped onto the couch, his front paws on the back of it as he nosed his way through the curtains covering the front window. He barked against the glass, and Briar shook her head as she reached for the doorknob.

She opened the front door and pulled it toward her, half-hoping a witch had visited Tarr in the night and cast a spell on him. He'd have to endure being an ogre, and then Briar wouldn't feel so inferior in his presence.

Sadly, Tarr had not turned into an ogre overnight, and the god of a cowboy stood on her front porch in a pair of dark wash denim jeans with a dark gray shirt tucked into an impossibly big belt buckle. He wore a black leather jacket over that, with that deliciously matching hat perched just-so on his head.

"Morning," he said in that smooth, bass voice that made Briar sigh.

"Good morning," she said back. "Do I need my purse?"

"I don't see why you would," he said. "Unless you want to walk around the shops or something."

Briar turned to get her purse, because she didn't go shopping very often, and she didn't know what might catch her eye in the area around Yolks Up. She didn't think Tarr would tell her she couldn't go somewhere she wanted to, and she shouldered her purse and turned back to find Tarr crouched down, lavishing love on Wiggins.

She smiled at the way he chuckled, at the way he loved her dog, at the memory of having those big, capable hands on her back and pressed against her side.

Something like happiness tickled through her, and she pulled in a breath. Tarr looked up, saw her, and straightened. "You okay, honey?"

She blinked, her normal coming back into focus. She may be going on a date with Tarr, but that didn't mean they were dating. She might be able to let down her guard a little bit with him, but that didn't mean he needed to know all her secrets. She could admire his good looks and strength, but that didn't mean she trusted him.

But maybe you can.

"Briar?"

"I'm okay," she said, shelving the thought for now. "I'm ready." She put a smile on her face and expected Tarr to turn and leave her house. He hadn't come very far inside, probably because he figured she'd glare him right back onto the porch.

Instead, he took the few steps to where she stood at the corner of the dining table and reached up to tuck her hair behind her ear. "You sure are pretty, Briar," he murmured.

She had no idea how to respond to that, and thankfully, Tarr dropped his hand to hers and laced his fingers through hers. He turned then, and she walked with him, the heat from his hand coating her whole body in the much-needed warmth.

"Thank you," she said when she stepped out of the house. Her manners had finally caught up to her, and she knew now how to respond to a cowboy calling her pretty.

Tarr stopped at the top of her steps and gazed up into the sky. "It looks and feels like snow."

Briar checked the weather religiously in the winter, and she nodded. "Yeah, it's supposed to start later this afternoon."

He made a sound of disgust and looked over to her. Briar tried smiling at him again, and it didn't feel so forced this time. "I think you look nice too, Tarr."

He blinked at her, pure shock marching across his face. She scoffed, her irritation with him, the situation, and herself going from zero to sixty in less time than it took for her to breathe in. "You don't have to look so surprised."

"You've never given me a compliment before," he said. "I'm allowed to be surprised about it."

"As if you don't know how devastatingly handsome you are." She rolled her eyes, pulled her hand away, and started down her front steps.

"Devastatingly handsome?" Tarr coughed, and then his footsteps ran after her. "Briar, wait up."

She did slow her step, which took her an extra moment, because she was used to giving in to her anger and letting it run her. But since her accident at the Goatel with the coyotes, she'd been trying to slow down, live more deliberately, and assess what she really wanted.

Tarr jogged in front of her and opened the passenger door, then turned back to her. "I checked the menu, and they have lots of non-egg options for you."

Briar came to a complete stop, though she only had a couple of steps to go to reach him. "I—checked the menu too."

The corners of his mouth tipped up. "What did you see that you wanted?"

Briar moved closer to him, hoping he'd casually lift his hand and encircle her in his arms. He'd done it before, and every move he made seemed so easy. She fiddled with the zipper at the bottom of his jacket, and he took his sweet Texas time putting his hand on her waist and sliding it around to her back.

She looked up at him. "I'm so tired, Tarr."

Alarm crossed his expression. "We can get breakfast to go. Maybe bring it back here and eat in the cabin." He raised his eyebrows as the question mark on what he'd said.

She shook her head. "I didn't mean I don't want to go."

"What did you mean then?"

"Let's just go," she said, sudden embarrassment filling her from top to bottom.

"Hey, can we agree on something first?"

"It's cold out here, Tarr."

"Then you better agree fast."

She sighed but looked up at him, gesturing for him to go on.

"I get you might not want to tell me everything on the first date. But...well, I'll just say it." He took a big, deep breath first, though. As he blew it out, he looked past her to the cabin, then brought his eyes back to hers, where they hooked and stuck.

"I obviously like you. I want to know everything about you, and that right there is where I know you're going to back out. So I just...I want us to agree that while we don't have to tell everything with every question...I want—" He blew out his breath again, clearly frustrated and unable to come up with the right words.

But Briar knew what he wanted. "You want us to talk about meaningful things," she said, giving him the words he lacked.

"Yes," he said, the word almost an explosion out of his mouth.

"You'll give me room to think about things before I talk about them," she said. "But you don't want me to ignore you and *never* circle back to talk about them."

"Yes," he whispered. "So you just said you were tired, but when I asked you what that meant, you shut down." He brought her closer and tucked her hair again. Briar found him to be so gentle and yet so stern too.

"And I want to know what you meant, but I can be patient while you figure out the right words to use to tell me. But in the end, I want you to tell me, whether that's today, or tomorrow, or in a couple of weeks or months." He ducked his head until she met his gaze. "Okay?"

She nodded, her emotions already wavering so close to the surface. Why, she had no idea. Something about Tarr simply undid all of Briar's defenses, and he'd been wearing her down for almost a year.

That was why she was tired.

She was tired of fighting him off. Pushing him back out whenever he somehow got inside her life. Rebuilding the walls around her cabin, her dog, her heart.

He was why she was so tired.

"Okay, Tarr," she whispered.

"Okay." He moved out of the way but kept his hand on the small of her back as she climbed up on the runner of his truck. "I like your boots, Briar."

"Thank you," she said again, dropping into her seat.

Tarr closed her door, then joined her in the cab of the truck. Feeling like someone had invaded her body, Briar reached across the console to take his hand in hers. He sucked in a breath, but Briar ignored it.

His low chuckle threatened to turn into a full laugh, but then he said, "Yeah, I think you like me too. You're just not sayin' it with words quite yet."

Briar ducked her head, her face burning as she untucked her hair so it would fall between them, effectively hiding the blush as it continued to bloom through her body.

Tarr let her stay quiet as he backed out of her driveway and rumbled down the dirt road to the highway. Briar breathed in and out, trying to come up with what to tell him. Her mind seemed to splinter in one direction in one moment, and then crack back the other way in the next.

As his blinker clicked through the cab, the pop songs Tarr loved so much in the background, Briar finally looked away from her side window and over to him.

"I'm going to get the special," she said. "Online, Yolks Up said they're doing a pumpkin spice pancake stack, with white chocolate chips and macadamia nuts."

"That sounds like it's totally up your alley," Tarr said with a smile.

"It comes with maple-pecan syrup, and I'm going to get so many sides of bacon, I hope you brought your platinum card." A true smile came to her face then, and when Tarr looked over to her, she actually laughed.

Tarr joined her, chuckling as he said, "You can have as much bacon as you want, sweetheart."

And she knew he could pay for it, because Tarr had been a champion in the rodeo for years. "Are you sure? Bacon is at a premium price these days."

He shook his head, clearly able to take her teasing. He squeezed her hand and said the best words on the planet: "You can have anything you want, honey."

Briar believed him, and she believed he'd do whatever he had to do to give her whatever she wanted. She'd seen him show up, day after day, even when she screamed at him to get out of her house and never come back.

He came back.

Every day, he came back.

He'd made sure she took her meds and got to her doctor's appointments. He'd fed her, and tucked her into bed, and held her when she felt so much pain, she'd cried and begged God to simply take her home to Him.

He'd never left her side, not once, since the coyote attack, and Briar cleared her throat, the words she needed to say about to vomit out of her throat.

five

Tarr shifted in his seat, the tension coming off Briar almost more than he could stomach. He wished she'd just be able to relax around him without the aid of a narcotic. He'd just glanced over to her when she opened her mouth.

"Thank you, Tarr," she blurted out. "I've been so mean to you, but you never gave up on me, and you kept showing up, and I really do appreciate it." She took a deep breath and looked over to him. "I've never said it, but...thank you. I've never met anyone like you, who...."

Just as quickly as she'd started blurting things out, she trailed off into silence. That adorable frown appeared between her eyes, and Tarr simply kept driving. He could barely comprehend that Briar had thanked him, because no, she'd never done that before.

Sure, he'd heard her be grateful to Tucker, to Ashton, the stable manager, to a random waiter who took her coffee order.

But him?

She'd never been grateful to or for *him*.

Warmth kindled in his stomach, and Tarr once again found himself shifting in his seat. "Who what?" he asked, wanting to hear the end of that sentence.

"Who didn't do exactly what I yelled at them to do—who left." She gave a cute little shrug, and Tarr's heart tore and bled for her. Just a little bit. But her eyes looked bright like pure ocean waves when she dared to glance over to him again, and that only made Tarr's hormones fire at him again.

"Tell me how you came to Deerfield," he said.

Briar drew in a deep breath and blew it out. "I wanted somewhere with the small-town feel of Western Canada, but I needed to get out of Western Canada."

He nodded, his memories returning—the ones of her slipping into a rodeo ambassador persona and talking about the Calgary Stampede. "Maybe you'll tell me more about why." He cleared his throat. "I came from Utah, from a rodeo there where I got injured."

"But not a career-ending injury," she said.

"No, I could've gone back." Tarr glanced out the window, this topic of conversation not what he wanted to be doing. He knew a few things about Briar, and one of them was that she hated the rodeo.

Funny, considering she'd definitely been part of it at some point.

"I didn't want to," Tarr said simply. "Tuck was really disappointed. He loves the rodeo. He lives for the lights, the jokes, the events, the scent of dirt." He chuckled. "I'd had enough of the travel, of living in a trailer—which is funny, considering where I'm living right now—in a new city every weekend."

He glanced over to her. "Tuck brought me to his family farm after my surgery, so I could recover, and I don't know. I've always loved the mountains, and I didn't want to leave this place."

She gave him a small smile. "Colorado is beautiful."

He sighed. "Yeah, this Texas boy can't quite understand the wintertime yet, but it's only my second one, so I'm trying not to flee too quickly."

She laughed lightly, and Tarr marveled at the sound of it. Briar didn't laugh easily, that was for dang sure. "I love the winter."

"Yeah? What do you like about it?"

"I don't know," she said, her voice a little too casual. That meant she did know. "There's something...simple about its beauty. Without the leaves, the trees are just bare. Open. All their jagged branches and flaws exposed. It's pretty."

"I like it when it snows and all the branches are covered in the white."

"Yeah, exactly that," Briar said. "I like that something so pretty can be made out of white, brown, and blue. It's...simple. A gorgeous kind of simple."

Tarr could sum her up the same way, and he yearned to know more about her. No, to know *everything* about what made Briar Prescott into the woman riding in his passenger seat in that very moment.

Tarr noted at least three hotels on the way to Yolks Up, and he managed to find a parking spot despite the busyness of the Black Friday shopping crowd.

He congratulated himself as he hurried around the front of the truck to let Briar out that they'd managed to have a semi-decent conversation on the way here.

"Yeah, about the weather," he muttered, but Tarr would take it, because having a casual conversation about the weather far exceeded fighting or arguing with Briar.

She joined him, and he once again tucked his hand in hers before facing the restaurant.

He wanted to ask her what she was doing for Christmas and why she never seemed to go anywhere for holidays. He wanted to find out if Tuck had hired her on for another year or indefinitely. And he wanted to know if she had any siblings and who her last boyfriend had been, why they'd broken up, and everything she knew about the rodeo.

He kept all of it tucked away and actually prayed that Briar would lead out in a topic of conversation.

As they approached the building, the front doors opened, and a cacophony of sound spilled out.

"Wow, they sound busy," Briar said.

"Yeah, but I got us a reservation," he said.

"Oh, honey, reservations don't mean anything." She grinned up at him, while Tarr's heart beat a little faster.

"They don't?"

She simply shook her head. "You've been a celebrity for far too long, Tarr."

"I'm not a celebrity," he said, and he tugged her through the fray of people to the hostess stand. "Tarr Olson," he said. "I had a reservation for two at ten o'clock."

"Mm–hm." The woman hummed as she looked down at her tablet. "Yeah, I can get you guys back in about ten minutes." She looked up, eyes hopeful. "Does that work?"

She lifted a buzzer from the stack, and Tarr didn't really see what choice he had. "Sure," he said, and he took the buzzer and towed Briar out of the way.

He managed to find a seat on the long, padded bench near the corner, and Briar squeezed in beside him. He lifted his arm around her shoulders, since his were too broad to share the space.

"I have a game I play with myself every day," Briar said.

"Oh, yeah?" Tarr ducked his head so his cowboy hat created a little pocket for just the two of them to talk.

"Yep," she said.

"Are you going to tell me what it is?"

"I guess it doesn't really have a name," she said. "Do you want to play it with me?" She blinked those oceanic eyes at him, and Tarr could only nod.

"I just try to tell myself one truth every day."

"One truth," Tarr repeated.

"Yeah," she said. "Sometimes it's the same truth every day, over and over, for weeks, and sometimes it changes."

"What's your truth for today?" he asked.

Briar stiffened at his side and crossed her legs. She pulled her crossbody bag up onto her lap and leaned into his chest. "Today, it's that I can do hard things."

"What hard things do you have to do today?" he asked.

"Go to breakfast with you," she said, her voice almost a whisper. "Be a good conversationalist. Accept and embrace my feelings." She cleared her throat and tilted her head slightly to look at him, her courage re-entering her gaze. "What about you? If you had to tell yourself the truth today, what would it be?"

Tarr's mind blitzed, and he honestly didn't know how to answer that question. After what felt like a long time of silence, but had probably only been several seconds, he said, "I think I need to face the reality that the RV is not going to sustain me through the winter."

Briar turned fully toward him then, alarm crossing her face. "What's wrong with the RV?"

"Everything?" He didn't mean to put a question mark at the end of it, but he so did.

"I thought it had heat," she said. "And running water."

"Why would you think that?" Tarr asked, because he'd certainly never told her that.

"They've started the cabin, haven't they?"

"Yeah," he said. "But there's no water or electricity on the property yet."

Briar's eyes widened and she searched his face. "How are you surviving there, then?"

"I installed a wood-burning stove last week," Tarr said. "But, well, the truth is...." He ducked his head and kicked an embarrassed grin at her. "I don't think I have the stovepipe exactly right, because I woke up in the night coughing, and the place was filled with smoke."

"Tarr," Briar said, plenty of chastisement in her tone. "That's not safe. You could have died." She exhibited the same fire and disdain for him that she always had and—oh—Tarr really liked it.

"Yeah, but God woke me up," he said. "I put the fire out, aired out the place, and crawled back under my down blankets and sleeping bags."

"Plural?" She frowned at him, an expression Tarr was quite familiar with, thank you very much. "You cannot live in a place without heat in the Colorado winter."

"Yeah, I was here last year," Tarr said. "Thanks, Mom."

Briar scoffed, but she didn't release his gaze as she cocked her head. "You should move back in with Tuck."

"I'm not moving back in with Tuck." Tarr lifted his head and looked out into the restaurant. "Maybe if a certain someone would loan me Wiggins, he could keep me warm at night."

"You are not taking Wiggins," Briar said. "I don't want you to call me in the morning and tell me my dog's frozen to death."

Tarr chuckled and shook his head. "Wiggins won't freeze to death." He sighed, completely unsure about what to do with his housing situation. Playing Briar's game, the truth was, the RV, in its current condition, was not going to last him through the winter.

"I think I'm just going to get a hotel," he said. "They have these long-term ones with kitchens and stuff, and it's not like I can't afford it."

Briar leaned back into him again. "Yeah," she said. "But then you'd have to drive onto the ranch, and sometimes that's really hard to do when it snows a lot. They close the roads here sometimes, Tarr."

"Yes," Tarr murmured.

And with Tuck, Bobbie Jo, and Rosie all going to Vegas for the NPR event, someone had to be there to maintain the farm, feed the animals, and keep things running.

"Maybe a hotel won't work," he said. "Maybe I could just stay in the house while Tuck's gone."

"I don't get why you can't stay there all winter," she said. "It's a seven bedroom house. It's practically like having your own apartment."

"Yeah, I don't know either," Tarr said. "There's just something telling me it's not a good idea."

His buzzer went off, and he lifted it so Briar could see the flashing blue lights. She stood first, and he followed her to an intimate table that he hoped would be able to hold their cups of coffee and a little pitcher of cream, let alone their breakfasts.

The conversation moved on, and Briar actually shared a

little bit about her wood crafts, and mentioned that she'd signed up for a watercolor class starting in January.

By the time Tarr turned off the highway and back onto the farm, he had self-congratulations running through his head for a great breakfast date.

"Take me by the RV," Briar said, no sign of a question mark in sight.

He eased his foot off the gas pedal. "What? Why?"

"I want to see the extent of the smoke damage." She looked at him out of the corner of her eye, and it sure felt calculating.

"Briar, it's fine," he said.

"Then let me see it." She turned fully toward him then, and she cocked one eyebrow at him in challenge.

"You're a real pill," he said, but he turned his truck to the left instead of the right when he reached the fork in the road.

"You should meet yourself," she shot back.

Tarr chose not to respond, and he caught the flap of the clear plastic sheeting that had been secured over his poured foundation as the wind picked it up and tried to rip it away. He went past that to the run-down RV, now thinking he simply needed a better one of these.

Water and electricity will still be a problem, he thought, the words hissing through his head.

He pulled off the road, as he didn't really have a driveway here. "All right," he drawled, bringing out his Texan accent. "Go check it, then." He nodded toward her side of the truck, where the RV now waited for her "expert inspection."

Briar glared at him, then turned to open her door. She sucked in a breath and recoiled away from the door. "What is that?"

Tarr leaned forward and tried to see past her. "What?"

"It's a porcupine." She gasped again and swung around to

look at him. "Tarr, the door to your RV is swinging open, and I swear that porcupine just came out from inside it...."

"No," he said, immediately dismissing the idea. Then he saw the way the door slammed against the side of the RV. His pulse dropped to the soles of his cowboy boots. "Stay here." He unbuckled his seat belt and left the truck running to go check on his temporary dwelling.

You can't stay here, ran through his mind in a multitude of voices. His. Tucker's. Briar's. His momma's. God's.

He saw the dark brown animal as it ducked around the front corner of the RV. Tarr came to a complete stop, his heartbeat hammering up in his ears now. The last of the quills on the chunky porcupine disappeared, and Tarr didn't dare take another step.

The door to the RV was open, and he didn't know how that had happened. Porcupines didn't have hands that he knew of.

"Come back," Briar called, her voice joining the whipping wind swirling around Tarr, through his head, down into his soul. "Tarr, come back to the truck. It's starting to snow."

That got him to look up into the sky, where yes, Mother Nature had started sending down white stuff through the gray sky.

He turned and went back to the truck, catapulting himself up and into the cab. He slammed the door and reached for his phone just as Briar said, "You should come stay with me tonight."

Tarr froze again, though his mind still moved a million miles a minute.

Briar reached over and gently extracted his phone from his hands. "Take me home, and I'll start getting my second bedroom ready for you. Then you can come back here, pack a bag, and then...."

She shrugged and didn't finish the sentence. But then again, she didn't need to. Tarr couldn't stay in the RV if wild animals were coming and going at will, if there was smoke damage, if he couldn't stay warm, and if he couldn't eat or bathe or anything.

"Fine," he grumbled, and he had to turn on his windshield wipers before he could back away from this spot of land that seemed to be betraying him at every turn.

six

Briar removed her current work-in-progress from the easel and moved to stash it in the bedroom closet. The easel folded up easily, and she put that away too. She loved the light coming in the west windows, though the storm had turned the day mostly the color of cold rocks.

She sighed as she turned back to face the couch, which stood against the wall just inside the door. Briar loved the dark leather, and a slip of weariness pulled through her as she reached to remove the back-rest cushions.

The full-sized couch only had two, and she set them on either side of the couch, then started pulling off the seat cushions as well. Straining, she lifted and pulled out the metal frame holding the air mattress.

The couch in the living room could be folded flat to make a double bed too, as the previous owner of this farm has used this cabin as a guest house for his family before he'd hired her.

His family had mostly stopped visiting by then, and Clive

had been going to see his daughters and stay with their families instead of them coming to the farm.

A wave of nostalgia that made no sense to her swept over Briar. Clive Hollowell had been incredibly kind to her, though, and he'd always treated her like his own daughter. She smiled fondly and reached for the remote to inflate the air mattress.

"More like a granddaughter," she murmured to herself. He'd been one of the first people in Briar's life who'd taken one look at her, smiled, and drew her into a hug. Even now, she could feel his arms around her, telling her she'd be safe here, and that she could move into this cabin.

Briar had treasured it every day since.

"But he left too." She supposed she couldn't blame him for passing away, and she didn't. Not really. His death had simply been a reminder that life was constantly in motion, and it wouldn't slow down or stop just because Briar wanted it to.

She had carved out a few years of peace and serenity here, but she'd been feeling a great change coming for several months now. Since the coyote attack, really.

"Since Tarr," she whispered.

The tall, dark, delicious cowboy hadn't arrived at the cabin yet, though he'd dropped her off a couple of hours ago. He'd texted only a few minutes after that, saying he wanted to go get some groceries and wondered if she needed anything.

She'd given him a few essentials, because if Tarr would bring her eggs, milk, and English muffins, why not? Then maybe he'd make her the breakfast sandwiches he once had after staying over to make sure she took her medication on time and wasn't in too much pain.

He made a mean sausage, egg, and cheese breakfast sandwich, and Briar needed to get her chub of breakfast sausage out of the freezer. She made up the bed with navy blue sheets and a blue, white, and gray-checkered comforter.

She replaced the cushions back on the couch to bridge the gap between the mattress and the back of the piece of furniture, and she turned to get the pillows out of the top of the closet. After fluffing them appropriately, she stood back and surveyed her handiwork.

"He should be comfortable here," she said, and she left the painting studio in favor of the kitchen. She had no idea how she'd be, sleeping under the same roof as him when she was whole and not hopped up on narcotics.

She busied herself in the kitchen, emptying her dishwasher and setting water to boil in her electric kettle. She stepped out onto the back porch and hurried to the lean-to to make sure she had gasoline for the generator.

She did, as she'd lived through many winters in places colder than Colorado, and she knew to be prepared.

She'd just ordered a cord of wood, and it had been delivered only a few days ago. She brought in several armloads, and then she stood in her living room, anxiety and impatience running through her in equal measure. "Where is he?" She pulled out her phone and checked the time.

Almost four o'clock.

She looked at Wiggins, who lay on the couch, curled into his typical ball. He only moved his eyes, and he'd lose his mind in a bark-fest if someone pulled up to the cabin. Therefore, Briar didn't need to go check.

She walked around the couch and out the front door anyway, telling herself she was checking on the weather. Sure, she'd just been out here to get her last armful of wood, but she hadn't specifically checked on the snowfall.

It wasn't currently snowing, but the wind had picked up. Briar wrapped her arms around herself and watched her driveway, then the road leading back to the cabin. Tarr's big black truck didn't appear, and she turned back to the cabin with a small huff.

The sun would set soon, as in the winter, the daylight would be gone in the next hour. She grabbed her phone from where she'd left it on the kitchen counter and tapped out a quick text to Tarr as she went down the hall.

I'm going to jump in the shower real quick. Then you can have all the hot water you want later.

Now that she knew the RV didn't have running water, she wondered what Tarr had been doing for showers.

"Probably stopping by Tuck's." She ducked into her bedroom and grabbed her robe, though she didn't normally use it. But Tarr could show up at any moment, and she didn't want to be caught having to duck across the hall in only a bath towel.

Just come in if you get here in the next fifteen minutes. Briar plugged in her phone and set it on her nightstand. Then she picked it up again. *Oh, and an ETA would be nice. Just saying.*

With that, she hurried into the bathroom and twisted on the water in the tub. Twenty minutes later, she stood in front of the mirror drying her hair when she heard Wiggins barking.

Her heartbeat leaped up into the back of her throat too, and when Wiggins stopped causing a racket, she figured Tarr had walked in the way she'd told him to.

"It's me," he called, and Briar heard him over the blow dryer.

"Okay," she called back. "I'll be right out." She never could quite erase the curl in her hair, but sometimes she really tried. Tonight wasn't going to be that night, though, and she stayed in the bathroom for a few more minutes before switching off the appliance and taking a deep breath.

She met her own eyes in the mirror, mentally told herself the truth for the day—*You can do hard things*—and went to meet Tarr in the kitchen.

She found him there, of course, holding open two cabinet doors as he looked inside. Irritation flashed through her, but she tamed it just as quickly. Still, she couldn't stem the feeling completely that her private space was being invaded.

"What do you need?" she asked.

He glanced over to her. "I got you a big box of those chocolate-vanilla pudding cups, and they don't all need to be in the fridge."

Briar moved over to the Lazy Susan in the corner. "I usually put stuff like that in here." She pushed on the door, and the turntable started to move.

He grinned at her and closed the cupboard, where she kept her coffee, tea, sugar, and other baking supplies. "I've got a few things too. Maybe they'll fit in there?" He turned and took the single step over to the island she'd installed herself after moving in.

He picked up several little cups of microwaveable macaroni and cheese, Pasta-roni, and Rice-a-roni. A grin burst onto Briar's face. "Your broccoli-cheddar rice? Yeah, I'm sure it'll fit in there."

"Are you making fun of my broccoli-cheddar rice?"

Briar lunged toward him as he lifted a tower of the cardboard cups and it started to tip. "No," she said as she grabbed a couple of the top containers. "I'm making fun of this…parmesan pasta."

"It's delicious," he said. "Ready in three minutes, and it goes great with chicken or steak."

Briar already knew Tarr could cook, and he did put together quick meals morning, noon, or night. He'd never fed her out of the microwave though, and watching as he put his favorites in her corner cupboard made her grin grow.

She took in the other groceries, which he'd already unbagged, and reached for the eggs sitting on the counter. She filled the fridge with the things he'd brought, while Tarr found a spot for the pantry staples. He shoved all the bags into one, and when they finished, he faced her and held up the ball.

"Do you keep these?"

"Yeah." She nodded to the slim cabinet between the stove and fridge. "I keep them in here." She took them from him and smashed them onto the top shelf with all the other grocery bags she'd brought home at some point.

She hardly ever used them, so they threatened to rain down on her, filling the kitchen with plastic, but she slammed the cupboard quickly before that could happen.

Tarr chuckled. "So I'm going to avoid that cupboard."

Briar didn't want this to be weird. She reminded herself that Tarr had spent plenty of time in her cabin. He'd slept in her bed with her, for crying out loud. This would be way tamer than that, and she nodded down the hall.

"Come see your bed for however long you need it."

Tarr took a couple of steps around the other end of the island and stopped in the mouth of the hallway. Briar thought he'd turn and lead the way—this cabin only had two bedrooms, after all—but he didn't.

"However long I need it? I thought I was just staying here for tonight."

"And yet, you brought twelve cups of Rice-a-roni." Briar's eyebrows went up. "And a pound of strawberries, and—"

"Those are for you."

"—almond milk, and—"

"Almond milk travels," he said.

Briar put her hand on her hip and tilted her head as she glared at him. "Tarr, do you think winter is only going to last for one night?"

"I can't move in with you for the duration of winter," he said.

"Then don't," she said. "But I can't in good conscience send you back to a porcupine-invested, smoke-filled, non-functional RV."

"My living situation isn't ideal."

"Ideal?" Briar shook her head and started toward him again. "Tarr, it's insanity." She gave him a pointed look and brushed past him. "I made up the couch in the studio. It's an airbed, so it should be nice."

She led the way, glad when Tarr's cowboy boots sounded on the wood behind her. She stayed out in the hall, but indicated that he should go in.

"You put your painting away," he said.

"It doesn't fit with the bed up," she said simply. "And I don't do a ton of painting in the winter."

Tarr dropped his duffel bag in the far corner and put his backpack on the bed. "I thought you were doing that sculpting class next month."

Briar's pulse blipped through her body, really jumping in the vein in her neck. "What? When did I tell you that?"

"You didn't tell me," he said. "You made me sign up for you months ago, as soon as the community center released their winter classes. You said it would fill up if you didn't sign up on the first day, but you had a bad headache and couldn't even look at your laptop for long enough to do it." By the time he'd finished talking, Briar had remembered.

"Oh," she said, because he had signed up for her.

Months ago.

"I think you said something about a hot shower?" Tarr unzipped his backpack and lifted out a toiletry bag. Of course. The man had lived on the road for a lot of years, and nothing about him was disorganized.

Briar nodded, swallowing hard. "Yeah, go ahead and shower. I'll make us something for dinner."

"If you want," Tarr said. "You don't have to cook for me, Briar." He came toward her, and Briar's nervousness reached new heights.

"Well, I have to eat too." She ducked away from him just as he arrived in front of her, and she practically ran down the hall and into the kitchen. Her heartbeat thundered up into the back of her throat, only calming slightly when she heard the click of the bathroom door.

The shower started a minute later, and Briar set about steeping herself a cup of tea and baking off a couple of ham-and-cheese-stuffed chicken breasts. She rolled some miniature white potatoes in olive oil, salt, and pepper, and added them to the oven.

By the time Tarr came down the hall, smelling like sage-brush and woodsmoke, dinner was almost ready.

"That was mighty nice," he said as he joined her at the bar. "Thank you, Briar." He put his arm around her and squeezed her a little closer to him. He always put off such great energy, and Briar allowed herself to relax.

"Where'd you go all day?" she asked. "Because it doesn't take almost five hours to get some groceries."

"Maybe traffic was bad."

"Tarr."

"Fine, I went through the RV and packed up everything I

thought I shouldn't leave inside. I took all of that to the barn storage. Then I made sure the RV was secured—no reason to give raccoons and porcupines—or anything bigger—to think they can live there this winer. Then, I went to town for groceries."

Briar still didn't think that would take that long, but she didn't press the issue. "Okay, well, I had some chicken cordon bleu, so I put that in with some potatoes. I'll just make a quick sauce to go with them."

She got up to do that, and she'd just flipped the gas on under the pan to heat cream, butter, salt, garlic, and parmesan cheese when the lights in the cabin went out.

Her breath left her body in a whoosh too, and Briar stood very, very still as she waited for the electricity to come back on. It didn't, and she turned around after several long seconds of silence.

"Great," Tarr said, and he sounded disgusted.

"I have a generator," she said. "And I brought in a ton of wood."

"Then we'll be fine," Tarr said.

The timer on the oven went off, and Briar spun to silence it and get their dinner out of the oven. "This is gas, so we should be able to cook." A franticness moved through her nonetheless, and her hands seemed to flap around as she started adding ingredients to the frying pan.

Then Tarr eased into her side and said, "Hey, we'll be okay," in that velvety, sultry voice. She'd long wanted to ask him if he'd ever thought about being in a country music band, but she'd never done it.

"I'll start a fire while you finish dinner, and we'll eat by fire-light, okay?"

She nodded, because Briar couldn't get her voice to say,

"Okay," in return. He stepped away from her, and Briar tipped her head back and pressed her eyes closed as she silently prayed, *Dear Lord, did the power really have to go out? Isn't the situation already awkward enough?*

She sighed. *I guess if this is how it's got to be, then bless me to come up with the patience and conversation I need to treat Tarr right.*

seven

Tarr knelt in front of the fireplace and exhaled a steady stream of air onto the flame to encourage it to grab on to the kindling he'd tee-pee'd around it. Behind him, Briar whisked, and the scent of butter and salt filled the air. Tarr had never felt so domestic in his entire life, and something good and homey made everything inside him calm right down.

The first crackle of wood uniting with fire met his ears, and he quickly reached for another handful of shredded newspaper.

The fact that Briar had newspaper at all made him smile, but she'd claimed that she kept it for art projects. He wanted to see so much more of her art—her paintings, her woodcrafts, her sculptures, anything she would show him.

His phone rang, and Tarr looked away from the bright fire to see Tuck's name shining on his screen. A zip of apprehension ran through him, but he reached to tap on the call.

After tapping the speaker icon, he said, "Howdy, Tucker."

"Hey, where you at?" Tuck asked. "The power just went out, and we drove by your RV, and it's totally dark."

"Yeah, I'm not there," Tarr said, knowing he couldn't dodge his best friend's questions. The walls of Briar's cabin suddenly closed in around him, and he felt like he was shouting when he added, "I'm staying at Briar's tonight."

The fact that Tucker said nothing spoke volumes. The hum of the truck came through the line, so Tarr knew they were still connected. Then Bobbie Jo said, "You can both come here if you need to."

"Yeah, that's right," Tuck practically yelled. "We've got a generator and lots of food."

"Briar has a generator too," Tarr said casually. "And you're on speaker while I build a fire, just so you know." He ducked his head in a covert way to look over his shoulder, but he couldn't see Briar, and he didn't sense her drawing close to him. "She brought in a ton of wood, and I went grocery shopping this afternoon, so I think we'll survive the night."

"Will you?" Tuck asked, and his question had sharp hooks.

"I think so," Tarr said, trying to keep his heartbeat as slow as his voice. Tuck and Bobbie Jo both knew that Tarr had spent more than one night with Briar.

But not while she's healthy and whole, his mind hissed at him, and the three of them seemed to know it.

"I'll check in with you in the morning," he said. "Our dinner is almost ready."

"All right," Bobbie Jo said.

"Did you guys want to come here?" Tarr rocked back on his heels, swiped up his phone, and stood. He turned toward Briar. "I'm sure we could rustle up enough food for you guys. If you're not even home yet—"

"We just ate dinner, and we were on the way home when everything went dark," Tuck said.

"At five-thirty?" Tarr asked. "You guys seem a little young to be eating the early bird special." He chuckled, and Briar turned toward him, a smile blooming to life on her face too.

"We were out shopping," Tuck said. "And decided to stop before we came home."

"Sure, all right," Tarr said easily. "Well, I'll touch base with you in the morning so we can go over the feeding schedule."

"All right." Tuck drew a breath in a way that Tarr had heard countless times before. He quickly tapped the speaker icon and moved the phone to his ear so Briar wouldn't be able to hear whatever embarrassing thing Tuck was going to say next. The man really didn't know how to hold his tongue, and most of the time, Tarr appreciated that fact.

"Hey, brother, just be careful, okay?" Tuck said. "I worry about your heart."

"He has a good heart," Bobbie Jo said. "Leave him alone."

"It's his good heart that I'm worried about," Tuck said. "Briar has punctured it before, and he just keeps going back for more."

"I'm still on the line," Tarr said.

"I know you are," Tuck griped at him. "I'm just worried about you."

"I appreciate the sentiment," Tarr said. "But I'm a grown man, and I think I can handle it."

Tucker, once again, remained silent—his way of saying he wasn't sure Tarr could handle it or not.

In all honesty, Tarr agreed with him. He could just see Briar squashing his heart again and then puncturing it with all of the thorns after which she was named. He'd retreat again, like a dog who'd been kicked, his tail between his legs.

But he'd come back. He knew he would, because something about Briar called to his soul, and just like he hadn't been able to leave her home alone yesterday, he couldn't imagine a scenario where he could turn his back on her and walk out of her life for good.

No, she would have to be the one to do that to him. And yes, then he'd have to figure out how to stem the bleeding from all the holes she would leave in his heart.

As he watched, she flipped off the flame underneath the pan where she had been making the sauce, and Tarr knew dinner was ready. "Hey, we're going to eat," he said. "I'll text you later."

"Bye, Tarr," Bobbie Jo called, and Tarr hung up as she hissed something else to Tucker about being more supportive of his best friend. Tarr knew Tuck loved him and supported him in anything and everything, and it sure felt nice to have someone worrying over him.

"Are they coming for dinner?" Briar asked.

Tarr shoved his phone in his back pocket as he took the few steps into the kitchen. "No, ma'am," he said. "They got dinner on their way home."

She nodded and indicated the pan, which now sat on her island next to the chicken cordon bleu and the roasted potatoes. "I don't have a vegetable, but we could open a bagged salad or something." She looked at him with apprehension in her eyes.

Tarr simply grinned at her. "I don't need to eat something green with every meal, honey. I'm an adult."

Briar's shoulders went down, and she ducked her head too. "All right. Well, then let's eat."

"Do you mind if we pray?" He'd left his cowboy hat in her spare bedroom, but he reached up in a nervous gesture and ran his hand through his hair. "I can just say it real quick, if you don't mind."

"I don't mind," she whispered.

In the quickening darkness, only punctured by the flickering firelight several feet away, Tarr reached for her hand as he bowed his head. His fingers fumbled over hers, but he managed to align them and tighten his grip before he said, "Dear Lord, I sure am grateful to be here in Briar's house during this winter storm. I'm pretty mad about the RV not working out, and I know I need a better solution for housing. I don't know what that is yet, but I'm grateful to have this warm, safe place, at least for a couple of nights, where I can figure it out.

"I'm grateful that Briar has finally allowed me to take her out on a date, and I'm grateful for this food that she made for us. It seems like I'm taking a lot from others around me, Lord, and if there's any way that I can give back, please inspire my mind and give me willing hands to do the work." He cleared his throat, suddenly anxious for this prayer to be over. "We're really grateful for all of Thy blessings in both of our lives, and I ask that if there is anything Briar stands in need of at this time, that Thou wilt grant it unto her, according to Thy will. Bless our food to nourish us and strengthen us and help us do good. Amen."

Briar did not repeat the *amen*, and Tarr lifted his head, his eyes automatically seeking hers. He found them and hooked, and something strong and powerful tethered the two of them together.

Tarr cleared his throat and reached for a plate. "I don't think we'll be going to church this weekend."

That seemed to break the silence, and Briar shook her head as she took the plate he handed her. "Do you go every week?"

"I try to," he said. "Part of my post-rodeo-Tarr persona I'm trying to become." He flashed her a smile and picked up the other plate she'd put on the counter. "I already know you don't go, and it's fine. It's not like I'm going to be pressuring you or anything."

She used the tongs to put one of the chicken breasts on her plate. He followed her down the line, and then he followed her into the living room to sit on the hearth, their backs soaking up the warmth of the fire.

"It's not that I don't believe in God," Briar said.

Tarr speared a miniature potato with his fork and dunked it in the puddle of ranch dressing he'd poured onto his plate. "Is that right?"

"Yeah," she said. "It's just...I guess I don't feel like I need organized religion in my life. I can believe and read the scriptures and pray on my own."

"Sure," Tarr said. "Those are all important. I guess I like feeling—I guess I like being around other people in a community who think and believe a little bit the way I do."

Briar nodded as she balanced her plate on her knees and cut into her chicken. "I can see that."

They ate in silence for a couple of minutes. Tarr finished in about half the time as Briar. He stood and took his plate into the kitchen. "I'll make us some dessert," he said. He put his dirty dishes in her sink and turned to the cupboard to get out the pudding cups. "I grew up in Texas, and my momma made dessert with every meal." He smiled just thinking about his mother. "Sometimes it was this big, elaborate sheet cake, and other times she'd give us miniature bags of M&M's."

He chuckled as the childhood memories ran rampant through his mind. "I don't hardly ever make elaborate desserts," he said. "But I always plan out a little something sweet for the end of every meal."

He opened her utensil drawer and pulled out a couple of spoons. He took the pudding cups back over to her and exchanged her now-empty plate for the dessert. After putting her dirty dishes in the sink and returning to the hearth, he peeled back the plastic lid on his pudding cup, the scent of chocolate rising up to meet his nose.

"I've only got the one brother," he said. "He's older than me, and, well, Wayne and I don't really get along. I don't talk to him much."

"What about your parents?" Briar asked. "Are they married? Divorced? Do you talk to them?"

"They're still married, yeah," he said. "Still in Stephenville. I talk to them all the time, especially my momma."

Briar nodded. Tarr told himself to eat slower, and he took one bite of his pudding, the creamy goodness of it coating his tongue. After he swallowed, he dealt with a pulse thundering like horses' hooves.

"What about you?" he asked, deciding to try to get a little bit personal with Briar. He'd called their breakfast that morning a date, and she hadn't corrected him. She'd invited him to stay with her. She'd made dinner, and they'd talked about religion, for crying out loud. He could certainly ask about her family. "You got any siblings? Your parents still alive? Together?"

He deliberately didn't look at her, because he didn't need to. She'd tensed up at his side and remained silent. He took another bite of pudding and then another, the questions starting to grow daggers and pierce the tension now filling the cabin.

"My parents are divorced," Briar finally said. "Though they both still live in Calgary." She looked up and over to him.

Tarr had never seen a more beautiful woman in his entire life than Briar in that moment, cast in shadows on one side of her face and a gorgeous orange glow on the other.

"I grew up there—Calgary."

He nodded, a silent gesture of encouragement for her to go on.

"I'm an only child," she said. "And I haven't really spoken to either of my parents since I left Canada about four years ago."

Surprise moved through Tarr for several reasons. One, that

she told him so much. And two, that she really did exist on this planet as an island, alone, all by herself here in Colorado.

His heart ached for her, and he took her empty pudding cup and stacked it inside his. He put their spoons inside and set them on his other side, and then edged closer to Briar and put his arm around her.

"So that's why you don't go anywhere for holidays."

"Yeah," she said. "There's just been a lot that's happened, you know?"

Tarr didn't know, but he nodded. "Families can be really complicated."

Briar seemed to melt into him for a couple of moments, and pure bliss moved through Tarr. He wondered if this would ever become commonplace for him—that he would come home to this cabin, and they would eat dinner together and talk, and everything would be comfortable and normal, filled with kindness and gentleness and love. He wanted it more than anything he had ever wanted before, and he wasn't sure why, as he didn't know Briar all that well.

She blew out her breath and straightened. Tarr pulled his arm back, and she stood. "Well, I hate to say it, but the generator is not meant to heat the entire cabin."

She took a few steps away from him and arrived in front of the couch. He'd slept there before, usually with Wiggins curled into his chest or covering his feet. Right now, she reached to pull the pillows off the couch, and she dumped them unceremoniously on the floor.

"I think we're going to have to sleep out here."

"Sleep out here?" Tarr repeated.

In the next moment, Briar released a catch on the couch, and the back of it laid down to create a flat surface. She turned toward him, and with the firelight shining in her eyes, he read the apprehension there without trouble.

"Yeah," she said. "The couch unfolds into a bed, and we can pull it closer to the fire." She flapped one arm toward the hallway. "We can close all the bedroom doors and seal the front door and the back door and try to keep all the heat out here. That way, the generator won't have to work as hard. It'll keep the fridge going, and we'll have hot water, but the furnace won't have to run as much."

Tarr stood too, his heart suddenly moving into palpitation mode. "All right," he said. His eyes dropped to the couch-bed. "We're gonna sleep in that together?"

Briar scoffed, and his eyes flew back to hers. She wore her usual fire and determination, and *ohhhh*, how Tarr loved it.

"That's right, cowboy," she said. "You've slept with me in my bed before. This is going to be no different."

"I think it's a *little* different now," he said.

She took one step toward him, and it felt a little menacing. "How so?"

"Well, for one, I've been holding your hand all day," he said. "We went out this morning." He cocked his head at her. "Are you seriously telling me it's not going to be different?"

Briar's jaw hardened, and Tarr knew he wouldn't get an answer from her.

"I'll go get our bedding." She turned her back on him and started toward the hallway. "You build up the fire, and we'll go from there."

eight

Briar's nose seemed to absorb all the chill in the air. She'd taken a few baby steps with Tarr—telling him a little bit about her family over her favorite pudding cups. Of course he wanted more, and she couldn't blame him. He had been holding her hand a lot, and Briar didn't even recognize her life for those few minutes while she sat on the hearth with his arm around her and everything warm and good permeating from him to her.

Of course, her old fear and familiar panic had set in, and she'd put a layer of distance between them once again. She'd spent too long fiddling with the pillows and blankets on their couch-bed for the night, while Tarr sat in the recliner he'd pulled closer to the fire, studying something on his phone.

He'd helped her lower blinds and close them, put weather-prevention strips along the floor at the front and back doors, and close off as much of the house as possible. The generator powered the hot-water heater, the refrigerator, the furnace, and the lights. She lowered the thermostat to sixty-four, thinking the fire would provide enough heat to conserve the energy and not kick the furnace on all night long.

She and Tarr had just finished the eighth or ninth round of a card game he'd played on the rodeo circuit, and she'd made a chilly escape to her bedroom to change into pajamas, and then to the bathroom to brush her teeth and take care of her other bedtime rituals.

Now, she stood in the mouth of the hallway and watched as Tarr wrestled Wiggins into a doggy sweatshirt, telling him things like, "You're the bestest boy ever," and "You look so handsome in this sweatshirt, buddy," and "This will keep you nice and warm tonight."

Wiggins never seemed to hurt for heat, and Briar hoped he would lay by her that night so she could be sandwiched between two warm, breathing bodies.

Tarr chuckled as Wiggins licked his face, and Briar regretted the little bit of attitude she'd let seep back into their relationship. "I'm done in the bathroom," she said.

Tarr twisted to look over his shoulder at her, his smile staying firmly hitched into place. "All right," he drawled.

He'd changed into a pair of basketball shorts and a T-shirt, and he didn't even seem to feel the cold. He approached where she stood blocking the entrance to the hall, and she simply watched him, her eyes traveling up his body to meet his when he arrived directly in front of her.

"Is there a password, sweetheart?"

She wanted to touch him, so she reached out and placed her hand against his chest. "No."

His smile faded into a more serious expression. Mother Nature could have blown down the front door and let in the blizzard raging outside, and Briar would not have looked away from Tarr Olson.

"I'm sorry about earlier." The words scraped her throat as she pushed them out. "I'm not good at letting people in."

"I know that, honey." He leaned down and swept his lips across her cheek. "I'm hoping the more you do it, the easier it will become."

With that, he brushed by her and went halfway down the hall and into the bathroom. The door clicking closed behind him jolted Briar out of her own mind, and she walked over to the dining room table where they'd been playing cards and picked up the electric lantern she'd found in her hall closet. She moved it to the end table in the living room and pulled back the blankets she'd laid on the front of the couch where she would be sleeping.

"Come on, Wiggy."

Wiggins jumped up onto the end of the couch-bed, circled a couple of times, and lay down. She tucked her feet right against his warm back and adjusted her pillow under her head to a more comfortable position.

Tarr came out only seconds later, and he sighed as he pulled back the covers on his half of the tiny couch. She slept in a queen-sized bed, and while yes, Tarr had held her there many times over the past few months as she healed from her injuries, tonight definitely felt different.

He wasn't her boyfriend—*yet,* her mind screamed—but he'd admitted that he liked her. He'd called her pretty. They had been on a date that day, and she had been holding his hand since last night. She'd invited him to stay here until more suitable housing could be found, and not only because she felt bad for him or because it was the right thing to do. She'd done it, because she wanted Tarr in her life. Why that was so hard for her to admit she didn't know.

She'd brought in a queen-size comforter for herself and the

one from Tarr's air bed in the guest room. She wouldn't have to touch him at all tonight. He'd just built up the fire, so when Briar reached and snapped off the lantern, plenty of light still filled the cabin.

With her back still to him, she asked, "Do you have enough room?"

"Plenty," he whispered.

Briar closed her eyes against the flickering firelight, but it didn't do much to dull the orange glow. Without thinking, she rolled over and piled her blankets behind her, creating more darkness. She scooted in closer to the middle of the couch, and in one effortless move, she lifted that side of her comforter and tossed it over Tarr's shoulder.

"We'll be warmer if we share blankets."

Tarr said nothing, but he held out the edge of his blanket, and Briar took it and pulled it over her body as she slid ever closer to him. Within moments, he enveloped her in his strong, warm arms, and she nestled deep into the comfort of his chest.

A sigh moved through her whole body, and Tarr actually let it out of his mouth.

"This does feel like when I used to stay over when you were healing," he said.

"Mm," she hummed, but she didn't know what else to say.

"Did you ever build a snowman growing up?" Tarr asked.

"All the time."

"Maybe after we take care of the animals tomorrow," he whispered, his voice entering her ears as well as rumbling through his chest and against her cheek. "We could make one. I've only ever made a couple."

"In your whole life?" she asked.

He chuckled. "In my whole life, sweetheart."

She tipped her head back. "If it stops snowing and we're all dug out, I'd build a snowman with you."

He pressed his lips to her forehead, and then she cuddled into his embrace again. "It does feel different, Tarr."

"Yeah, it sure does."

"I'm going to try," she whispered, though pure exhaustion pulled through her and all she wanted to do was go to sleep.

"Try what, baby?"

"To talk to you," she whispered. "To be nicer. To not panic about letting someone into my life."

"Someone," he whispered back. "Or specifically me?"

She thought about it for a few seconds, her brain so, so tired. "Someone," she said. "It's not you, Tarr, though it is you, because you're the one trying to get closer to me. What you don't get is...I don't trust anyone."

He ran his hand up the back of her arm and brushed her hair back off her face. "I'm really sorry about whatever happened to make you feel like that about everyone. Will you tell me about it one day?"

Briar didn't want to, but something deep in her heart told her that if she really wanted to share her life with a man like Tarr, she would have to figure out a way to tell him everything, kick down every wall, and let him walk through every door. The very idea sent her spiraling, and Tarr's arms tightened around her.

"Hey, it's fine, honey," he said. "You're fine. It doesn't have to be tonight. I'll be as patient as I can, I promise."

"I didn't even say anything," she said.

"Yeah, but your whole body turned tight."

Briar felt it then, and she took a deep breath and blew it all out, trying to send the tension with it. It worked a little bit, and she relaxed back into his chest, where she hoped she could find true rest tonight.

"My parents had huge expectations for me," she said. "They were both rodeo celebrities in Calgary, and my daddy still calls at the Stampede. Did you ever ride there?"

"Yeah, sure," Tarr said. "I didn't know any Prescotts, though."

Briar swallowed the lump in her throat, but the words wouldn't go with it. "That's because his name is Alvin Perry."

Tarr pulled in a sharp breath. "Oh...I know Alvin Perry."

"He's my daddy," Briar said. "I changed my name when I came to the US and became a citizen here."

"You did? Why?"

Briar exhaled again, but this time none of the tension left with the air. She kept her eyes closed, but the scent of Tarr's skin, his clothes, his cologne stuck in her nose. "So that they couldn't find me," she said. "He's big in the rodeo, and my momma was a championship barrel racer and stunt rider to boot."

"Yeah," Tarr said slowly. "What was her name again?"

He paused for a moment, and then they said together, "Regina."

"That's right," Tarr added. "I feel like I met her a few times."

"I'm sure you did," Briar said. "They used to host a dinner for the elite champions before the Stampede. They even did it after they got divorced."

"Yeah," Tarr said. "Though I think they'd stopped by the time I could have been invited."

"It's been about ten years." She tried to keep the memories at bay, but it took so much energy—energy Briar didn't currently have.

"Yeah, so just before my time," Tarr said. "But I think they were at a gala or something the last year I rode in the rodeo."

"Sounds like them." Briar didn't hate her parents. She simply didn't understand them.

"I just have to know," Tarr said. "Did you ride in the rodeo, honey?"

"No," she said.

"Then why do you hate it so much?"

Briar sighed, because the answer to that question couldn't be summed up with one sentence. It was like a thirty-sided die that, no matter how she rolled, a reason would come up for why she disliked the rodeo and the atmosphere surrounding it.

"There are a lot of reasons," she said. "Some of them small and some of them big. One of them has to do with the fact that every cowboy I dated came from the rodeo, and they all treated me badly. They all abandoned me when I got hurt, and they all took my parents' side when I desperately needed someone to be on mine."

Tarr let a few seconds go by, and then he said, "I'm real sorry about that, Briar."

He didn't press her to know more about how she'd gotten hurt, and when he breathed in deeply, so did she. She matched his slow, even exhale and whispered, "I like you, Tarr. Thanks for always being there," before she finally succumbed to her exhaustion, and fell asleep.

nine

Tarr woke when a blast of cold air slapped him across the face, there one moment and then gone with the snick of the front door closing. The warmth from the fire absorbed the chill quickly, and it caused a small smile to permeate his soul.

He'd gotten up twice in the night to rebuild and stoke the fire, and each time he'd eased back into bed and taken Briar right back into his arms without waking her. She wasn't there now, though, and he suspected she'd gotten up and gone to sit on the front porch.

She was definitely more of an early bird than he was. He liked to stay up late and sleep in, but he'd been here enough over the last few months to know that Briar got up early and took her coffee on the front porch while Wiggins ran around the yard.

Then she started her day over at the farm, usually helping Bobbie Jo with the goats and lambs and doing her rounds with the animals to check on their health and well-being. She'd chat with Tucker about the veterinary needs of the animals, and she usually disappeared into a tiny office in the rodeo barn just after lunch.

Tarr's Texas bones still felt chilled, and he tucked the blankets in all around him and stayed in bed for a little longer. He dozed, sleeping on and off, finally getting up when his need to use the bathroom and his desire for hot coffee couldn't be ignored any longer.

He set coffee to brew, surprised Briar hadn't done it yet, and then padded down the hall to the bathroom and then the guest room, where he got dressed in jeans, a T-shirt, and a sweatshirt his momma had sent him last week for Thanksgiving.

It was dark brown and said *GOBBLE* on the front in all capital letters, done in a burnt-orange, cream, and tan plaid. She'd made it, just as she had many other sweatshirts, and he had one for every season, holiday, birthday, and occasion. He even had a couple of old sweatshirts with his horses' names on them that he used to ride in the rodeo, and a couple that said *JUST FOR FUN* on the front, as that was the name of the bull that Tarr had ridden and conquered in the NPR finals to become the bull-riding world champion a few years ago.

Though the bedroom wasn't exactly warm and the call of coffee strong, he quickly tapped out a text to his mother: *Missing you today, Momma, but I had a real first date with Briar yesterday, and I survived my first snowstorm of the season. Of course I couldn't stay in the RV.*

He chuckled and shook his head. *You were right. It's not going to work for this winter, but Briar let me stay at her house, and I'm going to figure out something else.*

I was just about to call you, his momma said. *I saw the weather up there was really bad, and I wanted to make sure you were okay.*

Doing just fine, Tarr said.

A DATE WITH BRIAR???? came in next, and Tarr once again shook his head.

Don't make a big deal of it, Momma. It's Briar, remember?

From down the hall, she called, "Tarr?"

He looked away from his phone. "Just getting dressed," he called back. *I'll tell you more about it when I'm alone, okay? We're gonna eat breakfast and go work on the farm. Don't make a big deal out of this.*

I'm not the one making a big deal out of it, his momma said. *You're the one who told me in your first breath.*

Tarr grinned, shoved his phone away, though it buzzed in his back pocket, and went to greet Briar. "I was just coming to check on you," he said when he arrived in the front of the house. "Where's Wiggy?"

"I came in to get some treats for him." She opened the front cupboard on the island and pulled out a bag of dog treats. "He loves the snow so much, and I can't get him out of it."

She didn't sound super happy about it, but she did give Tarr a smile as she went by him and back out the front door. He followed her and found the dog romping through the snow, diving down into it and chomping at it as if he'd never seen the stuff before.

"He loves the snow," Tarr said, laughing. "I don't get it. This stuff is insane."

"We're from Canada," Briar said. "Snow is in our blood." She smiled as he came to her side. "I smelled coffee in there, and I was hoping you would have breakfast ready too."

"Oh, you were, huh?" He grinned down at her. "I suppose you want those breakfast sandwiches, because you requested the English muffins and all that."

"I mean, if you don't mind." She turned back to the front

yard and whistled through her teeth. "Come on, Wiggins. It's time to come in."

"I guess we have time," Tarr said.

"Yeah, you slept late."

"It's barely eight o'clock."

Briar grinned at him. "I like your sweatshirt."

He looked down at it, though he knew exactly what he wore. "Thanks. My momma makes them."

Briar's eyebrows went up. "She does?"

"Sure does. My daddy owns a T-shirt printing and design company in Texas, and Momma makes these and sells them at craft fairs and booths and stuff like that."

"Wow," Briar said, and she reached out and traced one fingertip along the G on his chest. "It's very festive."

She sighed as she turned back to Wiggins, who seemed no closer to coming in from his snowy romp. "This dog is going to be the death of me."

"Hey, better him than me," Tarr said, and he laughed as he brushed his fingers along hers and then turned to go back into the house to make breakfast.

He had just reached the doorknob when Briar said, "Tarr."

"Yeah?"

"My truth for today is that talking is good for me."

"That's a good one," Tarr said.

"What's yours?" she asked.

He turned back to her and found Briar watching him with interest and a hint of open vulnerability right there on her face. "I don't know," he said. "Can I think about it?"

"Yeah, sure," she said.

Tarr nodded and went back into the cabin. Before going to make breakfast, he opened all the blinds in the cabin, because the snowstorm had blown itself out, leaving the bright winter sunshine to reflect off all that snow and up into the house. He knew Briar loved the natural light, and he did too.

He thought about what his truth could be as he scrambled eggs and put them in the microwave to cook for her. She'd eat them if they were extremely dry and basically not egg-like at all. Tarr had come to appreciate microwaved scrambled eggs from his time on the road, when he didn't always have access to a stove and frying pan.

He made sausage patties and laid them in a pan, thinking about his truth for the day. The real truth was, Tarr would do anything to make Briar happy, but he didn't want to tell her that, and he also didn't want his own happiness to be sacrificed in favor of hers. He also wasn't as good at her game as she was, and he knew he was thinking too big-picture. She was talking about what she could do *that day* to move past some of the barriers in her life.

Tarr wasn't sure what barriers he had that he needed to hurdle, and his mind ran through his relationship with his momma and daddy, with Tuck and Bobbie Jo, with Briar, and finally with his older brother, Wayne. That relationship needed a lot of repair, and Tarr had no idea where to start.

"Perhaps with talking," he murmured to himself, as it probably wouldn't kill him to send his brother a text and ask him how he was doing. Did it matter that Wayne would never do that for him, that Wayne had not called once after Tarr had been knocked unconscious, hospitalized, and brutally injured in a rodeo accident? Did the slights and wrongs he felt had been committed against him mean that he could withhold his forgiveness from his brother forever?

Tarr didn't know, and he frowned, thinking about Briar and her parents and how she hadn't spoken to them in over four years. He'd believed the two of them complete opposites, but the more he learned about her, the more he realized they were more alike than he'd thought.

"Go on," Briar said from behind him. "He'll give you some sausage."

Tarr turned at the clickety-clack of dog claws on the hard-wood floor, and he pinched off a piece of cooked sausage from one of the patties he'd browned up. "You're finally coming in, huh?"

He fed the sausage to Wiggins and then grabbed a kitchen towel and scrubbed the dog's face and ears and down his back to get him a little bit drier. "You're soaking wet, bud."

"It's a heavy, wet snow," Briar said. "It's going to be a beast to dig ourselves out and get over to the barn."

Tarr looked at her and her unhappy expression, and then pulled his phone out of his back pocket. "I'll text Ashton, and he'll bring the tractor."

For once, Briar didn't argue, and she sat at the bar as he slid a plate with her hard-scrambled eggs, sausage, and cheese on a perfectly toasted English muffin in front of her.

"Thank you, Tarr," she said. "This looks amazing."

He tapped out a quick message to Ashton about coming to get them out at Briar's cabin, got a confirmation, and then looked back at the woman who had consumed his every thought for months now.

"I think my truth for today is that I don't need to be so stubborn," he said.

Briar blinked at him. "You? Stubborn? I don't think those two words go together." She grinned at him, and Tarr simply rolled his eyes.

He joined her at the bar and looked over to her. "Let's do favorites over breakfast."

"What does that mean?

"You know, like, I'll say something like 'animal,' and you tell me your favorite one."

Briar blinked at him. "Is this how dating works now?"

Tarr's eyebrows practically shot off his face. "Are we dating?"

Briar's expression settled into that familiar glare he knew so well. "Come on, Tarr. Don't act like that."

"Act like what?" he asked.

"Like...don't you want to go out with me?"

"Yeah, of course I do," he said. "I just didn't know that one date and one night in a snowstorm equaled dat*ing*. That usually takes a few dates and a conversation like this."

"Well, then let's have the conversation," Briar said. "I hate playing games."

Tarr laughed. "Yeah, honey, I know you do. Do you think I'm playing a game?"

"No," she said with plenty of saltiness in her tone.

"Does that mean if I ask you to dinner for tonight, you'll go?"

She searched his face. For what, Tarr had no idea. And then, in Briar's usual hot-cold fashion, her blue eyes became like pools of warm, inviting water as everything around her softened. "Yeah, I'd go to dinner with you tonight, especially if a certain cowboy wanted to take me to that place where they have the cheddar-cheese biscuits."

Tarr laughed again as he lifted his breakfast sandwich to his mouth. "I don't know much about you, Briar, but I've definitely learned that if I want to get you on my side, I have to feed you well."

She giggled with him, and after Tarr finished his first bite of breakfast, he asked, "Okay, favorite food?"

"Potatoes," Briar said, without missing a beat.

"Potatoes?" Tarr shook his head. "That's barely a food at all."

"Are you joking right now?" Briar pinned him with a sharp look and shook her head. "You can make potatoes into anything, cowboy. Hash browns, French fries, mashed potatoes and gravy. They're so versatile, and they're delicious with salt and pepper, and ketchup, or gravy and cheese. Poutine! Have you ever had poutine? Because it's *delicious*."

Tarr blinked at her and then burst out laughing. "No, but you're definitely gonna make me some of that this week for our third date."

ten

B riar smiled at the snowman standing sentinel in her front yard as she jogged down the front steps and hit the sidewalk running. She wasn't late, but no normal human being wanted to spend more time outside in frigid weather than they needed to.

She whistled at Wiggins and yelled, "Come on, you," as she reached the back door of her SUV and pulled it open. She'd come out fifteen minutes ago to start the car, because while she'd grown up in Canada and did enjoy winter, she *hated* scraping her windshield.

Wiggins barked and ran in a full circle around the snowman before galloping through the wet mess to the SUV. He leapt into the back seat, and Briar closed the door behind him and hurried around to the driver's side.

Blessed heat filled the vehicle, and she sighed as she reached to flip on the windshield wipers. They removed the melted ice, and Briar backed out of her cleared driveway and onto the dirt road that dead-ended at her house.

Nerves stampeded through her, because Tuck had said he would come find her that morning after he completed his morning farm chores. He and Tarr fed all of the rodeo animals, which included nine horses, several cows, over a dozen calves, and a couple of bulls. In addition to that, Bobbie Jo cared for more than one hundred goats of varying ages and breeds.

Despite being attacked there, Briar still loved going out to the Goatel, and she helped Bobbie Jo every morning with her herd. Then she'd walk through the stable and barns and pastures where the rodeo animals lived, checking on them as well.

Once upon a time, she'd aspired to be a farrier. She'd even taken a couple of classes, but she'd given that up quickly. Still, she could assess injuries and change horseshoes and do basic, minor things before she had to call in someone more skilled than her. She only held a veterinary technician certificate, so she wasn't a full-fledged vet and couldn't prescribe medications and other things that doctors could do, but Tucker had Kristie Higgins on speed dial, as she was currently engaged to the foreman at his family farm. She had come and done a few things here and there when the situation once again exceeded Briar's expertise and ability.

"He's going to hire you again," she told herself as she made the turn and the big rodeo arena and barns came into view.

She automatically glanced left, where Tarr's RV sat on the far corner of the parcel of land segmented by roads. His truck wasn't there, as he'd left earlier than her to do the feeding. She hadn't put an end date on when he would need to have somewhere else to stay, and since the power hadn't come back on yet, they'd shared the couch bed again last night.

As she started to drive by the arena, she noticed the lights shining from above the doorways. "So the electricity is on here," she said. It should be the same grid system, though she knew her lines were older and might need more maintenance.

The snow that had fallen had been filled with water—heavy and wet, perfect for making snowmen...and taking down power lines. The main city hub of Denver and most of its suburbs had gotten their power restored yesterday morning, but Briar had checked the website and knew that crews were still working on some of the outlying areas.

She passed Tarr's big black truck parked right next to Tucker's white one and continued around to the back of the facilities where the Goatel waited. Tucker also employed a facilities manager, and he and Bobbie Jo had just hired an agricultural specialist to help them plant the farm next year as well.

She put her car in park and took a deep breath, trying to soothe her worries with the fact that Tucker had said right to her face that he saw no reason to find someone else to take care of the animals. They discussed her salary, both thought it was fair, and he said he'd draw up another contract and get it to her "soon."

He'd texted a few questions last night about what her actual address was, and whether or not her last name had two Ts or one. A small smile touched her face as she recalled how embarrassed he'd been that he didn't even know how to spell her last name.

Briar thought about names as she got out of her SUV, released Wiggins, and the two of them made their way into the Goatel. All of the roads and walkways had been cleared by Ashton and the plow he attached to the front of the tractor. Tarr and Tuck and even Bobbie Jo had been out with shovels to clear the smaller spaces, and someone had been in the Goatel with a four-wheeler to move the snow to the fences.

She found Bobbie Jo in the enclosure, talking to some of her goats as she fed them. "Good morning," Briar said.

The blonde woman turned toward her, a smile quickly appearing on her face and then disappearing. "Good morning to you too." She watched as Briar reached for a pair of gloves on the shelf next to the door.

Briar hated nothing more than being watched. In general, she really liked Tucker and Bobbie Jo. She'd been very worried about the sale of the farm and the transition to a new owner, as she didn't always mesh with people. But, as it turned out, Bobbie Jo possessed an incredibly salty streak as well, and she was as no-nonsense as Briar when it came to work, caring for animals, and employing her passion about something she cared about.

Only Tuck seemed to soften her, at least from what Briar had seen, and no matter how early Briar came out to the Goatel, Bobbie Jo always beat her here.

"How are things here?" Briar asked.

"Just humming along," Bobbie Jo said. "The goats don't seem to mind the snow at all." She turned back to them, a fond smile reappearing on her face. Fine, the goats softened her too. "What about you? How are things at the cabin with Tarr?" She deliberately didn't look at Briar then, but Briar didn't mind the question so much.

"They're fine," she said. "We still don't have power, but we're making do with the fireplace and my gas appliances." She joined Bobbie Jo in front of one of the pens. "Are we letting them out today?"

"Yeah," Bobbie Jo said with a sigh. "I got a lot of the pasture cleared, and we'll let them get out there and frolic."

Briar nodded and dusted her hands together. "I'll go outside and get the gate open then."

"But you guys are doing okay with hot water? Your generator is still running?"

Briar met Bobbie Jo's eyes then, and she did find care and compassion in the other woman's expression. "Yeah, it's running okay," she said. "The furnace is the biggest energy hog, so if I can keep the fire burning to keep the place warm, it does great with the hot water heater and the fridge."

Bobbie Jo nodded. "I'm glad. You let us know if you two need to come stay with us, okay?"

"I thought Rosie was coming." Briar tilted her head and watched Bobbie Jo.

"She is," she said. "She was supposed to be here today, but the storm that we got moved north, and she decided to postpone her trip a couple of days." Bobbie Jo stuck another sheaf of hay into the feeder, though the goats had plenty. "We've got seven bedrooms, Briar. There's plenty of room for you, Tarr, *and* Rosie." She lifted her head and met her eyes squarely again. "And us. Tarr doesn't need to stay somewhere else."

"I know that," Briar said. "And you know that. Heck, even *he* knows that. He's just being stubborn."

"I don't get it," Bobbie Jo said. "It's not like me and Tucker are gross."

Briar smiled at her and shook her head. "No, you're not. I don't know why he's hung up on not staying with you."

"Maybe you could talk to him about it." Bobbie Jo looked so hopeful, and it almost seemed like her statement had a question mark at the end of it.

Briar blinked and then burst out laughing. "I don't think that's going to work," she said between giggles.

Bobbie Jo grinned at her and leaned one hip against the inside enclosure gate. "Why not? He likes you and respects you and will listen to you."

"Yeah, he likes *you* and respects *you* and will listen to *you* too," Briar said. "I don't think anything I suggest is going to be something Tarr will be raring to do."

"That's just not true," Bobbie Jo said. "That man would bend over backwards to make you happy."

The mood in the Goatel changed instantly, and Briar's smile dropped from her face at the same time her giggles dried up. "I've never asked him to do a single thing for me."

Bobbie Jo backpedaled as well, her eyes widening. "Everyone knows that, Briar," she said. "Just like he made it abundantly clear that *he* was the one who was going to take care of you after you got hurt."

Briar had no idea how to respond to that. She'd been in so much pain, she hadn't paid attention to anything beyond the walls of her cabin.

"I'm just saying," Bobbie Jo said. "Tucker's talking to his momma to see if she can get him to move in with us, and I just think that if he had another woman he really respected saying the same thing...he might seriously consider it."

Briar nodded and swallowed, trying to get her emotions to calm. Of course, she knew Tarr liked her. He'd said the words right out loud, and he held her with all the tender care Briar had ever wanted.

"If it feels natural, I can talk to him about it," she said. "Though I've asked him before why he doesn't stay with you, and he said it just doesn't feel right."

She nodded, hoping Bobbie Jo would get the signal that that ended the conversation, and then she left the Goatel and walked around the corner to open the outside gate to release the goats. They streamed out, some of them thrilled to be free, while others took their time, sauntering out when they were ready. She tied the gate back so that it wouldn't flop around in the weather and injure an animal or herself, and then she waded through the goats, most of them bleating and begging for her to open the outside gate that would let them into the pasture.

They had plenty of outdoor space here in the Goatel area as well, and Tuck and Tarr had reinforced the fences, adding several feet to their height and digging down into the ground so that the coyotes couldn't go underneath the way they had last time.

Briar opened the first gate, and of course the more eager goats flooded into the area between it and the second security measure.

"You guys," she said. "You've got to let me go through first. Noah, back up."

Noah did not back up. In fact, the senior goat pressed even further into the gate, forcing Briar to reach over his tall, bulbous body and struggle to unlatch that gate. She finally got it, and Noah himself pushed it out as he led the way into the pasture.

Briar flattened herself against the fence as goats continued to stream by her, and she laughed as a couple of the smaller kids ran and kicked up their back legs.

The sky shone a clear, crystal blue today, which only meant the air caused a cold sear deep in her lungs with every breath. Briar didn't mind it so much, though she did need to get her sunglasses or goggles if she was going to work outside for any length of time, what with so much sunshine glinting off so much snow.

In reality, this snow wouldn't last, and it would probably melt by the weekend, as they didn't truly have snow that stayed on the ground for longer than a few days until January—and usually only when they got back-to-back storms in close succession.

Despite the cold, Briar took a deep breath, closed her eyes, and tilted her head back, letting her entire vision fill with white light. She'd rather be here doing this than anywhere else.

"Thank you, Dear Lord, for leading me to this farm and giving me a place of sanctuary," she whispered.

"Morning, Briar."

She opened her eyes and turned toward the sound of Tucker's voice. He stood just outside the Goatel, and he lifted a manila folder in one hand. Briar's heart rate crashed through her body, and she quickly lunged at the outside gate.

"I just have to secure this," she called.

She did that for both gates, so the goats could come and go from their enclosure. By the time she started back toward the Goatel, Bobbie Jo had joined Tucker, and the three of them ducked back inside—"So I can breathe," Tucker said.

In the Goatel, he handed her the envelope, and Bobbie Jo extended a pen, her smile radiant and glorious. "Now, I gave you a raise," Tucker said. "It's not much—only about a thousand dollars a month, but...." He looked at Bobbie Jo, and she looked at him. Then they both swung their attention back to Briar. "You do a real good job here, Briar, and we don't want to lose you."

Briar flipped open the folder, her emotions balling up in her throat and cutting off her voice. She saw the salary sitting there at the top after her name and address, and she looked up.

"Tuck, it's too much. I already get to live in the cabin for free."

"There's a lot of expenses that come with living in a cabin like that," he said. "Firewood, gas for the generator, your utilities. It's not like that thing's airtight, and it needs a new roof."

Briar swallowed and nodded. "It does need a new roof."

"I know a certain cowboy who could probably help you with that," Tucker said. "Seeing as how Tarr's building his own place and all that. He probably knows how to fix a few cracks and repair a roof."

"I'm sure he does," Bobbie Jo said.

Briar looked up. "I don't need Tarr to fix my roof for free."

Tucker nodded to the packet of papers in her hand. "You're welcome to look over that and have your lawyer look at it. I used a lawyer to help me draft it. Bobbie Jo went over it, and we think it's pretty sound, but I'm happy to hear your thoughts on it."

"I don't have a lawyer." Briar took the pen from Bobbie Jo. "I still think the salary's too much, but I'm not going to say no to it."

After all, she knew Tucker was a billionaire and that he and Tarr weren't running their rodeo-animal training business for free. They sold those animals, and he trained Rosie Young for a fee. He'd just signed on another client as well, a man named Stretch Maughan, who'd be coming to the farm after the NPR finals next week.

Briar looked up every person who came to the farm, as meeting new people made her nervous and somehow posed a threat to this quiet, small-town haven she'd built for herself. Yes, things had definitely changed when Clive sold the farm to Tuck, but so far, none of them had been too damaging.

She signed the contract and handed it back to Tucker. "Thank you." She glanced over to Bobbie Jo. "Both of you. I really appreciate it. I love this farm."

"And we love having you here." Bobbie Jo stepped forward and hugged Briar. "Good. I'm glad that's done."

She looked at Tuck, and Tucker quickly stepped forward and hugged Briar as well. "How's Tarr doing?" he asked.

"Haven't you seen him already today?" Briar asked, because she didn't want to talk about Tarr with his best friend.

"Yeah, but he won't tell me anything," Tucker said.

Briar stepped back and grinned at him. "Well, if he's not going to tell you, I'm certainly not."

Tucker sighed and rolled his head, stretching his neck left and right. "You two are made for each other with your stubbornness."

Briar grinned even wider as a frown appeared between Tucker's eyes. "I just heard from Rosie. She'll be here tomorrow afternoon, and I want you to check her horses when she gets here."

"Yeah, of course," Briar said, though having to come face-to-face with someone active in the rodeo made her pulse skip and bounce through her body in an uncomfortable way.

Their little meeting in the Goatel broke up, and with Bobbie Jo and Tucker ducking outside first, Briar stayed inside and pulled out her phone, happiness streaming through her in a way she hadn't experienced in a long, long time. She'd been smiling so much more since Thanksgiving, and she knew it had everything to do with Tarr.

Good news, she texted to him. *I just signed an open-ended contract to stay on here at the farm!*

Wow, that's amazing, sweetheart, he sent back immediately.

Yeah, so you can't get rid of me now.

I don't want to get rid of you.

Briar sighed and smiled, and she could just hear Tarr saying that in his soft, Texan drawl. She imagined his hand sneaking around to her lower back and bringing her closer, and the scent of his skin and cologne in her nose. A flicker of panic moved through her that she'd started to feel so comfortable with him, and that he'd gotten in so close. She pushed it away, because today was a happy day, and she wanted Tarr in her life.

"You do," she told herself, that becoming her truth for the day. "I want Tarr Olson in my life, and that's the truth."

Now, she just had to figure out how to believe it, live it, breathe it, without falling into full panic mode.

93

<h1 style="text-align:center">eleven</h1>

"Go on, Davy." Tarr patted the horse's rump to get him to move out of the stall. He'd been rearranging animals for a couple of hours now in anticipation of Rosie Young's arrival at the facilities.

She'd been set to show up yesterday afternoon, but the storm had delayed her. Then her daddy had decided last minute to simply meet her in Las Vegas for the NPR finals, so she would be traveling with her older brother, Cole, and his wife, Rachel, instead.

Tucker and Bobbie Jo had been making appropriate preparations at the mansion for the past twenty-four hours, and that left Tarr and Ashton to prep the facilities, as Rosie would want to ride the moment she stepped out of the truck.

She reminded him so much of himself—travel wasn't his favorite part of being on the rodeo circuit, and that he sometimes itched for the wide open sky and the feel of a horse underneath him.

"Go on, you lazy thing. You're not even being ridden today,

so stop complaining." Tarr grinned as Davy finally started to move, and he strode along the length of the horse's body to his neck, grabbing the lead rope so Davy couldn't dictate where he wanted to go. The horse was one of their most stubborn, but Tarr loved him for it.

Rosie would be riding Pumpkin Spice, a pretty dark-orange horse, as well as a gray who knew how to cut close to the barrels. Tarr had been training them both for about a year now, and having a pro barrel racer here to work them would show him what they could really do. His own anticipation climbed as he got Davy settled in his new stall and went to get Cocoa Pebbles.

Rosie was bringing two horses with her, but it was a long drive from Coral Canyon, Wyoming, down to the Deerfield area of Colorado, and her horses would have been trailered for about ten hours by the time they arrived. Briar should be on-site to check them while Tuck, Bobbie Jo, and Tarr handled greeting the rodeo stars.

Cole Young had never ridden in the rodeo, but he worked at his wife's family's animal training facility—a ranch called Whispering Pines just north of Coral Canyon. They did all the same things that Tarr and Tuck were trying to do here: train animals for the rodeo.

Rachel's two older brothers, another man named Cole, and Warren both rode in the rodeo, retreating to their wintry farm for rest in the off-season. She had another brother named Harrison, who did manual labor around their facility and taught music lessons in town.

The Walkers were a huge rodeo family stemming from Wyatt Walker himself—the Rodeo King and one of the most winning cowboys ever to ride. Tarr had grown up *idolizing* Wyatt Walker, wearing his clothes and cologne and watching all of his videos. It took a special personality to be in the rodeo, because one not only had to have talent, but also charisma and presence—and Wyatt Walker possessed both in spades.

Tarr could still see the man's double-handed wave as he pulled off his cowboy hat and waved both it and his free hand to the cameras. He'd later told reporters that he did that special wave to tell his momma and daddy *hello, I love you, and thank you*, and Tarr loved the man's family values as much as he liked watching him ride.

Tarr's heartbeat bumped through his body, because he hadn't been this close to the rodeo in a long time. Tucker had been going to Texas to train Rosie for weeks on end. Sometimes Bobbie Jo went with him, especially now that they were married. Everyone would be leaving the farm by the weekend to get down to Las Vegas for the NPR finals, which started the following week.

Tarr had been checking the weather, and the ten-day forecast was barely out. So far—no snow. Having to deal with the farm and all the animals in a snowstorm like what they'd just gotten would be nearly impossible for him, Briar, and Ashton to handle by themselves.

Tuck had said they could call on the cowboys at the Hammond Family Farm, but it was over an hour for them to get here, and with snow covering everything, it would take even longer.

Tarr had simply been praying the weather would hold and the snow would melt until Tuck and Bobbie Jo returned.

He pulled a butterscotch candy out of his pocket and gave it to Cocoa Pebbles before even attempting to move her out of her stall. Once properly treated, the horse would do anything he wanted, and sure enough, she followed him without a lead rope into the stall down on the end.

The snow had melted a little bit more since Saturday, and his and Briar's snowman was looking pretty pathetic. Grasses had started to poke through in the fields again, and once Rosie arrived and everything was situated with her, Tarr would let the animals out to graze while Tuck ran Rosie through exercises and Tarr made notes on his horses' performance.

He finished up with the horses and washed his hands in the barn sink, turning just as Tucker and Bobbie Jo entered.

Bobbie Jo had grown up on a corn farm in Oklahoma and claimed not to know much about rodeo or animals, but she certainly knew how to work hard. Tarr admired her for jumping into whatever task was necessary around the house and farm. He'd grown up on a big farm like this, sans the rodeo facilities, and it had taken them both months to figure out all the chores and maintenance that needed to be done and how to accomplish it.

Tarr much preferred physical work over sitting at any kind of desk and looking at any kind of paperwork. Therefore he'd never gone to college, and he'd been riding in saddles since he was three years old.

"How's it looking out here?" Tuck asked.

"Great," Tarr said. "I just finished moving everyone, so we've got room for Rosie's horses when they get here."

"She's ten minutes out," Bobbie Jo said, glancing around as if she needed to hang a banner to welcome the barrel racer.

"Have you seen Briar?" Tuck asked.

"Not since this morning," Tarr said.

The electricity had come on midafternoon yesterday, and with the furnace now functioning, they'd both retreated to their separate bedrooms. Tarr had slept, but not well, especially compared to having the warm, soft, very female shape of Briar in his arms. He wasn't sure he'd ever truly sleep again without her.

His jaw tightened, and he swallowed, lest he blurt out anything he didn't want Tuck or Bobbie Jo to know. "I'm probably going to move into one of those long-term hotel rental things when you guys get back."

"You really don't need to," Tuck said. "You can have the whole top floor. It's two bedrooms and a bathroom."

"We've even put a microwave and a mini-fridge up there," Bobbie Jo said. "Because that's where Rosie and Cole will be staying."

Tarr nodded. "I'll think about it."

"We go out at the same time in the morning anyway," Tuck said. "And I know you—you're in bed by nine o'clock." He grinned, and Tarr couldn't help returning it.

"It would make more sense if you were on-site," Bobbie Jo said. "Especially in the winter."

"Now you're starting to sound like Briar," he said.

"That's because she's smart," Bobbie Jo said with a grin. "It's *seven* bedrooms, Tarr."

"Three levels. You could live in the basement if you want. It's just a lot cooler down there," Tucker said. "And we'd have to open up all the vents."

"I don't want to live in a basement," Tarr said.

The master bedroom, a guest bedroom, and two full baths sat on the main floor, along with an enormous kitchen, living room, and dining room combo with two-story windows. The steps led up to a loft that overlooked the downstairs living and sitting areas, and then the hallway branched down to the two-bedroom, one-bath suite Tucker was talking about. He'd even put a door on it, and out in the loft was the mini-fridge and the microwave Bobbie Jo had just spoken of.

"You can pay us rent if you want," Tucker said. "As much as the hotel rental, even." He glanced over to Bobbie Jo, grinning. "I mean, I'd take his money. Wouldn't you?"

"It would feed a lot of goats," Bobbie Jo said.

Tarr rolled his eyes. "How long have you guys been rehearsing this?"

"Just since this morning," Bobbie Jo shot back. "Really, Tarr, it's stupid for you to get a hotel, and you can't live in the RV."

"I mean, I guess you could keeping living with Briar," Tuck said. "But honestly, she's right across the hall, and you're sharing a bathroom. How is that less close-quarters and intimate than staying with me and Bobbie Jo?"

"I'll think about it," Tarr said again.

The basement at Tuck's mansion had three bedrooms, an additional one-and-a-half baths, a full kitchen, a theater room, and an open living room. The man definitely had way more space than he needed, even if he and Bobbie Jo started having kids immediately, though they both claimed they were going to wait a couple of years.

The sound of tires on gravel met their ears, and all three of them whipped their attention to the barn door.

"She's here," Tuck said.

"I don't know why you're so nervous," Bobbie Jo said.

"I don't know why you're not," Tuck said. "She's only seen this place in pictures and video. She's never ridden here, and what if she hates it?"

"Tuck, she signed a contract with you, bro," Tarr said. "She can't just quit. And besides, our facilities are the nicest in the state."

"They're nicer than where we train in Texas." Tuck swiftly moved toward the door. He exited first, his laughter bouncing around in the doorway, and then his too-loud voice saying, "You made it!"

A lower male voice said something Tarr couldn't quite make out as he followed his best friend outside. A tall, sandy-haired cowboy stood there, his hand in that of a blonde woman wearing a bright red, puffy coat.

"This is my brother Cole," Rosie said—the blonde powerhouse who'd hired Tucker to be her rodeo trainer and manager.

"So great to meet you," Tuck said.

Tarr moved right into Rosie and gave her a hug. "How was the drive, sweetheart?" he asked, really bringing out his Texas drawl and manners.

"Oh, it was a drive," she said. "This place is so nice, you guys." She beamed at Tarr. "I mean, look at this arena."

"It's huge inside," Tarr said. "Come on, I'll show you." He stepped that way.

"This is my wife, Rachel," Cole Young said before Tarr realized he hadn't met everybody properly yet. He shook Cole's hand, as well as Rachel's, sweeping one kiss along her cheek before stepping back to Tuck's side.

He introduced Bobbie Jo just as Ashton arrived and then took the truck keys from Cole Young.

"My own brother made me ride in the back seat," Rosie said, giving Cole a death glare.

She wore a pair of jeans, cowgirl boots, and a sweater the color of autumn leaves—bright gold. It matched her hair, and though she barely had any curves at all, she possessed plenty of sass.

"I think you said I could ride one of your horses when we got here," she said, hope entering her expression.

"Yep," Tuck said. "Ashton here is going to get yours

unloaded, and we've got our vet tech to check them." He shot a look at Tarr.

Tarr pulled his phone out of his pocket. "I'll text Briar right now."

"I am *so excited* to meet Briar," Rosie said, a new kind of energy pulsing out of her now.

Tarr abandoned his text-quest and looked over to Rosie. "You're so excited to meet Briar?"

"Yeah. You know who she is, right?" Rosie grinned at him and followed Bobbie Jo as she and Tuck started toward the arena doors. "She's only the best trick rider who's ever lived. I mean, you should see some of the stuff she did from the back of a horse."

She looked up at Tarr, who stumbled after her dumbly. Briar was a trick rider? "I think you're thinking of her momma," he said.

"No, I'm not," Rosie said. "She was incredible. She was at every rodeo for so long—the biggest ones too. The Stampede, the NPR—everything. She even did halftime shows at professional football games." She paused just inside the arena and glanced around. "I really want to meet her."

Tarr wanted to meet that woman too, as he'd assumed Briar must've been an ambassador. But a stunt rider?

He quickly fired off a text to her just as Ashton pulled the truck around to the back side of the arena.

"Tarr," Tuck said.

"I'm coming," Tarr said, and he followed everyone into the arena.

The scent of dirt and wood reached his nose, and he loved coming in here. It reminded him of the Friday-night lights of the rodeo, and in moments like this, small and fleeting as they were, he did miss his time on the circuit.

"Briar's right there," Tuck said. "Looks like she's got Pumpkin Spice ready."

Tarr's attention shot to the other end of the arena, where, sure enough, his gorgeous Briar was leading the pretty pumpkin-colored horse toward them.

"Wow, she's pretty," Rosie said, and surely she meant the horse. To Tarr, that statement was all about Briar. Always Briar.

As they closed in on her, Rosie squealed. She ran the last several steps to her and practically yelled, "I am so excited to meet you!"

Briar looked like she had been slapped across the face and then had ice water thrown in her open eyes. She blinked at Rosie rapidly, who grabbed onto her and hugged her.

"Oh, boy," Tucker said under his breath, and Bobbie Jo gasped.

Tarr simply stared while Cole said, "Rosie, give the woman space to breathe."

Rosie hugged her tight and then stepped back. She clapped her hands and bounced on the balls of her feet. "I can't help it. You're, like, a *legend.* I've watched every single one of your trick-riding videos online. And my daddy drove me to Calgary just to see the Stampede when you were headlining it. You were *incredible.*"

Briar stood there, and Tarr watched as every mask she'd ever worn stitched itself back into place. He could practically hear the bricks falling as she rebuilt the walls around her.

"I'm real sorry about your accident," Rosie said next. "I haven't seen anything about you online in so long."

Dreadful silence filled the arena, and Rosie finally seemed to clue in that she'd said or done something to cause it.

Tarr stared at Briar, trying to put all the pieces of her together. His chest pinched that he had to find out that she was a stunt rider and trick performer—and that was how she had gotten injured and left the rodeo scene—from someone who was a perfect stranger to both of them, though they knew Rosie by name through Tuck.

Cole moved to Rosie's side. "You'll have to excuse my sister. She gets really excited about other female legends in the rodeo."

"I'm not a female legend," Briar said curtly.

Tarr quickly moved to her side, wanting to touch her, but the electric energy she put off told him he'd better not.

"Briar is retired from that life," he said as softly and kindly as he could. "She's an amazing vet tech here at Deerfield, and she's going to take great care of your horses." He looked over to her. "Ashton's unloading them now, sweetheart."

Her eyes met his, and he almost fell back from the coldness she harbored there. She softened slightly and said, "I'll go take care of them." She nodded at Rosie, Cole, and Rachel. "It was great to meet you." Then she turned on her heel and marched away.

Rosie stared after her, and Tarr wished he could fix the situation for both of them. "She's just really private," he said.

"I didn't mean anything by it," Rosie said, turning her attention to Tarr. "Have you seen her ride? She's absolutely *incredible*. They said she wouldn't walk again, and I haven't really read or seen anything about her in years. I didn't mean to make things so awkward."

"I told you not to be so exuberant," Cole said. "And to let her lead. I said there would be a reason why you hadn't heard anything, and this is it."

"Briar's amazing," Tuck said. "She just gets a little...." He glanced at Tarr. "Well, she gets a little nervous meeting strangers, that's all. I didn't even know she was a stunt rider."

Tarr's gaze flew to his. "*You* didn't know she was a stunt rider?"

"She's only the best one who's *ever lived*," Rosie said.

Tuck shook his head. "We didn't know."

"Like I said, she's a really private person." Tarr really wished that didn't hurt so much, and that if there was anyone Briar trusted enough to tell about her former career, it would have been him. But she hadn't, and Tarr watched as she disappeared through the far door that led into the stables attached to the arena.

"It's fine," Bobbie Jo said brightly. "I'm sure we'll all hear more about it tonight at dinner."

Tarr's gaze flew to hers, his stomach now rioting. Dinner at the mansion. He'd forgotten that he and Briar and Ashton were joining everyone there tonight, and he started praying that he could actually get Briar out of the cabin and over to the mansion for that meal, because after that altercation...he didn't believe for one minute she would agree to go.

twelve

Briar had no clue how to get her pulse to stop throwing itself against every rib in her body. She stepped into the role of helping Ashton get horses out of the trailer, noticing that one of them seemed to have a little bit of gimp in his back foot.

They wore name tags, of course, because someone as polished and professional as Rosie Young wouldn't simply put her horses in a trailer for anyone to unload without knowing their names. Briar recognized all of the signs of someone who rode the rodeo circuit, and it only made the frown in her soul deepen.

She reached the deep brown animal and ran her hands down both sides of the horse's neck, using the equine's calm energy to bring her heart rate back to normal.

Briar had to be at least five years older than Rosie—maybe ten—and she hated the fact that the young woman had seen her ride and said so much about it in front of everyone else. At the same time, she understood looking people up online, because she did it for everyone she might encounter, including Rosie Young. She'd watched the young woman ride plenty of times since she'd signed a contract with Tuck.

But she wasn't used to people knowing *her* name or watching *her*.

It felt oddly invasive, though she'd literally looked up both Cole and Rosie last night, as well as their daddy, Jem. Cole and Rachel weren't supposed to come with Rosie on this trip, but when Tarr had found out that they would be there, he'd texted Briar to let her know.

She moved the beautiful gelding over to the indoor walking circle, going as slow as the horse wanted and causing him to nose up against her back. She didn't mind the horse trying to bully her, because Briar had grown up around horses and loved them with her whole soul.

She attached the animal to the line and said, "Go on now," in probably the kindest voice she'd used in weeks.

She moved to the edge of the fence as the horse started to walk. She looked back and forth between the two new additions to their barn, as Ashton had gotten the first horse on a walking line too. Rosie's horses both seemed glad to be out of the trailer, and as Briar watched, the one with the slight limp evened out its gait.

Her thoughts turned to Tarr then, though she would need to give these horses a complete check-over once they'd had a little bit of exercise. He'd come right to her side and defended her, and while part of her appreciated that, another part sent out sparks of irritation that he couldn't just mind his own business.

She didn't need Tarr Olson to fight her battles for her, though she'd literally been praying and wishing someone would take her side for years now.

"You can't have it both ways, Briar," she told herself. Then she ducked into the small vet office where she kept her mobile kit and went to tend to the horses.

Later that afternoon, someone knocked on her door, and Briar raised her head from that morning's paperwork, something she was completing a little bit later than normal thanks to Rosie's arrival.

"You haven't been answering any of the texts," Tarr said, leaning one broad shoulder into the doorjamb of her office.

She could only hold his gaze for a moment before she reached for her phone and flipped it over. "I forgot I put this on silent when I was dealing with the horses. It's nothing personal."

"Oh, I think it is." Tarr didn't enter her office, though she wished he would, so she could close the door and stop this conversation from leaking out somewhere else.

"It's about dinner, isn't it?"

"It's about dinner," he confirmed. "And Bobbie Jo's making herself sick with worry, so it would be great if you could reply."

Briar nodded, because no, she didn't want to upset Bobbie Jo or Tuck. She also didn't want to go to dinner tonight at their house with Cole, Rosie, and whatever Cole's wife's name was. Briar had been so inside her head, she couldn't remember it.

"I'm going to head back to the cabin and shower," Tarr said. "But there will be plenty of time for you to do that after me."

"I'm fine," Briar said.

"Yeah, I know you are," Tarr said. "No one's saying you're not."

"Can you come in?" Briar asked, and she got up and slipped by him to close the door herself. He moved further into the office, crowding into the corner by her desk, and she leaned her back against the wood.

"I didn't mean to act crazy," she said.

"You didn't act crazy."

"She threw me for a loop," Briar said, needing him to understand. "I haven't been recognized in years, and I certainly wasn't expecting it from a twenty-year-old."

"Well, you know how teenagers are," Tarr said. "They have online relationships with celebrities that feel real to them."

"I'm *not* a celebrity," Briar said.

"But sweetheart, you *were*." Tarr hooked her with his dark eyes and wouldn't let go.

Briar didn't look away. She heard the things he didn't say: *You were a celebrity and you didn't tell me.*

Why couldn't you tell me you were a stunt rider?

Why did I have to find out through Rosie?

His eyes said it all, as Tarr had never been good at keeping his thoughts and feelings off his face.

"I'm sorry," Briar said, her heartbeat thrashing now for a whole new reason. "Maybe I was a celebrity at some point, but that's not who I am now, and that's not the life I want now, and I don't know how to handle situations like that."

"She feels pretty bad," Tarr said.

"I'll apologize at dinner." Briar swallowed, because a public apology in front of her bosses and owners of the ranch wasn't exactly on her to-do list.

"You could say thank you too," he said.

"All right, *Dad*," she threw at him, instantly regretting the sarcasm. "I mean—" She sighed and sagged against the door. "I'm sorry. You're right. I should have told her thank you and been polite and talked to her like Tuck's client. I know they've been really nervous about her arrival, and I messed it up."

"You didn't mess anything up," Tarr said.

"How did you explain it?"

"We just said you're a really private person," Tarr said. "And we left it at that." He raised his eyebrows. "Did I get it wrong?"

"No," Briar said, because he could've said so many other things.

He nodded to her phone. "Please just text Bobbie Jo back so she can stop worrying."

Briar lifted her phone to do that, and with the task done, she shoved her device in her back pocket and repeated her truth for the day:

I want Tarr Olson in my life.

It was the same as yesterday, and at this point, she didn't know how many times she would have to repeat it to herself, and how many days it would be her truth before she finally accepted it. But she wanted the strength and comfort of his arms around her, so she rushed toward him, taking the two steps and practically barreling into his chest.

He grunted but wrapped his arms around her at the same time.

"I'm sorry," she said. "Please don't be mad at me."

"I haven't looked anything up online," he said. "But it has taken every ounce of willpower I have not to do that."

Briar swallowed and stepped back, her hands sliding along the top ridge of his belt and up his chest. "Don't look online," she said. "Please. Well—I mean, I guess you can look at my channel."

His eyebrows went up, every other feature about him so dark and stormy beneath the shadow of his cowboy hat. "You have your own channel?"

She nodded, her throat so raw. It felt like someone had wrapped it in rubber bands and was continuing to twist and twist and *twist* until she wouldn't be able to get a breath or speak at all. "I have a trick-riding channel," she said. "And it's positive. Some of the commentary that other people do is not complimentary."

"I can't imagine anyone not being complimentary of you," he said, his voice soft and yet so dry, and somehow it made Briar smile.

Tears filled her eyes. "I want you in my life, Tarr Olson. I'm really sorry I hadn't found a way to tell you about the stunt riding yet."

"You had a bad accident?" he asked. Everything about him remained unyielding, his mouth barely moving as he spoke. He kept his hands solidly on her back, holding her in place against him, so she had to lean her head back to see him.

"Yes," she whispered. "It was terrible. I broke both of my legs and a hip and shredded everything up my left side."

"So that's where you got those scars."

She nodded. "That's where I got the scars."

"Rosie seemed surprised that you could walk."

"There was a while there where they said I wouldn't be able to," she said. "I went through a couple of years of extremely difficult physical therapy and exercises—having to call perfect strangers to get rides to the doctor because my own family wouldn't take me, and all of my friends had abandoned me."

"Because you fell?"

"It was more than a fall." She pressed her eyes closed, and tears slithered out of the corners of them and down her cheeks. "I caused a huge accident, Tarr. One horse had to be put down, and another stunt rider was in a coma for a month before she woke up. Everyone blamed me—as they should have."

"I don't believe that," Tarr said.

"Well, people aren't perfect," she said. "And accidents happen."

"Yeah, so how could they blame you?"

"Like I said—some of the comments out there aren't very complimentary. There were people who analyzed the accident videos over and over and over, calling into question whether I'd caused the accident on purpose or not."

Briar had never felt so alone and so out of touch with her own body. "I couldn't believe it, because I had a pretty decent reputation of being kind, of volunteering for things I didn't have to, of leading little children around on their Stampede tours, of taking gigs no one else wanted."

She sighed and opened her eyes again.

Tarr reached up and brushed her tears away in one of the sweetest, most tender gestures anyone had ever done for her.

"But it doesn't really matter what's true or not, as long as they get likes and clicks and comments online, right?"

"No," Tarr said. "I don't care about what happens online at all. I care about *you*, and what's right and true."

"It was an accident," Briar said forcefully. "I didn't mean to hurt anyone or any animal, and it ended my career. How could I *want* that to happen? I was making hundreds of thousands of dollars as a rider, performing, and doing social media. Why would I want to ruin that?"

Tarr didn't say anything, and he didn't have to. He simply studied her and then slid his hand up to the back of her head and pressed it against his chest.

"I believe you, honey," he whispered, and better words had never been spoken.

"I did learn to walk again," Briar said. "And I've even ridden a horse a few times—though certainly not to do any of my stunts or tricks. As soon as I could, I left Canada and I changed my name, and I've been living and working here on this farm for four years now."

"Almost five," he said. "And now with a long-term employment contract in place."

Briar heard the smile in his voice, and she managed a small one of her own. "Yeah, if Tuck doesn't fire me after how I treated his only client."

"He's not gonna fire you, sweetheart." Tarr edged back and dropped his hand to hers. "Come on. Let's go home and get cleaned up for dinner."

Briar looked up at him. "Are we really okay?"

He thought for a moment and then nodded. "Yeah, we're really okay." He leaned down, and Briar thought for sure he'd kiss her. She pulled in a breath, and every muscle in her body tightened, but he only swept his lips across her cheek and then pressed his mouth to her ear as he whispered, "Because my truth for today, Briar, is that I want you in my life too."

She relaxed in his arms, though his words terrified her and struck a dissonant chord that echoed along with every heartbeat. She would have to find a way past this, to truly believe that he wanted her in his life when so many other people didn't, or she could lose this handsome cowboy prince forever.

thirteen

Deacon Hammond adjusted his jacket over his shoulders, wondering if he was trying too hard. Putting himself together after a long day on the farm for a dinner date automatically felt like too much work. In the past couple of months, he'd worn his best jeans, bought new shirts, cowboy boots, and even a new hat for the dates he'd been going on. He'd only made it to a second date with one woman, and then she'd confessed that he felt more like a brother than a boyfriend.

He hadn't asked anyone out from the farm again...until now.

"Alaska Whitby," he muttered to his reflection, wondering why he was entering this date with dread instead of excitement. Maybe because dating felt like a chore now, instead of something he could enjoy.

He did need to eat, and he enjoyed a steak he didn't have to cook, along with a loaded baked potato with as much bacon and ranch dressing as he could get.

He tapped a little bit of beard oil into his palm, rubbed his hands together, and smoothed it over his face.

Alaska was bubbly and talkative—everything Deacon struggled to do on a date—so he figured he'd at least have a good time. He could answer questions and add to a conversation, but he needed someone to get him started. He'd tried a date with a woman named Kara last weekend, and she'd been as quiet as him.

The meal had been awkward, and the walk over to downtown Ivory Peaks Park to check on the ice skating rink had been filled with tense silence.

He'd been asking out women he knew from church, work, or through a friend that he'd met at least once, but the pool of potential dates was quickly drying up. He didn't want to do anything online, and if Opal or Jane offered to set him up on a blind date one more time, he felt sure he'd lose his mind.

His phone chimed out the familiar alarm notification, and Deacon abandoned looking into his own eyes to pick up his device. It was a calendar reminder for tomorrow's barrel racing finals, which Rosie Young was riding in. Tucker and Bobbie Jo had gone with her, and Deacon wanted nothing more than pure success for his brother, because he knew Tuck wanted more clients.

If he could get Rosie to win in her rookie year as a pro rodeo rider, he would have people knocking down his door and begging to train right here in Colorado instead of in San Antonio.

He swept away the reminder and saw that he'd missed a text from his father. He tapped on it and read: *Call me when you can.*

Deacon quickly checked the time and saw he had about fifteen minutes before he had to walk out his front door and over to the cabin community where Alaska lived, which would take him less than five minutes. So he tapped to call his father and listened to the phone ring three times before his daddy's familiar bass rumbled through the speaker.

"Howdy, son."

"Hey," Deacon said. "Sorry, I just saw your text. I'm getting ready for yet another first date."

Daddy chuckled. "You don't sound too happy about it."

"Why would I be?" Deacon griped. "I don't understand dating at all. Why can't I just meet someone, and fall in love in five seconds, and we can be married?"

Daddy full-on belly-laughed then. "I'm putting you on speaker with your mother."

"Really? This is a speaker call?" Deacon's mood worsened. "If I'd have known that, I would've waited until after the date."

"She likes hearing about your dating escapades," Daddy said.

Deacon groaned even as his momma said, "You can't go into it with such a bad attitude."

"I don't have a bad attitude," Deacon said. "I'm dressed up real nice, and it's Alaska. Besides, she thinks anyone who talks to her has hung the moon."

"So you don't think she's a potential serious girlfriend?" Daddy asked.

"I don't know what I think." Deacon sighed. "You wanted me to call?"

"Yeah," Daddy said. "It's only a couple of weeks until Christmas, and Jane and Cord are coming up here. I know it's hard to leave the farm, but we wanted to know if you might be coming with them."

"I don't think so," Deacon said. "Mission will be around, but four of our other cowboys are leaving the farm for a few days for the holidays."

"Yeah, I figured," Daddy said. "It's a hard time."

"What are you going to do then?" Momma asked. "Uncle Wes and Aunt Bree are out at Gerty and Mike's."

"Yeah, they invited me to eat with them," he said. "But I don't know if I'll go."

"Well, you can't have Christmas at that farm by yourself," she said.

Deacon wanted to ask her *why not?* but he held his tongue.

"Matt and Boone also invited me," he said. "They're doing stuff with their kids, and I thought that might be a good place to go."

"Tuck and Bobbie Jo are going to Oklahoma," Daddy said.

"Yeah, they sure are," Deacon said. "And Hunter and Molly are going to be in town with her folks. Tarr and Briar are going out to Mike's, and so are Steele and his girlfriend—probably his fiancée by Christmas."

"Yeah, I heard he bought a diamond ring," Daddy said.

"He did," Deacon confirmed, trying not to be too salty about it. But he wanted what Steele had managed to do: meet a woman, ask her out, hit it off within minutes, start dating, and six months later be planning to propose.

He didn't want to go hang out with couples, and that was all who would be out at Mike and Gerty's farm, while Matt and Boone, who'd both worked the farm while Deacon grew up, had teenagers and single young adults. Keith and Lindsay would be there with their new baby, and so would Britt and Lars—and she was due with their first child just after the first of the year.

But Deacon wouldn't be the only single one there; he wouldn't be this massive fifth wheel, taking up too much space at the dinner table.

"Yeah, I'll probably go to Matt and Boone's," he said. "I'll text him and see what he wants me to bring."

"Well, we'll miss you," Momma said. "Maybe you can come up in January or February for a visit."

"I'd like that," Deacon said.

"I know Uncle Wes was going to ask you to follow them back," Daddy said. "They're staying through West's birthday at least, but they like having help if something happens on the roads between here and there."

Deacon nodded to himself. "I can coordinate with them." He looked out the window above his kitchen sink. "I'll look at my cowboys' schedule and talk to Mission, because it would be nice to get away from the farm for a couple of weeks."

"You need that sometimes, son," Daddy said. "That place will eat you alive if you let it."

"I know, Daddy."

His father had told him that many times. Deacon loved the farm and loved the work; he loved the sky and the fields and the cattle; he also loved the horses and the cowboys and cowgirls who worked with him. He loved the horseback riding lessons and the children who came to the farm, bringing it life and vitality.

But Daddy was right. The work was never-ending, and the farm never slept.

"Wish me luck on this date," he said. "Are you guys watching the rodeo finals tomorrow?"

"Sure are," Daddy said.

"Tuck's been texting about it nonstop," Momma added. "I've been praying so hard for both him and Rosie."

Deacon hadn't been doing that, but he made a mental note to add Tuck and Rosie and Bobbie Jo to his prayers that evening.

"All right, well, I better go," he said. "It's not a good idea to show up late on the first date when she lives next door to you."

He chuckled, glad when his momma and daddy did too, and the call ended.

Deacon silenced his phone and stowed it in his back pocket as he left the bathroom of the generational house where he lived. Hunter and Molly and their kids lived in the main farmhouse, and if Deacon ever got married and had children, he knew that place would become his one day.

"Lord," he sighed out as he left the house and took quick steps down to the front sidewalk. He turned right and headed across the lawn toward the family barns and stables. On the other side of that ran the dirt road that led straight through the cabin community where the hired help at the farm lived.

Alaska shared a cabin with another woman from the staff—Ruth. Deacon hoped he wouldn't have to go through a rigorous round of roommate questioning before he could take Alaska to dinner. His legs felt especially tired as he went up the front steps and knocked on the door.

Ruth opened it and stepped back, her face alight with a healthy glow. "Hey, Deacon," she said. "Alaska just ran down the hall to grab her earrings."

"I'm right here," Alaska called, bursting out of the hallway in the small cabin with both hands still fiddling at her right ear. "I'm ready."

She wore an enormous smile to go with her little black dress, and Deacon was really glad he had put on a collared shirt with buttons down the front and his best brown leather jacket.

"Wow, you look great," he said.

She tipped up onto one toe and cocked her red cowboy boots. "It's the boots, right? They really make the look."

Deacon grinned at her, his heart sending out an extra beat, though he hadn't really felt anything romantic for Alaska before now. "Oh, it's the boots, all right," he said.

She came over to him, and Deacon put one hand lightly on her back as he leaned in to kiss her cheek. "Are you ready for dinner?"

"I am *starving*," Alaska said, her usual exuberance on display. "And I hope you packed your platinum credit card, cowboy, because I want the surf and turf."

Deacon chuckled and offered her his arm. "I've only got the one card, Alaska, but I think it'll cover your surf and turf." He nodded to Ruth. "Good to see you, Ruth."

She giggled. "You too, Deacon," and he finally escaped the cabin with Alaska on his arm.

Normally that contact disappeared pretty quickly as they had to go down steps and navigate back over to his house to get his truck. But Alaska slipped her hand into his the moment they reached the bottom of the stairs, and Deacon glanced over at her.

Heat filled his face, because he wasn't sure how he felt about holding hands with Alaska, and he didn't want to give her the wrong impression. He also didn't want to yank his hand away and make everything awkward before they'd even left the property.

So, while his discomfort continued to stream through him, and he second-guessed even asking her out, he continued to hold her hand as he led her back toward the generational house and his truck.

Why does dating have to be so hard? he thought, glad at least that Alaska seemed able to carry a conversation almost entirely on her own with only an occasional nod or hum from him.

At the same time, that wasn't the kind of relationship he wanted to have, and after he got Alaska situated in the passenger seat of his truck and walked around the hood to get behind the wheel, he knew he would not be the one to ask her on a second date—and he would have to turn her down if she suggested it.

Talk about awkward, he thought. *And this is why you should not date anyone who works and lives here on the farm.*

Hadn't he learned that lesson yet?

Apparently not.

fourteen

Tarr padded around the kitchen in the mansion, putting together a quick and simple breakfast of chocolate chip pancakes and bacon.

After all, his momma always made him this breakfast on his birthday. He snapped a picture to send to his parents before pouring maple syrup over his pancakes.

His momma had texted him at 3:14 that morning—the exact minute he'd been born, thirty-three years ago—to say happy birthday.

He'd chatted with her already that morning, and now he sent the picture of pancakes and bacon, along with the words, *Love you guys. I hope you have an amazing day today.*

You too, Daddy said. *And happy birthday.*

HAPPY BIRTHDAY!!! his momma wrote, and then she sent several emojis, ranging from cakes to poppers to birthday gifts.

Tarr grinned and chuckled, then settled at the bar to eat. He'd been staying at the mansion for a couple of days while Tucker and Bobbie Jo were in Las Vegas with Rosie. Since she'd won Rookie of the Year, as well as the national championship in barrel racing, Tarr knew they would've been out late celebrating last night.

He did expect both Bobbie Jo and Tuck to text him and say happy birthday, but no one else would. He hadn't told Briar that today was his birthday, and the only other person who knew was Wayne.

Tarr tapped on his social media as he took a bite of his bacon and immediately remembered that *the entire world* knew it was his birthday. He'd ridden in the NPR finals several times in his life, and many announcers had said "Let's put our hands together for Tarr Olson, who's celebrating his birthday today!" right before his eight-second ride. He'd also put the date on many of his social media profiles, and everyone from childhood acquaintances to perfect strangers had already started sending good wishes.

He quickly closed out of those apps, completely dissatisfied with getting messages from people he didn't know.

With Tuck gone, he'd been doing the feeding himself while Briar took care of the goat herd. That put them a little bit behind, but he went through her veterinary rotation with her, and then he started training just after lunch, about the time she disappeared into her office. Thankfully, there had been no more snow, and Tarr could admit that he liked living in the mansion.

He'd been looking online for hot plates he could put on a countertop, so he could make his pancakes and bacon, scrambled eggs, or a grilled cheese sandwich with the mini-fridge and the microwave upstairs. It really would be an excellent place to stay until he could get his cabin finished.

He'd scheduled a call with Les Davenport at Portside Construction next week, because Tarr had originally thought he would build the cabin himself, but now knew that the task was beyond his abilities and the amount of time he had to dedicate to it. If he hired someone, he could probably move in by spring, and if he did it himself, it might be another year.

He'd just finished breakfast when the doorbell rang, someone knocked, and then the front door opened, all in the span of a single second.

Tarr sat far enough back in the house that he couldn't see the front door, but the alarm system said "Front door open," so he knew someone had come in.

"It's just me," Briar called. "Wiggins, get out of the way."

Tarr stayed on his barstool and watched the mouth of the hallway that led toward the front of the house, where Tuck had a formal office and a formal living room off the ten-foot-wide foyer the front door opened into.

Briar's steps sounded short and stilted, and the moment she appeared, Tarr understood why: she carried at least two plastic grocery sacks on each arm and balanced an enormous birthday cake in her hands.

"What in the world?" Tarr jumped to his feet and went to relieve her of the dessert. "What's this for?"

"What's this for?" she repeated, her voice filled with daggers.

Tarr slid the cake onto the counter at the same time Briar lifted the bags and let them crash down. "It's your birthday, Mister Olson, and you did—not—tell—me."

She freed her hands and arms from the plastic loops and planted one hand on her hip, her glare fixed perfectly on him.

"It's not a big deal," he said.

"It's not a big deal?" Briar shook her head. "That's ridiculous. Birthdays are a big deal."

"Oh, yeah? When's yours, then?"

"March," she said, lifting her chin in a haughty movement.

"Now, it smells suspiciously like chocolate in here, which means you've already eaten—and that's fine. I'm going to feed the goats, and then I'm going to come back here and make your birthday lunch."

She dove into the plastic bags and started pulling things out of them, including potatoes, shredded cheese, sour cream, vegetable oil, and brown gravy packets.

"What have we got going on here?" Tarr asked. "What are you making for lunch?"

"Poutine," she said.

"Honey, it's *my* birthday." He grinned at her, but she maintained her forceful glare.

"Yes, and we missed our poutine date last week, because *someone* needed to go horseback riding with the big celebrities."

"Hey, I invited you along."

"Yeah," she said. And she'd had fun going with Cole and Rosie and Rachel in a more relaxed manner.

"Their dads are rodeo-famous."

"Yes, I heard." Briar stepped around the island and started to put things in Tuck's fridge. "So we're going to have lunch, and then we're going to spend the day watching movies in the theater room downstairs."

"I can't do that," he said. "I've got two horses I'm working with."

"Ashton's going to do it."

Tarr scoffed, the noise angry and loud and not really reflective of how he felt.

"It's your *birth*day, Tarr," Briar said as she turned back from the fridge. "And it's a weekend. You don't have to work yourself to death." She took one menacing step toward him and poked her forefinger into his sternum. "And you should have told me it was your birthday."

"I didn't want it to be a big deal."

"How would you feel if it was my birthday and I hadn't told you?"

"Well, that tracks for you," he said.

"Which makes this even weirder." She glared at him and went back to un-bagging groceries. "I got the cheddar cheese and caramel popcorn you like for the movie—which I'm going to let you pick, by the way, because it *is* your birthday—and Bobbie Jo said the theater room is full of blankets, and we can turn on the space heater down there if we don't want to uncover the vents."

"You've talked to them about it?"

"How do you think I found out it was your birthday?" she asked. "I had to find out from Bobbie Jo, for crying out loud."

"Yeah, kind of like me finding out about your stunt riding from Rosie Young."

Briar whipped back to him, her vulnerability combining with her ire and making her absolutely stunning in the morning light coming through the back windows. "I apologized for that."

Tarr grinned at her and drew her into his arms. She tried to resist him, but in the end, she eased into his chest and wrapped her arms around his back, making him feel strong and steady.

"Well, I'm sorry then, sweetheart," he murmured. "December birthdays are kind of hard, you know? It's like every-thing's overshadowed with Christmas."

"All the more reason you should have told me," she said. "Then I wouldn't have had to make an emergency run to the grocery store, panic-buy everything I saw, and hurry here so I could catch you before we had to go do our chores."

She stepped back and gazed up at him. Tarr's eyes dropped to her mouth as he found himself thinking about kissing her more and more often.

"I'm afraid my presents are pretty lame, and I'm going to save one of them until later today, but you can have the first one right now."

"Oh, yeah?" He raised his eyebrows. "And what would that be, sweetheart?"

"Well, one, I'm making you lunch."

"Dang," he said with a grin. "I thought you were going to say I could kiss you."

Briar sucked in a breath and stepped back. Tarr dropped his hands from her body, realizing that while they had been getting to know each other over the past couple of weeks and becoming more and more friendly, she definitely wasn't ready for kissing.

"It's fine," Tarr said, waving his hand. "What's present number two?"

She reached for the plastic bag still sitting on the counter and wrapped the ties all the way around something rectangular inside. "This is for later, and I still have to wrap it," she said. "But number two is that I'm going to leave Wiggins with you all day, and he can sleep here with you tonight."

Tarr's smile widened even further, and he laughed as he grabbed Briar and spun her around in the kitchen. "That's the best birthday present ever, honey. Thank you."

It felt natural to him to lean down and kiss her, so he did, but he planted his lips right on her cheek instead of her mouth.

"Really, thank you, Briar," he whispered in her ear. Then he straightened again and beamed at her, turning toward Wiggins, who had pivoted from the back door where he'd been watching for possible intruders—or probably just birds.

"Hey, buddy, did you hear your momma's gonna let you stay with me tonight?"

Wiggins smiled and his tongue dropped out of his mouth as

he panted. Tarr crouched and scrubbed him along the ears, the sides of his face, and under his neck.

"I mean, I don't need you to keep me warm anymore, but I sure do love it when you're in the bed with me."

"Oh, brother," Briar muttered from behind him, but Tarr didn't much care. He did love Wiggins—the dog was a good friend—and he straightened and turned just as Briar closed the cupboard where Tuck and Bobbie Jo kept the sugar bowl for their coffee and their salt and pepper shakers.

"Don't you be looking in there," she said. "We need to go do our chores."

"Yes, ma'am." Tarr walked back over to Briar and took her hand in his. "Thank you, Briar. Really."

He watched her fingers meld with his, a slip of happiness stealing through him. "I was just thinking about how only my momma and daddy have texted me for my birthday, and the only other people who knew were Tuck and Bobbie Jo."

"And everyone online. Have you forgotten you're a celebrity, Tarr?" Briar asked dryly as they went into the foyer and out the front door.

"I'm not a celebrity," he said.

She scoffed and flipped up the hood on her coat.

"Hey, if *you* can say you're not, then *I'm* not." He went down the steps with her and climbed into the passenger seat of her SUV. "But I'm really not," he said.

The interior was still warm, as she'd left the car running while she'd come inside.

"And you definitely still are," Tarr added, because he didn't have people squealing and fan-girling over him the way Rosie had with Briar last week. He'd only been out of the rodeo for a couple of years now, true, and Briar had been gone for almost five, but he'd watched several of her videos on her stunt-riding channel, and she had been incredible.

"I've never performed at the halftime of an NFL game," he said as she pulled up to the arena. "So I definitely think one of us has more celebrity status than the other."

"In a very small circle," Briar said. "The rodeo is much bigger than stunt riding."

"Is it?"

"I'm not arguing with you about this." Briar threw him a dirty look and got out of the car.

Tarr chuckled and followed her. She had to go toward the back of the building and the Goatel, and he just had to go inside, so he rushed around the hood and grabbed her before she could stomp away. "Hey, you're not really mad, are you?"

"I'm absolutely mad," she said. "We're *dating*, Tarr, and you didn't tell me it was your birthday."

"I'm still struggling to think that we're dating," he said.

"Why is that?" A cute little line appeared between her eyes. She seemed genuinely confused, and she pinched the zipper on his coat between her thumb and forefinger and pulled it up and then back down, up a few inches and down a few more, up and down.

"Because, sweetheart," he said. "I usually don't think about myself dating a woman until I've kissed her."

"The kissing again." Briar looked up at him, her big blue eyes full of fear. "I don't know, Tarr."

"About kissing?" he asked. "It's pretty natural."

She gave him a gentle push against his shoulder. "You said you'd be patient with me."

"I am," he said. "This is the first time we're even *talking* about kissing. I didn't just rush in and do it."

She pressed her lips together and looked over his shoulder. "I just haven't kissed anyone in a long time."

"How long?" he asked.

"I haven't had a boyfriend since I moved here," she said. "And I know you've dated a lot."

"Not a lot," he said. "I've only dated one person since my injury."

"Well, that's one hundred percent more than me then, isn't it?"

Tarr reached out and tucked her hair behind her ear, then cupped her face in his palm and gently guided her to look back at him. "And you think you're not going to be good at it? Or I'm not? Or you're not going to like it?"

"I think I'm going to like it," she whispered. "And that scares me. I'm not sure *you're* going to like it, and that scares me too."

"Sweetheart, there's nothing to be afraid of. It's just a little kissing."

"No," she said, but it didn't carry the power of her usual argumentative self. "Kissing means something, Tarr. You just said so yourself—it's how you know you have a girlfriend."

"Yeah, that's right." Because Tarr could agree with that. It did mean something to him to kiss someone. He didn't go around doing it all the time. "Don't worry, Briar. I'm not going to be upset if the third gift isn't a kiss."

"Well, it's not," she said. "I wrapped up the third gift in that plastic bag and shoved it in the cupboard."

"Well, maybe I could get four gifts." He grinned at her, then shook his head, his smile falling away. "Seriously, Briar, no pressure. It'll happen when it happens. And honey, don't worry. It's going to be amazing."

With that, he pressed a kiss to her forehead and stepped by

her to go inside the arena. He didn't hear her footsteps crunching through the gravel as she walked away, and he paused at the door and turned around to look at her. She still stood exactly where he'd left her, her hands hanging limply at her sides and her head held high.

He really wished he could dive into her head and see what she was thinking, if only so that he could understand her better and try to reassure her that he wasn't going to kiss her and then dump her.

The way his heartbeat pranced through him, Tarr could not imagine any world, any scenario, where he would not enjoy kissing Briar Prescott, and he really wished she could see herself the way he did.

"I can feel you staring at me," she said.

"Well, you're just standing there."

She muttered something, then walked away. Tarr noted that she didn't stomp or march, and he smiled at her back before ducking into the warmer barn so he could feed the horses.

It's going to be a great year, Tarr told himself, getting better at Briar's game of speaking a truth to himself each day.

Yep. It's going to be a great year if you can keep getting to know Briar, make her your girlfriend, and finally settle down the way your momma has always wanted you to.

He loved his parents, and in that moment, he realized he loved his brother too, despite the differences they'd had over the years.

So, before he got too involved with his chores, he pulled out his phone and tapped over to Wayne's name to send his brother a message. He honestly had no idea if Wayne even knew today was Tarr's birthday.

"It doesn't matter," he muttered to himself, and then he

typed, *Hey, Wayne—just thinking about you today, and I hope you're doing well.*

He sent the message, not quite sure how he wanted Wayne to respond, and tucked his phone away and went to spend his birthday with horses, Wiggins, and his beautiful Briar.

fifteen

Briar whisked the gravy vigorously, ignoring the home security system in the mansion as it alerted her to the front door opening. The familiar *click-clack* of claws on expensive tile met her ears, as did Wiggins's excited panting.

"Hey, buddy," she said, but she did not stop stirring the gravy.

"Something smells good in here," Tarr said, and Briar managed to send one beaming smile in his direction.

"Lunch is almost ready," she said.

"Holy cow." He paused at the end of the island. "Did you make these French fries?"

"I sure did. They're double-fried and perfectly crispy."

She'd never fed goats so fast and gotten them out in the pasture before returning to start on his birthday lunch—the biggest pile of poutine she'd ever made.

"This is restaurant quality, honey." He eased into her side, and it took all of Briar's energy not to sag into his strong warmth.

"The gravy is almost done," she said. "And then I'll put it all together for you."

"So it's beef gravy?" he asked.

"It is beef gravy," she said. "And I put some shredded meat in it." She nodded to the plastic container on the other side of the stove. "I had to use one of those microwave meals, because someone didn't tell me that his birthday was today, so I couldn't put in a roast last night."

Tarr's arm snaked around her, and Briar relaxed into his side. "It's going to be amazing, hon. Do you always make it with a roast?"

"My favorite is elk," she said. "And I would have ordered white cheese curds, but again, I had to make-do with what was at the store."

She reached up and flipped off the flame underneath the gravy. "You really should have the most authentic poutine when you try it for the first time, but this will have to do."

"I think it's incredible already," Tarr said. "My mouth is watering."

She looked up at him, expecting to find his gaze locked on the beef gravy she had made. Instead, he watched her, and warmth started in Briar's stomach and spread up into her face.

"We'll go sit down at the table," she said. "I've got everything set." She'd been back at the mansion cutting French fries, frying them, and decorating the table for his birthday for the past hour.

"Oh-my-lanta." Surprise flowed in every syllable Tarr spoke. "Briar, you didn't have to do all this."

"I know," she said. "But it's your birthday, Tarr."

"I'm thirty-three," he said. "Not five."

"I think birthdays should be even more celebrated as an

adult," she said. "Because you made it through another year, and that's an amazing accomplishment." She picked up the pan of gravy and turned with it to the island, where she had already laid out a trivet. She put the pan there and then reached for the big metal pail she'd bought in the gardening aisle at the grocery store.

The *gardening* aisle.

"One of my favorite shops is in a little town called Drumheller," she said. "It's a couple of hours from Calgary, and you drive out through all these hoodoos and amazing land formations, and it's this tiny hole-in-the-wall place." She dumped the fries unceremoniously into the metal bucket. "They serve their poutine like this, and it's family-style—you just go all in."

She cut open the bag of cheese curds and sprinkled them over the fries, using her fingers to nudge a few out of the way so the cheese got all the way down into the pail.

She glanced over to the dining room table when she realized that Tarr had not responded. He stood there, staring at the blue cloth she'd spread over Tuck and Bobbie Jo's table. Her helium balloon display had been delivered mere moments after she'd returned from her farm chores.

The bouquet lifted into the air from the center of the table, and she'd ordered tan, white, and navy blue regular balloons, some that had *Happy Birthday* printed all over them in a fun, cartoony font.

Then she'd added two mylar balloons in the shape of threes, since he was thirty-three years old today, and one galloping horse who wore a navy-and-white bandana and tied the entire thing together. All the strings attached to a balloon weight with white confetti spilling out the top.

Next to that, Briar had managed to wrap her grocery-store

gift and set it on the table, along with two plates, two forks, and a big roll of paper towels.

"Do you want to watch the magic?" she asked.

Tarr turned toward her, a semi-blank look on his face, as if he'd forgotten she was there. He stepped closer and stood on the opposite side of the island from her, with the big metal bucket of almost-finished poutine between them.

"So, it's fries," she said. "And you want them to be crispy, though I kind of like it when the gravy softens them up." She smiled, her nerves on high alert. She loved poutine, and she loved Canada, and for some reason, she wanted Tarr to as well. "And then there's cheese curds. The fries start to melt them a little bit, but the gravy is the real magic."

She lifted the pan, gripping it tight due to the weight. "And then you pour the gravy in." She did that, the chunks of shredded beef falling with the brown gravy, and she swirled and twirled it over all the fries and cheese curds.

Steam lifted up and painted her soul with a smile. It showed on her face as she quickly scraped out the last drops of gravy and turned to set the pan in the sink. When she faced Tarr again, she gestured to the pail. "And then you eat."

"It's like meat and potatoes and gravy all in one thing," he said.

"Right. It's incredible." She reached for the handle and lifted the bucket. "You can't grab the bucket by the sides, because it'll be hot."

"Does everyone serve their poutine in a bucket?" Tarr followed her over to the table, where Briar hefted the poutine pail in the center and then went around to the far side of the table, with the windows at her back.

"I just told you," she said. "This is how they do it at my favorite place in Drumheller."

"Oh, right. I heard that."

She nodded to his chair, and he sat down hastily, as if he'd forgotten how to do some things.

"You're acting weird," she said.

"No one's celebrated my birthday like this in ten years," he said, and he pinned her with that dark-eyed gaze that left her feeling naked and vulnerable, like he could see more than she wanted him to.

"Birthdays are a big deal to me," she said simply.

"I'm making a note of that," Tarr said. "You said yours was in March?"

"March fifth," she said.

"How will I know what you want?"

Briar jumped to her feet. "I forgot the tongs."

She hurried into the kitchen and opened the same drawer where she had gotten out the whisk and the rubber spatula. When she returned, she pressed in close to Tarr and picked up his plate.

"You just go in, cowboy," she said. "This is messy, hole-in-the-wall, Canadian food, and it's delicious."

"When do I get to open my present?"

"Later." She put plenty of French fries and cheese curds—all of it dripping with the beef gravy—on his plate and slid it in front of him. "It's a pretty salty dish, but I think you'll love it."

Tarr looked up at her and swept his black cowboy hat off his head. "It smells amazing, Briar. Thank you so much."

He hooked his arm around her waist again and pulled her into him, pressing his whole head against her ribs. She balanced the tongs in the bucket and went around the table to sit down across from him.

"Did you want to pray?" she asked.

Tarr had already stabbed a bit of shredded beef and a French fry, and he raised his eyes to hers. "Sure, we can pray."

Briar nodded, so much saliva in her mouth she had to swallow. "I'd like to try, if you don't mind."

"Absolutely not." Tarr wouldn't look away from her, but Briar squished her eyes closed and dropped her chin. She could still feel him watching her, which annoyed her a little bit. She pushed that away and tried to focus on how she felt and what she wanted to say to God.

"Dear Heavenly Father," she said, the words still not quite lining up. "We come before Thee on a very special day and thank Thee for the bounteous blessings that we enjoy here on the farm. I'm personally grateful for the health of the animals and a good cabin to live in, and Wiggins—though I told Tarr he could have him for the evening. He loves that dog, Lord, and bless him that he'll get a lot of joy out of the gift of sleeping with him tonight.

"I'm grateful that the poutine turned out pretty good, and please bless Tarr to pretend to like it if he doesn't. After all, it's just food and it won't poison him, even if it *is* his birthday and he should have everything he wants."

Briar gave herself a little shake, as her prayer had definitely gone off the rails. "Anyway, I'm—no, *we're* really grateful for everything Thou hast given us, and we ask Thee to bless the food and bless us to do good and to find a way through the things that trouble us to the other side of them, where we can find happiness and peace and joy with ourselves, with each other, and with Thee."

Briar's throat felt like she'd swallowed a handful of nails. "Amen," she managed to push out, and everything in her body relaxed as she opened her eyes and lifted her head. She pulled her hands back off the table and tucked them between her knees as she looked at Tarr.

"Amen," he said, plenty of sincerity and punch in his tone. "That was a really beautiful prayer, Briar. I'm not going to have to pretend to like this. It's French fries and beef, for crying out loud."

"Still," she said, and she watched him put his first bite of poutine in his mouth.

He groaned in an over-exaggerated way and tipped his head back.

"Okay, you don't have to overdo it." Briar reached for the tongs so she could serve herself a heaping helping of poutine too.

"I'm not exaggerating," Tarr said. "You're right—it's salty, but it's *sooo* good."

He went right in for another bite, spearing a cheese curd with his fries and gravy this time. Briar did the same, pure satisfaction driving through her that he liked what she'd made him for his birthday lunch.

Her own stomach growled just as she put her first bite in her mouth, and the creamy, hot gravy coated her tongue with its salty, savory goodness. The French fry added the right texture—crisp and creamy at the same time—and the cheese curd squeaked against her teeth.

"Oh, I've forgotten how much I love this stuff." She wanted to shovel the food into her mouth with both fists, but she carefully arranged another bite, this one with a hefty shred of beef to go with her potatoes and cheese. After she finished that bite, she looked across the table to Tarr again.

"It would be great if you could give me your top three movies," she said. "And I'll see where we can stream them for our movie afternoon."

Tarr grinned at her. "You'll watch anything I want?"

Briar's first reaction was to say no, of course not. They could find something they both liked, couldn't they? But she forced herself to casually shrug one shoulder. "It's your birthday, cowboy."

"Did you get everything you wanted on your birthday growing up?" he asked.

"Yeah," she said. "My mom and dad would take me wherever I wanted to eat, and we'd do whatever I wanted that day. From the time I was one until the time I was eighteen, they got me the same number of presents as my age, which I might have done for you if I'd had ample time to prepare."

"Well, now you know my birthday is December eleventh."

"Exactly two weeks before Christmas." She smiled at him and took another bite of poutine.

"I like all kinds of movies, Briar. We could do action-adventure with something like *National Treasure*, or we could do a musical like *The Greatest Showman*, or we could do a rom-com...."

Briar grinned at him. "You don't know the names of any rom-com movies, do you?"

He burst out laughing and shook his head. "No, ma'am. I sure don't."

"So, action-adventure," she said. "Maybe *Jumanji*, or—"

"The new one." He pointed his fork at her. "I don't like the old one."

"The new *Jumanji*," she said. "*Jurassic Park, National Treasure*...."

"There's also that new one with the guy from *The Office*," Tarr said. "I don't know the name of it."

"I think I know what you're talking about," she said. "It's on one of the streaming services."

"Yeah. Or we could watch something like a documentary. I like those ones about people living in Alaska, or the guys who rock climb."

Briar wanted to wrinkle her nose and shoot him down, but she said, "Yeah, I can look those up," instead.

"Are we having cake now or later?"

Briar glanced over to him and found that his plate had been emptied. "You can have more if you want," she said.

"I'm deciding based on whether we can have cake now or later." He grinned at her. "You know what? It's my birthday, and I should've had cake *before* lunch."

"I'll get it." Chuckling, Briar got up and hurried into the kitchen, where the enormous cake she'd had to buy off the shelf waited. If she'd had more time, she would have ordered something custom, maybe put Wiggins on the top of it or something. As it was, this was a male-themed birthday cake decorated in black, yellow, and blue, and it said *Happy Birthday* in perfectly piped cursive letters.

She grabbed two fresh plates and a spatula server on her way back to the table, then returned to the kitchen to get a knife.

"The yellow is kind of gaudy," she said.

"It's perfect, Briar."

She cut into the corner of the cake. "I know you love frosting, so you can have this corner piece." Extra piped frosting decorated every edge almost an inch high, and she cut him a healthy piece, slid it onto the plate, and put it in front of him.

Before she could pick up the knife to get herself a smaller portion, he grabbed her hand and tugged her closer.

"Tarr," she warned as her balance started to fail her.

"Just sit with me for a second."

She practically fell onto his lap, and he grunted, which caused a stream of embarrassment to erupt inside Briar's chest.

"It's my birthday and all."

She wrapped her arms around his shoulders and tilted her head back as he nuzzled his face into the soft skin there.

"You smell amazing." He placed a kiss against her skin, and Briar shivered. "Yeah, this is going to count as my fourth birthday gift," he whispered.

Little by little, Briar relaxed as Tarr held her and placed gentle kisses along her neck, ear, and jaw. At this rate, she wasn't sure why touching her lips to his would be that big of a deal, and she pulled back to look him in the eye.

Just then his phone rang, the shrill sound of it piercing the tender, intimate moment between them.

"That's Tuck." He pressed her closer with one hand while he released her with the other so he could silence the phone. "I'm not talking to him right now." He got the ringing to stop and refocused his attention on Briar.

Her heartbeat stampeded through her whole body, and she swallowed, not quite sure where to put her hands or what to say.

In the next moment, a beep unlike she'd ever heard before filled the house, and then the electronic voice of Bobbie Jo said, "I got it. Tuck—it's working. They should be able to hear us."

"Tarr!" Tuck practically yelled, and Briar's eyes shot to the intercom system on the other side of the kitchen. The security voice talked through that when doors or windows were opened.

Tarr swore under his breath as he twisted toward the security system panel too.

"Hey, brother," Tuck said. "Uh, hey, we're just letting you know that we've got cameras in the house, and we can see and hear everything you and Briar are doing."

"Well, turn it off," Tarr said.

Pure humiliation ran through Briar, and her eyes immediately swept the corners of the room and along the ceiling where cameras might be hidden. She didn't see them at all—the mark of what a lot of money could buy.

"I don't know how to turn it off," Bobbie Jo said.

"You don't have to watch," Tarr called.

"We get a notification every time there's movement," Tuck said. "And we're not sure how to turn that off either."

Tarr swore again, and with everything shattered between them, Briar managed to slip off his lap, serve herself a piece of cake, and return to her seat.

"Sorry, Tarr," he said.

"And Briar," Bobbie Jo called. The irritating beep filled the house again, lasting for a good three or four seconds and reminding Briar of the way her dryer alarm went off when the cycle had finished. She ducked her head, glad she'd removed her ponytail after feeding the goats that morning. Surely she was the color of a bright red boiled lobster, and she put a bite of cake in her mouth without even tasting it.

Across from her, Tarr's thumbs flew across his phone screen, and after a minute or two, he threw it down in disgust.

"Cameras on the front porch," he said. "All over the main living areas and in the backyard."

Briar looked up. "I feel like I have to text you so I can talk to you now."

"Yeah, it feels stupid, doesn't it?" He wore a dark look of disgust, and Briar really missed the way his hands had felt on her waist and her back, and the soft warmth and urgency in his touch against her neck and cheek.

"What about the basement?" she asked.

"Tuck said he wasn't sure, because they never go down

there," he said. "When we go down for our movie afternoon, he'll let me know."

Briar swallowed and left the rest of the cake on her plate in favor of the poutine. She knew her house didn't have any cameras, but she didn't know how to invite him back there for his birthday dinner. Would that be too forward? And would he make assumptions about how far he could go? Not only that, she wasn't even sure she was ready to kiss him yet, which made no sense, as he'd definitely just kissed her a couple dozen times. No, not on the lips, but in intimate places nonetheless.

She dove into her phone too, looking for the movies Tarr had mentioned, so she'd have something to distract herself with.

As Tarr served himself another piece of birthday cake, Briar snuck a look at him. No matter what, she was definitely falling for a cowboy, something she'd vowed she'd never do again.

But things change, don't they? she asked herself, immediately agreeing with the sentiment, because if there was anything Briar had learned about living life, it was that it changed constantly, and she needed to adapt with it, or she'd always be broken.

Tarr healed so many cracked and bleeding things inside her, and she decided right then and there that falling in love with him wouldn't be so bad after all.

sixteen

Tarr jogged down the stairs, a newfound giddiness prancing through him. "I've got great news, sweetheart," he called as his foot reached the bottom step.

Tucker had a huge, 70-inch TV in the main living area in the basement, but he also had a theater room down the hall in the corner, and it actually sank lower into the ground, with eight more steps down to the screen there.

Briar had taken his caramel-cheese popcorn in there, and he'd also found a cooler with his beloved Diet Dr. Pepper and root beer, iced and ready to go.

The stuff that she knew about him wasn't lost on Tarr, and he could admit that he loved being taken care of by her. No, doted on. Briar had been *doting* on him all day, and it felt very adoring. No one, besides random strangers, had treated Tarr like that for a long time.

Briar emerged from the theater room as he started down the hall. "Good news?"

Tarr held up his phone. "I found the camera and disabled it, so we're good on the entire basement level."

Briar grinned at him. "That is good news."

"Sorry I had to go take those phone calls." He didn't slow his pace as he reached her, and he wrapped her in his arms and lifted her right off her feet. She squealed and held on to his shoulders until he put her down.

"Who called?" she asked.

"The first was the general contractor, and he said he's going to be out on Tuesday to look at my site and see what we need to do to get the house built by spring."

"That's great news," she said.

"And I'd put out a few feelers about a different RV," he said. "Though I think the one I have is fine if I can get it hooked up to water and electricity."

"Yeah, but how are you going to do that?" Briar stepped back and laced her hands through his. "I thought we'd sit in the second row, so we're still pretty high up, but we're not right by the door."

"Sure." Tarr didn't care where they sat in the theater room at all. He let Briar lead him down a couple of steps to the second row of luxury loungers, where she'd positioned the cooler on the floor between their feet and the popcorn and red licorice on the armrest between them.

"My friend Jentzen is going to come move the RV next to the barn," he said. "I talked to Ashton, who said he stays in the loft sometimes when he can't get off the ranch due to weather, and he said there's a semi-bedroom up there—just a queen bed with a blanket and a pillow. And of course there's a bathroom in the arena. Tuck has a space heater out there for the winter, and it does okay, because, you know, we keep the arena air-conditioned and heated."

"Right," Briar said.

"But Ashton then said we can just hook the RV up to the water and electricity in the arena, and if I park it on the south side, I'll get all the winter sunlight and get some shelter from the wind."

He sank into his chair and looked over to Briar as she did the same. "You're going to sit all the way over there?"

"I'm not going to sit on your lap during the whole movie," she said, with some measure of disgust in her voice.

"There's plenty of room in this chair for both of us, sweet-heart." He grinned at her, but Briar just rolled her eyes.

"Eat your treats first, and then maybe I'll come sit by you."

"That would be gift number five, that's all I'm saying. I'm pretty sure we could get to thirty-three." He lifted the bag of popcorn. "This could be number six. The Diet Dr. Pepper, number seven. Root beer, number eight. Red Vines, number nine."

Briar smiled and simply shook her head, but Tarr's happiness would not be contained.

"So Jentzen said he can come look at my RV, help me with the stovepipe, and help me move it, since I'm not sure I can get it off the corner of the property where it is right now."

"That's great," Briar said. "When's he going to do that?"

"Wednesday," Tarr said. "And Bobbie Jo and Tuck don't get back till Thursday, so I might be able to get out of here before then."

"You could just stay here with them," Briar said. "I don't get why you don't want to. You have your own suite up there on the second floor, and they're a really sweet couple."

"Yeah, I know," Tarr said. "I just feel lame. And besides, Ashton said that Tuck's new client is going to be living here with them, and Rosie is going to stay for a while too, so I can't have the suite and then put both of them down here."

"Why not?" Briar asked, in her usually salty way. "There are *three* bedrooms and *two* bathrooms down here. How much room do you think they need?"

"I don't know. It just feels weird, with them not being married at all. It'd be nice if they could each have their own floor."

"Well, I'm sure Tucker and Bobbie Jo can explain the situation to them."

"Yeah, but if I can get the RV moved next to the arena, then I can steal some of that electricity and water, and if it's really bad, I can sleep in the room where Ashton sometimes does."

"Well, it sounds like you've got a plan," Briar said. "I didn't know there was a bedroom in the arena."

"He said it's up on the second floor, along the row of offices. And he said it's pretty bare, but he's managed to make do with a case of water and some beef jerky. And then, of course, he can come to the house and eat with Tuck and Bobbie Jo."

"Maybe you could put a microwave and a mini-fridge there."

"I've got that stuff in the RV," Tarr said. He couldn't stop grinning, and he faced the big screen, which sat paused on the movie that Briar had found and he'd approved—*Jumanji*, with Dwayne "The Rock" Johnson.

"Are we ready?"

"I'm just waiting for you to stop talking, cowboy."

Tarr chuckled, and he really did want Briar in this luxury lounger with him, instead of all the way over there with the cooler and drinks and so many armrests between them. He'd been surprised that she'd let him kiss her so much at the dining room table, and he felt certain that if Tuck and Bobbie

Jo hadn't interrupted, he'd have his kiss on the mouth by now.

That would be worth thirty birthday gifts, Tarr thought, and his pulse jumped just thinking about it.

They'd finished their poutine lunch about an hour ago, and he'd helped her clean up and opened his birthday gift—a brand-new pair of winter gloves to work around the farm—before they'd come downstairs to start their movie afternoon. Then he'd gotten distracted with calls and texts and trying to disable the camera, but in the end, he felt all of that would be worth it.

Briar got up to go start the movie. She'd attached her laptop to the cables coming out of the wall, so she didn't have a remote for it. She hurried back down the aisle, and Tarr waved her closer, as if she were an airplane and he wanted her to park right on his lap.

First, she bent over the cooler and got out a can of his Diet Dr. Pepper. He took it and put it in the cup holder on his left so he could hold Briar on his right. She slid into the space, and he opened his arm and put it around her, her hips butting right up against his. Then she twisted onto one side and leaned into his chest.

"Is this okay?" she whispered, as if there were other movie-goers who would be bothered by the two of them talking.

"It's perfection," he whispered.

And while he wasn't a hormonal fourteen-year-old who could make out with his girlfriend during the whole movie, Tarr suddenly wanted to. At the same time, he really needed to let Briar lead in all things physical.

He ate his popcorn slowly and then opened a package of Red Vines as he enjoyed the movie. Being with her was enough, and he didn't want to pressure her or make her feel like it wasn't.

He also didn't believe that she would stay awake for the duration of the movie, and sure enough, about halfway through, a soft snore met his ears. He gently leaned the luxury lounger back even further so she could rest more completely against his chest.

Tarr's new favorite thing was holding Briar while she slept when she wasn't hopped up on narcotics, or hurt, or needed him to stay warm. No, she lay in his arms now by *choice*, and she only needed him for him, not because she had a medicine schedule to keep or she might freeze to death without him.

Tarr, too, closed his eyes, though he didn't think that he would doze. He just wanted to breathe in the purity of this moment and enjoy the shape of Briar in his arms, the scent of her in his nose, and the fact that, for this soft moment in time, she was his and he was hers.

Briar had dinner delivered to the house—a complete steak-fajita meal—which completed the third meal of Tarr's favorite things.

He hadn't kissed her during the movie, and they'd taken their fajitas down to the big couch in the basement so they could talk without Bobbie Jo and Tucker overhearing them. The hour had grown late, and Briar had been yawning for a good half-hour by the time Tarr stood up and said, "We should get you home, sweetheart."

"Yeah." She sighed as she got to her feet as well and started helping him gather up their plates, napkins, and plastic containers.

With everything upstairs and the house clean, Briar bent down and wrapped her arms around Wiggins's neck. "You be a good boy for Tarr," she said. "I left you some food on the counter, and he'll feed you in the morning, and I'll see you out at the Goatel, okay?"

Wiggins licked her face and she giggled as she stood up. She tucked her hands in her back pockets, a showing of vulnerability for Briar that Tarr really loved.

He certainly wasn't going to kiss her right there in the kitchen or the foyer or the front porch, and if he wanted to do that for his birthday, he'd have to drive her back to her cabin, which seemed a little bit ridiculous.

"Thank you," he said, pulling her into his arms again. "This was the best birthday I've ever had."

"I'm glad."

Tarr pressed a kiss to her neck, and then just below her earlobe, and then her cheek, before pulling away. "Thank you for lending me Wiggins for the night."

"You know you could get your own dog." She moved over to the couch where she'd tossed her coat at some point during the day.

He helped her put it on. "I could," he said. "But I think I'm going to wait until I have a permanent house to live in."

"Will you really let me come to your meeting on Tuesday?" she said. "I love blueprints."

He grinned at her. "I said you could come. Tuesday, one-thirty. In fact, maybe we could meet in your office." He raised his eyebrows as a silent question mark.

Briar nodded and reached up to cradle his face in one of her hands. "That would be great. Happy birthday, baby."

"Thanks."

She dropped her hand and stepped back. He walked her toward the front door, with his phone buzzing in his back pocket. "That's probably Tuck. I told him to call tonight and that you'd probably be gone by now."

Sure enough, he pulled his phone out and saw Tucker's name. "Give me just a sec, okay?"

She paused just outside the doorway to Tucker's office while Tarr slid on the call. "What's up, brother?"

"We're getting alerts that the northeast door on the stable is open," he said. "Bobbie Jo's trying to pull it up on the camera, but it's been pushed sideways and we can't see."

Tarr frowned. "Briar is on her way home. We'll go check right now."

"Something's definitely wrong," Bobbie Jo called.

"I'll call you back," Tarr said, and he ended the call and jogged back into the house to get his own coat. He slid on his new winter gloves as he joined Briar on the front porch and filled her in on the situation.

She drove them over to the arena and then down to the back side, where their stables stood.

"Oh yeah, that door's flapping open," Tarr said.

The big barn door that they usually only opened when they got a big delivery for pallets and whatnot slammed into the side of the barn as Tarr watched.

"I don't know if I can get that closed in this wind," he said. "I might need to call Ashton."

"Let's try," Briar said, a note of urgency in her voice. "The horses will be cold."

"Yeah." Tarr unbuckled his seat belt and slid out of her SUV. The wind whipped his hat right off his head, and he yelped, then called, "Be careful, Briar!"

It hadn't started to snow yet, but this wind wasn't playing games. He wasn't sure he could muscle the door closed against it, and if the wind grabbed on halfway through and flung it into the barn, it might damage the mechanisms, and he wouldn't be able to secure it anyway.

Inside the barn, the shriek of a horse met his ear, and Tarr took off running. His heart pounded in his neck, his ears, and up into his head as he tried to make sense of what he was seeing.

"Gemini is loose!" he yelled as he spotted the pretty, cream-colored horse down at the opposite end of the stable. "How did you get out, bud?"

Briar cried out behind him, and Tarr spun back to her, torn between helping a woman or a horse. He went toward Briar and grabbed her hand and pulled her into the barn.

"We'll have to deal with the door in a minute," he said. "Gemini is loose."

She sucked in her breath, and then another one. "Okay," she said. "It's okay. Let's just calm down."

She smoothed her hands through her hair as Tarr tried to steady his own galloping pulse. *Gemini first,* he told himself. *Door second.* "You okay?" he asked, automatically putting Briar at the top of the list.

"Yeah." She nodded in a still semi-frantic way. "Yeah, I'm okay. Really."

She moved down the corridor between stalls, reaching out to touch the nameplates of the horses as she went by each one. Tarr liked watching her steady herself with each tap, and she held up one hand toward Gemini as she said, in the kind, soothing voice he'd only heard her use with animals, "Hey there, fella. You're all right."

A moment later, she twisted slightly, barely turning her head toward him. "Tarr, I think he's hurt."

Tarr followed a little bit behind her, because he was a bigger figure that could spook Gemini, and he didn't want that to happen. "I've got a lead," he said, pulling one off a hook as he went by.

Briar extended her hand behind her for it, and Tarr put it in her fingers.

"Hey, bud," she said, and Gemini let her walk right up to him. She slid her hand up his nose and gently slipped the lead around his neck. "We've got to get you back in your stall, bud. It's not safe for you out here."

With Gemini roped, Tarr turned back to his stall. Several strides later, he arrived in front of it, realizing how the horse had gotten out.

"His stall is damaged," he said. "That big barn door must have swung in."

His eyes roamed all over the area where the stall met the outer barn wall. The door had definitely swung in—probably more than once—and damaged this area enough to get Gemini's gate to unlatch.

Horses were prey animals, and he'd probably spooked away from the door in search of safety.

He heard the clomping of hooves behind him, and he turned toward Briar, who gently led Gemini toward them.

"He can't go back in here," Tarr said. "We've got to get him another place."

Thankfully, they were nowhere near capacity here at the facilities, and he and Briar got Gemini settled in another stall.

"There's something wrong with his back leg, Tarr," she said. "I don't know what. I think we should call Kristie."

Tarr set his jaw and nodded, as the big barn door outside once again smashed into the barn. "I've got to get this door secured," he said. "I'm going to call Ashton and see if he can come help."

Briar nodded. "I'll check on all the other horses and make sure everyone else is okay."

They left Gemini's stall together, and Tarr continued toward the gaping doorway at the end of the aisle while Briar paused at the next stall down.

He grabbed a couple of ropes as he went, thinking maybe he could get the rope through the door handle and then pull it closed without having to be right next to it, where the wind could toss both him and the door like rag dolls.

"Tarr!" Briar called, and he heard the edge of panic in her voice.

He turned and walked backward. "What?"

"Please be careful." She wore nothing but concern on her face, and Tarr tucked that away in his heart before he turned around and faced the challenge of the wildly swinging barn door.

seventeen

Briar couldn't calm down. She'd dealt with a lot of stressful situations in her life, but not very many of this caliber since moving to Colorado.

Tarr worked some magic with ropes and muscle, and he managed to get the door tied closed. Without the wind howling inside, the barn started to warm, the furnace pumping hard to get it back to its regular temperature.

Briar had gone stall by stall and put blankets over each horse, murmuring comforting things to them that she didn't quite feel herself.

"Briar?" Tarr called, and she lifted her head from where she sat on a stool in the corner of Gemini's stall.

"I'm with Gemini," she said, trying not to raise her voice too much and spook the horse.

Tarr's heavy footsteps came closer, and then he gently opened the door.

"We're all right," she told him instantly, heading off the

question she knew he would ask. "Kristie was out at Mission's, and they're both on their way."

"Oh, good." Tarr swept one of his big cowboy hands over Gemini's shoulder. "How you doing, buddy?"

"He's not putting much weight on that back foot," she said. "But he lets me touch it."

Tarr ran his hands along Gemini's back, then down his flank. The horse snuffled a little, clearly warning Tarr not to do too much more.

"Yeah, I'm just gonna let Kristie look at it, bud. Don't worry." He faced Briar then, and she offered him a weak smile.

"All the other horses and stalls were secure. I covered them with blankets since it was getting cold, and we can remove those any time."

"They like them." He let out a hissing breath as he slid down the wall near her stool and sat in the straw in the corner. "It'll warm up fast in here."

"How'd you get the door closed?" she asked.

"Kind of like a pulley system," he said.

Briar nodded as if she understood, but she'd had a very busy day—waking up before usual and making a trip to town to get everything she needed for Tarr's birthday. Then rushing through her chores and cooking lunch only added to the list of things she'd done. She'd slept for an hour that afternoon while Tarr finished *Jumanji*—something he teased her about, but something that told her how comfortable she was with him.

She reached over and brushed her fingers along his hairline. He looked at her wearing an expression of weariness that she felt deep in her bones.

"He's going to be okay," she said. "It's not a life-threatening injury."

"No?"

She shook her head. "No."

Tarr threaded his fingers through hers, and Briar loved the way it made her feel—claimed, less alone.

"What are you doing for Christmas, sweetheart?" he asked.

"I think you already know the answer to that." Briar leaned her head back against the wall and let her eyes drift closed. "I'll just be here at the farm."

"Tucker's cousin Mike has invited us for dinner—well, it's really lunch—on Christmas Day. They're eating at one-thirty. And with Tuck going to Oklahoma and all, I thought it might be nice to go out there."

"Isn't he the CEO of some big company?" Briar asked.

"Yeah," Tarr said. "But his wife's got a little hobby farm south of Ivory Peaks, and his sister is out there too. She married one of the cowhands from the farm, and she's due with her first baby any time." He blew out his breath. "Their parents are there too."

"Not Tuck's parents," she said.

"No, it's his aunt and uncle," Tarr said. "His parents are in Coral Canyon, and his sister and her husband are going to visit them. His other brother, Deacon, might be there. I haven't heard. It'll be a lot like going to the Hammonds' for Thanks-giving—a good time with good food and nice people."

"Are you asking me to go with you?" Briar asked.

"Was that not obvious?" Tarr chuckled. "Yeah, Briar-Thorn, I'm asking you to go with me."

Briar-Thorn. For some reason, that prickly nickname burrowed straight into her heart and warmed her from the inside out.

"If you don't want to, we can have our own private Christmas celebration here at the farm, but then that would be me and you cooking, sweetheart."

"I'm not a bad cook," she said. "And neither are you."

"Mm, true. It just feels like so much work."

"You don't want to go home to Texas?"

"I can't," he said. "Who's going to take care of the farm if Tuck's in Oklahoma?" He looked up at her. "It's me and you again, sweetheart, but we could get the chores done for the day, head out for lunch, and be back in time for the evening feeding."

"Yes, we could," she said. "I mean, why not? The Hammonds act like everyone's family, don't they?"

Tarr chuckled again. "They sure do, sweetheart."

"Hello?"

Briar lifted her head and then scrambled to her feet at the sound of Kristie's voice. "We're in here," she called, and then hurried to the door to unlatch the gate. "Thank you so much for coming." The lights in the barn blazed brightly against the dark night, almost fooling Briar into thinking it wasn't an hour past her bedtime.

"Our barn door got blown loose, and it broke Gemini's gate down there on the end. He got out. He was in the barn when we found him, but he's favoring his back leg."

"Let's take a look." Kristie gave her a quick smile and then got down to business.

Tarr came out of the stall and extended his hand toward a cowboy Briar had only met once or twice. "Howdy, Mission."

"Howdy, Tarr," he said, his voice even and his gaze watchful. "What do we need to do with that door?"

Tarr glanced over to Briar. "Do you remember meeting Briar?" He reached for her and tugged her forward. "She's our vet tech here. Briar, this is the foreman at the Hammond Family Farm, Mission Redbay."

"Sure," she said. "I think we've met a couple of times."

"At the State Fair," Mission said, and he smiled as he shook her hand. "I think you'd just been injured...." He flicked a look over to Tarr.

"Yeah, I had a run-in with some coyotes this past summer," Briar said.

"That's right." Mission shook his head. "You guys haven't had any trouble with them since, have you?"

"Nope," Tarr said. "We made the fence taller and deeper and haven't had any problems."

Mission nodded, and Tarr indicated the door. "Let's go see what we need to do with this, and then Ashton and I can come in the morning to get it all fixed up."

They left to do that, and Briar hovered in the doorway of the stall where Kristie now sat on the stool she'd been resting on, examining Gemini's back hoof. She applied a bandage, sighed, and ran her hand up the horse's leg as she let him settle back onto it.

"It's nothing serious." She looked over to Briar before she started repacking her vet kit. "He has a small laceration on the inside of his hoof. I got it back together, and he'll just need to be watched."

"Should I put him in the walking circle tomorrow?" Briar asked.

"Yeah, see how he does," Kristie said. "It's really minor. It probably would have just healed up on its own. I put a couple of steri-strips there—you'll be able to see them—and covered it with a small bandage."

Briar nodded. "Thank you so much, Kristie."

"Of course. I'm happy to come." She closed her bag and gave Gemini a good pat along his shoulder. "I gave him a little numbing agent in the area and some painkiller." She held out her hand, and Briar did the same so Kristie could drop a couple of pills into her palm. "He can have these in the morning, if he's acting like he's in pain."

"He can eat and drink and everything?" Briar asked.

Kristie nodded. "Yep. Sure thing."

Briar tucked the pills into her pocket and followed Kristie out into the aisle. "Is the wind bad out on the west side of town?" Briar asked as she watched Mission and Tarr examine the broken and cracked part of the interior wall of the barn.

"Not as bad as here," Kristie said. "But Mission talks to a lot of other foremen and farmers, and Keith Whettstein lives on the north side of town, and he said it's bad at Blackhorse Bay."

Briar nodded and hugged herself. "Well, I hope you guys won't have any trouble getting back."

"We shouldn't," Kristie said. "And we're closer to my house now, so we could stay there if we needed to."

Briar nodded. "You'll bill Tuck?"

"Oh, I'll bill Tuck." Kristie gave her a smile and then went to join the cowboys.

Briar followed her, but she hung back and just listened to Tarr and Mission brainstorm what needed to be done with the barn door. They finished up a few minutes later, and she left the barn with Tarr and drove him back to the mansion.

"Well, that was an eventful evening," she said as she pulled up in front of the house.

"Yeah, I'm exhausted," he said. "Can we go out an hour later tomorrow?"

Briar looked over to him. "Have you met goats? You want me to delay their release by an hour? They'll eat me alive by the time I show up at the Goatel."

Tarr laughed, and Briar joined him, a new release of joy eliminating some of the fear she'd been harboring for so long.

"You do your chores whenever you want, cowboy. I'm going to be out in the Goatel at eight-thirty as usual."

"Well, I'll see you at some point," Tarr said. "Because I've got to bring Wiggins back."

"You sure do," she said. "The gift is just for one night of doggy snuggles." She grinned at him, but they both looked out the windshield as the wind rocked her SUV.

"All right, I'm gonna make a run for it," Tarr said, and he leaned over the console and swept a kiss across her cheek. "Text me when you get back to the cabin so I know you made it and didn't get blown into a ditch."

"Okay, cowboy," she whispered, and then Tarr launched himself out of her car and ran for the front door of the mansion.

Briar drove herself home alone, missing Wiggins more than ever, which was ridiculous, because half the time the dog annoyed her. But Tarr was right. He was a good friend, and she did miss having him in bed with her that night. Thankfully, with everything she'd done that day, she was so tired that she didn't have a chance to miss him too much before sleep claimed her—and Tarr starred in her dreams all night long.

Briar had just finished putting away her notes on Gemini when she heard male voices out in the arena. She jumped to her feet and exited her office so she could greet Tarr and the general contractor who'd come to help him finalize plans for his house and take over the build. She had no doubt that Tarr could build a house, but she also knew he didn't have time to do it, keep up with the farm, and train all the rodeo horses.

He laughed with a man probably fifteen years older than him before his eyes settled on Briar. "This is my girlfriend," he said. "Briar Prescott. Briar, this is Les Davenport, the man who's going to build my house."

"It's great to meet you." Briar extended her hand for the man to shake.

"Are you the final approval?" he asked, grinning.

"Oh, I doubt it," Briar said. "This isn't my house."

Les tossed a look over to Tarr, and the two of them stared at one another for far too long, which meant Tarr had definitely said something about Briar already.

"Did you *want* me to be final approval?" she asked.

Tarr's gaze flew back to hers.

"I just wanted to see the blueprints, because I love stuff like that—floor plans, layouts. It's so fun to imagine what it will look like."

Tarr lifted a few pieces of paper. "I've got them right here, and yeah, I'd kind of like to know what you think."

"Well, come on in," Briar said, and she backed up into her office. "I brought in an extra chair and moved my table out a little bit, so we should all be able to gather around."

She went around the table and squeezed herself between it and the wall, leaving the other side for the thicker, broader-shouldered men.

Tarr took a seat and spread his papers out. "I don't need it to be a mansion like Tuck's, but I bought four acres from him, and I'm thinking long-term."

"Like you're going to live here forever?" Les asked.

"Yes," Tarr said without looking at Briar. "And if my momma had her way—with a wife and children."

Les pulled the nearest paper toward him. "Yeah, I see what you've got going on here. Where'd you do these?"

"Just a website I heard about from a rodeo buddy of mine,"

Tarr said, and he glanced over to Briar now. "I've lived a fair few places in my life, and I have an idea of what I want."

"Primary suite on the main floor," Les mused. "With a master bath...but...this isn't a very big closet, Tarr."

"No?"

Les eyed it and then reached into his bag and pulled out a pencil. "This is a two-story house—basement and main level. With a wife, kids...your wife's definitely going to want a bigger master bedroom closet than this."

He sketched something out and continued on with his thoughts about storage, linen closets, laundry rooms. When he finished one sheet, he passed it to Briar. Her imagination brought the space to life—colors for curtains and couches with cushions, art on the walls and granite countertops in the kitchen.

After she looked at both floors, as well as the expanded garage, a shed in the backyard, and outdoor parking for trucks, boats, and RVs, she finally looked up and met both men's eyes.

"Well?" Les asked. "Does it get the girlfriend's seal of approval?"

Briar wanted to shoot something salty back at him, but instead, she simply grinned and said, "It sure does."

Les looked at Tarr. "And what about you, Tarr? Does it meet your approval?"

"Yeah, it's great," Tarr said. "What are we talking for a timeline?"

"Well, based on what I saw out there, your foundation looks really good. I don't think we need to expand the footprint of that...except maybe for the back deck." Les pulled that paper closer to him again. "Which will be fine. This extra square footage here—" He circled something. "We can do a window seat or just not have anything in the basement beneath it."

"All right," Tarr said.

"I'll get it on my schedule," Les said. "I'm thinking we'll come first week of January, get the walls up, get the roof in and insulation going, and it should go pretty quick from there."

"Thank you so much," Tarr said.

The two men got to their feet. Briar went with them all the way to the exit, where Tarr shook hands with Les again, and they both waved as the general contractor got in his truck.

The energy level decreased significantly, but Briar's adrenaline still pumped through her. She stepped in front of Tarr and gripped the collar of his shirt. "Let's go to dinner to celebrate," she said.

Tarr grinned down at her. "Yeah. A celebratory dinner date —that sounds amazing."

Briar bounced on the balls of her feet and lifted up onto her toes. She pressed her lips against Tarr's cheek, right above where his beard grew. "Give me fifteen minutes to get home and feed Wiggy and change my clothes, and then you can come pick me up."

"Yes, ma'am." His voice barely sounded like his as it ghosted between his lips.

Briar wasn't sure what she'd done that surprised him so, but she stepped back and said, "I've just got to grab my keys from my office."

As she moved by him, he reached up and covered where she'd kissed him with his hand, almost as if he could capture the touch and hold it in his palm.

Briar smiled to herself that she seemed to have such an effect on him, and then she hurried home to get ready for their date to celebrate the fact that Tarr would be living permanently on the same farm as Briar very, very soon.

eighteen

Tarr couldn't believe what a difference two weeks made. Just before Thanksgiving, he'd been feeling downtrodden and dejected, and now he followed behind his RV as his friend Jentzen pulled it with a tractor toward the arena. They were maybe moving five miles an hour, and yet Tarr felt like he was soaring on top of the world.

Ashton would meet them at the arena, and the three of them would work on the RV to make sure it was level, stabilized, and hooked up to electricity and water before anyone left for the day. Tarr had enjoyed his stay in the mansion, and the longer he was there, the more he could see staying with Tuck and Bobbie Jo.

However, they weren't home, and Tarr knew the moment they returned, he would not want to be there. He knew no one understood it—heck, he didn't even understand it—but they'd have two other people living with them, and he didn't want to be the third.

So he inched along, watching the curtain sway in the back

window of the RV, and then came to a stop as Jentzen master-fully turned it in a wide arc around the corner and continued. They had to make one more turn, this time right, and then Ashton started waving Jentzen toward the long, south wall of the arena.

He parked it correctly the first time, much to Tarr's aston-ishment, and the three of them met at the door that sat halfway from each end of the RV.

Tarr grinned and grinned. "It looks great right here."

"Yeah, you could set up a whole patio and an outdoor area," Ashton joked. "I thought this would be the best place, because we have an outdoor outlet right here, and we should be able to get your whole rig plugged in."

"Let's get it level first," Jentzen said. "I've got cinder blocks and pallets if we need them."

He set about doing that, and he set up an area in front of the RV with pallets to make a decent front porch where Tarr could escape the snow and mud, clean his boots, and then go up the steps and inside his temporary home. The three of them crammed inside next, and Ashton took one look at the wood-burning stove and said, "I don't think you need that."

"No? Just space heaters?" Tarr looked from the stove to the facility manager and expert cowboy here at the farm.

"If we sealed the roof up right, the wood-burning stove could be out here, and you could use a space heater inside in your bedroom," Jentzen said. He took the few steps to look inside the back bedroom, poked his head in the bathroom, and then started opening cupboards. "Are you showering in this thing?"

"If there's hot water," Tarr said. "I could shower out here."

"We could probably do some sort of gravity system," Jentzen said. "Especially if you've got water hookups to the arena here."

"We should be able to do that," Ashton said. "But it might take a hose."

"Won't a hose freeze in the winter?" Tarr asked.

"Yeah, probably," Ashton said. "But I wonder if we could feed it out the second-floor window and kind of use gravity the way Jentzen just suggested." He looked up to the ceiling, as if he could see where to place a hose coming from…where?

Tarr had no idea—and that was why he'd tried living in the RV without utilities.

"Or you could not shower out here," Ashton said. "But all of your dishes and everything you need water for—washing your hands, cooking—would have to be done with ice-cold water—if it doesn't freeze."

Tarr honestly didn't know how any of that would work. "What about a water tank?" he asked. "That I keep inside the RV, so it won't freeze. What could we do? Fifty gallons, one hundred?"

"You could do that," Jentzen said. "And it would be what-ever temperature it is inside the RV. But you could heat it for dishes, or coffee, or washing your hands."

"And I could just shower at Tuck's," he said. "Or Briar's."

Ashton nodded. "Yep, that's what I would do. I don't think you need to shower out here."

"What about the bathroom?" Tarr asked. "If I had a hundred gallons, would I be able to use that?"

"I would just use the bathroom inside the arena," Ashton said. "You're only twenty-five feet from the door, and you'll be able to get in and out real easy."

Tarr nodded, though that didn't sound entirely ideal, but he had Les scheduled to work on the house now, and Tarr told himself he could do anything for five months. Heck, he'd done a lot of things he didn't like for a lot *longer* than five months.

"So I'm going to shower inside somewhere. I'm going to go to the bathroom inside. But I'm going to have electricity, and if we do a water tank, I can wash my dishes and have water come out of my kitchen faucet for tea, coffee, cooking, and small clean-up jobs."

"Yeah, all that," Jentzen said. "Your stove here will work with the electricity. We put an electric heater in the bedroom, fix up the wood-burning stove out here, and you've got a microwave." He smiled as he looked left toward the back of the RV and right toward the front. "It's not a bad place, Tarr. It's actually really nice."

Tarr thought so too. He entered the RV to a dinette set that was really a booth on three sides. He had a living room down on the front end, closest to where someone might drive the RV, and that included a full-size couch and a recliner, with a TV mounted to the wall above the chair.

His kitchen was galley-like, and on its way to the bathroom and bedroom—which housed a king bed and a tiny closet in the back of the RV. He had plenty of blankets, pillows, and sleeping bags, and the wood-burning stove just needed to be shored up and properly vented.

Jentzen set about doing that while Tarr stepped out of the RV with Ashton to get it plugged into the electricity.

"I can head to town and get you that water tank," Ashton said. "I think we can put it in the bathroom, above the shower, and run the lines into the kitchen. That's what I would do."

Tarr nodded, and it only took a few minutes to find the right cords and outlets and get things plugged in. When he climbed the steps back into the RV and saw the lamp shining above the only free counter space in the kitchen, he whooped. He grabbed his cowboy hat and threw it right up into the air. "There's electricity in here!"

The other men laughed, and as they quieted, Tarr appreciated nothing more than the hum of electricity in his house.

"I need a few supplies for this stove," Jentzen said. "I'm going to have to make a run to the hardware store."

"I'll go with you," Ashton said. "I'm gonna get the water tank."

"Let me send you guys with my card." Tarr fumbled for his wallet and pulled out his credit card. "Get anything we need."

"Do you need anything else?" Jentzen asked. "You've got silverware? Food? All that?"

"I've got stuff at Tuck's that I can bring out," Tarr said. "But otherwise, yeah, I'm good."

"If you think of anything, text me," Ashton said, and the two of them left together, chatting with one another easily, though they'd just met.

Tarr stood out on the pallets that Jentzen had used to create a clean area for him. They ran two deep and three long, and he'd be able to wipe his boots clean before he had to go into his house. Then he turned in a full circle and surveyed his RV, which had once looked like a dump but now shone like a palace. Grinning, he went back up the steps and into the RV, letting the door slam behind him.

He straightened up the things that had fallen and moved while the RV had rumbled down the dirt road, made his bed, and decided to convert the bathroom to a storage space since he wouldn't be using it.

He got behind the wheel of his truck and drove to Tucker's house, collected his groceries and clothes and everything he'd left there, and moved it to the RV, because he'd sleep there tonight ahead of Tuck and Bobbie Jo's return.

When he pulled back up to the RV, he found Briar's SUV parked in front of his pallets. She sat on his front steps despite them being metal and probably freezing, and she raised her hand in a wave as he parked beside her.

"Hey, you," he said. "Did you come to check it out?"

"I like this front porch-patio area." She smiled at him, got to her feet, and came to collect some grocery bags. "You're moving in today, huh?"

"I don't see a reason to wait, do you?"

"Yeah, I do, Tarr. It's called *comfort*."

Tarr simply shook his head and led the way up the steps and into the RV. "I've got electricity now, sweetheart. I can make breakfast. I can store things in the fridge and have them stay cold. I'm going to be using an electric heater in my bedroom, and we're going to fix up the wood-burning stove for out here."

Briar walked into the living room and then came back by the dinette, trailing her fingers across the top of the table. With the two of them standing shoulder to shoulder and simply turning around, they put away his groceries and other goods. Tarr returned to his truck and grabbed his duffel bag and took it into his bedroom.

When he came out, Briar stood next to the table holding a wooden sign in her arms. Tarr came to a complete stop and drank in the beautiful woodcraft she'd created for him.

"Home Sweet Home," he said, noting the carved dog between the words *Home* and *Sweet* and the horse between *Sweet* and *Home*. "Briar, this is great."

He moved over to her and took the sign from her. "Is it indoor or outdoor?"

"This is an indoor sign, baby," she said, leaning her head against his bicep and linking her arm up and through his. "I was thinking maybe you could hang it in the living room here."

She walked over to it and indicated a blank spot on the wall, where he'd duck under to get to the driver's seat. "You're not using the loft, right?"

"Nope," he said. "But, I mean, it could be a guest bedroom." He grinned at her.

She giggled. "Some guest bedroom. How do you even get up there?"

"There's a ladder that comes out," he said. "See that knob right there?"

"Oh, right here?" Briar reached up just above her head and pulled on the knob. A ladder came shooting out, and she lowered it all the way to the ground, then climbed up a few steps to look into his "loft."

"There's no mattress or anything."

"I'd put an air bed up there," he said. "Wiggins would love it."

"You would never get Wiggins up this ladder." She grinned down at him as he positioned the sign on the solid wall there. "I think it'd look real nice right there."

"I'll have to find some hammer and nails."

"I brought some," she said. "I'll go get them."

Before he could protest and say he would get them, she hopped down from the ladder and scampered out of his RV.

Tarr gazed down at the hand-cut and sanded wood shaped into letters and glued to another slab of wood that had been lovingly stained a dark brown. The letters were more oak-colored, and she'd painted the dog and the horse with colors. He ran his fingertip around the outline of the gray dog with the black nose, his heart expanding with every breath he took and every thought of Briar making this for him.

She returned after only a minute, and as he exchanged the sign for the hammer and nails, he asked, "When did you make this?"

"In the past few days," she said. "Now that my guest bedroom is back to being an art studio, I've had time."

He hammered a nail into the wall and then turned and reached for the sign. "You've been staying over at the mansion until nine-thirty or ten every night with me." He lifted his eyebrows. "So when have you had time?"

He still hadn't kissed her, because he usually walked her out to her SUV, hugged her, and waved to her as she drove away—all while Tucker or Bobbie Jo could see them. Maybe now that he'd be living in the RV, Tarr could drive her home and kiss her there—or kiss her right here in the RV. Or he might spend evenings with her at her house for *comfort.*

"I've been staying up a little bit late," she said. "It's too high on the left, Tarr."

He lowered it and looked over his shoulder to her. "Now?"

"Yeah, it looks nice."

She smiled, and when she did, she transformed into a pure angel. Tarr put the ladder away and went to join Briar, easily lifting his arm around her shoulders. "Yeah, that's real nice, Briar. Thank you so much."

"You need some art for these walls, Tarr," she said. "This looks like a 1970s nightmare."

"Hey, it's from the nineties," he said.

She giggled. "That's still thirty years old."

"Well, I wish I knew *someone* I could commission for some art for a thirty-year-old RV." He grinned at her.

Briar beamed back at him, turning fully into him. "What do you like, cowboy?"

She wore her hair back in a ponytail, so Tarr couldn't tuck it behind her ear. He lifted his hand anyway, and he ran his fingers up the side of her jaw and along the curve of her earlobe to the ponytail. He tightened his fingers around it and then pulled them down, letting the hair slip through.

"I like you, Briar."

She swallowed, then said, "I like you too, Tarr."

"And I like that there are no cameras here." His heartbeat picked up its pace, especially when Briar turned slightly tense in his arms. He leaned down and let his eyes drift closed as he drew in a breath of her hair, her skin, her perfume.

"I like that you made me that sign, and I'll like any art you make for me at all."

Briar's breath tickled as it moved across his chin. "And I'd like to kiss you, sweetheart."

"Do it, then," she whispered.

Tarr didn't second-guess or ask twice. He moved slightly, sensing where Briar was right in front of him, his hand sliding up to cup her face on one side and hold her steady at the waist with the other.

His lips touched hers, and every magical, fantastic thing Tarr had imagined would happen when he kissed Briar came true.

Sparks and pops moved through his whole body, and she tasted like that cherry Chapstick that made her lips a little bit pink. She pulled in a sharp breath, and then her hands landed in his hair, his cowboy hat somewhere else, and all of Tarr's focus went solely to kissing Briar—again and again and again.

nineteen

If Briar had known kissing Tarr would rock the earth off its axis, she would have done it on his birthday five days ago. Or maybe sooner. Maybe the very evening she'd met him, when she'd accused him of stealing Wiggins instead of figuring out how to get his lips on hers.

He kissed like the champion he was, and Briar went along for every moment of it.

She let her mind go blissfully blank and allowed every cell in her body to experience and feel the warmth of his hands in her hair and along the side of her face, to enjoy the softness of his beard against her skin, and the way he absolutely couldn't seem to get enough of her. She definitely breathed him in through her nose and swallowed his very essence.

She had no idea how long they stood there kissing in his RV, but when he pulled away, everything inside her told her it had not been long enough.

Tarr's shoulders rose as he breathed in, trying to catch his breath. "See," he whispered. "It's simply incredible, right?"

Briar wanted to agree, but she didn't have time before his lips claimed hers again, and the best ride of her life started over.

* * *

Another weekend arrived, and with it, Mother Nature sent hail, followed quickly by snow, with the forecast calling for more of the same in the next few days leading up to Christmas. Bobbie Jo decided to move the goats out of the Goatel and into the arena ahead of her trip to Oklahoma to see her parents.

She and Tucker were flying to Tulsa, where they'd spend a week before returning to ring in the New Year here on the farm.

Tucker had signed two more rodeo stars—another barrel racer and a bull rider like Tarr. They'd both be coming to the farm and facilities in January. Briar had already looked them up, and she couldn't complain that there would be more rodeo personalities here. This was what Tucker and Tarr did, and she'd begged God to let her stay on this farm.

She also wasn't going to complain about moving the goats into the arena, though it would definitely be a big mess they'd have to clean up later. It would make feeding them easier and warmer, and Briar could admit she was looking forward to only doing the holiday schedule around the farm for the next couple of weeks.

Tarr wouldn't train, and he and Ashton would focus on keeping the roads cleared and the rodeo animals fed, while Briar took care of Bobbie Jo's goats and tended to any veterinary needs of the animals living here.

Though Wiggins was no herding dog, the goats didn't seem to know that, and they followed one another in a steady stream from the front gate of the Goatel to the back door of the arena. It was simply because Bobbie Jo had gone that way, and Tucker,

Tarr, and Ashton had made a human fence on one side while Briar and Wiggins manned the other.

When every last goat had been moved indoors, all of the humans went inside too, with Ashton securing the door behind them.

Briar helped Bobbie Jo feed the goats while the men peeled off and went into the stables. They'd moved some horses from their main stable to what they normally used for their rodeo stars, freeing up space in the barn for the goats.

Once they had been cared for, Briar started her rounds, dictating notes on each animal as she visited them.

Near the end of her daily assessment, she found Rosie in the walking circles, with both of her horses going round and round and a restless energy pouring off her.

"How are they doing?" she asked as she joined Rosie at the fence.

"Great," Rosie said brightly, and she seemed so down-to-earth for being the new barrel racing champion of the world.

"Can I sit with you?" Briar asked.

"Absolutely."

She didn't need to move down on the fence, as there was plenty of room for Briar to climb up next to her, which she did.

"You were really great in Las Vegas," Briar said.

Rosie's entire persona puffed up at the compliment. "Thanks. My daddy says I should just own the success, and I try to, but it really was lucky that Leanna didn't have a good ride."

"Yeah...something about her horse?" Briar asked.

"Yeah, she couldn't ride her normal horse," Rosie said. "He had tripped or something. Daddy says half of the rodeo is luck anyway, and not to feel like I didn't win, because I did."

"You sure did," Briar said. "And who cares if it was luck anyway? Maybe next time the bad luck will be on your side."

"That's right." Rosie beamed over at her. "So you've been living in Colorado all this time?"

"Mm hm," Briar said, some of her defenses automatically flying up. She took a breath and tried to tamp them down, telling herself *you don't want to have to apologize to Rosie again, and the young woman genuinely admires you.*

"Are you going home for Christmas?" Briar asked, smiling at the younger blonde who reminded her so much of herself. When she blinked, she saw herself sitting on the fence in Rosie's place. She'd worn cowgirl jeans like that before, and a plaid shirt and cowgirl boots and a hat everywhere she went. Rosie wasn't one for makeup when she wasn't riding, but Briar had seen plenty of it in the finals.

"Yep, I'm going home on Tuesday," Rosie said. "I'll come back in the New Year, and I guess Tuck's gonna have a couple more people here, so the mansion will be pretty full."

"Oh, are you all going to be staying with him?" Briar asked.

"I know I am," Rosie said. "And I know Stretch is too. I think he's coming back early next week—even before Tucker and Bobbie Jo."

"I have a schedule somewhere," Briar said, but she didn't have to concern herself with the comings and goings of the rodeo stars on the farm, so she didn't. "Do you know the other barrel rider that he signed?"

"Yeah," Rosie said, her voice perfectly neutral. "Jessa Lilly. She's a third year, and she's pretty good."

"Do you get along with her?"

Rosie frowned out at her horse. "As well as I get along with anyone."

Briar nudged her with her shoulder. "Hey, you get along great with people."

Rosie looked up at her, pure vulnerability streaming from

her. "Do I? My daddy says I'm almost as salty as the ocean, and I don't know how to hold my tongue."

Briar laughed, because she'd certainly been called prickly and thorny her whole life. "I'm sure you don't say anything that's not true."

"I try not to," Rosie said.

"And it's not like you're mean on purpose," Briar added, her eyebrows going up. "You're just calling it how it is. And yes, sometimes you'll have to learn when not to say things, but for the most part, Rosie, your qualities are good. They make you a good rider, and good with animals, and you do just fine with people too."

"Thanks," Rosie said with a sigh.

"I mean, I'm the one who acted like a complete fool the first time we met. Remember?"

Rosie grinned at her. "It was fine...and honestly, it made me feel better about myself."

They giggled together, and then a timer went off on Rosie's phone. "That's it for these guys today." She hopped down from the fence and looked up at Briar. "I know this is really stupid, but can I get a picture with you?"

Briar climbed down in a much more careful manner than Rosie had, because while she possessed some athleticism, she had been injured quite severely in the past. "It depends," she said, trying to keep the snap out of her voice. "I know you're a big rodeo star and all that, and you probably have to post on social media, but...well, I don't want my picture or name to be on social media."

"I didn't think you would," Rosie said. "This would just be for me, because I really did love watching you ride. I'll just send it to my daddy and my momma." She wore that young hope that Briar prayed the rodeo wouldn't beat out of her.

"And I'll tell them that they absolutely can't post it on social media or anywhere else."

Briar nodded and stepped next to the girl. "That's fine, then."

She posed with her, bringing out her stunt rider smile—the one she'd used when she'd done interviews and posed for headshots.

"My cousins are going to *flip out*," Rosie said, grinning at her phone. "Don't worry, I'll tell them all that they can't post. Our daddies are kind of famous, so we get it."

"Yeah, country music stars right?"

"And the rodeo celebs," Rosie said. "My daddy and Uncle Blaze."

"And Harry Young too, right?" Briar asked. "Isn't he your cousin?"

"Yeah, he sure is," Rosie said. She finished sending off the picture and looked up at Briar.

She nodded down to her phone. "Would you send that to me too, please? I mean, *you're* the celebrity between the two of us, and I'd like to have it to show my friends that I know the barrel racing champion of the world."

Rosie's face turned red, and she shook her head. "I don't feel like a celebrity."

"Well, stick around the rodeo a little longer," Briar said. "And you will."

With that, she ducked through the rungs in the fence. "I'll get Snowdrop and meet you back at the stables."

"Wait," Rosie said. "I don't have your number."

Briar turned back to her and recited it, her heart glowing with happiness in the same way that Rosie's face took on a new light.

"All right, I'm sending it," Rosie said, and Briar's phone vibrated in her back pocket.

She helped Rosie put her horses away, and then she continued down the line, checking every animal and making notes until she got to Gemini. It had been a week since his accident, and Briar stepped into the stall with him to check his hoof.

"How you doing, buddy?" she asked.

Gemini was definitely one of the more vocal horses, and he actually snuffled at her as if to say, *Oh, I'm still alive,* in his best horsey-Eeyore-voice.

"I've got to look at your foot," she said, and she positioned a farrier stool so Gemini could rest his knee joint on it while she gripped his hoof between her thighs.

"It's looking good," she said, noting that the bandage she'd put on yesterday contained no blood spots today. "I don't even think you need a bandage anymore, bud."

The tiny cut had healed up nicely and seemed to have a pretty healthy scab on it. Gemini hadn't given her too much trouble when she re-bandaged it, and he hadn't had any pain pills since the morning after the wind had blown the door into the barn.

They'd finally fixed that only last night, as it had caused more structural damage than Tarr and Ashton could do themselves. They'd hired a foundation specialist to come out, and he jacked up the barn and held it in place while they removed the compromised wood and replaced it. The barn door had to be rebuilt and replaced with all new hinges, and it now bore a much beefier lock than it had before.

Briar finished up her rounds and went into her office to transcribe her dictation. She'd only taken one step inside when she realized someone already sat at her desk.

The scent of Tarr's cologne hit her nose next, and she

blinked at him—sitting there with his feet up on her desk and his hands clasped behind his head.

"What are you doing?" she asked.

"Waiting for you," he drawled, that sexy smile on his face. "I saw you talking to Rosie."

"Yeah," she said. "And Gemini is looking great."

"Great." Tarr got to his feet and reached for her hand. He pulled her further into the office and used the toe of his boot to nudge the door closed.

She grinned up at him as she twined her fingers behind his neck. "What are you *really* doing in here, cowboy?"

"I told you," he said. "I was waiting for you."

"I've got work to do," she said.

"Hmm. It can wait." He lowered his head to kiss her, and Briar certainly wasn't going to complain about that. He'd come over to her cabin every night that week, and when she'd said she could come to the RV, he claimed her couch was more comfortable.

He kissed her for several blissful moments, and then he pulled away. "Briar, honey?"

"Yeah?"

"I've been trying to guess at what would make Christmas amazing for you, and I finally admitted to myself that I'm not good at guessing. I just need you to tell me: how can I make Christmas amazing for you this year?"

Briar kept her eyes closed and tucked herself against Tarr's chest. "We're going out to Mike and Gertie's farm, aren't we?"

"Yeah, but honey, that's just a meal. I'm talking gifts, tree decorating, and Christmas Eve dinner. Do you want to go out? Do you want me to make something? Can I get you new boots, a vacuum, one of those espresso machines?"

Briar straightened and looked at him, joy dancing through

her senses. "My momma used to tell my daddy that if he got her something that plugged in, he'd failed." She grinned at him. "But I do need a new vacuum, and I *have* been telling you about how much I would like an espresso machine...."

Tarr grinned at her. "And the boots you're wearing have a hole in the bottom, honey."

"They do not," she said. "It's actually in the top where my pinky toe pokes through."

He grinned at her and hugged her closer. "So all of the above?"

"Honestly, Tarr, it doesn't matter. I haven't gotten gifts from anyone at Christmastime in five years."

"I'm real sorry about that," he said. "I think I'm just feeling a lot of pressure, because you made my birthday so awesome."

"How about this?" Briar ran one hand down the side of his face, simply because she liked touching him. "I've got a Christmas tree we can set up in the cabin, and you don't have one in your RV. So let's do Christmas Eve at my house, and I'll cook, and you can bring all the gifts, stockings, cards, music, whatever you want."

"Okay," he said. "I think that sounds great."

Briar did too, and she stretched up to kiss him real quick before she settled back onto flat feet. "Come on. We better get over to the mansion to say goodbye to Tuck and Bobbie Jo before they leave for Oklahoma."

He groaned and prevented her from stepping out of his arms. "Do we have to? Can't we just stay here and kiss a little longer?"

"No," she said with a giggle. "Now, come on."

twenty

Taggart Crow smiled and started to sink onto the couch as he extended the mug of hot chocolate to his wife, Opal. "Here you go, honeybee," he murmured.

"Thank you." She took a sip, her own smile prevalent as they both watched four-year-old West play with his trucks and toys.

"All right, sorry about that." Gerty exhaled heavily as she came out of the hall leading further back into the farmhouse where she lived with her CEO husband, Mike. She perched on the arm of the couch and beamed at her son. "Are you ready, baby? We're going to do our Christmas Eve presents."

West jerked his head up and looked at his mother. "Cwristmas pwesents?"

The little boy would be five next month, and he really was the most adorable thing on the planet—even Tag thought so.

"Remember, you can only pick one from your stocking, and Momma and Daddy have one to give you."

West got to his feet and parked himself right in front of the Christmas tree. "Not one of these."

"Nope, not one of those, buddy," Mike said. "Momma's got your present over here. You get to pick one thing from your stocking."

Tag happened to know that there was only one present in the stocking. After all, Santa Claus hadn't come yet, so how could there be more?

He and Opal had spent Christmas with Mike and Gerty last year, and he did enjoy their family traditions of opening pajamas on Christmas Eve and putting one small amazing thing in their son's stocking.

A year ago, Opal had helped West pick his present from the stocking, but today she remained steadfastly on the couch. Only ten days from delivering their daughter, she moved much slower these days than she had last year or even last month, and Tag reached over and threaded his fingers through hers. He cherished her every day, thanking God that He'd allowed Tag to meet her and somehow orchestrated it so she fell in love with him.

She looked over to him and smiled, and Tag returned it, mentally mapping out their own family Christmas traditions for a year from now. They'd have so many firsts this year, and Tag wanted to experience all of them.

"All right, has everyone got their present?" Mike handed Opal a pair of packages as he spoke. She kept the one wrapped in bright red paper with twinkling gold stars and passed him the one that looked like a Christmas Eve night sky, the navy blue and gold reminding him so much of what he imagined the night Christ had been born looked like.

"Ready, Daddy," West said, his package perched on his knees as he knelt in front of the Christmas tree.

Mike got down on the floor with his little boy. "All right, let's open 'em."

The sound of ripping paper and crumpling filled the air, and then West gave the biggest gasp any small child could do.

"Momma!" he yelled. "Mine be Buzz Lightyear!"

He jumped to his feet, shaking the last of the wrapping paper from his pajamas—which wasn't a two-piece set, but a onesie.

"I wear it right now, Momma! I wear it right now!"

Gerty set aside her pale blue silk pajamas as West threw his Buzz Lightyear onesie at her and started taking off his shirt.

"Yeah, you can put it on right now, buddy," she said. "But Daddy's down there to help you."

She tossed the pajamas over to Mike, who caught them and flapped them out, saying, "Come over here, bud. I'll help you."

West had already stripped down to his underpants, which coincidentally, were also Buzz Lightyear-themed, and with his chubby toddler body, he rushed over to his father.

"Put 'em on, Daddy."

"I'm putting them on. Turn around, my friend." Mike got West to turn and back right into him, and the little boy practically sat on Mike's shoulder as he lifted one foot and then the other to put on his new pajamas. Mike zipped him up to the waist, and then turned him so he could finish, and Tag started to clap.

The others joined him, and then West thrust both hands up in the air as if he had transformed into a superhero, and he buzzed and made truck beeping noises as he flew around the room.

"What'd you get, Gerty?" Opal asked.

Gerty showed her the blue silk pajama set. "They're my favorite. I'm like an otter in the sheets, slipping around." She grinned and nodded back to her. "What about you?"

In Opal's condition, she didn't exactly enjoy wearing pants, and she'd been opting to wear big, loose dresses for the past couple of months. Thus, Tag had picked out a nightgown for her in a pale peach color that highlighted the darkness in her hair and the olive tone of her skin.

"Oh, that's so pretty," Gerty said as Opal held up the night-shirt. "What'd you get for Tag?"

Tag looked down to his lap and lifted his black and white pajama set. "This seems to be made of flannel. I'm going to be way too hot in these."

"No, they're shorts." Opal reached over and moved aside the top to reveal the bottoms.

Tag lifted them, and sure enough, the pajama set didn't come with pants.

"And they have that cotton bamboo lining," she said. "It's cooling." She put her fingers under the collar of the shirt and pushed it out so that he could see the inside lining of the fabric.

"Wow," he said. "These are really nice, honey. Thank you so much." He leaned over and pressed a kiss to her temple.

"I'm the lumberjack," Mike said, and he belted out a loud laugh as he lifted a pair of soft, elastic-waist pants that were the color of denim and a plaid shirt in red, brown, and white with an ax printed on the chest pocket.

Tag laughed too as the women giggled alongside them.

"You're always saying you wish you had more time to be a cowboy," Gerty said.

"You know you could quit," Opal said. "You've been the CEO for a long time."

"Five years is not a long time, sissy," he said. "Daddy did it for thirty."

"Well, you're not Daddy," she said.

Mike and Opal's parents had been staying with them since Thanksgiving, and Tag glanced over to the pair of them. Opal's father was a tall, broad-shouldered man whose personality, intelligence, and quick wit had not been diminished by age. He was pushing ninety now, as he hadn't married his wife, Bree, until he was fifty years old.

"What'd you get, Momma?" Opal asked.

Bree lifted a very sensible set of pajamas that would work for a Colorado winter as well as it would a Wyoming one. She loved purple, and this eggplant set came with white trim along the cuffs, hems, and collar.

"I'm pretty sure this is the same set your father got for me last year," she said, beaming at him with all the love in the world.

"Hey, when you've found a good thing, you don't deviate," Wes said. "I got a couple pairs of those slicky shorts I like," he added, holding up a gray pair.

"Do you not wear a shirt to sleep, Daddy?" Mike teased.

"I do," Daddy said. "Whatever I had on that day does a good enough job, so we don't need to be spending money on a shirt just to wear to bed."

"Yeah, it's not like you don't have the money. Right, Daddy?" Opal grinned at him, and while she and Tag had talked extensively over the past couple of weeks about having her parents so close, and how sometimes her mom treated her like she'd never lived on her own, Tag knew Opal loved her parents with everything inside her.

She would sob uncontrollably when they finally had to return to Coral Canyon. She'd been the last one to get married and the last one to start having babies, and Tag had known her long enough to hear her pray over her father, begging God to preserve his health and life just long enough to walk her down the aisle and then to meet their baby girl.

"Well, now that we all have pajamas," Gerty said. "It's probably time for some of us to get to bed." She grabbed onto West, who erupted into a fit of giggles. "I mean you, mister. Come on."

"I don't want to go to bed, Momma."

"Well, Santa won't be able to come until you're asleep," she said. "That's the rule straight from the North Pole."

West sobered then and looked right into his mother's eyes. "Do we have to follow all the rules, Momma?"

"Yes," she said. "You have to follow *all* the rules." She grinned at him. "It's how you get the most blessings."

Mike groaned as he got to his feet. "Come on, buddy. I'll take you to the bathroom, and then Momma will come, and we'll tuck you in."

He swept his son up into his arms and paused at Gerty's side. He whispered something to her, and she nodded. He turned around and stood at her side.

"Before we go put West to bed," she said.

The atmosphere in the quaint, homey farmhouse changed on a dime. Opal pulled in a breath and reached for Tag's hand.

"Mike and I wanted to announce that we're going to have another baby next year." Gerty grinned around at everyone, and then at her husband. Mike put his arm around her, tucking her into his side while he held West on his opposite hip.

"Oh, praise the Lord," Bree said, and she pushed her way to the edge of the loveseat and stood. She reached Gerty and Mike first, enveloping them both in a hug.

Wes joined them, and Tag got to his feet and offered his hand to Opal, because he knew she would want to congratulate her best friend and sister-in-law.

"This is so exciting," Opal said as she waited for her daddy to finish hugging Gerty. She took her turn, gripping the lithe, strong woman tightly with her giant pregnant belly between them. "When are you due?"

"Not until July," Gerty said. "July fourth, in fact."

Opal's hand dropped to her belly, her eyes widening. "Oh, there's a little bump there."

Gerty grinned and shook her head. She wiped her eyes and said, "No, there's not. That's just my food baby."

"Congratulations," Tag said, and he hugged Mike and then Gerty, turning to find that Opal had wandered into the kitchen with her mother.

She nibbled on a shortbread cookie, because she never really ate very much these days. She wasn't the tallest woman, and their baby had definitely moved a lot of her organs around, finally protruding straight out. She couldn't see her feet anymore, and she couldn't put on her own shoes. Watching her smile and laugh, though he knew how very miserable she was, made his heart fill with love for her all over again.

She was bringing *his* baby into this world, and no greater sacrifice could be made.

"Come on, Westy," Gerty said, taking the boy from his father. "It's time for bed."

"Auntie Ope have a baby," he said.

"Yep, Auntie Ope's gonna have a baby," Gerty said. "And Momma is too, in a few months."

"Momma baby?" West asked, turning and putting his hand on his mother's face.

She slid him to his feet and took his hand. "Yep, Momma's going to have a baby, and you're going to be a big brother." She led him down the hall with her hand in his and Mike trailing along behind.

"Not long until you two will have your baby," Wes said as he came to Tag's side. "Have you guys decided on a name?"

"I think Opal's pretty set on Rose," Tag said. "But she

changes her mind every now and then. So it could be Lily or Marigold. She really likes Mary, but not plain."

He shook his head because he didn't have much of an opinion on what they named their daughter. He only wanted Opal to be happy and healthy and have everything she wanted.

As he watched, she put one hand on her belly, then leaned into the counter with the other. He heard her gasp even from across the room, and something inside him shifted once more.

He immediately started toward her. "Opal?"

She swung toward him, her eyes wide and afraid.

"Hey, what's going on, baby?" he asked, arriving in front of her only a moment later. He put both hands on her belly and felt how incredibly *tight* it had become.

"My water just broke," she gasped out.

Tag backed up a step and looked down, and sure enough, the faintest trickle of liquid had puddled on the floor. Pure panic reared inside him, and every thought he'd ever had simply vanished. The farmhouse disappeared, and his ears ceased functioning.

He looked up at Opal, and when their eyes met, sound and life and the world rushed right back at him. "Let's go," he said.

"Momma, my water broke," Opal said, her voice as panicky as Tag felt.

"Wes, can you help me get Opal in the truck?"

"Absolutely," her daddy said, joining them as her momma said, "It's fine, Opal. You guys have mapped the way to the hospital, and no first baby comes in only a few minutes."

"Some people's do," Opal said.

Tag strung his arm through hers. "Opal, honeybee, we are not going to panic. We can have a baby here, or in the car on the side of the road, or at the hospital. It's not going to matter. Okay?"

She looked at him, and after only a moment of hesitation, she nodded.

Tag adored the trust she put in him, and he got her outside and into the truck before racing around to the other side to get the engine started. He forced himself to drive at a normal speed as he trundled down the road the half-mile to their house.

"You stay right here. I'm going to run in and grab your baby bag. I know right where it is, and it's packed."

"I don't want to have the baby on Christmas Eve," Opal said.

"No problem," Tag said. "You probably won't have her tonight at all, and she'll be born on Christmas Day."

With that, he jumped out of the truck and ran inside. Opal did have her baby bag waiting at her bedside, sitting in front of her nightstand, packed and ready to go. Tag grabbed it and ran back outside, tossing it over the driver's seat at the same time he climbed in.

Opal had both hands on the top of her belly, and as he pulled his seat belt across himself, he said, "Tell me what's going on."

"I had a contraction," she said. "We probably need to start timing them."

His eyes flew to the clock, and then he dug his phone out of his pocket. "Yep. Let's start tracking 'em." He fumbled to get to the timer app and then pushed start. "We can add—what? Fifteen seconds to this when you have another one?"

She nodded vigorously, like it was all her head knew how to do. "Yeah, maybe fifteen or thirty seconds."

"All right," he said, handing her the phone. "Let's go."

He swung around their circle drive and aimed the truck down the dirt road, praying with everything he had that they could make it to the smoother, more solid asphalt quickly, so he could get his beloved Opal to the hospital. Because while he had just said they *could* have a baby on the side of the road, he certainly didn't want to do that.

twenty-one

Briar could admit she loved the scent of pine trees mingling with freshly baked bread; it exuded a sense of quaintness and home. With the furnace running and a fire crackling in the hearth, she felt like she'd created a tiny slice of perfection against the cold and darkness beyond the cabin's front door.

She'd just glanced at the clock when loud thumps landed against the front door.

"Briar, it's me," Tarr called. "My hands are full, sweetheart."

She rushed to open the door for him, pulling it all the way open until it touched the wall. She found him carrying a laundry basket stacked with wrapped Christmas presents and a few grocery bags slung over one forearm.

"Those better not all be for me," she said as he quick-stepped it past her.

"Did you invite anyone else to this party?"

"No." She closed the door behind him and gave Wiggins a

glare as he had to *bark-bark-bark!* his hello to his favorite person.

"Then these are all for you." Tarr lifted the basket over the back of the couch and groaned as he set it down.

She glanced over to the Christmas tree they'd started decorating that morning after their chores, and that they planned to finish tonight. Plastic crinkled and something that sounded like canned goods grumbled as he set the bags on the counter, and then he turned to face her.

She couldn't clear the frown from her face before he caught it. "What's wrong?"

"I think I got you three presents," she said, because she might as well be honest.

"Briar, honey, I asked what would make this Christmas perfect for you, and you told me I could do whatever I wanted."

"I didn't know you were going to bring a laundry basket full of presents."

Tarr stepped toward her, his gait even and slow. Everything about him was like that, and Briar actually really needed the steadiness in her life.

"I don't care. I wouldn't care if you got me nothing," he said. "Every single one of mine reminded me of you, and that's why I got them. It's not a contest."

He brushed his fingers along hers, his gaze dropping down to her hands. "Your fingers are cold, sweetheart."

He wrapped them in his, and though he'd just come in from the winter cold, his hands were warm and hers fit inside easily. He lifted them and slid both of their hands into the pockets of her hoodie, where Briar pressed her palm flat against her stomach and Tarr covered her hand with his.

"It smells good in here," he said, inching closer. "I brought the whipped cream, the oats, and other stuff you asked for."

Briar raised her gaze to his. "Thank you."

With his free hand, he reached up and smoothed her hair back. "Honey, today was supposed to be perfect. You can't seriously be mad about the presents."

She caught his hand as it dropped from her face. "Just surprised, I guess."

He gave her a small smile, one that spoke of his mischievousness. "You underestimated me. Is that what I'm hearing?"

A smile slid across her face too. "No," she said. "Now stop it."

"How's your stomach today?" he asked in his usual caring fashion. He pressed his hand tighter against hers, as if he could read her stomach issues that way.

Briar had learned that she could tell Tarr something once, and he'd remember it and come back to it later. She released him and slid her other hand into her hoodie pocket and sandwiched his between them.

"I feel better," she said, though it hadn't really been her stomach that had been bothering her. She certainly didn't need to get into her female problems with her boyfriend, especially after only one month of true dating. With a heating pad, lots of Gatorade, and a few doses of painkillers, Briar could usually get herself back to the land of the living within a couple of days.

She slid her hands out of her pockets, and Tarr immediately wrapped her in his arms, a sigh coming out of his mouth. "Merry Christmas, honey," he whispered.

Briar breathed in the goodness of him, getting a little bit more pine and that tangy spice from his cologne, and the cottony scent of his shirt, and the warmth of his skin. She fell back one step and looked up at him. "Merry Christmas, cowboy."

She tilted her head back so he would kiss her, and Tarr could read her body language exceptionally well, because he did just that.

Though she'd been letting Tarr in more and more, and faster and faster, she'd never truly felt herself falling for him until that moment. Her first instinct was to stop and catch herself, pull back and rebuild the wall—anything to protect herself from future heartache and pain when he left—but he stroked his lips against hers with absolute surety, and Briar let herself go.

She felt wild and free and absolutely out of control. But instead of flailing, she focused on the steady strength of Tarr's arms around her. He would not let her fall, and he'd done everything in his power to help her heal—mostly focusing on her physical wounds from the coyote attack, but also in other ways he certainly didn't know about.

He pulled away when a timer went off in the kitchen. "What's that for?" he asked, turning that way.

She watched him walk through her house as if he lived there. He'd definitely been here a lot in recent months, and she liked the way he fit inside the small cabin with Wiggins—and inside her life too. The dog followed him into the kitchen, where Tarr silenced the timer on the stove and then pulled open the oven door. "You want me to check this, honey?"

"Yes," Briar said, coming back to her senses. "I'm going to go change."

After all, she couldn't wear a sweatshirt to their private Christmas Eve party, even if it did have the word *JOY* on the front. She left him to tend to the turkey breast, and she hurried down the hall and into her bedroom.

Tarr had been wearing a dark-washed pair of jeans, a forest-green polo with white and gray stripes, and his sexy cowboy hat. It was Christmassy without screaming it, and Briar quickly shed her leggings and sweatshirt and stepped into a much louder representation of the holiday.

Her dress bore red-and-white plaid with green stripes through the white and had long sleeves and a cute V-neck collar. It fell to her ankles, and she pulled on a non-skid pair of red socks to match.

She glanced in the mirror above her dresser, fluffed her hair out, and slipped on some pink lip gloss before returning to the kitchen.

Tarr now stirred the creamed corn on her stove while Wiggins ate something he'd been gifted. No wonder he liked Tarr best. The cowboy looked over to her, and Briar put one hand on her hip and pushed the other one out.

He abandoned his tasks in the kitchen instantly, his expression growing hungry. "Wow. Look at you." His smile filled his whole face as he came closer. "This is a gorgeous dress, and you are a beautiful woman."

He took her face in his hands and kissed her again, and Briar didn't care what was in any of the packages. Having him here was the greatest gift of all, as she had celebrated the holidays alone for the past few years and she didn't want to be alone anymore.

Briar had never thought such a thing would ever be true again.

She wrapped her arms around Tarr and slid her hands up into his hair, pressing closer into him as she kissed him deeper. She wanted him to know how she felt without having to use words. Since he was so good at reading her—and he absolutely couldn't hide his thoughts or feelings—when they broke apart and she looked into his eyes, she knew he had gotten the message.

A tickle of embarrassment ran through her, and she ducked

her head, her gaze landing on the plastic grocery sacks he'd brought. "I just need to finish the topping for the apple crumble," she said. "And I'll get that in the oven."

She stepped away from him to do that, and Tarr let her go. He was patient, and kind, and so good-looking, it almost hurt to look at him sometimes.

After a few seconds, he joined her in the kitchen, holding out a square present that had been wrapped in silver paper with navy blue snowflakes on it. "I should have given you this this morning."

Briar dusted her hands together, though she'd only gotten out a bowl to start making the crumble topping. She smiled as she took the present, noting that it was soft and flimsy and probably held something like a shirt. The paper was thick, and she wondered where he'd gotten it as she ripped it open and found green, flowered fabric inside.

"What is it?" she asked as she pulled it out. Then the ties became apparent, and the front of the apron dropped down.

"I don't want you to get this pretty dress dirty," he whispered.

As he took the apron from her, she faced him, feeling like something intimate and important was about to happen. Tarr looped the apron over her head and pulled her hair out so it wouldn't be stuck to the back of her neck.

Briar stood very still, every cell in her body on fire, as Tarr smoothed down the front of the apron over her dress and then grabbed onto the ties at the waist. His eyes never left hers as he slid his fingers along her waist, his hands moving oh—so—slow, and tied a bow against her lower back.

He stepped away, that powerful gaze now sweeping down to her socked feet and back to her face, his smile absolutely devastating. "There," he said. "Now you can keep making the crumble."

Briar looked down at the apron too, finding the fabric thick and big pockets stitched onto the front. She tucked one hand into it, the dark green fabric a contrast to the lighter, flowery main pattern.

"I love this," she said. "Thank you so much."

She looked up and met his gaze again, and to her horror, every emotion inside her suddenly wobbled. Tears filled her eyes, and she actually sniffled as she quickly whipped her attention back to the bowl on the counter and then turned her back on him to get a pair of scissors to open the bag of brown sugar that he'd brought.

Tarr, in all his goodness and glory, let her retreat, and he moved into the living room with Wiggins, giving her space to figure out why an apron that had probably cost him twenty dollars had unraveled her completely.

It was more than the apron. She knew it was what the apron represented—that Tarr knew her and understood her, cared about her and liked her.

Briar hadn't felt liked in years. Not even at the height of her stunt-riding career. Sure, she'd been well-known, but even then, she hadn't had friends. She'd had people who wanted to use her, including her own parents, so that they could get ahead, they could get the fame and the next booking, or a keynote speech, or a sponsorship.

Briar let the memories stampede through her mind. Instead of corralling them the way she usually did, she let them go. They ran and raced, sometimes close to the wall the way her stunt horse had in a tight circle as she did tricks all across his back and shoulders, and then they simply galloped right out of her life.

She didn't have to hold them anymore.

They didn't get to hurt her anymore.

She went through the motions of making the crumble topping, coming back to reality about the time she started sprinkling it over the apples she'd already laid neatly in the casserole dish. She turned and slid that into the still-hot oven, then glanced over to Tarr and Wiggins in the living room.

He'd taken all of his gifts out of the laundry basket and piled them under and around her tree, and he currently lay on the floor, his feet flat against it and his knees up, Wiggins curled right into his side. Tarr had one arm around the dog and was scrubbing his back leg and hip with one hand and stroking the other along his face as he murmured something—probably Christmas wishes—to Wiggins.

Briar felt herself falling again, and with everything set in the kitchen for now, she joined them in the living room, carefully gathering her skirt at her knees as she got down on the floor with Tarr and Wiggy. She curled into Tarr's other side as he chuckled, and she giggled when Wiggins licked the back of her hand as she slid it across Tarr's stomach and between him and the dog.

"Yeah, this is real nice," Tarr whispered.

"Best Christmas ever," Briar said, committing this moment to memory so she could relive it any time she wanted to.

twenty-two

Deacon lay in bed on Christmas morning, the silence around him somehow holier than usual.

Molly had invited him for breakfast, set to start in a half-hour, and to watch the kids open their presents so he wouldn't be entirely alone on this Christmas Day.

So many texts had been coming in since last night, and he certainly didn't feel alone. He marveled that technology could connect people across so many miles, and time zones, and boundaries. But it did, and he'd really enjoyed the steady stream of news, travel updates, and well-wishes that had been hitting his device.

On the big group community-family text thread Deacon belonged to, Steele Harris had led them off last night with a beaming, bright picture of him and Hazel Monson, grinning at the camera, her left hand up and showing the giant diamond ring she now wore.

Yep, that was how he'd announced his engagement to his friends and family. And honestly, Deacon didn't blame him.

His stomach did tighten, though he was happy for Steele. He knew the other cowboy had often struggled with where he fit in the world, in his community, and in his family.

Deacon knew exactly where he belonged, and it was right here on the farm. What he didn't know was if he'd have to endure this life he really loved alone or not.

After a really great, really friendly date with Alaska, Deacon had decided to take a break from dating. He didn't ask anyone new out, and while he saw Alaska several times each week, they'd both agreed that the date hadn't really held any romance for either of them. That actually brought Deacon a lot of relief, as the exchanges between him and Alaska—an employee here on the ranch—weren't as awkward as they could've been.

Mike had sent a picture of West in his new Buzz Lightyear pajamas, and then, only twenty minutes later, Gerty had chimed in that Tag and Opal had gone to the hospital only moments after her water had broken

Deacon was one of those early-to-rise, early-to-bed type of cowboys, and he hadn't seen any news of the baby since going to bed last night. But this morning, he'd awakened to a whole slew of texts, including one of Tag half-laying in the hospital bed with Opal while she cradled their new infant in her arms.

They'd both been crying, and Deacon sniffled as he looked at the photo now, his own emotions at what a miracle a Christmas baby was catching him a bit off-guard.

Opal likes the name Mary, Tag said. *But she thinks it's real boring, and she always wished she had a nickname, so we decided to name her Marigold Sapphire Crow, and we're going to call her Mari.*

His next text read: *But not like 'Merry Christmas,' even though she was born on Christmas. And Opal wants me to make sure y'all know that we're going to have two different celebrations, a birthday for Mari and Christmas every year, and she doesn't want them combined.*

Deacon smiled and added his own congratulations to the text string, both for the engagement and the newborn.

At that point, Gerty, Poppy, Molly, and Gloria started talking about what to do about Christmas dinner. See, Opal and Tag were supposed to be hosting at their house this year for Gerty and Mike, Uncle Wes and Aunt Bree, Tarr Olson and Briar Prescott, and Steele and Hazel. But with Opal in the hospital and unable to cook, Molly had invited anyone who wanted to come to her parents' to do that, citing that there would be plenty of food.

Anyone can come here too, Gloria said. *It's us and Boone's family, with Travis, Poppy, and their kids.*

Deacon certainly couldn't help in terms of food prep, unless everyone wanted to eat scrambled eggs and toast for Christmas dinner.

Poppy came on and said, *Travis and I are going to take the kids out to Gerty's and help with the food and do everything that Opal would have done. So we'll go there instead, okay, Gloria?*

That's totally fine, Gloria said.

That meant Deacon's dinner party had just been reduced to himself with the Whettsteins—Matt and Gloria and their still-single kids—Boone and Cosette and theirs, and Keith and Lindsay, their baby Nash, and Britt and Lars.

We are not having any more babies born on Christmas, okay? Keith said. *Britt, Lars, you hearin' me?*

I'm not due for another three weeks, Britt said. *Opal was due in only a few days.*

Ten days, Mike had said. *Twenty-one is not that many more.*

We're not having any babies on Christmas, Keith said.

His text only reminded Deacon of how protective Keith was

of his sister. Britt still worked at Pony Power, though she would be taking leave come the first of the year. Deacon knew she was scared, and she never got more than a few feet away from Cosette or Gloria while she was working. He'd advised all of his cowboys and cowgirls to keep an eye on her too, just in case she went into labor and needed help while dealing with horses or kids.

Big news for us again, Mike said. *My parents are thinking of moving here to Ivory Peaks.*

Wow, Hunter said.

That's amazing, Jane said. *They should, since both you and Opal are having babies left and right.*

That's what they said. Mike sent a grinning emoji, and the conversation switched after that to *Merry Christmas!* and *Happy Holidays!* and pictures of Christmas trees from various couples and families from around Ivory Peaks. Deacon loved them all, even the tree in Oklahoma that came from Bobbie Jo's parents' house and held individual ears of corn that lit up, as if that was an appropriate holiday ornament.

He'd been getting texts from his brother for several days now about his mother- and father-in-law, as Tuck had never really spent a lot of time with them while dating Bobbie Jo or since they'd been married. Blending two families certainly wasn't the easiest thing in the world to do, and instead of spouting off and causing a problem, Tucker had matured enough to simply text his brother and vent things out instead.

Deacon had a smaller family text that included his parents, Jane and Cord, Hunter and Molly, and Tucker and Bobbie Jo, and he sat up and took a selfie of himself with rumpled hair and his black sleep shirt.

Merry Christmas to everyone. I love you all, and hope that maybe we could have the holidays here at the farm next year together.

If he started planning now, he could avoid a situation like what he currently found himself in.

All of the adults in his family replied, sending selfies of themselves as well, some with the hashtag *#SaturdaySelfie* or *#ChristmasComeAsYouAre.*

Jane and Cord were still clearly in bed, their heads pressed close together on one pillow as they grinned up at the camera. Daddy sat at the bar at his house in Coral Canyon, and Momma pressed her cheek to his, the two of them, the half-dark and half-light combo that Deacon found inside Tuck every time he saw his older brother.

Tuck had a picture of just himself on the back deck, saying he'd come outside for a bit of fresh air while Bobbie Jo helped her momma make pancakes for breakfast. Molly had extended her hand way out in front of her to capture her face in the lower part of the picture and Hunt whisking something on the counter in the house right next door.

Satisfied and filled with love for his family, Deacon finally abandoned his phone on his nightstand and went to shower.

* * *

Several hours later, Deacon pulled up to Matthew Whettstein's house, the man who had basically been a second father for him growing up. Matt had been the foreman at the Hammond Family Farm for almost thirty years, and Deacon wasn't even that old yet. He was as steady as the sun and just as warm, and he stepped out onto the front porch before Deacon had even retrieved the three dozen rolls he'd stopped by the bakery and brought along for today's meal.

"Merry Christmas," Matt called, and he tucked his hands in his denim jacket pockets. "Looks like the weather held off. It's good news for those people going up to Coral Canyon and over to loved ones'."

"Sure is." Deacon put a smile on his face and jogged up the steps and into Matt's arms. "Thanks for having me."

"You're always welcome here, Deac." He clapped him on the shoulder and then turned to lead him inside.

Deacon found that he had arrived last, behind Keith, Lindsay, and baby Nash. Britt and Lars sat cuddled together in one oversized recliner, looking at something on her phone. When he saw Deacon, Lars jumped to his feet. "Hey, Deacon, how you doing?"

He was a nice guy, an eternal optimist. Deacon wondered what that would be like—to perpetually see the good and feel happy about almost all things. He'd definitely inherited some of his daddy's quietness and grumpiness, and Deacon did like things that were slow and steady, a little bit old-fashioned, and that felt good and downright homey. He didn't need flashy technology or bright lights or the rush of a bull beneath him the way Tuck did, and he'd never aspired to be anything but a cowboy, a simple farmer.

He supposed God had put him last in his family for that very reason, as he'd never have to feel the pressure of being the CEO of the Hammond Manufacturing Company the way his uncle had, and then Hunter, and now his cousin Mike.

Jane had fought for her place in town with Cord and among everyone in the Hammond family, whether they were there by blood or not, but Deacon had never felt like that either. He fit, and he belonged, and he had his space. He always had. He'd never needed more.

He leaned down and swept a kiss across Britt's temple. "How you feeling, Britt?"

"Really good today," she said. "The baby's moving a lot, though."

Deacon smiled at her and then turned toward the kitchen, where Lindsay worked with Cosette, Boone, and Gloria. He went to the cusp of the linoleum and took off his cowboy hat. "Howdy, everyone."

Cosette moved right into him and hugged him hard. "Merry Christmas, Deacon. We're so happy you're here with us."

He wasn't sure why he hadn't wanted to go out and see his aunt and uncle and his blood cousins, and he'd thought for a few minutes that perhaps it had something to do with Steele. But with Opal having the baby and then Gerty making another announcement via text and pictures, he knew it was something more.

After breakfast, she'd sent several of West opening his presents, and then one of her and Mikey, both wearing shirts—hers that read *Momma x2,* and Mike's that said, *I'm going to be a daddy again.*

So they were pregnant again, and due in July, and Deacon should be happy for all the amazing, good things his cousins and siblings and friends were doing. And he was; he absolutely was.

So he shook Boone's hand, gave him his cowboy hat to hang up, and then hugged Gloria and Lindsay. After the greetings finished, he turned to return to the living room, only to come face-to-face with Keith holding his six-month-old.

"I'll take him," Deacon said.

"He needs to be fed," Keith said. "And I'm supposed to help candy the ham. Do you mind?"

"Not even a little bit." Deacon took the little boy from Keith and then the burp cloth and the bottle.

"My momma's got a rocking chair back in the guest bedroom," he said.

Deacon nodded and went down the hall. Though he didn't know where the guest bedroom was, and had never been there, it certainly wouldn't be hard to find. He found it in the first bedroom on the left, and he settled into the chair in the room with the blinds closed, the sunlight dimmed and pure serenity streaming through it.

Little Nash gave a wail, and Deacon shushed him and tucked him securely into the crook of his arm, holding him tightly against his body, and smoothing the burp cloth over the baby's chest. Then he offered the bottle, to which Nash glommed onto eagerly, his eyes also locked on Deacon.

Despite what he didn't have, peace streamed through him, and Deacon somehow knew that God hadn't abandoned him. He wouldn't abandon him. He didn't even know *how* to do that to one of His children.

"So maybe I just have to hold on a little longer," Deacon murmured. "Is that it, Lord? I just have to hold on a little longer?"

Yes, my son. Deacon heard the words in his mind, and as much as he didn't like them, he supposed he'd have to find a way to live with the truth.

He leaned his head back against the rest of the rocking chair and gently toed himself back and forth as his eyes drifted closed.

If that's what I have to do, he thought. *Then bless me with the strength to do it.*

twenty-three

Tucker Hammond lay on his side, his arm draped over Bobbie Jo's waist. She breathed deeply in his arms, but he knew she hadn't fallen asleep.

"It'll be fine, sweetheart," he told her, his voice barely audible to his own ears.

"We just have to draw really firm lines with them," Bobbie Jo whispered back.

Tuck hated seeing his lovely wife so tense and irritated. She'd been working on curbing her temper since he'd met her a couple of years ago, but finding out her mom had lost her job at the elementary school six months ago, and that her daddy didn't make enough at the hardware store to cover their bills, had sent Bobbie Jo's irritation to the stratosphere in only one second.

Tucker's default reaction was stunned silence while Bobbie Jo scoffed and stomped around. In the end, her mother and father were going to lose this rental in only another week, and they had nowhere else to live. Nothing lined up.

Bobbie Jo turned in his arms and slid her hand along his ribs and under his arm. "I just don't get what they thought would happen," she whispered fiercely.

He moved his hand to push her hair back off her face.

"Did they just think a miracle would manifest itself out of nowhere?"

"Yeah, sweetheart," he murmured. "I think that's what they thought."

"It's just *ridiculous*," she said. "Who thinks like that?"

"I think what they thought...is that they would tell you when we came for Christmas and we'd do exactly what we did—offer for them to come live with us."

"If that's true, I don't want them to live with us."

Tucker didn't want her parents to live with them in the mansion at all, but he couldn't say that, and he couldn't leave them here in Oklahoma without proper housing.

"We're going home tomorrow," he whispered. "And we'll make sure everything's ready in the upstairs suite, and it will be fine. We're out on the farm all the time, and they'll have that second bedroom to set up as a den or a living room, and Tarr said he would text me pictures of the electric stove top when he goes to the store tomorrow."

"I guess it's really lucky that we have someone who's thought about living up there without bothering us," she said.

Yes, Tarr had already done all the research about how to make the second-floor suite more independent. They'd put a microwave and a mini fridge in the loft, but the moment Tucker had called and practically screamed at his best friend that his in-laws were going to have to come live with them, Tarr had said, "No problem. I'll make sure that suite is everything they could possibly want, and we can put a two-burner stovetop on the countertop out in the loft, and Briar knows how to install islands for more storage and counter space, and they can even make a reading nook in that loft. It's *huge.*"

He'd gone on to detail how they could stage the second bedroom as a living room, and they had a full bathroom and a bedroom with a linen closet as well. "It'll be great," Tarr said.

And hey, they have no other options, Tuck thought.

"Do you really think it will be temporary?" he whispered.

"I don't know," Bobbie Jo said. "I'm sorry, Tuck, but I really don't know. My parents have always been self-sufficient, and I just don't know what's happened in the last few years."

She sighed and rolled over again, and Tucker had the very real feeling that this was just the beginning of a long night of tossing and turning and talking as they both tried to filter through their feelings and figure out what to do.

A couple of days later, Tuck found himself standing on the elevated edge of one of the pallets in front of Tarr's RV. He gestured on that side, while Ashton waved in another trailer opposite from him.

"There." Tarr had called his friend Jentzen again, and he'd just arrived with a heavy-duty extension cord, a bag full of surge protectors, and a one-hundred gallon water barrel.

Tuck had been inside Tarr's RV since he'd moved it to this location on the south side of the arena, and while he wasn't super pleased with the mobile home community going in on his property, he also recognized it as a great blessing from God Himself.

With John and Linda due to arrive from Tulsa tomorrow, Tucker's house had suddenly become one-third smaller. He and Bobbie Jo would stay on the main level, where all of the amenities were, and her parents would take the second-floor suite.

Rosie Young and Jessa Lilly would live in the basement, in that three bedroom, two bath area with a full living room and the theater room. It had space for a kitchen down there too, and Bobbie Jo was handling the arrival of a full-size fridge and stove to complete that area, so his rodeo clients could live comfortably in the basement.

Everyone would have to come and go through the front or back door, and Tuck reminded himself that he'd grown up on a farm with a revolving door that anyone and everyone walked through at any given time, day or night. He actually didn't mind it so much, but he really worried about Bobbie Jo. She wasn't like that at all, and she liked her privacy and her quiet time in the evenings.

He thought of the main level suite, where they had a full master bedroom with a sitting area and a fireplace, a connected master bath and a door that led into the nursery. He had already ordered furniture to make it Bobbie Jo's office and a reading nook, so she would have somewhere private and quiet all to herself. He could handle the rodeo stars and her parents anytime she needed to escape.

As the beeping stopped on Alex Monterro's trailer, Tucker thanked the Good Lord Above that he had this farm to provide for the needs of his friends and family. Tarr was super happy in his RV—warm and watered with restroom and shower facilities only a few steps away. He'd said that he'd start showering at Briar's to leave the mansion for the rodeo stars and Bobbie Jo's parents, and Tucker loved Tarr's thoughtful heart.

Alex dropped out of his truck, his grin as wide as the sky. "This is going to be so great," he said. "Look how close I got to those pallets."

Tuck looked, as the edge of the trailer had gone right by him, and he hadn't even noticed. "Your steps go right on the pallets," Tarr said. "And then you can get out of the mud and get everything clean before you go inside." He turned back to the arena. "I'm thinking we need some retractable awnings here, though. Sure would be nice if this patio area was covered."

"Don't call it a patio," Tuck growled. "It's a bunch of pallets."

Tarr turned toward him, his eyebrows raised. They had a whole conversation in only one look, and Tarr's face settled back into a regular expression. "You're right. It's not permanent. You probably shouldn't put anything permanent on the side of the arena. We'll figure out if we can set up some poles, maybe put some tarps that will slope down over the pallets to slick the snow away, so we can have this dry area where the pallets are."

"It'd be great to make it through the winter," Alex said.

Tuck took a deep breath and tried to calm his inner beast. It didn't come out very often, as he was definitely more like Momma and Hunter, who both saw the bright side of life, while Jane and Deacon had inherited their daddy's more grumpy personality.

"I can fund a tarp-roof for your pallets," Tuck said. "If you guys want to look into it."

"If you're talking some sort of roof structure," Jentzen said, as he stepped up onto the porch-pallets with them. "You could put in some four inch posts or poles, but they'd need cement."

"Just QuickCrete, probably," Alex said.

Tarr looked back and forth between the two of them as if they were speaking another language, and Tuck felt the same way. Sure, he'd grown up on a farm, but he lived with all the modern conveniences of life these days, and he employed people to build fences; he didn't actually do it himself.

"It'd be really easy to adjust the pallets or cut through them," Jentzen said. "I've probably got some posts at my place." He started pacing off the distance between the two trailers. "Probably twelve foot tall," he said as he reached Tarr's RV steps.

"And you'd only need three." He turned to face them again. "We could put one right behind Tarr's RV, one here in the middle, and one on the other side of your trailer, Alex." He returned to their huddle, and Tuck wanted to leave it. A headache stretched across the back of his neck and up into his skull, and he just wanted to go home and take a nap.

"What would you use for the roof?" Tarr said. "A tarp? And where would you attach it?"

"We put lower posts on either side." Jentzen looked right and then left, indicating the trailer-less sides. "They'd match up with the three main posts, so you need six more—mm, probably eight foot posts, so you could walk underneath them."

"That doesn't give you much of a slope," Alex said.

"True. We could make the back side even lower," he said. "Keep the front open for where you guys are going to park and walk in, and make the back side go all the way to the ground. Then we could stake it and keep it nice and tight."

Jentzen actually looked excited by this project, and Tuck turned away from the conversation. He let them continue to brainstorm as he unhitched Alex's trailer and got it level and settled. He pulled his truck forward and parked it next to Tarr's, and then got out to find Bobbie Jo exiting the arena through the side door that Tucker had once thought they'd never use. Now, it was one of the most trafficked entrances and exits of the arena, and he, once again, took a moment to acknowledge the blessings in his life.

After all, having a property like this that had once felt too big and completely ridiculous for a single man to purchase now provided shelter and life for almost a dozen people.

"How'd it go at the house?" he asked, moving to meet Bobbie Jo.

"Great," she said. "The fridge and stove are in. Everything's plugged in and works. When the girls get here, everything's ready for them down there. Beds, toiletries, all of it."

Tuck drew her into a hug. "Thank you, sweetheart. Tarr and I got everything ready for your mom and dad on the second floor." He stepped back and gestured to the trailers parked on the property. "Alex and Tarr are going to be out here. Stretch said he found a room with a friend not far from here—only about fifteen minutes."

"That's great," Bobbie Jo said. "And he can stay at the mansion if he has to. There *is* a third bedroom in the basement."

"I just worry about those young ladies," Tuck said, though he wasn't that much older than Rosie and Jessa. Their daddies had entrusted *him* to take care of them, and he didn't want to put a cowboy directly across the hall from them, even though Stretch was one of the most amazing men Tucker had ever met.

"This is really cozy," Bobbie Jo said, a smile coming to her face as she faced the trailer yard. "Have you ever thought about living in a trailer, Tuck?"

"I've lived in plenty of trailers." He chuckled. "Where do you think Tarr and I stayed most of the time?" He nodded over to his best friend's RV. "Somewhere far worse than that, let me tell you."

"I can't believe you guys sold everything when he retired."

"Well, we didn't need it," Tuck said. "And I never would have predicted this."

Bobbie Jo wrapped her arms around him and leaned into his side. "Me either," she said. "I'm really sorry, Tucker."

"Hey, you have nothing to apologize for," he said. "They're your parents, and we have to love and honor them, and if that means giving them a place to live, then that's what it means."

"I'm going to make sure they know that they need to find jobs and look for a place of their own," she said.

Tucker nodded, his throat tight. Bobbie Jo's parents were in their early sixties, and he wasn't even sure what employable skills they had. He knew he could take care of everyone on this farm for the rest of their lives, because he had been abundantly blessed simply by being born with the last name Hammond.

"Maybe your daddy can work around here," he said, making a mental note to call his father and thank him for the bounteous blessings in his life.

"He'd probably love it," Bobbie Jo said. "There are tons of schools here, so something will come up, right?"

"I'm sure," he reassured her, though he wasn't sure, and he didn't really know.

Sometimes, Tuck just wanted life to go back to normal. As he stood there and listened to Tarr laugh about something Jentzen had said, and watched Alex point to something on a piece of paper they'd wrangled up to start designing their tarp roof, Tucker realized that this *was* normal.

Every day was different in a normal life, every day brought challenges, and every day had the potential to bring joy too.

He turned as more tires crunching over gravel met his ears, and he wasn't surprised to see Briar pulling up in her SUV, nor that Tarr immediately abandoned the design-fest happening on the patio and went to greet her. Tarr never talked much about the women he dated, but he'd already told Tucker that he'd kissed Briar. So it wasn't that shocking to watch him jog the last few steps to her, wrap her in his arms, and lean down and kiss her right on the mouth.

"They're so cute together," Bobbie Jo whispered. "I really hope she can handle him."

"Are you kidding?" Tuck whispered back. "It's *him* who has to learn how to handle *her*." He looked at his wife, and she searched his face just as hard as he did hers.

"This is what people said about us, isn't it?" she asked, her smile growing and growing.

Tuck laughed and wrapped her up fully in his arms. "I'm sure they did."

Now, if he could just survive her parents moving in with them tomorrow, Tucker was sure the Lord would stop surprising him with big challenges he needed to solve in a short amount of time.

Please, Dear God, he prayed as he stepped back from Bobbie Jo and went to see what Briar had made to welcome Alex to the farm. *No more surprises for a while, okay?*

twenty-four

Tarr tipped his head back and drained the last of his peach-almond punch, Tuck's grandmother's recipe. The atmosphere in the mansion carried a more upbeat and festive vibe than Tarr had thought it might.

Of course, it was New Year's Eve, but Tucker and Bobbie Jo had been unusually stressed since learning of Bobbie Jo's parents' financial issues and then moving them into the second-story suite less than a week later.

Tarr had seen his best friend stressed before, worried about things, and struggling through his own thoughts to arrive at what he thought was best, but nothing like this. Tarr actually missed the way he and Tuck used to go get breakfast at two in the morning and talk through everything troubling them.

But the truth was, Tucker didn't need Tarr for that anymore. He had Bobbie Jo, and though Tarr knew that life shifted and changed and that Tuck absolutely should be confiding in his wife and not his best friend, he still felt like he'd lost something important to him.

The Hanks had moved in on Wednesday, only an hour ahead of the cold front and snowstorm that had been swirling over the Denver area since. Snow removal, keeping the horses fed, and spending time with Briar took all of Tarr's time and energy, and living alone in the RV—while exactly what he wanted—had left him feeling lonelier than ever.

None of it made sense, because he found himself surrounded by a fun, loving group of people at this very moment, and he had a new neighbor on the south side of the arena in Alex Monterro. The man was probably pushing thirty, but he'd only turned pro last year. He'd gone to college and actually worked as an accountant for the NPR before finally deciding to throw his hat into the ring and ride professionally.

Jentzen hadn't had time to construct anything like a pavilion roof yet, and so he and Alex had been shoveling the snow off their pallets and putting down salt. Tarr had grown tired of it quickly, and as a New Year's present for himself, he'd purchased heat mats that he could plug in, and they stayed warm all the time. They'd melt the snow and ice and leave him a path from the parking area to his RV's front steps; he'd covered those with an awning that extended out from the vehicle.

Jentzen had worked some sort of magic with the wood-burning stove, and there'd been no more smoke issues. And with the space heater in the bedroom with a thermostat on it, Tarr always came home and had somewhere warm to be. He didn't dare leave a fire burning while he wasn't home, and he put his space heater at sixty-five, hoping that it wouldn't spark all day long and cause a fire.

Being so close to the arena helped, and some of his anxiety propelled him outside regularly, just to check on the trailers to make sure they were still standing. After all, the last thing he needed was his house going up in flames and taking Tuck's arena with it.

"You must be thinking about something," Briar said, and Tarr looked down to meet her eyes.

"I'm sorry. Was someone talking to me?"

She grinned up at him. "Yep, you were definitely thinking about something."

"I was just wondering if I needed to run back and check on the trailers to make sure they haven't caught fire." He chuckled and shook his head, though losing everything to flames certainly wasn't something to laugh about. "My daddy was a volunteer firefighter," he said. "And he drilled fire safety into me, but I always extinguish the fire before I leave in the morning, so I know it's not going."

"I don't know how you live out there at all," Jim said, and Tarr simply stitched on his smile for Tuck's father-in-law. He'd dealt with plenty of personalities as a rodeo star, and he'd only met Bobbie Jo's parents and had brief exchanges with them a couple of times in the past couple of days.

Still, he could see why Tuck and Bobbie Jo were frustrated with them and why Tuck didn't think they'd ever be best of friends. Jim and Linda complained about everything, even the brand-new carpet on the second floor, where they were living in a two-bedroom suite with a bathroom and a modified full kitchen, fully furnished, for free.

Bobbie Jo eased into her daddy's side. "Did you guys get enough to eat?" she asked. "I'm going to be putting away the appetizers, because Tuck is going to bring in the smoked salmon and smoked turkey, and we'll have dinner."

She threw a nervous glance at Tarr and then Briar.

"I'll help you," Briar said, and she moved into the kitchen to start reboxing crackers and put cheese dip in plastic containers.

"I do want some more of that krab dip," her daddy said. "Your momma makes the best krab dip in the world."

Her father moved over to the island where the charcuterie boards waited, and Bobbie Jo sighed. "He's not bothering you, is he?" she practically hissed under her breath.

"He's fine," Tarr said.

"That krab dip is disgusting." She shook her head and then turned and walked into the kitchen to join Briar.

Tuck sat on the couch with Alex and Deacon, and Bobbie Jo's mom sat in a recliner, knitting. Yes, *knitting* at a party. Tarr wasn't sure what to make of her, because she certainly knew how to keep herself busy while not doing anything helpful. He turned his back on the whole living room scene and moved over to the drink dispenser to get more punch.

"She's got hot chocolate on the stove," Briar said, taking his punch cup from him. She took a sip of it and then smacked her lips.

"Hey," he said. "That's my cup."

He wished they were bringing in the New Year alone so he could hold her on his lap as they watched a movie neither of them cared about, and he could kiss her as much as he wanted to. As it was, he didn't dare leave Tuck and Bobbie Jo here with her parents, though he'd already heard each of them say that they probably wouldn't make it past ten PM.

Briar wasn't a night owl either, but Tarr and Tuck had spent years staying up late for rodeos and after-parties and breakfast for dinner at one in the morning. Tarr still loved that lifestyle, and he didn't have to be riding the circuit to stay up past midnight and groan when his alarm went off in the morning. He'd have to get back to training horses on Tuesday, which was when Tuck had declared the end of their vacation schedule.

Briar extended her hand to give Tarr his cup back, but he shook his head. "You're right. I want the hot chocolate."

"She made plain milk chocolate," Briar said. "And then she's got these oils that you can put in it for mint, or orange, or raspberry."

"I want the orange," he said.

Briar wrinkled her nose in the cutest gesture ever. "I'm going to have mint."

"That tracks for you." He grinned at her and hooked his arm around her waist, pulling her flush against his body.

"Tarr," Briar warned under her breath.

"What?" he asked. "There's like five people at this party. It's not like I'm gonna make out with you in front of strangers." He leaned down and touched his lips to her cheek. "There's no paparazzi here to get our pictures and post them online."

She relaxed in his arms then, leaning her cheek against his chest as she hooked her fingers in the belt loops at his sides. He liked that, because it made him feel like she needed him to stand up.

He ran his hand down over her left hip. "How are you feeling tonight, sweetheart?" he asked. She'd told him that the colder weather made her hip hurt, and it had gotten worse this year because of the coyote attack.

"It's sore," she said. "I should probably take some more painkillers now, so I can take some before bed too."

"We can sit at this party," he said, as Tucker and Bobbie Jo had plenty of furniture in their house and only eight people here. Rosie and Jessa had not arrived for their training, and Stretch had opted to attend a party with the friend he was staying with.

"I'll get us some hot chocolate," he said. "You go claim us a spot on the loveseat."

She stepped back and nodded. "All right."

He managed to make it out of the kitchen before the hour bell rang, and Tuck popped to his feet. "It's eight o'clock," he yelled to the house as if no one knew. A grandfather clock chimed, and they all stood there and waited for it to play its little song and then bong eight times.

By then, Bobbie Jo had gone into the office and then come back with a bunch of balloons that had been reduced from eight. They had popped a balloon at five o'clock when the party started and were planning to do so every hour until midnight.

Tarr had attended fancy balls, and award ceremonies, and galas, but he much preferred this small-town brand of fun to anything he'd done in Las Vegas or Calgary or San Antonio.

"Momma, it's your turn to pop," Bobbie Jo said.

Her mother sighed, as if Bobbie Jo had told her she had to go outside and stand in the snow for fifteen minutes. She set her knitting on the arm of the chair and stood with a groan. "Oh, all right," she said. "How do I do that?"

Bobbie Jo held out a big crochet pin used to hold down blankets to foam pads. It was metal and a couple inches long and shaped like a T, so that someone could actually hold it.

Tarr had not popped a balloon yet, as Tucker had done the five o'clock, Alex the six, and Bobbie Jo the seven. He had no idea what the order was, but he figured Bobbie Jo's parents would be next, so they could go to bed any time after nine PM.

"Any balloon, Momma," Bobbie Jo said, grinning at her like the woman had never annoyed her in her life. Tarr admired someone who could hide their emotions and feelings like that, because he really couldn't.

Her mother fretted about which balloon to pop, and just as Bobbie Jo exchanged a glance with Tuck, she selected a lavender one and jabbed the pin at it. It popped with a loud noise, of course, and her mother shrieked and jumped back. Confetti fell out of the balloon, and Bobbie Jo caught some of it in her hand.

"It's orange and yellow," she said, turning back to Briar.

She held a laminated card in her hand, and she scanned it for a moment. "Orange and yellow are the Peach-O Rings for our hourly snack, and it's game hour." She made it sound like a grand thing, and Tarr grinned at her, because he knew that she did not enjoy board games. They'd played cards when the power was out, but he couldn't get her to do much more than that.

"All right," Tuck said. "We've got lots of two-player games here, like Connect Four, and Tarr and I know lots of card games that just take a couple people."

"We've also got Pass the Pigs," Bobbie Jo said. "It's one of my favorites. And Tuck just put a pool table in the front living room to make it a game room."

"We also have video games in the theater room downstairs," Tuck said. "And we can put a movie on after that if anyone wants to go down there."

"We also have real food ready," Bobbie Jo said. "Tuck just needs to bring in the smoked meats, and I've got scalloped pota- toes, vegetable beef soup, hot rolls, and grilled asparagus to go with it."

"And the Peach-O Rings are right here," Briar said, indi- cating a big bowl on the end of the counter. Their seven o'clock snack had been chocolate-covered pretzels, and a bowl of those still sat there as well, along with the peanut M&M's from their six o'clock balloon pop and their party-opening bowl of caramel popcorn.

Tarr loved to eat, and he left Briar to claim a spot for them at the dining room table with their mugs of hot chocolate while he went to get their food. Deacon and Alex started a game of Connect Four, but as soon as Tarr finished eating, he made eye contact with Briar and said, "You want to try a video game in the theater room?"

He didn't think for one moment Tuck or Bobbie Jo would leave their party and go into the basement. Nor would her parents. Alex and Deacon might come down, but Tarr was hoping he could enjoy some time alone with Briar if he snuck away under the pretense of playing video games in the theater room.

"You go get it started," she said. "And I'll help Bobbie Jo clean up a little bit." She was always hyper-aware of that, and Tarr didn't want to argue, so he left her to do that.

He did go downstairs, the noise of the chatter and games fading into blissful silence. He turned on the game machine and navigated with the controller to some of the mini-games that he and Briar could play, just in case anyone else came downstairs.

It took Briar fifteen minutes to join him, and she also made no pretenses about playing a video game. She simply climbed into the same luxury lounger as him, tucking her shoulder under his arm and draping her arm across his waist.

"This was a great idea, cowboy," she said. "Maybe if we take a mini-nap, we'll actually make it until midnight."

"You think I brought you down here so you could have a mini-nap?"

Briar giggled. "Mister Olson," she chastised. "Why else would you bring me down here?"

Tarr chuckled with her and smoothed the ends of her hair down over her bicep. "When I was younger, my mom and daddy always made us set goals for the year on New Year's Eve."

"Oh, yeah?" she asked. "And what would childhood Tarr set a goal for?"

"It was usually some sort of weightlifting goal," he said. "An increased weight or a faster time in the sprint or, you know, to get one-hundred percent on my times tables. Stuff like that." He smiled just thinking about it. "I gave up doing it when I left home, because I thought it was kind of stupid."

"Do you want to set some goals for this year?" she asked.

"I don't know." He closed his eyes and enjoyed being in the moment with Briar. "What would they be? Train five horses? My life is pretty simple."

"You can still have meaningful goals," Briar said.

"What would one of yours be?"

She remained quiet for several long seconds before finally saying, "You're right. It's harder than it sounds."

Tarr swallowed, his nerves suddenly lodged in his throat. "I know we're still new and all, Briar," he said. "But I do have a goal to get married—doesn't have to be like, this year or anything, but I sure do like you more than anyone I've ever dated before."

She lifted her head then, and Tarr felt her watching him before he granted her the gift of opening his eyes. "Have you ever thought about getting married?"

"A long time ago," she whispered back. "When I still believed in things like that."

"What would it take to make you believe in that again?" he asked.

"I don't know," she admitted. "I swore off cowboys when I left Canada, and yet, somehow I'm dating one again."

Tarr nodded. "So maybe we'll just keep talking through things and see how things go," he said, though he didn't want to admit how shattered he would be if he and Briar didn't work out. He'd already started thinking more long-term, but he watched when the slender column of Briar's neck shifted as she swallowed, and then he ran his hand along her lower jaw and guided her mouth to his.

He kissed her exactly how he wanted and for as long as he wanted. When he finally pulled away, he murmured, "Happy New Year, sweetheart."

"Happy New Year to you too, Tarr," she said, and then kissed him again in that needful way she had that told him she had more to say and didn't want to say it. He wasn't complaining... for now.

twenty-five

Briar knew she couldn't keep kissing Tarr without telling him more. She always seemed to have more to talk about than he did, though he'd just admitted that one of his goals for next year was to get married.

Briar had given up on marriage a long time ago—maybe even before her first serious boyfriend. She'd been stunt riding since the age of ten, and as her talent for it became more and more obvious, and the spotlight shifted away from her parents and their roles in the rodeo to their star of a daughter, her mother had started telling her that men only wanted one thing from "girls like her."

At the time, she hadn't been sure what a girl like her was, but her more casual dating had told her that men liked her curves and were sometimes more interested in kissing her than anything else.

She'd put up a pretty impenetrable wall at that time, which had only been reinforced by her mother telling her that marriage would only trap her in a place or tie her to a person she might not want to be trapped or tied to forever. When her parents had gotten divorced, Briar, once again, wondered why anyone would get married.

She'd started dating a man seriously after that, and he'd been like a child in a big body. She didn't want to mother her husband. Yet, every man she'd dated seemed put together on the outside but could barely function inside his private life.

She'd told Tarr almost nothing about the men she'd dated and why she didn't like cowboys, and how she'd nearly lost everything after trusting one with a boyish face, a quick smile, and sugared lips.

She finally got control of herself and stopped kissing Tarr. She loved being physically close to him, but she'd be lying if she said it was enough. She knew it wasn't, and Tarr did too, though he'd kept his promise and had never pushed her to tell him more than she was ready to tell him.

She pressed her lips together and swallowed. "I think maybe I could believe in love and marriage again," she said. "With the right person."

Tarr simply hummed and rubbed his thumb up and down from her elbow to her wrist, where he circled the bone there and then let his fingers start the journey again.

"I dated a lot of losers," she said. "Two bull riders and one roper."

Tarr said nothing, and Briar took a deep breath to center her thoughts. "But it wasn't just them that broke my confidence that men could be good, and that someone could love a woman for more than her status."

"I don't care about any of that," Tarr said, his voice somewhat defensive.

Briar didn't need him to reassure her, but she gave a quick nod against his chest. "Anyway, my parents didn't have a good marriage," she said. "And my mom told me she wished she'd never married my dad. She said men—especially cowboys—just want their women in the kitchen, and I was meant for greater things than that."

Briar closed her eyes, and once again, she simply let the memories wash through her, hoping they too would drain away the way the ones at Christmas had. "For a long time, I believed her," she said. "I was stuck-up and snobby. I didn't have any friends, only people who wanted to be associated with me because I was good at stunt riding."

Tarr slid his hand down past her wrist, aligning his fingers between hers.

"I let myself feel like I was more important than them," she said. "And I trusted the wrong people. Then, of course, after the accident, I realized that I had created the bed I now found myself sleeping in.

"Of course no one was going to be on my side. I had never been on theirs. They weren't going to back me up. I had been taking from them at every opportunity. I think most of them were delighted to see me fall, though they probably didn't wish two broken legs and a hip replacement on me to do it."

"I don't know that woman at all," Tarr said.

"I'm a completely different person now." Briar's voice turned tinny as she struggled against her emotions. "But Tarr—"

Her voice quit, just simply quit on her, and her throat had narrowed so much she couldn't even swallow. She felt like she might choke, and panic reared through her. She sat up and sucked at the air.

"Hey, it's all right," Tarr said.

She shook her head as air finally went in right. "I'm okay."

He didn't reach for her or demand she lay back in his arms. She took another breath and looked at the bright screen with colorful pictures that Tarr had pulled up, the video games they had come downstairs to play somehow comforting her in that moment.

"Baby, there are consequences to how I used to be," she whispered. "And not just that I'm really salty sometimes or that I don't trust people yet, but, like, physical consequences."

"All right," Tarr said, easily.

"Sometimes my hip really hurts," she said. "And I'm real stubborn about going to the doctor about it. And sometimes—"

She couldn't look at him, though she needed to. She took another breath and swallowed. "You know how sometimes my stomach hurts?"

"Yeah," he said simply.

"It's not really my stomach," she said. "It's my...female stuff. I'm kind of messed up inside. The doctors told me they aren't sure if I'll be able to have kids."

Her voice broke, and Tarr reached for her then. She snuggled back into his chest and let herself cry.

"I didn't care at the time," she said, her voice nasally. "Because there was no possible way on this planet that I would ever want a child. But now...now I'm thinking maybe I should go to the doctor and get that stuff figured out."

"So you do want kids?" he asked, his voice a little rougher around the edges than she'd heard it before.

"I don't know," she said. "I've never considered myself to be very nurturing, and like I said, dating and marriage and kids were never in the cards for me until—" She cut off and reached for her inner well of bravery. "Until *you*, Tarr. You've made me think about things and reevaluate them and want something different than I've ever wanted before."

"Good things, I hope," he said calmly.

"Yeah," Briar said. "But you should know, Tarr, if one of your goals is to get married and have a family, I might not be able to do that, and you might want to find a woman who can have your kids."

"Stop it.'"

"What do you mean, stop it?" Briar asked. "It's a real thing, Tarr. What if I can't have babies? I've known people who've broken up because of that. It's a real thing."

"I'm not saying it's not," he said, that frown coming between his eyes that told her he was thinking. "And while I'd take a baby girl who looked like you any day—even with all your fire and sass and saltiness—there are other ways to build a family."

His eyebrows went up as he searched her face. "Aren't there?"

A tear streamed down Briar's face as she nodded, and Tarr's composure crumpled. He gently brushed her tears away with his thumb, pure compassion shining in his eyes. "All right, sweetheart. Just lay down. It's okay."

He shushed her again the way he would calm a small child or a frightened foal. "It's okay," he whispered. "It's all going to be okay."

And because Tarr had never given her a reason to doubt him, she believed him.

* * *

The first Wednesday of the year arrived, and with it, so did Briar's watercolor class. She hurried through her morning

239

chores and only made it to half of the animals before she had to leave.

"It just goes until twelve-thirty," she said to Tucker. "And then I'll be back to finish."

"Yeah, no problem," he said from where he stood at the rails watching Jessa go through her warm-up. He called something to her about keeping the horse up off her left shoulder, and Briar turned to leave the arena.

It hadn't snowed for a couple of days, but that just meant the world existed in ice and snow and freezing temperatures, everything within sight flat and white and gray. Excitement bubbled inside Briar because she loved learning new things and being creative, and this watercolor class would provide both.

She drove the half hour to the community center and collected the bag of supplies she'd pre-purchased for today's class. She smiled at another woman walking in, and after they'd both checked in for the watercolor class at the front desk of the community center, the woman said, "My name is Teri. Have you done watercolors before?"

Briar shook her head. "I've painted other things, but not watercolors. I'm Briar."

"It's great to meet you." Teri smiled like she really meant it. "I did an oil painting class last year, but mostly I've been painting walls and cabinets in my house as we remodel." She gave a light laugh, and Briar smiled at her.

"I mostly do crafty types of art," she said, surprised that she was talking to this woman at all.

"What do you mean by that?" Teri asked.

They turned into the classroom, which had huge windows facing south, bringing in a plethora of natural light. A dozen stations had been set up with easels and canvases, and Briar stopped for a moment just to breathe it all in.

"I cut wood and stain it and make signs," she said. "I can show you some."

She and Teri picked out two stations in the middle row on the right side, and Briar set down her bag of supplies to swipe through her phone. She found the sign for the Goatel and showed Teri. "I work out on this farm in the Deerfield area," she said. "And the owner has over one hundred goats, and I made this Goatel sign."

"Oh, that's adorable," Teri said, peering at the phone.

"If you swipe, you can see a sign I made for my boyfriend," Briar said. "It says *Home Sweet Home.* He's a former rodeo rider, so I put on a horse, and he loves my dog, Wiggins."

"Oh, that's cute," she said as she swiped. "Do you cut these with a jigsaw?" She looked up, interest in her eyes. "My husband does custom cabinetry, and I've never thought about cutting out wood and doing stuff like that."

"It is a jigsaw," she said. "Stabilized with a table, so I guide the wood, not the saw." Briar swiped one more time. "This is one I made for one of my boss's clients. He's a current rodeo rider—a roper."

She could see the *Eat, Sleep, Rope, Repeat* sign in her mind that she'd made for Alex Monterro. He'd laughed and laughed when she'd given it to him, and he'd placed it above the small window in his trailer, where he could see it every day.

"The lasso was really hard on that one," she said. "I cut through it three times before I finally got it right." She took the phone back and smiled at Teri. "Do you have any of your oil paintings I could see?"

Teri dove into her phone too, because of course she had pictures of her art. Briar realized at first glance that this woman was far more talented than she was, and she gushed over the woman's fall landscapes—reds with such vibrant golds, tangerine, crimson, and even green, as leaves didn't change color all at the same time.

"These are incredible," Briar said.

"All right, everyone," the instructor called, and Teri quickly took her phone back, smiled at Briar, and the two of them settled onto their stools. The instructor stood up on a platform so that they could see her past their easels, and she wore a light-blue dress with an art apron over it.

Briar had not brought an apron, as it had not been on the list of supplies she'd been told to bring, and she glanced around to see if anyone else had.

"My name is Arantha Adams," the woman said. "I know it's a pretty weird first name—my mother was from Colombia—and I mostly go by Ari."

She smiled and extended her arms wide to both sides. "I've been painting since I was a child, and I attended art school at the Art Institute of Chicago." She grinned and scanned the students. "We're going to be here together for the next twelve weeks, learning and experimenting with watercolors, and I've brought you all a gift."

She stepped over to a table where she also had an easel. "Now don't all rush up at once, but you can come forward and get your art aprons. I sewed these myself, and I make one for all of my students, because you need somewhere to wipe your hands or your brush, and you don't want it to be on your clothes." She grinned out at all of them. "Though I suppose with watercolors, it would wash out easier than other types of mediums."

She held up one apron that had been done in a bright patchwork quilt of colors with black rickrack between the squares. "Come on; don't be shy. Come get your aprons."

Briar stood up and followed Teri past her easel to the aisle, suddenly anxious to get her art apron. This was the second apron that had meant so much to her in the past couple of weeks, and as Briar tied it around her waist, she could almost feel Tarr's hands doing it for her.

She felt like she'd climbed so many mountains in such a short time and turned several corners, and as she settled back at her station for the first lesson, that same feeling descended upon her.

I see you ran through her head, and it took her a moment to realize that it was a message from God. Warmth filled her from head to toe, because while she believed in God and even prayed to Him, she hadn't felt like He knew who she was or cared where she went or saw anything she did, but the words *I see you* rang through her mind again, as did *I always have. You are mine, and I will never abandon you.*

Briar's vision blurred behind tears, and she quickly blinked them away as Ari was already demonstrating the first lesson—blending colors to make skies—and she didn't want to miss a moment of this class.

She also didn't want to miss another moment of living her life, and she realized that the past few years had been exactly that: her trying to hide from who she'd been and trying *not* to live her life. She hadn't become the person she should be, the person God wanted her to be.

"And this is just the first step," Ari said, and Briar could apply that to almost every aspect of her life as she started mixing her paint and her water and swishing her brush across the canvas.

Some of the burdens she'd been carrying simply washed onto the paper. She didn't have to carry them anymore. The canvas could. She never had to carry them again, because Christ would.

As her class finished and Briar started packing up her things and looking at Teri's sky and gushing over how she'd gotten the blue and indigo to fade so perfectly together, she couldn't wait to get back to the farm and tell Tarr everything, from how she'd made a new friend, learned a new skill, and realized that she was a child of a God who had *not* forgotten her.

twenty-six

Tarr swung himself up into the saddle, a familiar position for him, and one that made his heartbeat settle into a new rhythm as it attempted to match the horse's. "That's a good girl." He leaned down and patted Daisy Chain's neck.

He'd been working with her for a few months now, and he'd been increasing her speed coming out of the turn around the barrels. Now he needed her to make those turns tighter.

Horses didn't like getting close to objects—certainly not when they had to be almost horizontal to go around them. She practically came to a stop as she turned, and then he expected her to explode back toward the other side of the pattern. But one thing Tarr loved most about horses was the same thing he loved about dogs: their loyalty and their ability to be trained.

He could teach and reward, teach and reward, teach and reward—and the horse would do it every single time. Not only that, but they loved him for it, and he loved them right back.

"All right, DC," he said. "I'm gonna pull you real tight in this time."

He urged her to move, and then trot, and then gallop. He took her around the full circumference of the arena before aiming her at the far barrel and spurring her into a barrel-racing run. "Let's go, let's go, let's go!"

He yipped and leaned low over her head the way his rider would. He weighed far more than a female barrel racer ever would, and that only meant that Daisy Chain would be able to handle whoever rode her.

"Tight, tight, tight," he yelled as he pulled hard on the left to get her to go closer to the barrel than she'd ever gone before. She hit it with her shoulder, and he cursed mentally but urged Daisy toward the next barrel, impressed with the way she picked up her gallop—the exact way she'd been taught.

He cut her in tight on the right this time too, and she refused to do it. Tarr straightened and slowed her, not bothering with the third barrel, which would be another turn to the right.

He needed her to get left and then right correctly before he moved on. "All right, sweetheart," he said. "Let's try again." He moved her into an easy canter and then a gallop, and then aimed her for the far barrel again.

She cut close to this one, and he managed to keep her from knocking into it. She still wasn't as tight as he wanted her to be, but he told himself he'd only been leading her around the barrels at a walk. She knew them, obviously, but he wanted her to be able to sense them and cut close, using her strong legs and hooves to get her where she needed to go in less time than ever before.

They approached the second barrel and Daisy Chain fell out of her gallop. "Hey, what's going on?" He straightened again, the reins in his hands tight, giving her no room. She loped around the barrel, clearly not wanting him to make her cut that close.

"All right, let's just do an easy one, then." He took her around the barrels and this time aimed for the one that was usually on the side. She cut around it just fine, moving at probably half the speed as before. He approached the barrel she wouldn't go around, and she did that one fine too, and the third one.

"So you're just being lazy today. Is that it?" He chuckled as he imagined Daisy Chain saying, *You worked me hard, cowboy. I'm allowed to have an off-day.*

And she was. He just didn't want it to be during a competition. Animals had to be mentally strong as well, and that required training too.

Tarr ran her through a few more exercises and then spurred her toward that far barrel one more time. "Come on, girl," he yelled. "You gotta get it once."

She once again cut close to that first barrel, far more hesitant to get close to the second. She did it, though, at her usual distance, and Tarr yipped as he ran her toward the third and final barrel. She cut right for this one, and she did that extremely well. She'd always been better at going right than left, which made that first turn even weirder.

He waved his arms left and right, though he didn't carry a whip with him during training, and urged Daisy all the way to the end of the arena at her fastest clip. His adrenaline pounded through his body as he eased up and the horse slowed. He kept her galloping and then moved her into a canter, simply going around the arena at an easy pace.

"That was incredible, girl."

He heard someone whistle, and he looked over to find Briar

sitting on the top row of their bleachers. She grinned and waved, and Tarr reached up and lifted his hat to her.

Daisy ran for a few more minutes, and then Tarr moved her into a walk. Her sides heaved, and he went around and around with her, checking the enormous clock at the end of the arena to make sure he had time to rake things out before Rosie arrived for her training. She'd been meeting with Tuck to go over things on paper and run through them in her mind before they showed up at the arena, and Tarr had been using that time to train his horses.

He hoped Daisy Chain would be ready for this summer's rodeo season, and he had another month or so before he'd need to put up videos and start trying to find a buyer for her.

He brought the horse to a stop in front of Briar. "How long you been sitting there?"

"Just for the last ride," she said. "She's looking good."

"She's not cutting tight enough on that second barrel." He stroked a hand down Daisy Chain's neck. "But we'll get 'er there."

"She's beautiful," Briar said.

Daisy was a gray with mostly white hair and a dark mane and tail. Tarr would clean her up good and blow out her hair and probably put ribbons in it before he had Tuck film for the listing. Once, he'd paid someone to come braid a horse's mane, and she'd sold in fifteen minutes. He knew it was more than aesthetics, but he also knew that cowgirls liked their horses to look as good as them, and showing that a horse had patience to have her hair braided went a long way.

Briar came down the few rows of bleachers and then climbed up a couple of rungs on the fence. "What are you doing later?"

He grinned at her. "The same thing I do every day, sweetheart."

"Yeah, but you work with different horses," she said. "And my paperwork is light today. I was thinking I'd go home and make chicken pot pie soup, and you could go grab us some bread bowls."

"Oh, I see," he said. "You want to use me for my shopping ability."

She grinned at him. "That's right, cowboy. I wouldn't be opposed to some of that broccoli salad that you somehow manage to find in the deli."

"It's always there," he said with a chuckle.

"I've never been able to find it. That's all I'm saying."

Tarr fell a little bit more in love with Briar every single day, though he'd been trying to hold himself back. She called him on the way home from every one of her watercolor classes—three weeks running now—and he loved listening to her talk about all she'd learned and then seeing the product in her studio later that day.

"Did you cancel your doctor's appointment?" he asked. "I thought that was today."

"It's next week," Briar said, some of her shininess fading. "And I'm going to be bringing home dinner that night, so will you have a roaring fire going in your RV?"

"You want to eat at my place?" he asked.

She nodded. "Yeah. You're going to have Wiggy already, and I'll bring dinner, and we can put a movie on your big screen." She grinned at him, and Tarr simply shook his head.

"I'm so sick of you making fun of me about that TV," he said. "It works, and it *is* big for the wall it's on."

Briar tipped her head back and laughed, revealing that slender throat that, oh, Tarr loved to kiss.

"All right, well, I should be home anytime after two-thirty," she said. "Soup will be ready by four."

"Four o'clock," Tarr said, glad to have a mini-date on the horizon, though he saw Briar every single day. They usually spent evenings together in her cabin, which was far bigger and more functional than his RV.

Sometimes he cooked and sometimes she did, or sometimes they made a meal together. Then they'd play cards, or she'd show him her paintings and she'd paint while he ran through social media and answered emails. Sometimes she put on a movie while he made notes about his horses, or he'd watch one of his documentaries while she transcribed her veterinary notes.

He'd taken her on formal dates to restaurants and movie theaters, but it was cold, and neither one of them minded staying home and simply spending time with one another.

Briar started to get down from the fence, and Tarr's heart-beat skipped and bounced at him. "Hey, real quick," he said.

She turned back to him, her expression open and unassuming.

"I was thinking, since you're so caught up," he said. "Maybe you'd want to come to church with me this weekend."

She'd have to get pretty far behind in only one day to not be able to go with him, and yet she hesitated. Tarr could go to church by himself, and he did. He also knew a relationship would be easier if their religious beliefs were the same, and she could encourage him when he didn't want to attend church, and he would do the same for her. Having to be the strong one all the time wore on him, and while Briar supported him in lots of other ways, he wanted his faith to be included on that list.

"All right," she said, her voice pitching up into a slightly higher octave. "I think I can probably go."

"You've got lots of real pretty dresses," he said, as if that would help her decide.

She nodded and pressed her lips together. "I've heard you and Tuck talk about the pastor, so maybe it'll actually be good."

"It varies," Tarr admitted. "But most of the time it's great, and it's only an hour, and I'll get to hold your hand." He grinned at her.

Briar smiled back. "All right. See you later." With that, she swiped her clipboard up from the bottom bench in the bleachers, tossed a wave over her shoulder, and continued toward the stables.

Tarr went that way too, entering through a different gate and taking his time as he went through Daisy Chain's cool down and aftercare. He finally put her in her stable with a bag of oats and fresh straw, and then he went to stand at Tuck's side and watch Rosie ride. It wasn't surprising to him at all that she'd won Female Rookie of the Year and been the barrel-racing champion. She was incredible in the saddle, and her horses trusted her explicitly. She never made a mistake, and as she finished her ride, Tarr said, "How do you even train her?"

Tucker sighed. "I have to look stuff up on the internet, man." Then he ducked through the fence and started walking toward her, calling, "That was good, but your left elbow is coming up too much when you make that second turn."

Tarr chuckled to himself. "Left elbow." No barrel racer needed to be told about their *left elbow*. But Rosie was paying Tuck good money to be here to train and to become the best, and Tucker did know how to bring that out in a rider.

Tarr left the arena, automatically falling into a prayer. First, that everyone at the farm would be kept safe, animal and human alike, and second, that he and Briar would have an amazing afternoon and evening together.

"Bless her to like me," he whispered as he got behind the wheel. It was something he'd asked God for several times in the past, but as Tarr uttered the words, something dark entered his mind.

This was not the thing he should be asking for.

He couldn't make Briar like him any more than God could, and he didn't want her to be coerced anyway. He frowned to himself as he adjusted the heater, pressed the button to get his seat warming up, and backed away from the arena.

"I just feel like she's such a match for me," he said, starting to puzzle through his feelings by speaking out loud. "And why would I feel like that if she's not meant to feel the same?"

God, of course, did not answer him, but Tarr continued to talk, telling the Lord, "I do want to get married and have a family, whatever that looks like. And not only because my momma wants me to, Lord, but because it feels like what *I* want. And you know, I want it with her."

He looked left and right when he reached the stop sign and then pulled out onto the highway, heading for the grocery store to get the bread bowls and broccoli salad that Briar liked. "She's a good woman," he said next. "And that's all I need: someone good who can keep me in line and remind me that I want to be good too. She gives me someone to work for, because I want to be the man she deserves. That's not bad, is it?"

He didn't want to change *everything* about himself, though part of him thought he might for Briar. "No," he said out loud. "I want to be who You want me to be. And hopefully that's the man that Briar needs, too."

He finally felt like he'd reached a resolution in his thoughts, and he quieted. No matter what, he knew he shouldn't be praying for Briar to like him, but perhaps for his own heart and mind to be opened, so he could see her clearly, and come to know for himself if he really could spend the rest of his life with her.

Tarr had never been very good at fitting into a mold, and Briar had never asked him to. He went up and down the aisles at the grocery store, getting more of the steel-cut oats she liked for breakfast, in addition to the bread bowls, the broccoli salad, and another bag of the gourmet Caesar that she liked.

She'd told him that she loved winter for lots of reasons, one of which was that it was soup season, and she loved nothing more than a soup-and-salad-dinner on a blistering winter night. He grabbed another bag of rolls from the bakery before getting himself a new container of protein powder, some frozen mixed berries to go with it, and a pound of sun-dried tomato turkey to make his sandwiches for lunch.

With his grocery shopping done, he returned to the farm, and as he pulled up to Briar's cheery cabin—under a sky that was already darkening at four-thirty p.m.—Tarr realized that he should be praying for things he could control and change, and that wasn't anything about Briar.

It was only about himself.

So, as he killed the engine and looked at the bright yellow squares of Briar's windows, he murmured, "Bless me to know how to change and what not to change to be a man that she could love and marry."

He wasn't sure if he was that man right now or not, and he wasn't sure if Briar had reached the point inside herself that she believed in love and marriage again. She'd told him she was trying, and that he had caused her to start thinking and feeling things that she hadn't felt or believed for years. Just the fact that she had a doctor's appointment next week told him that, and he added one more prayer to his hour-long conversation with the Lord:

"If it be Thy will, bless her with good news at her appointment...when she finally gets the courage to go to it."

twenty-seven

Briar tugged the dark green dress down over her thighs so it would reach her knees, immediately deciding that she didn't want to wear this dress to church today. She had already changed twice, and everything felt so *hard*. Growling under her breath, she reached for the hem and practically ripped the dress over her head.

She had plenty of choices, as Briar loved a good sundress and often wore them all summer long. She eyed the two still lying on her bed—one a soft lavender she felt washed her out, though she spent plenty of time in the sun and had a tan to match. The remaining dress bore a dark brown color with cream-colored appliqués all over it, and Briar felt like she aged herself ten years whenever she wore it.

Still, she had a beautiful pair of heels she could wear with it, and since it was the middle of January and not Easter or summer, the rich, earthy color felt more appropriate. She bypassed the purple dress and reached for the brown one.

It flowed over her shoulders and skin easily, and Briar

sighed into it. Yes, this was what she wanted to wear. She could hide inside brown, and perhaps Tarr's towering presence and giant personality would further dwarf her and keep attention on him instead of her.

"Who are you kidding?" she asked as she moved over to the mirror and made sure the crisscrossing folds of fabric in the front lay correctly over her chest. "Everyone's going to be staring at *you*, because you'll be holding hands with *him*."

Briar sat with the thoughts as she moved into the bathroom and brushed her teeth and braided her hair back on the sides. That way, some could still hang over her shoulders, but she wouldn't constantly be pushing it out of her face. She'd already fed Wiggins, as well as all the goats, and as far as she knew, Tucker and Bobbie Jo would attend Sabbath day services today as well.

Briar moved into the kitchen and pulled open the fridge, though she'd eaten and her stomach vibrated with nervous energy that told her not to do so again.

Then Wiggins burst into a round of barking, which sent Briar spinning and her pulse crashing through her veins. "Wiggins, stop it," she hissed at the dog at the same time the front door opened.

"It's just me, honey," Tarr said, and his eyes first landed on hers before he dropped into a crouch to greet her dog. "What are you always barking about, you rascal?" He laughed as he scrubbed Wiggins's jaws and ears. "You gotta learn to be quiet when someone comes to the door."

He straightened and looked at Briar again. "Are you ready?"

He wore his black leather jacket, unzipped over a white shirt and tie, which he'd tucked neatly into a pair of black slacks and then positioned that championship belt buckle just-so.

"That's a pretty dress," Tarr said. "The darker color makes your eyes seem a little bluer."

"Thanks," Briar said, though she wasn't sure if that was a compliment or not. The part about the dress was at least. She moved to the end of the couch and picked up her coat. "I hate to say it, but it feels colder out there."

"The sky is as clear as glass," Tarr said, moving to help her with her coat. It was black and puffy, and Briar suddenly worried about it clashing with her dress. Did people wear brown and black together? She honestly didn't know, and she looked down to her brown leather heels, suddenly feeling very drab from head to toe. Then Tarr took her hand, which usually filled her world with color, and led her toward the still-open door.

"We'll be back in a little bit, Wiggy," he said to the dog, and then they left.

He helped her into the cab of his truck, as he'd done many times before, and Briar sat rigidly until he joined her and pulled his seatbelt across his body. Only then did she unfreeze and do the same. She glanced over to him at the same time he looked at her.

"If it's too much, we don't have to go," he said, his voice soft and low, the way she imagined he spoke to his horses when they were spooked.

"No, I want to go," she said.

"All right." Tarr put the truck in reverse and backed out onto the street. "How long has it been since you went?"

Briar swallowed. Her memory was quite good, but she couldn't recall an exact date. "A long time," she said. "More than a year—two years. I haven't gone to church since I came to Colorado."

The confession almost freed her as it left her mouth. "My faith was something I lost with everything else."

Tarr reached over and took her hand, then lifted it gently to his lips. "But you said you believe and you pray."

"Yeah, I do," Briar said. "But it's only been in the last couple of weeks that I've started to think and believe that God didn't abandon me the way everyone else did." She watched the snowy landscape go by out her window, her hand tightening around Tarr's.

"I fear it's another thing you're going to have to be patient with me about."

"I'm going to be winning awards and certificates and gold stars for patience." He chuckled and then dropped her hand to put both of his on the wheel as the truck slid around a particularly icy corner. "I keep forgetting to tell Ashton about that," he said, glancing in his rearview mirror. "It's not the main way on and off the farm, so I forget."

He hadn't deposited them in the snowbank on the side of the road, and Briar relaxed further as the heater in her seat calmed her.

Tarr left her to her thoughts on the quick fifteen-minute jog to church. As she dropped to the ground, he linked his arm through hers. "You just stick right with me, sweetheart. I promise nothing bad is going to happen here."

Once again, Briar believed him, and she stepped with as much feigned confidence as she could. The bright white brick of the church house called to her; the steeple rose into the sky, practically puncturing it. As they stepped inside, heat warmed the air in her lungs, and she was able to relax her shoulders.

Tarr led her through a foyer and a set of double-wide doors that had been thrown open. Gentle piano music came from inside, and the moment she entered, she pulled in a breath and held it.

In front of her, the entire Garden of Eden bloomed to life in gorgeous, delicately colored panes of glass. Hundreds of them sat arranged to make trees, shrubs, flowers, rocks, and waterfalls. A deer caught her eye on the left side, and bright light came through the very center top window, which was white and seemed to halo directly above Adam and Eve, who stood peering up at the light from behind a tree.

"Wow," Briar said, all of her artistic genes admiring the scene before her. "That's incredible." She turned to Tarr. "Can you imagine making that?"

"I sure can't," he said. "But I love walking into the sight of it every week." He took a step, and Briar went with him.

The chapel had three sections with longer benches in the middle and shorter ones on each side. He led her down only a few rows and then gestured to the pew on the left. She entered it first and left him plenty of room to sit beside her on the end. He sat right next to her easily, lifting his arm around her shoulders and cradling her against his chest.

Briar blinked, and in that moment, other people came into focus, though none of them seemed to turn around and whisper about her being there with Tarr—or her being there at all. That helped her calm even more, and Briar closed her eyes and used all of her other senses to experience being back in church for the first time in five years.

Only a minute later, the music stopped and her eyes flew open at the same time the pastor said, "I am delighted to welcome you to your Sabbath day service today. My name is Pastor Johnson, and I'm thrilled to see so many people here, even though it's not Christmas or Easter."

A few people twittered, but Briar couldn't look away from the charismatic man standing at the pulpit. He too wore a white shirt and tie with a jacket over it, but his was a regular suit coat and not cowboy leather. He also didn't wear a cowboy hat, though with one quick sweep of her eyes, Briar realized that several other men did.

"We're going to be blessed to hear a couple of hymns from our choir," he said. "Apparently they had a few more to sing for our Christmas program, but it had to be trimmed due to time, and then one of our own, Jeremy South, will give us our invocation."

Briar stayed seated, though others stood to sing along with the choir. Tarr stayed steady and silent at her side. As Briar continued to soak up everything happening around her, she felt akin to a sponge—just taking everything in and letting its goodness wash through her. By the time the prayer had been said and the pastor stood in front of the mic again, Briar had already decided to come back to church next week.

There was a difference between attending and not attending, as her belief and faith could be cultivated here in a way she couldn't do alone. There were so many things that Briar couldn't do alone, including put the leaf in her table for holiday meals, sometimes opening that sticky jar of pimento—and apparently feeding off the faith and testimony of others. Probably because she'd isolated herself in every way possible, and the church community Tarr had spoken of couldn't be achieved if she was the only one in attendance.

"Today, I want to talk about the ninety and nine," Pastor Johnson said. "This may be a familiar parable to many of you, but there's a reason why we study the scriptures over and over throughout our lives. We don't get the same thing from them each time we read them, because we bring ourselves to the equation. Every time we turn a page, the experiences you have today shape what your thoughts and feelings are for tomorrow. And even if you read the Bible last year or last month."

He grinned with all the wattage of the sun. "You are not the same person today as you were last year or last month. Your unique and new perspective comes with you each time you open the Bible to read a passage from God. So while the story of the lost sheep may be familiar, perhaps you'll indulge me as who you are today, in this moment, and what you can take from this parable into your life moving forward."

Briar really liked that, because it reminded her that people changed, and it was actually okay—no, *necessary*—to change.

She did know the story of the lost sheep decently well, but Pastor Johnson had a captivating, deep voice that entertained, and she found herself being swept along as she listened to the story of the Good Shepherd tending his one hundred sheep and realizing that one had wandered away and had been lost.

"Perhaps you see yourself in one of the ninety-nine sheep who stayed," the pastor said. "I want to make it clear that the Lord did not abandon them in favor of another. He knew they were safe, and His demonstration of leaving them to go find the one that had wandered only further solidified to those who had not that they too would be rescued if they ever found themselves walking in a dark path. So for those of you who don't feel like the one, be reassured that God knows and sees and understands you as well—and that if you do ever find yourself lost or forgotten, remember that the Good Shepherd will come."

Tears pricked Briar's eyes, because while she didn't feel like one of the ninety-nine who hadn't strayed, she found so much comfort in the pastor's words. *Be reassured that the Good Shepherd will come.*

Briar needed to do that with more faith and more obedience, and as the pastor finished his powerful testimony about God's love for all of his children and the choir got up to sing, Briar once again felt like she herself was being personally tended to from on high.

She felt certain God had led her to this farm, knowing that Tucker Hammond would eventually buy it, and Tarr Olson would come with him. God knew that Tarr would be the only person who could tell Briar she had ten minutes to change her clothes or he was hauling her to Thanksgiving dinner in her pajamas. And God had known she would go.

God had also given her space and time to get to this place in her life where she was ready to feel His spirit and hear His voice again, and she marveled at how masterfully He could intertwine multiple lives in order to provide blessings for each of His children.

"All right, honey," Tarr said, and Briar blinked over to him. "It's over. You made it through."

She turned fully into him and wrapped him in a tight hug. "Thank you for inviting me," she said, glad her emotions had not gotten the better of her and made her voice wobble. "This was incredible."

He hugged her back just as tightly, everything gentle and good about him coming out in that hug. "I'm glad you came," he said. "Did you like it?"

"Yes. It was so good." Briar pulled back and studied his face. "You say he's not like this every week?"

"Oh, he gives a good sermon," Tarr said. "Sometimes it's a little boring, or maybe my mind just wanders. I don't know. Today was great, though. It really was."

Briar got to her feet and held Tarr's hand as they moved out into the foyer to leave. "I don't want to talk to him," she said when she saw the pastor there with a wife in an emerald-green dress at his side.

"No?" Tarr asked. "Why not?"

"I don't know," Briar said. "Do we have to talk to him?"

"No, not at all." He shuttled her along the back of the line of people waiting to speak with the pastor.

The winter air outside blasted her but also provided a sense of escape for Briar. Back in Tarr's truck, he turned toward her. "All right, do you want to get some lunch?"

"Yes," she said. "Will you please take me to that Brazilian steakhouse you've been bragging about?"

Tarr chuckled and flipped the truck into drive. "Your wish is my command, honey."

Briar liked the sound of that, though she knew Tarr could hold his own with her as well—and she liked that too. As she snuck a glance over to him, Briar realized there was very little about Tarr that she disliked, and she let her eyes drift closed as she thought through the sermon once more.

The Good Shepherd is coming. What a wonderful promise— and one that Briar clung to with everything inside her.

twenty-eight

Deacon had been waiting for ten minutes past the pickup time for his orange chicken and beef lo mein. He glanced down the row of parking stalls, trying to remember if any of them had left and new people had parked while he'd been sitting there. He hadn't exactly been paying attention, as he'd escaped the seventy-five-degree heat of his parents' house in favor of picking up dinner that night.

His daddy had definitely gotten old, and he liked the house hot. Uncle Wes and Aunt Bree had stayed through Valentine's Day, and Deacon had finally followed them up here to Coral Canyon a few days ago.

No one should live in Wyoming in February, Deacon knew that, and he reached to start his truck again, as it had gone off while he'd been waiting.

He wondered if his parents should come back to Ivory Peaks too. They'd only just retired here a couple of years ago, but Tucker was married now, with Jane having her family in Ivory Peaks too.

"They don't need to worry about you," he said with a scoff, though he knew his momma fretted over him continually. If they moved back to Ivory Peaks, she'd be able to do it much closer.

As the heater started to blow, Deacon picked up his phone and navigated to the group chat that only had his siblings on it.

You guys should see Momma and Daddy. They've gotten old. Well, Daddy at least.

Have they? Tucker asked. *But they're all right, right?*

Yeah, they're fine, Deacon said.

I do need to get up there and see them, Hunt said.

We just saw them at Christmas, Jane said. *They were wonderful.*

I just think, Deacon said, letting his fingers fly. He was the youngest of the Hammonds, but he possessed a pretty level head. It was the lawyer part of his father he'd inherited.

We all live in Ivory Peaks, and a lot of us are still young, having families. It's like Uncle Wes and Aunt Bree. Why are they living up here alone?

He sent the text, wondering what his brothers and sister would think. They wouldn't hold back, Deacon knew that.

I'd love to have them here again, Jane said. *Do you think they'd come?*

Daddy's brothers are up there, Hunter said. *That's why they went,.*

Yeah, but now Uncle Wes is moving back here, Deacon said.

We should talk to them about it, Tuck said. *I wonder what the real estate market is like in Coral Canyon.*

Deacon blew out his breath, knowing the answer to that. Not good. It took a long time for houses to sell in Wyoming right now, and in February?

No one in their right mind would move here in the winter. No, they'd have to be wooed by the summer months, after someone had prayed for months for fifteen minutes without any wind.

His stomach growled, reminding him that he still didn't have his food. He left the siblings chat for now and tapped on his order confirmation for The Darling Dragon. A number sat there, and Deacon tapped on that next. The line simply rang and rang and rang, and irritation drove through him all over again. What was the point of an online order and curbside pickup if none of it worked?

His stomach growled, and that propelled Deacon out of the truck and toward the Chinese restaurant. The din of laughter and chatter and music all combined into one, creating a froth of noise that drove Deacon insane the moment he walked inside. At the same time, it fed his soul—a kind of energy Deacon hadn't experienced for a while, since he'd taken a break from dating. He didn't visit too many restaurants, and certainly not on a weekend night.

The Darling Dragon had a pickup counter, and Deacon joined the line for it. Someone else joined him almost immediately, and he listened to the woman behind him talk to someone on the phone.

"I just said I don't know," she said, her voice light and airy and yet also tinged with frustration. "If you can't talk right now, it's fine. I'll get dinner and see you later. No, I don't know why they don't have it. I've been waiting outside in the stall for fifteen minutes. I just came in to check on it."

Another pause came on her side of the conversation, but Deacon felt a sense of validation move through him, because she'd clearly ordered for pickup and hadn't gotten it as well.

"I clearly have a phone that works, Jonathan," she said next, her voice turning snowy and crisp. "And I know how to make a phone call, thank you very much. Yes, I called.

No one answered. I'm inside, in the line right now to find out. Okay, I'm just gonna hang up. No, I'm hanging up because you didn't even listen to the first half of this conversation, and now you're trying to mansplain to me what I should do to get the food. I know what to do. I'll see you later."

She sighed mightily and muttered something Deacon couldn't catch. He wanted to commiserate with her about The Darling Dragon's inability to bring out a curbside order, but decided against it. On the best of days, he didn't want perfect strangers talking to him. And with his order twenty minutes late now, he figured it best to wait to talk to female strangers until he wasn't hangry.

The line inched forward, and Deacon peered over the shoulder of the man in front of him as a woman yelled, "If you're new to the line, we're having a problem with our curbside orders, and we really apologize. We need all curbside people over on the left. We probably have your order ready right now."

Deacon shuffled to the left along with only one other person in front of him.

"We didn't get any names printed on the orders," the woman called. "So please listen and know what you ordered."

She started firing off an order as she lifted a brown paper bag up to her eye level. Deacon fumbled for his phone because he wasn't exactly sure what his momma and daddy had put into the app. He caught the word *shrimp*, though, and knew immediately that would not be his.

No one should be eating seafood in Wyoming in February, he thought, adding it to his list of strikes against the state.

His momma had a mild shellfish allergy, while Daddy simply didn't like the stuff, so thankfully, Deacon didn't have to explain the rules to them. He found his order and pulled it up as another man went to get his food.

"Orange chicken," the woman called. "Beef lo mein."

Also Deacon's.

"Vegetable tempura."

His momma's.

"Hot honey chicken with fried rice."

Deacon stepped forward, because the woman had just named everything on his order. "That's mine," he said as he approached the counter.

"No," a woman said, coming to his left side and planting herself against the counter as well. "It's mine."

Deacon looked at her, recognizing the voice as the woman who had been on the phone behind him in line. She had long blonde hair that cascaded in waves over her shoulders and romantic eyes that sat somewhere between blue and green.

Deacon turned his phone toward her, trying to ignore the pounding of his heart and the way his voice caught in his throat as he said, "I'm pretty sure it's mine."

She didn't even look at his device. She turned hers toward the woman holding the brown bag. "It's mine, Howdy. Sally."

Sally looked at her phone and handed her the bag.

"Wait a second," Deacon said, and he showed his phone to the woman at the counter. "I've got the same order."

"What's the timestamp?" Sally asked.

Deacon looked down at his phone again, struggling to find where that was.

"Mine is six-twelve," the woman beside him said.

"I know we did our order before that," Deacon said.

"Just a minute," Sally said, and she moved to get another order from the counter behind her. The woman with Deacon's food stood there, her grip tight on the paper bag.

"Can you believe we got the same order?" he asked, which was probably the worst pickup line in the history of mankind.

She blinked at him, a small smile finally touching her lips. "Are you going to eat all this by yourself, cowboy?"

"No," he said. "Are you?"

She shook her head, her smile growing. "No, this is for me and my boyfriend and my older brother."

Everything inside Deacon deflated on the word *boyfriend*.

"I've got another order right here for that," Sally said. "Timestamp, six-nineteen."

"That's mine," the woman said.

"If they're the same, it doesn't matter." Deacon reached for the bag still in Sally's hand and took it from her.

"Sorry about the curbside fiasco," she said.

"You're fine." Deacon nodded at her and then turned away from the pickup counter. He made his way through the busy restaurant and back outside, where it hurt his lungs to breathe in for more than two seconds.

"You didn't say who your food was for."

He turned toward the woman, catching a whiff of her perfume now that it wasn't covered by sesame oil. She smelled like peach blossoms and sunshine and something citrusy that Deacon really needed in his life.

"It's just my momma and daddy," he said.

"Oh, so you still live at home?" she asked, something guarded coming into her expression under the harsh street-lights outside.

"No," he said. "I'm visiting them. I don't even live here."

She blinked, clearly not expecting that answer. "Oh."

He gave her a dry look and turned away. "Enjoy dinner with your boyfriend and your brother." As he walked off, he could practically feel the stunned energy coming off the woman. Part of him cared, but a louder, grumpier part totally didn't. He'd told her the truth. He didn't live in Coral Canyon, and why should he get this woman's number? He only came up here a couple of times a year, and she had a boyfriend already.

Deacon had never had a problem getting a date, but he certainly didn't think he could woo a woman away from her current boyfriend to be with him. "With your quick wit," he muttered to himself as he got back in the truck and put the Chinese food on the passenger seat. Deacon could barely carry on a conversation over a meal, so a long-distance relationship that would require texting and talking on the phone absolutely was not for him.

She seemed like a local, and like she'd been one for a while, especially if she knew the name of the manager at The Darling Dragon.

He reminded himself that he wasn't really a local of Coral Canyon. Sure, he'd spent summers here for a couple of decades, but he'd mostly palled around with his cousins and siblings and didn't concern himself with making friends. He had those back in Ivory Peaks, where he lived during the school year.

Deacon returned to his parents' single-level house they'd moved into only a couple of years ago. He'd been in Coral Canyon for about a week now, and he had needed a break from the farm. He loved his parents, and they treated him like gold. If Deacon ever needed anything, he could ask Momma or Daddy, and they'd patiently and lovingly teach him and lend him their advice.

He knew plenty of people didn't enjoy the blessings he had in his life, from an amazing family, to acres and acres of land, to a couple of billion dollars in the bank. And while Deacon got down on his knees every night and thanked the Lord for those things, he could also recognize the gaping hole in his life.

He rolled his neck, stretching out some of the tension there as he fought against the prompting running through his mind. "I don't want to date again," he muttered to God.

His parents had a security system and surely knew he sat in the driveway, in his truck, their food getting colder by the moment. At the same time, they'd all waited twenty extra minutes for it.

He figured he had time to reinstall a dating app where he'd set up his profile once and never come back to it. "This is what I've reduced myself to," he muttered. "A dating app."

It downloaded, and he tapped it open. Of course, the app wanted his login information, and of course, Deacon did not remember it.

Growling yet again, he flipped off the ignition in the truck, grabbed the food, and headed inside. He could look at the app later that night, after he had been fed and had more time when his parents wouldn't be tracking him.

"It would be great if I didn't have to use a dating app at all," he said, and then he went inside to eat his Friday-night dinner with his parents, feeling more pathetic than ever.

twenty-nine

Chapelle McRae woke up with the same bad taste in her mouth she'd had since Friday night.

"Something has to change," she whispered to herself, but she wasn't sure what that should be.

She worked for the city of Coral Canyon as a soil engineer in their landscaping and agricultural department, and while it had been a good enough job out of college, she now found the Wyoming weather almost unbearable. She'd only been in town for about four years, and her gypsy soul itched for a change. Not only that, but she knew she needed to—

"No, what you *need* to do," she told herself as she swung her legs over the side of her bed. "Is get rid of Bryson."

She barely liked her boyfriend anymore, and thankfully he'd gone back to Jackson Hole last night. Chapelle wouldn't have to deal with him lounging around her apartment and bothering her roommates while she went to church. And if Chapelle needed anything right now, it was divine assistance with where she should be and who she should be with.

She showered and, as she soaped and shaved, admitted to herself that she'd only started dating Bryson because he was her older brother's best friend. "Such a cliché," she said into the shower spray.

Because she'd gotten up early, she had plenty of time to blow-dry her hair until it was long and shiny and straight.

She lived with two other women, and they all had a private bedroom and bath in a farmhouse that sat in a suburb here in the small town of Coral Canyon. It had grown a lot in recent years, but it still had the feel she loved—where neighbors knew one another's names and would notice if they hadn't seen someone for a few days.

Chapelle wasn't much for cooking, so she ate out a lot, and she had her favorites where she knew the waitresses and managers. Her mind automatically flowed to the dark-haired, dark-mannered cowboy she'd encountered on Friday at The Darling Dragon. She hadn't gotten his name, and he hadn't offered it. He'd said he was visiting his parents, and he'd dismissed her with all the coldness of a Wyoming winter before walking away.

The last thing Chapelle needed was an ill-tempered cowboy. The man she currently dated—a lawyer at a firm in Jackson Hole—couldn't be further from that, and Chapelle didn't like him either.

"Maybe you need new everything," she said to her reflection as she finished buttoning her denim skirt and pulled her sweater vest down over the waistband.

She found her roommate Laurel in the dining room sharing breakfast with her boyfriend.

"I'm going to church," she said.

Laurel jumped up. "Oh, Chapelle, could you stop by the animal clinic on the way back and pick up Rockford?"

"You didn't get him last night?" Chapelle froze, her arm reaching for her purse. "Laurel, that's going to be, like, a three-hundred-dollar charge."

"We were just so late coming back from the concert," Laurel said. "They were closed already."

"I would have gone to get him," Chapelle said.

"But you know Bailey McAllister, right?" Laurel asked. "Won't you see her at church?"

"I don't know," Chapelle said, disliking this level of responsibility her roommate was laying on her. "She might be there, but it's not like I keep track of her."

"Well, if she is, can you grab her and both of you can swing by there and get Rockford? He's there alone. She said there would be someone there, but not all the time."

"Yeah. You probably caused her a problem, Laurel."

A frown finally appeared on Laurel's face. "Can you talk to her or not?"

"Will you text her first?"

"Yeah, I'll text her." Laurel turned and huffed and then stomped back to the table, as if Chapelle was the one doing something wrong.

Chapelle grabbed her purse, glared at her roommate's back, and pulled open the hall closet to get out a coat. She had to wade through no fewer than eight of Victoria's coats to find one of hers, and she had no idea why someone needed so much outerwear. Of course, Victoria had grown up in El Paso—right on the southern border of the United States—and she'd never seen snow until she came to Wyoming. She worked in the luxury lodge business here in town, of which several more had been going in recently.

Chapelle stepped outside and made the quick drive to the little church where she'd been attending since she moved to

Coral Canyon. They often had a lot of visitors, as it sat at the mouth of the canyon where one of the luxury lodges welcomed guests, as well as a gated community that the wealthy owned but didn't live in. They rented those houses.

Chapelle had quickly realized that half the people in Coral Canyon in the summer were tourists. In February, though, she wouldn't have to deal with that, and she hurried inside the little chapel, catching sight of an aisle spot in the middle section, about halfway down.

She slid into the seat there, realizing a beat too late that someone's phone and Bible already sat on the pew. She glanced around and didn't see anyone, and gently pushed the book and device further in. There was still plenty of room for someone to sit there.

A cowboy and his wife sat a little bit further down. They both looked at her and blinked, and Chapelle's face filled with heat.

"Do you make it a habit of stealing people's seats?" A man's voice tickled her eardrums and his breath washed across the back of her earlobe.

Chapelle startled and turned, coming face-to-face with the gorgeous cowboy from Friday night.

"You weren't here," she said, taking in the length of the man's eyelashes.

"I left my book and my phone," he said, standing at the end of the bench. "So I could talk to my daddy's neighbor for five seconds."

He glared at her, and Chapelle's first instinct was to glare right back. "There's plenty of room," she said. "Are those your parents down there?"

"Yes." His mouth barely moved as he said the word.

Chapelle did what any reasonable person would do. She

turned her knees to the side to give him room to step past her. When he didn't immediately do so, she looked up at him and said, "Well, go on."

He muttered something that sounded dangerously close to, "I wanted to sit on the end," and did everything he could not to touch her as he brushed by, almost as if she was diseased and he would catch it if he got too close.

In the tiny space between the bench and the back of the pew in front of them, he leaned down to pick up his Bible and his phone. He glared at her as he sat down in their place. "Is your brother coming?" he asked. "Your boyfriend?"

Chapelle's throat tightened, but she shook her head. "No. They don't live here."

"You're dating someone who doesn't live here?" His eyebrows went up in pure cowboy judgment.

Chapelle gave his grouchy attitude right back to him. "I don't see how this is any of your business."

"You took my dinner *and* my seat," he said. "Seems like everything you do is becoming my business."

"Hey, Deke," a man said, and Chapelle's eyes flew to him.

Deke got to his feet and looked uncertain, though it was clear he wanted to shake the man's hand, and he wasn't sitting or standing on the end of the aisle.

"Hey, Luke," he said.

Luke moved to the bench in front of them, and he and Deke shared an awkward embrace over the back of the pew. "Did you get my message?"

"Yeah, I sure did," Luke said, glancing at Chapelle. "You can come over any time. Should be fine."

Of course Chapelle knew who Luke Young was. The man was a legend from a legendary country music band. And while Chapelle had grown up in Idaho and not Wyoming, she'd come here for a reason. She adored small towns and a slower way of life. She'd become a dirt scientist, for crying out loud—listening to country music was practically part of her job description.

"I'm thinking maybe tomorrow," Deke said. "I've got a massage with your wife, and maybe we can meet after."

"Sure. What time's that?" Luke pulled out his phone.

"Ten-thirty."

"Let's do lunch, then," Luke said, and they shook hands. Luke smiled as he left to go sit with his family while Deke sat back down and threw Chapelle a look out of the corner of his eye.

"Wish I hadn't told you I have a massage tomorrow at ten-thirty. You're probably going to try and steal that too."

Chapelle's mouth fell open, and then the choir began to sing, so she couldn't even respond. She'd seen how quickly Deke changed from broody cowboy to "hey, it's great to see you, Luke" and back again, and part of her really wanted him to turn his charms on her.

That would be a change, she thought as she got to her feet and started to clap along with the choir. Deke did not—which seemed to track for him—and Chapelle couldn't help the wicked thoughts that ran through her mind.

I wonder how hard it would be to find out Luke Young's wife's name and what massage studio she works at, and call and insist on a ten-thirty appointment.

Chapelle wouldn't really do it, of course, but it was fun to fantasize about. And with that, Chapelle knew for certain that she needed change in her life, as she was now resorting to torturing complete strangers for no reason whatsoever.

As the song ended and she sat back down, she closed her eyes and prayed, *Guide my feet, Lord, and I will walk in thy way. Oh —and it would be really great if the path led somewhere warm.*

<h1 style="text-align:center">thirty</h1>

arr sat in the corner of his dinette station in the RV. The wood stove filled the small space with plenty of heat, and Tarr had been praying that they'd now made it through the coldest weather they'd have until next winter.

No matter what, his house should be done by then, and Tarr wanted to go by the build site on his way to Briar's that afternoon. His stomach twisted, because after a couple of appointment postponements and then one cancellation by the doctor, she was *finally* going to see the OB-GYN about her suspected fertility issues.

Tarr had once again been trying not to pray for things he couldn't control and ask for blessings that felt outlandish, focusing instead on something he could change within himself.

Not that he thought praying for such things was bad. Just that, for him, in this moment of time in his life, he wanted to focus inward on his own habits, personality, and behavior. He couldn't make Briar's health problems—which she'd suffered from a fall and injuries five years ago—better today simply by praying.

Or maybe he could. After all, Tarr did believe in miracles, and Jesus had raised people from the dead, restored their sight, and cured lifelong ailments.

Briar had admitted she still wasn't sure if she wanted to have kids at all, and Tarr had been thinking on the issue since she'd told him on New Year's Eve. He did want kids, but was it a deal-breaker? If his wife didn't or couldn't, would they adopt or foster? Or would Briar take the answer as she wasn't meant to be a mother?

He blinked at the notebook in front of him, trying to clear the worry from his mind. She was at her appointment right now, and he couldn't change what the doctor was going to say any more than he could make time go backward prevent her fall and injuries. He focused on the list in front of him, which was something he'd been putting together for weeks in preparation for Briar's birthday.

It was next Thursday, and he'd already talked to Bobbie Jo and Tucker about both of them having the entire day off. He'd said he would call in people to come help with their chores and feeding, but Tucker said he would handle it.

Briar loved breakfast sandwiches, and Tarr wanted to pamper her with breakfast in bed, and he'd scheduled her a pedicure for midmorning. He'd already scouted restaurants near the nail salon for their birthday lunch date. And then, in a bold move, Tarr had scheduled them a couple's massage at a ritzy hotel and resort only twenty minutes from the farm. He'd asked Briar casually about getting a massage, as it was one of his favorite things to do while riding the circuit.

He liked going to someone who also had some certifications in chiropractic care, and he'd inquired about such a person at the resort. He'd been assured and reassured that it would be fine, and that they would have the couple's suite ready with the hot sea-salt stones for both him and Briar, and an aromatherapy called Water, which promised "crisp notes with hints of citrus."

Oh, how he hoped Briar liked citrusy aromatherapy. "She does," he murmured to himself. Her perfume already gave him that idea, and Tarr had been taking notes on the things Briar had said for months now.

He tapped to open his phone and moved to the note-taking app that he'd colored green, one of her favorite colors. He'd ordered balloons in purple and silver as well, and he'd recruited Bobbie Jo to decorate the cabin before they returned from their couple's massage. Tarr planned to spend that evening with Briar in her cabin, and he flipped to the page in his notebook to get to the ingredient list that would form his grocery shopping.

He wanted to offer her a choice for her birthday dinner, and he wasn't sure what she would pick. Briar was a mood eater, and she might not want something heavy after his homemade breakfast sandwiches and then a lunch out.

She loved soups, and he'd put baked potato soup and taco soup on his menu. But another quick glance at his notes told him she'd also made hamburger stew that winter and a delicious chicken-corn chowder as well.

"If I do the stew," he said, tapping the end of his pen against his notebook, "I could use those heart-shaped molds for cornbread."

Tarr suspected he was being a little bit extra when it came to Briar's birthday, but he couldn't help it. He wanted everything to be absolutely perfect for her. Christmas had been such a success, and now he had a really high bar to meet.

His alarm went off, and Tarr closed his notebook and left it where it sat on the table. He scooted to the end of the bench and stood up. He first moved over to the wood-burning stove and closed the oxygen valve that would kill the fire, as Tarr didn't dare leave it burning when he wasn't home.

They had eventually gotten the poles put in and the tarp roof constructed over the outdoor pallets between his RV and Alex's trailer. Jentzen had fashioned it with clear plastic sheeting used by painters, and it honestly had turned the outdoor area into somewhat of a greenhouse that had helped keep the trailer warmer than Tarr thought possible. As spring approached, Tarr didn't need to leave the space heater on either. In fact, he moved into the bedroom and turned it off.

He shrugged into his coat and ran into the arena to use the bathroom. He came back out and checked to make sure that the fire was fully snuffed out. Then he got behind the wheel of his truck and headed over to Briar's. He didn't think she would be there, nor that her front door would be locked, so he climbed the steps and opened the door for Wiggins, who'd only barked once.

"You're really off your game today, buddy."

His favorite friend in the whole world came over to him, his whole body wagging back and forth. Tarr laughed and gave the dog plenty of love before Wiggins trotted down the front steps and started sniffing along the sidewalk. Briar's cabin faced south, and they hadn't had a snowstorm in a couple of weeks, so a lot of her snow had receded into the higher piles, leaving the edges of grass and flower beds bare for Wiggins to do his business. Tarr sat on the top step, glad when the dog came to join him, and he simply gazed out at the serene country setting in front of him.

"Thank you, Lord," he whispered, because Tarr's life had not been this calm and peaceful since he joined the rodeo circuit fifteen years ago.

He comforted himself as he waited for Briar by stroking his hand absently down Wiggins's head and neck. By the time Briar pulled into the driveway, the dog practically sat in his lap.

Wiggins barked and leapt away from Tarr, then greeted his owner. Tarr honestly felt the same way, and he forced himself to stay seated on top of the steps as Briar killed the engine of her SUV and got out.

"Hey, you," she said fondly. "Did Tarr let you out? Did he? Were you keeping him company?"

She disappeared down the other side of the SUV as she bent to pat her dog, and then she straightened and came around the back end of it. Their eyes met, and Tarr's heart leapt up into the back of his throat. He wasn't sure if the news would be good or bad, because Briar kept everything caged up behind shutters and walls, and he honestly wondered how she did that.

"Hey," he said, but he didn't get up from the steps. "How'd it go?"

She sighed as she reached the bottom of the steps and started to climb. "It was fine," she said.

"Oh, that doesn't sound fine, honey." He rose and took her hand as she reached the porch. "Tell me about it."

She paused and looked over to the chair where she sat in the morning, sipping her coffee. Without thinking too hard about it, Tarr stepped that way, tugging her with him. He sat first, and she settled easily onto his lap—something she'd once protested about but now did as if it were second nature. She'd talk to him easier, too, if she didn't have to look him straight in the face, and Tarr could hold this woman in his arms forever and never grow tired of it.

He pushed them back and forth while Wiggins circled and lay down next to the chair.

After a few rocks, she said, "It's not bad news, Tarr, but it's not exactly good either."

"All right," he said.

"She wants to check my fallopian tubes for damage. She says there could be some uterine scarring that may affect implantation, which would obviously make conception difficult. Along with that, if there's a lot of scarring around my uterus or fallopian tubes, that could cause narrowing in the tubes, and obviously then I might not have eggs that can be fertilized."

She drew a breath. "She said she'd put me in the reduced-fertility or unknown-impact category, and she wants to do more tests so we can see if there's any of that scarring from the hip replacement or pelvic injury. Something called an HSG."

"All right," Tarr said. "You want to do that?"

"Yeah," Briar said. "I have an appointment in another couple of weeks for that."

"I can drive you," Tarr offered.

Briar drew in a long breath, and it shuddered through her chest. Tarr's heart broke for her. He really didn't want her to have to go through this alone. He also knew he'd have to force himself on her if he really wanted to drive her to do the testing, because Briar still resisted help from almost everyone.

"She said that it's entirely possible that I can get pregnant," Briar continued. "But she then has a lot of concerns about carrying a baby and delivering it properly. Because of my hip replacement, my pelvic width might not be big enough, and it's very likely that I would have to have a C-section. So there are lots of things."

"Well, we can deal with things," Tarr said. "Things that we know about are far better than things that we don't."

"Yeah." Briar sighed and got to her feet. "I don't want to talk about it anymore." She reached for both of his hands and playfully pulled him to a stand. "Take me to dinner?"

"Yes, ma'am." He wrapped her in his arms and leaned down, hesitating only millimeters before his mouth touched hers. "Thanks for telling me, Briar," he said, using her name in a rare showing of saying it out loud. "Where do you want to go eat?"

She closed the distance between them and pressed her lips to his. Tarr quickly deepened the kiss, the sense of knocking down even more of Briar's barriers flowing over him. He didn't go on too long before he whistled for Wiggins and put the dog back in the house. Wiggins barked a couple of times as Tarr brought the door closed between them, and he turned back to Briar with guilt streaming through him.

"Oh, he's fine," Briar said. "I want to go to that gourmet hot dog place."

Everything Tarr knew about Briar shifted. "You want a gourmet hot dog?"

"After the doctor's appointment that I've been anxiously awaiting and dreading at the same time? Yeah, I want an all-beef foot-long with caramelized onions and spicy brown mustard," she said. "And maybe some of that tangy sauce they put on yours last time." She grinned at him. "It sounds good, doesn't it?"

"Hey, I'm always up for a gourmet hot dog," he said.

With that, he led her toward the truck, and after she climbed in, he pressed in close to her and rested his arm across her lap. "I've been thinking a lot about it, sweetheart," he said. "And even if you can't have kids, it doesn't make you less."

Her eyes met his, searching and searching as if he might not be telling the truth. "You really mean that?"

"Yeah," he said. "It's one tiny little part of who you are. It doesn't define you, and it's definitely not a deal-breaker for me, because you're amazing exactly how you are."

Briar cradled his face in her hand and let her eyes drift closed. "Thank you, baby. That means a lot."

Tarr kissed her again, still a little surprised that something he'd fantasized about for almost a year could actually happen now. He wanted to provide a safe harbor for her in every way possible, and as he stood there in her driveway, the sun slowly sinking into twilight and reminding him that it was far too cold to be carrying on for very long, Tarr definitely started falling in love with Briar. And maybe if he managed to provide the perfect birthday for her, she could fall in love with him too.

thirty-one

Briar woke up on her birthday, the scent of bacon filling her senses. She'd figured Tarr would help her start her birthday in the best way possible—and that meant breakfast sandwiches.

She opened her eyes to find darkness still covering the windows. That also made sense, though the days were definitely getting longer and longer. She noticed that her bedroom door stood more ajar than she usually left it, and she felt around with her feet for Wiggins. He was gone, and of course he was. The dog loved her unconditionally, and though Briar had been resisting the cowboy's charms with everything she could, she also knew why Wiggins felt the way he did about Tarr.

Tarr knew how to take exceptional care of those around him, and it helped that he fed Wiggins whatever he wanted. With a start, Briar realized Tarr did the same thing to her. She dictated where they went for dinner, and he was currently in her house right now, preparing to feed her exactly what she wanted.

So she and Wiggins weren't all that different.

Part of her wanted to shower and get dressed before she showed her wild morning hair to Tarr and inflicted her morning breath on him. But he'd seen her plenty of times in her pajamas —and quite literally at her worst when she'd awakened in the hospital and found him at her side—so she left on her pajamas and padded down the hall in bare feet to the kitchen. She paused just out of sight so she could drink in Tarr's tall, dark form as he whisked something on the stove.

In the end, Wiggins gave her away, catching sight of her only a moment later and barking a good morning to her. *Bark, bark, bark-bark!* he went as he wagged toward her, and Briar imagined him to be saying, *Happy birthday, my human.*

Briar bent to pat her dog, effectively getting him to quiet down. "Morning, Wiggy," she said to him, leaning down to scratch along his neck and down his back.

"Hey, there you are." Tarr abandoned the work on the stove and came to greet her. "Happy birthday, honey."

She let him wrap her up tight in his arms—something else Tarr was incredibly good at.

"You're cooking?" she asked. "I thought you said we were going to lunch."

"We are going to lunch," he said. "But you have three meals on your birthday, and you gotta start the day strong."

Briar leaned back in his arms and smiled up at him. "You're going to be annoying all day about this, aren't you?"

He chuckled. "You know, some might call it attentive."

Briar stretched up to give him a morning kiss. "If you get sick of me, you can leave," she said.

"Don't worry. It's not me who's going to be sick of you, but I've built in some alone-time for both of us."

"You have? Do tell."

Tarr took her hand and led her back into the kitchen. "I've got the schedule right here on the whiteboard."

A whiteboard? Briar did not own one of those, but Tarr obviously did, as one now stood on an easel at the end of her dining room table, an enormous vase of blood-red roses beside it. His cowboy handwriting was nowhere to be found, and instead Briar recognized the more feminine slant of Bobbie Jo.

She moved to the end of the counter to read the schedule, frowning after only the first line. "Our chores aren't on here."

"Nope," he said. "Because you're not doing chores today, and neither am I. It's a day off."

Briar turned toward him. "The whole day?"

"Just read the schedule, sweetheart." He flicked off the flame on the stove and moved the pan to the counter. "I'm going to be toasting the English muffins and doing eggs next, and then we'll be ready to eat."

"Okay," Briar said absently, her gaze locked on the schedule once again.

After breakfast, he'd scheduled a pedicure for her. That would apparently take ninety minutes, as their next appointment was lunch sometime between eleven-thirty and noon. After that, he'd put "open first round of presents," and then by three they needed to be somewhere.

Briar's breath left her body. "A couple's massage, Tarr. You've got to be kidding."

"I don't think any man is stupid enough to be kidding about something on their girlfriend's birthday." He grinned over at her. "You said you used to like massages when you were stunt riding."

"I did. I do." She gazed at the board. "I just haven't had one in so long."

"It's just laying there," he said. "I think you'll remember how to do it." He grinned at her. "And I'll be in the room too."

"Yeah?"

"They assured me we could be as private as we wanted. You can go in first, for example, and get situated under the blankets, and I'll come in after you. We have access to a swimming pool, sauna, and hot tubs afterward," he said. "So we can take our swimming suits and stay until they close."

"What time is that?" she asked.

"Mm, I think they're open until ten," he said.

Briar knew they would not be staying until ten o'clock, because the next thing on Tarr's schedule read "dinner with Wiggins." She reached down to pat Wiggy, who stood right at her side. "Where's dinner?" she asked.

"Right here," he said. "Back at your place. There will be a choice menu, and you'll tell me what you want and I'll make it."

"You didn't plan the meal?"

He'd returned to the stove and was cracking eggs into a sizzling pan. "I planned three of them," he said.

Of course he did.

"Because I knew what we were having for breakfast, but I don't know what you'll choose for lunch, and I know you're a mood eater, so I wanted to make sure I have different options for dinner."

"This looks like a lot of eating and pampering," she said.

"Which is all anyone should ever do on their birthday," Tarr said without missing a beat.

She looked back at the schedule, her eyes quickly spinning through it again. She did love to eat. And to get her toenails looking good again? She was all for that, because it had been far too long.

"This looks like the perfect day," she said.

That caught Tarr's attention. He stood at the stove, the spatula frozen above the pan, everything about him warm and wonderful and quiet and good.

"Yeah," Briar said. "It's pretty much all my favorite things, Tarr—bacon sandwiches, a pedicure, lunch out, time with my dog, a massage...."

Tarr expertly slid his spatula under the eggs in the pan and flipped them. "And time with your favorite person, right?"

"Oh, did I not mention that?" Briar teased, though she knew Tarr needed reassurance from her from time to time. Heck, probably more often than she gave it to him.

"No, I didn't hear that part." He grinned.

"Yes," she said. "A perfect day includes time with my favorite person."

"And that's me, right?"

"Would you just let me finish a thought?"

Tarr glanced over at her, his expression open and vulnerable. "I'm sorry, honey."

She moved into the kitchen with him. "Of course it's you, Tarr. I haven't spent my birthday with anyone in years, and I certainly wouldn't do it now if I didn't like you." She met his eyes. "*Really* like you."

"As much as Wiggins?"

She grinned and shook her head. "Don't press your luck, cowboy. Wiggins is one of a kind."

"Oh, boy, I know it," he said.

She linked her arm through his, though he still needed the use of it to scramble the eggs. "Thank you, Tarr. This looks amazing in more ways than one."

"Do you approve the schedule?" he asked.

"Does it matter if I don't?"

"Of course," he said. "I'm not going to make you do something on your birthday that you hate."

"Well, I definitely don't think there's anything there that I hate," she said. "I've never done a couple's massage, and maybe I'm a little nervous about it, but...."

She drew breath, glad when Tarr gave her a moment to finish her thought. "It's me and you, so what could possibly go wrong?"

He grinned at her. "Exactly. And don't worry, sweetheart; I'm not expecting anything out of it. It will be dark and soothing, and I won't peek at all."

Briar didn't think he would, but she still said, "That sounds great, Tarr."

"Do your parents attempt to talk to you at all on your birthday?" he asked.

Briar shook her head. "They haven't."

"Do you check their social media or anything? Maybe they post?"

Briar turned away from him, but not because his questions irritated her. Fine, they did a little bit. She took a moment to think through them, and then said, "I've checked in the past, and when there was nothing, it hurt too much to keep doing that. But I guess anything is possible."

"I just don't get it," he said. "How do you have kids and then just not talk to them?"

"I don't know," Briar said. "Have you ever heard back from Wayne?"

Tarr's jaw hardened and he shook his head. "Nope, nothing. My momma keeps me up-to-date with him, so I know what's going on with him, and I assume she does the same and tells him about me too."

"Yeah, probably," Briar said. "Does that bother you?"

"Yeah," Tarr said. "But I think it makes my momma feel good, and I don't want her to be upset about anything." He once again flicked off the flame. "All right, sweetheart, you've got to let go of me so I can put together your sandwich."

He grinned at her, and Briar backed up to give him more room behind the counter. She took a seat at the dining room table behind the whiteboard and waited for Tarr to bring over the two immaculate plates of her favorite food: a toasty breakfast sandwich with cheese on a toasted English muffin.

He put one plate in front of her and slid the other one across the table. Then he swept his arm around her and leaned down. "Happy birthday, Briar," he whispered.

Oh, how she loved hearing him say her name in his sexy cowboy tenor. When she first met him and he'd called her *sweetheart*, she'd found it demeaning. Then she realized he was as Texan as anyone she'd ever met, and he called everyone *sweetheart*, including goats, sheep, and sometimes Wiggins. Having him use her name felt significant.

Briar definitely felt the loss of his presence at her side as he moved around the table and took his place across from her.

"Can we pray?" he asked.

Briar immediately folded her arms and bowed her head, though the call of the delicious salty bacon tempted her to skip prayer for once. She and Tarr had prayed together many times now, but she still appreciated the sound of his voice saying, "Dear Lord," and the sentiment with the words that came after that.

"I'm sure glad to be here celebrating with Briar today on her birthday. Thank you so much for opening her heart and allowing me to have a chance to be in her life. It has been a blessing to me for these past few months, Lord, and please bless us both that we'll be able to have a good day today—especially

Briar, as it's her birthday and she deserves everything good in the world to come her way."

Tears gathered behind Briar's eyes, because she had never heard herself described as a blessing in someone's life. She almost wanted to scoff and remind Tarr that he shouldn't tell lies, but he spoke with such sincerity that she believed he truly found her to be a blessing to him.

Briar wasn't sure she'd ever been a blessing to anyone, and a warm, bright feeling filled her from head to toe.

"Amen," Tarr said.

She'd missed the rest of the prayer, but it didn't matter. She'd heard the part her heart needed to hear. She glanced over to Tarr as he picked up his breakfast sandwich and took the first bite. He moaned the way Tarr always did, and Briar shook her head at the way he patted himself on the back—the way she always did.

She giggled, this birthday off to a perfectly salty, delicious, cowboy start.

thirty-two

"You want me to go in first, sweetheart?" Tarr asked.

Briar, who'd pulled her hair back into a messy bun, looked at him with big, soulful eyes above her puffy white spa robe, and nodded. He wanted to reach for her and tell her how gorgeous she was, but he reminded himself that he'd already done that right after bringing her a little cup of home-made granola and a glass of ice water infused with green apples. He'd never indulged in the treats in the waiting room before a massage, but Briar had told him that was half the fun.

He could still taste the apples. They weren't disgusting, but they certainly weren't the best thing he'd put in his mouth that day.

Tarr let his fingers brush against Briar's as he moved past her and followed his spa attendant into the couple's massage room. His eyes adjusted quickly to the low light, and his attendant was a five-foot-nothing brunette with a wide smile.

"Any injuries I should know about?" she asked.

Tarr shook his head. "I called in about my girlfriend's hip."

"Her attendant will ask her," the woman said. "Don't worry—Wendy is our most amazing chiropractic masseuse."

Tarr grinned at the woman he'd been assigned. "Okay. I don't have any injuries, and I've done massages plenty of times."

"Great," she said. "I've got the Himalayan pink sea salt stones for both of you." She indicated the counter behind her and another counter behind the second table. "And I have you both doing the Water aromatherapy."

"That's right," Tarr murmured.

"There's a hook here for your robe, and you can just leave your slippers there. Any loose items go over here in this bowl," she continued, explaining that she'd then send in Briar and he should lie face down.

Tarr had been through all this before and knew what to do. She finally stepped out, and he shed his robe and hung it on the hook, practically dancing over to his massage table.

He'd spent plenty of his life with people watching him—millions through cameras—and he had to give interviews before and after his ride, but somehow he felt more self-conscious as he climbed under the blanket for his massage than he ever had in his life.

He got all settled, the heat from the table seeping into his bones and muscles and helping him relax. A moment later, a knock sounded on the door.

"Are you ready?" a woman asked.

"Yes, ma'am," he called, and he kept his eyes closed, though the light was already dim.

As the attendants brought in Briar, her masseuse went through the same quick instructions and stepped out. Tarr's pulse thundered through his body, making his circulation feel like a herd of wild mustangs stampeding across the plains.

Briar said nothing—not even to double-check with him to make sure he wouldn't peek. He heard the soft swishing of fabric and then movement on the table only a few feet from his. It made a slight noise as she laid down, and then she sighed, finally.

"This feels great," she whispered.

"I'm glad," Tarr whispered back, because it felt like they definitely couldn't talk louder than that in this room.

"Is your table heated?"

"Sure is."

It seemed to take the attendants a long time to come back, but they finally did. The lights lowered even more, the music turned up slightly, and Tarr settled in for an amazing experience. As his massage therapist put both hands on his upper back and leaned into him, he felt her grounding him. He sighed out as she pressed her hands down his back, along his hips, and then came right back up to his neck. Only then did she pull the blanket back, and she repeated the motion, this time with his bare skin against her hands.

Tarr breathed in deeply when she told him to, the scent of eucalyptus and orange further relaxing him, and he could tell with the first stroke of his masseuse's hands down his right side that he was going to feel amazing at the end of this.

* * *

A couple of hours later, he opened Briar's door for her, and she climbed into his truck. He joined her and glanced over to her, then leaned over, reached past her, and opened the glove box.

"I know it's still early," he said. "And we're gonna go by the build site, but I'd love for you to choose the dinner menu." He held up the file folder, wiggled it back and forth, and handed it to her.

"What's this?" she asked.

"It's your birthday menu," he said.

She eyed him for a moment, then flipped it open. He'd hand-written the menu on a single sheet of paper that spanned front and back and explained the starter, main course, and dessert.

"Tarr," she said. "How are you going to make all this in one day?"

"Oh, the starters are easy," he said. "It's chips and guacamole or baked potato soup."

"I do love baked potato soup," Briar said, her eyes scanning the sheet. That menu came with steak and roasted asparagus. The one with guacamole came with chicken and carne asada tacos, and the third choice was something not quite as elaborate but just as delicious—at least in Briar's world—green salad and spaghetti and meatballs.

"The desserts are all birthday cake," he said. "But there is an assortment of ice creams."

"I think that's for you, cowboy." Briar grinned over at him and flipped the folder closed. "I think I want the soup and steak."

Tarr took the menu back from her and tucked it down into the side of his door.

"Is that okay?" she asked.

"Of course it is." He glanced over at her. "It's your birthday, sweetheart. You can have anything you want."

"I think we've proven that that's not true," she said. "Because I wanted a really relaxing massage, where a certain someone wasn't snoring next to me."

Tarr scoffed and put the truck in reverse to pull out of the parking spot. "I was not snoring."

Briar continued to giggle. "Yes, you were. Both of the masseuses even said so."

"Oh, they don't even know what they're doing in there," he said.

Briar full-on laughed, and she reached over and took his hand in hers. "I think it's great you got a little nap, baby. You work too hard sometimes."

He looked over to her, surprised. "Do I?"

"I think so," she said. "Especially now that spring is here and your house is coming along. Aren't you going to put in the flooring yourself?"

"Yes," he said.

"And Bobbie Jo told me that you took Tucker to the big hardware store to have him help you pick out paint. Are you doing that yourself too?"

"I'm not going to do all of the painting," he said. "But I am going to do the flooring and the finishing work on the cabinets and shelving. I really like seeing those little details come together."

"Yes, I can see that about you," she said, and Tarr wondered what she really saw in her head when she thought of him.

They made the drive back to Deerfield quickly, and Tarr rumbled past her road and around the corner to the far end of the square where his house had come to life over the past couple of months.

All of the walls and roof stood proudly against the sky, and Tarr smiled as he pulled in and parked in front of the house. "Looks like they put the gutters on," he said, eyeing the new rain gutters on the house.

"This barely counts as a cabin," Briar said.

"Never once did I say I was building a cabin," he told her for probably the fifth time. "It's always been a house, Briar."

He shook his head and got out. She joined him, and he led the way up what would become the front sidewalk to the house. He had a two-car garage and plenty of room for parking bigger vehicles—like his RV or a boat, four-wheelers, or anything else oversized that Tarr wanted—down the side and toward the backyard, which he planned on fencing and replanting with some of the native trees that they'd had to take out to build the house.

"I do love this porch," Briar said as she climbed the steps to it.

Tarr stopped and admired it as well. It extended across the full front of the house and wrapped around the far side, where it extended all the way to the back corner over there. The master bedroom took up that corner, and he'd have a sliding glass door which led out onto a private side porch. Tarr had admitted—only to himself—that he'd designed that for Briar, so she could take her coffee on the south side of the house, in that rocking chair she loved.

Tarr pushed open the door and walked into the house. "Oh, they've come a long way," he said, as he could now see the kitchen laid out with spots for the appliances and the cabinets that had been brought this week.

The front door faced east and the back door west, and as he'd been spoiling Briar all day for her birthday, the sun had started its descent toward evening. Tarr moved in that direction, where a pair of French doors would let him out onto a back deck and into his backyard. He'd be able to see the arena from here, even if Bobbie Jo and Tucker grew big stalks of corn in the fields in between.

"It's looking good," he said, turning back to Briar.

"They've hung doors this way too, Tarr," she said, peering down the hallway.

He joined her, drinking in all the new things that they'd done in the house since he'd been here last. He really tried not to come every day, because it simply fed his impatience.

"What do you think?" he asked, putting his arm around Briar.

"I think it's amazing," Briar said.

He swallowed, not wanting to ruin anything since they still had dinner to go for her birthday. But he couldn't stop himself from asking, "What do you think, my thorny Briar? Do you think you could live here with me one day?"

Briar leaned further into him and looked down the hall as if someone had painted a gorgeous mural on the walls and only she could see it.

Irritation drove through him when she didn't immediately say, *Yeah, of course, Tarr,* and he said, "Forget it. Don't answer that, okay?"

"Tarr—" she said, but he had already turned to leave.

"Let's get back to your place," he said, making his voice as bright as he could. "I've got to put a three-course dinner on the table."

She followed him, and when they were both in the truck and headed back down the lane, she said, "It's not a hard question, Tarr."

"Well, you didn't answer it."

"I don't know if I'm ready to start talking about marriage," she said. "And I know that's not the answer that you want to hear, so I was trying to figure out how to say, 'Yes, I'm thinking about living in that house with you,' without it turning into a big conversation about marriage."

Tarr's throat burned like he'd swallowed acid, and he forced himself to nod. "Why don't you want to talk about marriage yet? Are we going too fast?"

"Not exactly," she said. "But remember, I'm still getting used to the idea of me being married at all, and it has nothing to do with you, Tarr, and everything to do with me."

He nodded, though he wasn't entirely sure he believed her. Wouldn't the heavens open and angels be singing for Briar if marrying him was the right thing to do? Couldn't God give her that reassurance or those experiences, or whisper in her ear, the way He had about other things, to help her along this road a little bit faster?

Tarr coached himself to be patient. He pulled up to Briar's house, and they got out and went inside. He snatched her hand just before she reached for the doorknob. "Hey, I just want to ask you one more thing," he said. "And then I swear I'll drop it until you bring it up again."

She sighed and turned back to him.

"And if you don't want to answer, you don't have to answer. It's your birthday, and that's always been our rule. But I guess I'm wondering what you need to see, or have happen, or something in order to see yourself getting married. Is there anything I can do? Because I don't know the words to tell you that I think you're absolutely stunning in every way, and you're smart and you're beautiful, and you're funny, and you make me smile. And I just—I don't think *you* feel like you're amazing, but you are, and I don't know how to tell you that."

Her chin shook as she moved closer to him, stepping into his arms. "You just did, cowboy."

"But you don't believe it," he said, finally putting the pieces together. "That's it, right? You hear me say it, but you don't believe it."

She nodded, her eyes falling closed. "You're right. I don't believe it. Can we please not talk about this on my birthday? I don't want to be reminded of the things that made me this way, or why I'm choosing to be like this. Everything about this day has been perfect, Tarr. Including you. So can we just table this until another time?"

"Of course," he said, because he'd gotten the answers he needed already. He didn't have to like them, but at least he'd gotten them.

thirty-three

Bobbie Jo Hammond glanced over to her mother. "Mom, you got the job." She gave her a smile and focused on the highway in front of her again.

"Yes." Her momma sighed, and Bobbie Jo wished she could feel the same relief driving through her.

"So...are you going to go look at that condo?" Bobbie Jo refused to look at her mother, though they'd had a couple of conversations about the temporary-ness of the current living situation.

If Bobbie Jo wanted to stay married—and she did—she really needed her parents to have a plan—a real plan—to get their own place.

"I suppose," her mother said. "Your father is enjoying the work at the farm."

"I'm glad." Bobbie Jo made her voice as bright as possible. "That condo is really close to both places." She wouldn't let this go; she couldn't.

Her parents never found satisfaction in anything, though they smiled and laughed and said things like, "Your father is enjoying the work at the farm."

At least Daddy had found a job working with horses at a training stable and wasn't working for Tucker anymore. That had only lasted a couple of weeks, and apparently, winter in Colorado was far harsher than those in Oklahoma.

Bobbie Jo had experienced them both, and she knew they were about the same.

Exactly the same, she thought dryly. But she tamed that inner grump, and sweetened all her saltiness.

"Mom," she said. "Tucker and I wanted to talk to you about perhaps building a house on the farm." She flicked a glance over to her mother, but didn't make contact. This road sat straight and long, but Bobbie Jo's nerves rioted.

"There's a great parcel right on the highway," she said, her words rushing over each other now. "Easy on and off the property, and you'd have your own place."

"Oh, Bobbie Jo." Her mother sighed again, but this time, it didn't carry any of the relief as before.

"What?" she asked. "Tarr knows a great general contractor, and his house is almost done."

"I can't let you two give us land and build us a house."

Bobbie Jo blinked, because her mother and father had taken everything—every single thing—she and Tuck had offered them since they'd arrived in Tulsa a few days before Christmas.

"So...."

"We're going to go look at the condo next week," her mom said. "I'll call the realtor today."

So she hadn't even done that yet. Bobbie Jo gritted her teeth, but she didn't know what to say. She didn't want to mother her mother,

"Okay." She swallowed. "But Mom, really. Tuck's cousin is building a place for his parents on his farm, and Tuck and I are more than happy to do that."

She and Tucker had gone across the city to Mike and Gerty's farm, and they'd seen the construction happening on the new house there. Nothing big, as it was just Tucker's aunt and uncle. But then, Wes and Bree would be living close to two of their children—and their grandchildren.

Bobbie Jo wasn't pregnant, and she and Tucker hadn't even been married for a year yet. But her parents were here, now employed, and she supposed anything could happen at any time.

"I know you are, dear." Her mother patted her hand, and her third sigh wasn't one of relief, or frustration, but of...resignation. "We really appreciate everything you and Tuck have done for us."

Bobbie Jo nodded.

"But we do need somewhere without so many *stairs*."

The way she said it made Bobbie Jo feel like the second-story suite—complete with furniture, a made-for-them kitchen, loft, and den—wasn't good enough.

Oh, and they'd been living there for three months for free.

But you know, the *stairs*.

Bobbie Jo held her tongue, and changed the words she wanted to say into different ones. "Yeah, Daddy's knees can't handle those stairs for much longer."

"No," her mother said. "Don't you worry, Bobbie Jo. We'll be out of your hair before you know it."

Bobbie Jo caught her mother's smile in her peripheral vision, and all she could do was pray that her mother hadn't just lied to her.

Please, please, please, she thought, sending her pleas heavenward. *Please bless my parents—and me and Tuck—that this condo will be somewhere that can give us the answers we all need.*

thirty-four

Briar sat in front of the mirror in her bedroom, carefully plaiting her hair into several smaller braids.

Doing intricate up-dos came with the territory of being a cowgirl in stunt riding, and Briar had learned from an early age how to do it herself. She hadn't been able to count on her momma for such things, and since she'd left her former life at the border, she'd been doing ponytails or letting her curls roam free. But today, she and Tarr would be attending the very formal western wedding of the foreman at the Hammond Family Farm, Mission Redbay, and Briar's friend and vet, Kristie Higgins.

She smiled at her reflection, because she'd seen the two of them together, and Kristie adored her cowboy fiancé while he made himself a planet to her sun, revolving around her and caring for her in any way he could.

Briar's thoughts, of course, moved to Tarr, and though a month had passed since her birthday, they'd still only talked about marriage that one and only time. "And we didn't even do that," she said to her reflection.

The reason they hadn't was because of her, and when Tarr made a promise, he kept it. He had not brought up living in his house with him, or marriage, or anything related to it since.

Briar spent every morning and evening with Tarr, first out in the arena and then either at his place or hers. She'd let him take her to her doctor's appointment for her scans and subsequent doctor's appointment where they had not found anything that would prevent her from having a baby.

"How I can talk about that and not marrying Tarr, I have no idea."

They went by his house all the time now, as the general contractor had just scheduled the final inspection, and anything after that would be cosmetic. Tarr would do the finishes himself before he moved out of the RV and into his new permanent house.

"One of his goals checked off," she said quietly to herself.

Tarr had been very clear with her. He wanted a permanent home after living on the road, traveling for rodeos, and staying in someone else's house for way too long.

He wanted a wife. He wanted a family. And he wanted this small-town existence that prevailed here on the farm, with Tucker and Bobbie Jo. Knowing Tarr as she did, Briar believed every goal he'd set for himself would be achieved.

She still felt lost, adrift at sea, not quite sure who she was yet. She'd enjoyed her watercolor class—it had ended only a few days ago—and the same teacher would be doing an advanced class in the fall that Briar had already signed up for. She loved her job on the farm, and with her contract now open-ended, she didn't have to worry about that going away.

No, the only unknown in her life stemmed from her relationship with Tarr.

As she started to pin and clip her hair to hold it in place until she could twine it all into an elegant updo, she had the distinct feeling that he would not wait for her forever, despite the promises he'd made.

And you don't need to test him. That thought sat heavy in her mind, and Briar wanted to kick against it.

"I'm not testing him on purpose," she whispered, but God thought differently.

She tilted her head and looked into her own eyes.

Hasn't he proven to you that he's trustworthy? The thought lingered, and Briar had no idea what to do with it.

"He has," she finally said, her fingers finally getting every last braid twirled into a crown and pinned in place. "But Lord, why can't I trust myself? What if I've just fallen for him, because he's so handsome, and so funny, and so good? Haven't I gotten myself in trouble like this before?"

She thought of her previous boyfriends, and yes, they'd been handsome, and they'd been known to show kindness, but she wasn't sure she would label any of them as specifically *kind* and *good.* Briar had never thought anyone was good the way she thought Tarr was.

"So why does he like me?" she asked herself as she got up from the vanity and moved to step into the pretty purple dress she'd bought for today's wedding.

She'd barely buckled the silver sandals she hoped she wouldn't regret wearing when Wiggins flew into a barking fit, rushing toward the door and then back over to where she sat on the edge of the couch, finishing with her shoes.

"Come in," she called, because she expected their visitor to be Tarr himself.

Sure enough, the devastatingly gorgeous cowboy opened the door, chuckled as he praised Wiggins for his excellent guard-dog skills, and then straightened to look at Briar. They'd been to church together several times, and he wore something similar now to what he usually did then: black slacks, white shirt, tie, and a jacket. Today's wasn't leather, though, but one that matched his navy-blue pants.

"Wow, you're looking amazing, honey." He drew her into his arms and kissed her.

"I'm worried about my shoes," she said, lifting one heel so he could see them. "They moved their wedding up a whole month, and I don't know if it's warm enough to wear an open-toed shoe outside for very long."

"I don't think we're gonna be outside for very long," Tarr said.

"No?" Briar asked. "Last time I talked to Kristie, she said they're definitely getting married outside at the farm."

"Yeah, but I think all the dancing and everything is inside the barn, and it's heated."

"Oh, so I might be okay," Briar said.

"I'm sure you'll be fine," he said.

Outside on the porch, the sun shone brightly down. Briar took a deep breath of the springtime air and watched Wiggins as he trotted along the fence line that bordered the front yard from the fields beyond.

"I think if I ever got married," Briar said, noting the way Tarr whipped his attention to hers. "I would want it to be in the spring like this." She moved carefully down the steps, holding up her dress so she didn't trip.

"With a lot of flowers, and a big blue sky with still a little hint of crispness in the air, and all the trees blooming." She smiled out to the still-leafless trees. "I think April is too early, because those trees don't even have buds yet, and I want there to be greenery everywhere."

"Noted," Tarr said, his tone a little bit scratchy.

"I've been thinking a lot, Tarr," she said as she carefully laced her fingers through his. They slowly walked down her sidewalk toward his truck. They had plenty of time to talk on the way to the farm, as it took eighty minutes without traffic, and she didn't expect any on a lazy Saturday afternoon.

"I think one of the reasons that I haven't been able to really think too much about getting married is because I would want my parents there."

"Would you?" he asked, plenty of surprise in the words.

"I think so," she said. "And that means I have to reach out to them and try for a reconciliation, and that feels really hard."

"I'll bet it does," he said.

They reached his truck, and she turned toward him, looking up into those deep, dark eyes that had captivated her from the moment she'd seen him. "You know how it is; you've tried with Wayne."

"Yeah," he said. "I do know how it is."

He opened the door for her and ran his fingers from her elbow to her wrist. "And let me tell you, sweetheart, it's only that first text or call that's hard."

"He still hasn't responded to you, has he?" she asked.

"No," Tarr said, shaking his head. "Because making that first call or text is hard, and he doesn't know how to do it. So you don't have to figure out everything with your parents, you just have to figure out how to make that first call or send that first text."

Suddenly, everything felt less overwhelming, and Briar nodded as he whistled for Wiggins to come get in the truck. She had no idea what she would even say to her mom or dad as she got into the passenger seat. The terrifying thought of what they might say back to her ran through her mind.

"What if they say nothing at all?" she wondered aloud as she watched Tarr circle the hood to get behind the wheel. How did he put up with that rejection day after day? Briar wasn't sure she could, and she realized then that one of the reasons she hadn't tried to get in touch with her parents was because it would hurt too badly if what she suspected was true—that they really were done with her.

A fresh wave of hurt ran through her even as Tarr asked, "Hey, you okay, sweetheart?"

She nodded. For right here, in this moment, she was okay. Overall, she was okay. When she thought of her parents ignoring her the way Wayne did Tarr, she wasn't okay.

"How do you deal with the rejection?" she asked him.

Tarr glanced over to her, his eyes searching hers in a silent show of questioning.

"The rejection from your brother," she said. "Tarr, what if my parents don't respond the way Wayne hasn't? What if they *do* respond and say they don't want to talk to me or don't want to come to the wedding?"

A troubled look crossed Tarr's face, and to his credit, he didn't immediately answer. After several seconds, he said, "There's only a few things I know, and one of them is that just like I get to make my own choices, so does everyone else on this planet. I can't choose for them, and I can't change them. So sometimes the problem is with us, and we have to fix what we've done wrong. We can apologize, we can send cards, we can try to make it right. But in the end, the other person gets to decide what to do with all of that. They get to decide what to do with the *I'm sorry* and the restitution. We don't get to decide that, so we have to do the best we can and get to a place where we know we've done all we can do."

"But how do you know that?" Briar asked.

"God tells me," Tarr said simply. "And after a couple of weeks, when I think of Wayne again, and I ask, *Should I text him again?* If God says yes, then I do it. I'm still new at it too, especially when it comes to Wayne, but I'm getting better at listening to my gut and asking for help and then doing what feels right, even if it's uncomfortable."

Briar nodded, her thoughts moving in several directions now. Before she knew it, they had arrived at the Hammond Family Farm, a place that Briar had been several times since Thanksgiving. She smiled as Tarr rounded the bend past the big pine tree that stood sentinel over the farm.

"Man, I love this place," Tarr said.

"Yeah?" Briar asked. "Why is that?"

"I was in rough shape when Tuck brought me here," Tarr said. "And this place provided the exact refuge that I needed in my eleventh hour." He sighed, gazing out his side window. "It saved me in a lot of ways."

He glanced over to her. "Do you have a place like that?"

"Yeah," she whispered. "Deerfield."

Tarr nodded. "Then you get it."

"Yeah, I think I do," she said.

The farm she'd visited casually suddenly looked different now that she knew what it meant to Tarr.

He pulled up to the red barn, where several other cars and trucks had already parked. "Looks like the party's already started," he said jovially, as he loved nothing more than a good party.

Briar wasn't as fond of them as he was, but she sure enjoyed his boyish enthusiasm, and she let him come collect her from the passenger side. She linked her arm through his and followed the signs and the balloons around the side of the red barn to a meadow on the west, where the afternoon sun painted everything in glorious hues of gold and warmth.

Cowboys mingled in jackets and boots and hats, most of them holding flutes of sparkly liquid in their hands. Briar and Tarr joined Tuck and Bobbie Jo, who stood with Tucker's brother, Deacon, and an older couple that Briar had not met.

"This is my momma and daddy," Tuck said, indicating the people at his side. "This is our vet tech. She works a ton with Bobbie Jo and the goats, but she checks on our rodeo horses every single day too."

"It's great to meet you," Briar said. "I didn't catch your names."

"Gray," the older man said, reaching out to shake Briar's hand. "And my wife, Elise."

She looked at Tucker, who seemed to be made of half of each of them, and then Deacon, who'd definitely come from his daddy but sure didn't have a lot of his momma's lighter features.

"Deac's looking to build himself a new house here," Tarr said, his voice entering the conversation easily. "Because Gray and Elise here are planning to move back to Ivory Peaks."

He beamed at them like they'd made a great choice. "Is that still the plan?"

"Yep," Deacon said, while Gray and Elise simply nodded along.

"It's a beautiful day for a wedding," Briar said into the somewhat awkward silence.

"It sure is." Elise smiled at her and added, "Tuck and Bobbie Jo speak very highly of you." She shot a glance over to Bobbie Jo herself.

"Oh, well, I'm glad," she said. "I love working at Deerfield."

"And we love having her there," Bobbie Jo said.

"If we could get everyone to come into the tent," an older gentleman said into a mic, drawing everyone's attention. "The wedding is going to begin in ten minutes."

"Let's go, sweetheart," Tarr said, and he guided Briar with a hand on the small of her back.

She went with him easily, flowing with the rest of the wedding guests, and marveling that she had no problem believing Tucker and Bobbie Jo when they said they loved having her work for them at the farm.

She didn't doubt her abilities as a veterinary technician, and in fact, she knew where her limits were and operated inside them. But somehow, she didn't believe it when Tarr told her she was an amazing person.

How can I know I'm a good vet tech and not a good person? she wondered as she took her seat beside the man who had first forced her to this farm for a Thanksgiving meal.

He lifted his arm around her and leaned his head down. "I would love to know what you're thinking right now," he whispered in her ear.

"I don't even know how to sum it up," she whispered back. "Why does life have to be so confusing?"

Tarr pressed his lips to her temple, the gesture warm and full of compassion. "I don't know, sweetheart. But I do know that if there's anyone who can figure it out, it's you."

Irritation fired inside her—an emotion she used to aim at Tarr but now reflected back on herself—because *she* was the one telling herself she wasn't smart enough, wasn't good enough, and could never be loved for who she was. She knew those thoughts had roots from her childhood, but they had grown deep, and Briar simply didn't know how to pluck them out and discard them.

Yet.

thirty-five

Mission Redbay adjusted his collar and told himself it was only a tie. A strip of fabric. A knot he'd redone three times while his cabin sat in afternoon quiet and the clock on the stove advanced toward four o'clock.

He pulled in a steadying breath, because he'd been waiting for this day for months now. Even though he and Kristie had moved the wedding forward, his impatience to have her living here with him had reached a peak weeks ago.

The front door opened, and his granddad walked in. "I told everyone to take their seats," he said.

And then he'd walked over from the barn, so Mission only had a few minutes to get back over there. He smoothed his hands down the front of his Granddad's jacket. "All right."

"Boy," Granddad said, his eyes bright and his own cowboy hat perched on his head just-so. He didn't say more, and he didn't have to. Mission grabbed onto him and hugged him, breathed in the cedar-and-shaving-cream scent that had always belonged to Granddad, and immediately steadied on his feet.

"Good?" he asked.

"Good," Mission said. "I'm ready."

He led the way out onto the front porch and automatically looked right toward the Rocky Mountains. He loved the way they waited like witnesses and the Lord's peace sat like a soft hand on the back of his neck. He breathed, then smiled, because the Hammond Family Farm had always settled him.

Early spring sunlight lay across the front lawn and the still dormant fields, and a faint wind pushed toward him. He kept pace with Granddad, the energy buzz increasing with every step closer to the white tents.

He counted each crunch of gravel under his boots, not to measure the distance, but to keep his nerves from consuming him.

He was ready. *You are,* he told himself sternly. *It's a few minutes that's important, and everything else is for show.*

No, everything else was for Kristie. She'd made the difficult decision to invite her family, and they'd declined to attend. Mission's heart beat faster for a moment, then slowed again, which made him feel whiplashed emotionally.

He rounded the back of the stable, the big tents appearing in front of him. Rows of white chairs split by an aisle that extended underneath the canvas, and strings of bulbs glowed against the afternoon sunshine.

They reminded him of bottled stars, and Mission smiled at the imagery in his mind. They weren't planning to keep their guests outside past dark, as the earlier date had already been tempting Mother Nature to actually snow on their nuptials.

Mission took his place at the altar and hugged his granddad one more time before he bustled off to join Kristie in the barn. Since her father had not come, she'd asked Granddad to walk her down the aisle, and Mission once again tugged at the blasted tie around his throat.

Friends filled almost every seat—Hunter and Molly and their kids, his cowboys and cowgirls from the farm, all of them in clean boots and pressed shirts, Pony Power counselors tucked together like a flock, Poppy and Travis Thatcher with their kids, Tuck and Tarr in jackets that didn't know what to do with their shoulders, Bobbie Jo and Gerty laughing with Opal, who sat in front of them.

The Whettsteins took up a row, and Mission's heart squeezed mightily when he caught Deacon beaming at him from the front row, his parents tucked tightly in next to him. Mission nodded to them, his emotions spiraling up and then plummeting toward the earth the way a roller coaster did.

Kristie's baking friends—Lennie, Jocelyn, and Harper—sat in the front row on the bride's side, as did many of her veterinary clients, Keith, Lindsay, and Nash, with Britt and Lars and their new baby, Sullivan, way down on the end.

Mission's heart filled with love for all of them, because everyone who came to the Hammond Family Farm knew how to open their arms and welcome anyone and everyone.

Kristie would come from the left, from the little path lined in mason jars and pink roses. He'd walked it with her last night when they'd checked the tent and the chairs and the way the wind moved under the canvas. Her laugh had been soft and quick and it had stayed with him long after they'd said goodnight with a whisper of hands and the promise that tonight's dance would be theirs alone.

His granddad appeared at the end of the aisle, and Mission met his eyes and pulled in a breath.

One minute. Sixty seconds until he'd see his lovely bride in her wedding dress for the first time. Granddad disappeared again, and the music changed. People rose from their seats, the melody curling up toward the ceiling of the tent and continuing right on through it.

Mission shifted his feet nervously, but when Kristie appeared, every part of him quieted.

Her dress was simple and entirely her: a clean, graceful line that moved when she moved, cap sleeves, a skirt that whispered instead of announced, with shiny fabric that caught drops of mountain light and kept them in the fibers.

She wore her hair down, because she didn't want to "look bald" in the pictures, and it fell in soft curls around her face, with the rest tucked away at the nape of her neck. The veil spilled out from that and trailed behind her, the wispy edges of it just visible riding on the train of her gown.

Her bouquet boasted darker-than-spring colors like burgundy, sage, and pumpkin. She seemed to have her eyes open wider than normal, but her smile radiated happiness and excitement. Those things hit him when her eyes locked on his, and he found his anchor.

Kristie had long been the person he wanted to run everything by, the only woman he wanted to impress, and the love of his life.

His chest did that tight, squeezy thing it did when something sacred walked into the room. Outside, he stayed steady. He didn't lift a hand toward his tie again. He let his eyes do all the speaking they needed to do. He felt every step she took and silently encouraged her to keep going.

She nodded to people in the crowd, her eyes skipping down rows and back to his over and over. Granddad kept his arm steady in hers, their pace toward him slow but sure.

She almost seemed to be looking for someone, and when she didn't find them, her gaze came back to Mission's and held there. So she'd been hoping her family might change their mind and make the drive to Ivory Peaks.

She reached him, and Granddad slipped her arm into Mission's. "My blessings go with you," he whispered in his gravelly voice, and then he moved to sit beside Deacon on the front row.

Mission bent his head down and touched the brim of his cowboy hat to Kristie's forehead. "I'm here," he whispered. "And you're here."

They'd talked that it didn't matter who came to the wedding —and who didn't. All he needed was her, and all she needed was him.

She nodded slightly, took a breath, and together, they turned to face the pastor who'd come to marry them.

"I love officiating weddings in April," Quinn Benson said. Molly's father had retired from leading a congregation, but he still held the credentials to marry people in the state of Colorado, and Mission had known him for years.

"Because my wife and I got married in April, on the day of the biggest snowstorm of the season." He beamed his exuberance out into the world, and Mission found himself smiling. "Today, only the wind wishes to destroy your amazing day, but don't worry. Nothing can actually do that. God loves marriage, and whatever happens today will only add to the main event."

As if he'd called it, the wind rustled against the side of the tent, apparently unhappy it couldn't come in and witness the I-dos. Mission looked to the left as a few people twittered in the crowd.

"I know neither Mission nor Kristie likes to stand in the spotlight for very long," Pastor Benson said. "And I've promised not to go on too long, but one of the things I like to do when I marry someone is offer some advice."

Mission swallowed, because he felt sure whatever Pastor Benson counseled him to do, he'd try to do.

"Keep your marriage small," the pastor said. "And work on it daily. Pray by yourself, and then pray together. Think first, and speak second. Keep your problems between the two of you, and work on them together."

Keep your marriage small. Mission had been instantly confused, but the more Pastor Benson said, the more pieces fell into place.

"Life can get very loud," the pastor continued. "And you both have a whole lot pulling you in different directions. Come home to each other every night. Mission, look her in the eye and tell her how amazing she is. Kristie, put your hand in his and ask him how his day went."

Kristie's hand in Mission's actually tightened, and they exchanged a glance.

"Find a simple ritual that you can do every week. Some couples I know counsel together every Sunday night and share three good things they noticed the other doing that week. Some chat in the dark before they fall asleep, and lay out the things they need in the near future. No matter what, find something that works for the two of you, for no one else is in your marriage but the two—of—you."

He spoke the last words with enough emphasis for Mission to pay attention.

"Do the small things, and the Lord will make the reward big." Pastor Benson nodded, and he smiled widely as he looked from Kristie to Mission, and then out to the crowd. "Now, it's my understanding that the couple has put an advice wheel in the barn, and they'd love for you to write down *your* best marriage advice for the two of them."

He clapped his hands. "All right, Mission," Pastor Benson

said. "I'm going to pass the mic to you." He did just that, and Mission adjusted it in his grip while he dug into his pocket with his other hand.

Mission pulled out the index card where he'd scribbled down a few of his thoughts. "Kristie," he said, and a faint breeze lifted her veil and let it settle again, as if even the air wanted to look full in her face. He swallowed, but the lump sitting there stayed.

"I promise to be your constant champion, let you bake as much as you want, host chocolate night at our house, and get as many horses as you want."

"Oh, boy," someone said behind them, and a smattering of laughter moved through the crowd.

"I thank God every day that He allowed us each to get out of our own way and start living our lives together instead of apart. I'm grateful you forgive me, and I'm glad I have you to set me straight when I feel crooked."

His emotions surged again, and Mission tucked his card away, as he didn't need it. He lifted his free hand toward the mountains and then took hers in his. "I love you. Yeah, that's it. I love you, and however many dances the Lord gives us, I'll take them all."

Her eyes shone with unshed tears, and she cut a quick glance at Pastor Benson, who gestured for her to go ahead with her own vows.

She looked at him again, and Mission grinned at her, so glad his part was over. "Mission," she said. "Something about you has called to me since the moment we met. It used to irritate me to no end, and I thought it was because you were arrogant and rude."

He ducked his head, though he'd heard all of this before.

"But being quiet is not the same as being arrogant. Being

knowledgeable and speaking the truth doesn't make you rude. You have taught me so much about how to be myself, and I love that you live a life according to exactly who you are."

She released his hand and reached up to wipe the corner of her eye. "I promise to love you for exactly who you are, because I know you're doing that for me. I want to bake and bring home horse rescues and sit on the rooftops and watch the sun go down."

Mission met her eyes, wanting all of those things too.

Kristie wiped her eyes again. "And I know you'll let me bake when I'm happy, and when I'm sad, and when I'm upset, and I think you're going to regret letting me have as many horses as I want."

Mission chuckled and shook his head.

"I've loved dancing with you for the past year, and somewhere in there, I've learned the steps to peace. I promise to hold that with you, to follow and to lead, to love you in the wide daylight and the narrow night."

Mission couldn't stop smiling, because those promises were beautiful, and they both looked back to the pastor.

"That was wonderful," he said. "Let's do the most important thing, shall we? Then we can move on to the second most important thing—dinner."

Mission laughed again, quickly sobering when Pastor Benson said, "Kristie Jenise Higgins, do you take unto yourself, Mission Hawkeye Redbay, to be your legally and lawfully wedded husband? And do you give yourself unto him to be his legally and lawfully wedded wife, in honor, trust, and fidelity, as long as you both shall live?"

"I do," Kristie said, not a hitch of hesitation in her voice at all.

The pastor turned toward him. "Mission Hawkeye Redbay,

do you take unto yourself, Kristie Jenise Higgins, to be your legally and lawfully wedded wife? And do you give yourself unto her to be her legally and lawfully wedded husband, in honor, trust, and fidelity, as long as you both shall live?"

"I do," he said, relieved he hadn't stuttered or sounded like he'd swallowed rusty pennies.

"Then, by the power vested in me by the state of Colorado and the Good Lord Above, I pronounce you husband and wife." He lifted both hands toward the corners of the tent. "Everyone, Mister and Missus Mission and Kristie Redbay."

He smiled for all he was worth and gestured for Mission and Kristie to seal their union with a kiss. Mission pulled her flush against him and pressed his lips to hers as the crowd whooped and hollered and applauded.

Their adrenaline rushed through him, and when he pulled away, he tucked Kristie against his side. "Our first dance," he shouted over the still-cheering crowd.

Oh, and the country music, which suddenly blasted its way into the tent. He grinned at her, and Kristie smiled right on back.

Then he took her hand and they danced their way down the aisle in perfect time to the song they'd danced to at the Summer Stroll last year.

thirty-six

Opal Crow sat on her front porch, her precious Mari snuggled into her chest. She patted the baby's bottom, though the little girl had been asleep for the past thirty minutes.

Her parents should be here any moment, and Opal's pulse skipped though the scene surrounding her testified of pure country stillness.

Blue sky, rich earth that Tag had just overturned this past week in preparation for planting season, a gentle breeze through the new leaves that had just come back to the trees.

"It's a beautiful day, baby," she whispered to her infant daughter. "Daddy will be home soon, and Grandma and Gramps are coming today too."

Opal looked down the lane, expecting to see her father's big, black SUV. He'd traded in his truck for something a little easier to get into, and now that her parents were leaving the harshness of the Wyoming winters, they didn't actually need a pick-up.

They did need single-story living, with accessible entrances and exits. They'd been staying in the cabin where Tag had once lived while they'd been in Ivory Peaks previously, and their house sat over around the bend from the stable where Gerty kept her rescues.

They didn't want land of their own, but her parents had paid for the construction. They'd be closer to Mike and Gerty than Tag and Opal, and that was okay with her too.

She was just thrilled they'd listened to her and Mike and decided to move here. "Now, we just need Uncle Easton and Auntie Ali."

Her younger brother lived and worked back East, and he and Allison had two children. Opal missed them, and she pulled out her phone and sent them a quick text, all with only the use of one hand.

Honestly, since Mari had been born, she'd gotten so good at doing everything with only one hand.

"Hey, honeybee." Tag stepped out onto the front porch and swept his lips along her hairline. "They're still not here?"

"Not yet." Opal tossed another look down the lane. "You're done already?"

"Gerty wanted to get back to the house to start dinner." He sighed as he sat on the rocking chair opposite of her. "She's really out." He gazed fondly at their daughter, and Opal had never seen a more devoted daddy than Tag.

"Yeah." Opal reached to un-strap the sling. "I'm getting hot. Do you want to go lay her down?"

"Sure."

Opal passed the baby to Tag, who made no move to get up and take their daughter down the hall to her crib to finish her nap. In fact, he snuggled the baby and laid his head back, his eyes drifting closed as if he'd join Mari in her afternoon siesta.

Opal couldn't be unhappy about that, and in fact, her heart-strings thrummed with pure love for her husband and daughter. She stayed in that moment for a few seconds, pure gratitude filling her for the good things God had given her.

Then she rose to her feet and swept her fingertips through Tag's hair. "I'm going to go start the ice cream."

His eyelids fluttered open. "All right, honey-darlin'." He grinned up at her. "You want to kiss me first?"

Opal grinned at him. "I was hoping you would ask." She leaned down and touched her lips to his, getting lost in the simplicity and perfection of her life.

She left them to snooze on the porch, and she went into the kitchen to get the ice cream base out of the fridge. She poured it into her electric freezer, plugged it in, and pressed a button to get it going.

It didn't take ice or salt, but froze the bowl as it turned. She'd told Gerty she'd bring dessert to dinner that night, and then they'd all go over to the build site to see how the house was coming along.

She'd just put a sheet pan of blondies in the oven when the front door opened and the quick wail of Mari entered the house. Opal automatically looked that way and found her daddy holding and shushing his granddaughter.

Joy leapt into the back of her throat. "You're here." She quickly set the timer on the stove and went to greet her momma. "Mm, you're later than I thought you might be."

"Oh, your daddy had to stop for a hamburger." She hugged Opal tightly, and tears pressed into Opal's eyes for some reason.

Her hormones still felt a little out of control these days, and she told herself she was just so excited for her parents to be so close. She stepped back and smiled at her mom. "Is Hillie still there?"

"Yes," Momma said. "And still a flirt." She threw a glance

over to Daddy, who paced in the kitchen, his mouth bent close to Mari's ear as he whispered something to the baby. "Your dad eats it right up." She shook her head.

"She wasn't flirting with me," Daddy said from the kitchen. He hadn't even looked over to them, and Opal grinned at him. He wore his ten-gallon cowboy hat in his customary black, a pale yellow polo, and jeans.

Opal had never known her father as the power-suit who ran the family company as the CEO. To her, he'd always been super devoted to his family, present for everything, wise, and her biggest champion.

She moved over to say hello to him, and she found Mari's dark eyes wide open, staring up at her grand-daddy. She sucked on her pacifier, and her calm, sometimes a little too quiet, demeanor reminded Opal so much of Tag.

He'd followed her parents into the house, and now he stood in the kitchen, looking at the stovetop. "Honey, this timer isn't on."

Opal's gaze flew to him. "Shoot. Take it down a couple of minutes, and start it for me, would you?"

"Yep." Tag started doing that, and Opal turned her grin on her father.

"Did you bring me anything from The Burger Babe?"

He lifted his eyes to hers, and oh, she found his usual mischief there. "We're eating dinner at Mike and Gerty's."

"And yet, you stopped."

"We stopped for lunch," Daddy said.

Opal glanced over to the clock on the microwave. "Daddy, it's three-thirty."

"That's because he couldn't stop accepting rounds of applause." Momma joined them and started to take Mari from Daddy. "My turn, Wes. You can take Opal and Tag and get the car unloaded."

Opal smiled at her mother as she melted into complete Grandma mode.

"Oh, hello, my beautiful girl," she cooed to Mari.

"She can eat anytime," Opal said. "There's breastmilk in the fridge. It's fifteen seconds in the microwave."

"Mm hm." Momma moved over to the recliner in the living room and eased into it.

"There might be an earthquake in a few minutes," Opal said.

"Okay," Momma said.

Daddy started to laugh, and Tag shook his head as he smiled. Opal shook her head too, and she moved over to Tag. "I think they brought some things we'll need your muscles for."

"Non-essentials," Daddy said. "Christmas stuff, and winter clothing."

"And we're just putting it in the cabin?" Tag asked.

"Yeah, Mikey said we can use it as a storage shed." Daddy grabbed onto Tag and hauled him in for a hug. "I didn't even say hello to you."

Tag chuckled as he clapped Daddy on the back. "I know who you guys are here to see, sir." They both laughed, and Opal's heart filled to bursting to see her husband and her daddy getting along so well.

Of course, Tag got along with everyone, and so did Daddy.

"Let's go," Daddy said. "We filled the SUV to the brim, and Gerty's been texting up with a tempting birria."

Opal let them lead the way out, and she stopped in front of her mother. "Momma," she said. "There's a timer on the oven. When it goes off, you have to get the blondies out, okay?"

Her mother met her eye. "Okay, I can do that."

"The ice cream machine will stop when the ice cream is

churned. You can take the whole bowl out and put it in the freezer in the garage."

Her mom smiled at her. "I can do that too."

"With Mari?" Opal raised her eyebrows. "You don't have to carry her everywhere." She indicated the swing and the sit-and-play. "She loves to stand in that, and if you feed her and put her in the swing, she'll go back to sleep."

"I just can't stand to put her to sleep," Momma said. "She has such beautiful eyes."

Opal smiled at her mom. "Okay, but you have to finish the desserts for me if you want me to go unload your stuff. I told Gerty I'd bring it tonight."

"I can do it," Momma promised, and Opal went to join Tag and her daddy.

Her father drove back down the lane where, a half-mile away, sat Gerty and Mike's expanded farmhouse. The walking circle, the stable, and two barns made up the main epicenter of the farm, with acres and acres of fields surrounding it all.

A half-circle of cabins sat behind the second barn, and that was where Momma and Daddy stayed. Steele and Hazel would live in one too, once they got married next month.

Opal loved this little community on this little farm, and her emotions threatened to overwhelm her again. Thankfully, Daddy didn't turn to go back toward the cabins, but kept driving.

He went through the gate, made a left, and the construction site that Opal walked to everyday with Mari opened up before them.

"Ah, there she is," he said fondly. "It's coming along nicely."

"They're out here workin' on it everyday," Tag said.

Opal had watched them pour the foundation, then put up

walls and attach a roof. Since then, it seemed like not much got done—at least from the outside.

She had to go indoors to see the forward momentum of the build, with sheetrock going up, being taped, and then mudded. The outline of appliances and cabinetry had gone in, but the windows had arrived, and they'd started on the back deck too.

"Only two steps up, Daddy," she said, eyeing the wide, barely-there steps.

"Yeah, and only four inches," he said. "Gray needs something like this."

"Did they decide to move here?" Opal asked. "I never saw the end of that conversation." Opal was a full-time mom and hadn't done much with her medical foundation either. So she definitely had time to keep up with the family texts, though sometimes they came in at a furious pace.

"Yeah," Daddy said. "They're going to come back." He smiled at her in the rear-view mirror, then opened the door and got out. He pulled open her door too, and Opal slid to the ground and stepped into her daddy's arms.

"I'm glad. Then you and Momma won't be alone," she said.

"We'd come without them," Daddy said.

"I know." Opal stepped back and went with her dad toward the back of the SUV. Tag beat them there and pressed the button to open the lift-gate. "But you've loved living in Coral Canyon with your brothers."

"Yeah, I have." Daddy gave her a smile that told her it would be hard for him and Momma to move here. They'd lived in Coral Canyon for over thirty years, and all of Momma's friends were there.

"Uncle Gray's decided to stay until their house sells." Daddy pulled out a duffel bag and handed it to Opal. "The market in Coral Canyon has cooled considerably, so it could be a while."

"But that's okay," Opal said. "Right? I mean, they don't have anywhere to live here either."

"They could stay at the farm," Daddy said. "Or Twilight Fields. They'd have a place."

"Sure, of course." Opal led the way toward the cabin, the grunt of her husband behind her telling her he carried something much heavier than her. "But they want to be on the farm, right?"

"Right," Daddy said. "And the cabins are full."

"Well, they're not full here," she said, an idea forming in her mind.

"They're going to move into the generational house. It's what it's for, after all."

"What about Deacon?" Opal asked, surprise running through her as she dropped the duffel bag and turned back to her father. She didn't think for a moment that Deacon would move into a cabin here to run the farm he owned ten miles north.

"He's the one who'll build himself a new house." Daddy smiled. "We're goin' over there tomorrow for a little bit. He wanted me to help him scope out a plot of land for his house."

"So they'll have two homesteads," Opal said, not really asking.

"Deacon needs it," Daddy said. "And Hunter and Molly still need their house too."

"Hey, I'm all for it." Opal watched as Tag slid the box he carried onto the dining room table. They made a couple more trips from the SUV to the cabin, and then Opal's phone rang.

"It's Momma." She swiped on the call and turned her back on the men. "What's goin' on, Momma?"

She expected to hear Mari wailing, but she didn't.

"I'm just wondering if you have any more of that Mexican vanilla."

Opal's pulse bounced strangely in her chest. "I'm sure I do... why?"

"Oh, I thought the blondies needed a few more minutes, and well...."

"You burnt dessert."

"It just got away from me, and there's time to make another batch."

Opal sighed and shook her head. "Are you holding Mari?"

"It's fine," Momma said. "I've made thousands of brownies in my life."

Opal suppressed her sigh, suddenly wondering if she could survive having her parents living so close.

Of course you can, she thought. She loved her parents and wanted them here for as long as God would let her keep them.

If only her mother could take blondies out of the oven when the timer went off. But did it really matter? Opal had more butter, brown sugar, and yes, Mexican vanilla.

"The vanilla is that slim cupboard between the microwave and the fridge, Momma."

"Oh, that's right."

Opal heard some scraping, but Mari once again made no noise. "

"Yep, here it is."

"Remember, Momma, it's stronger, and you don't have to use as much."

"Right," her mom said, about the same way she'd promised to take the dessert out the first time. "Thanks, Opal."

Mari squawked then, and Momma added, "Oh, she must finally be hungry. Gotta go."

The line went dead, and Opal lowered the phone and looked at it. "Unbelievable," she whispered.

"Everything okay, honey?" Tag looked at her phone and then her.

"Yeah." Opal watched as Daddy pulled out a rolled-up rug and hoisted it onto his shoulder. "Baby, go help him with that."

Tag looked over to her father, then took off at a jog, calling, "Wes, let me do that."

Opal sighed and ran her hands through her hair. "Really, Lord? Is this what I'm dealing with now? A father who thinks he's half his age, and a mother who's so distracted by a baby she can't pull blondies out of the oven?"

If so, Opal wouldn't have it any other way—and she really couldn't wait for her parents to be here permanently, and now, for Uncle Gray and Aunt Elise to join them.

After all, Momma and Elise had been best friends for decades, and surely that would soothe Momma a little bit.

thirty-seven

Hunter Hammond pulled up to The Burger Babe and killed the engine. "You ready?" He looked over to his son, who'd had his head bent over his device for the entire drive from the farm to the burger joint.

Ryder's thumbs flew over the screen, and then he looked up. "Yeah."

"Maybe we should leave your phone here." A certain measure of weariness moved through Hunt,

Ryder frowned. "I'll participate appropriately." He opened the door and jumped down from the truck. "Besides, it's lunch with your brothers and sister. I don't know why I'm here at all."

"You're here, because your mother needs a break from babysitting an eighteen-year-old." Hunt's irritation with his son spiked, and he followed Ryder out of the truck. He slammed the door behind him and strode around the front of the vehicle. "I want the phone on silent, and I don't want you to huff, sigh, or check it every fifteen seconds."

He must've spoken with enough seriousness, because Ryder

blinked, the fight in his shoulders deflating. "Okay," he said, and he silenced the phone and stuck it in his back pocket. They faced the burger joint together, and Hunter exhaled slowly to get his frustration in check too.

"Did Momma really say she needed a break from me?" Ryder asked as Hunter stepped up onto the curb.

He shot a look over to Ryder. "Buddy...yeah. Okay? Yeah. You stress her out with your insistence that you and Clementine aren't going to break up, that you're late all the time, and that you can't seem to do the few simple chores she asks of you."

Ryder wore a hint of worry in his expression. "I don't mean to do that."

"Really?" Hunter pulled open the glass door and cocked his eyebrows. "If you didn't mean to be late to dinner, you'd be on time. If you didn't mean to cause us grief over your girlfriend, you'd break up with her. If you wanted your mother to worry less, you'd feed the chickens, pick up Lisa and Charlotte on time, and clean out the stalls you're being paid to clean out."

Ryder glared at him now, and he'd just started past Hunter when Tucker called, "Hey-o, boys."

Hunt grinned at his younger brother. "Hey, you." He laughed as he detoured over to Tucker and hauled him into a hug. "You live so far away, and I feel like I haven't seen you in so long."

Tucker laughed too, and he hugged Hunter hard. He possessed all of their daddy's height, just like Hunter, and they grinned at one another as they parted. "We've been really busy with that agricultural specialist we hired. She's got us doing all kinds of soil tests and water purification."

He looked over to Ryder and hugged him too. "Hey, buddy. You're not in school today?" Tuck stepped back and looked at Hunter.

"He has three weeks of school left, and apparently, none of it is important." Hunter shot Ryder a look, who smartly kept his mouth closed.

"Jane's inside," Tucker said. "Deac texted to say he was running a minute or two late."

Hunter nodded, then turned and led the way into The Burger Babe. Sure enough, he found Jane holding down a big corner booth by herself. She sat on the very end of it, and she glanced up as if sensing her brothers' arrival.

They'd met for a late lunch, so the place wasn't terribly busy. Hunter suspected he had about fifteen seconds before Hillie would be out front, causing a fuss over him, so he leaned against the half-wall and called to Jane. "Did you order?"

"Sure did," she called back.

Hunter lifted his hand in a wave and continued toward the ordering kiosk. He'd just tapped when he heard Hillie's laughter.

"Look at you, young man," she drawled, and Hunter glanced over to find her pulling Ryder into a hug. His son knew to go along with it, and in fact, everyone loved Hillie.

"Howdy, Hillie," Ryder said, and Hunter had to abandon his order to hug her hello too.

She hipped him out of the way and tapped with the pad of her finger, her long, red fingernails not getting in the way of her use of the kiosk. "You want the beer-battered fries, baby?"

"Yes, please," Hunter said. "I was putting it in, Hillie."

"Yeah, you sure were," she said. "Tell me what to add, now."

Hunter nodded to Ryder, who came closer and gave Hillie his order. Tucker followed suit, and by then, Deacon had walked in.

Hunter waited out of the way, and once Hillie had tapped in her code and made their food free, he was able to grab onto his youngest brother and hug him. "Hey, is everything okay at the farm?"

"Yeah," Deacon said. "It's just busy this afternoon as we're getting all the equipment out."

"Sure, yeah," Hunter said, though he'd never really run the farm in a full-time capacity the way Deacon did. He'd been the CEO of the family company, HMC, in downtown Denver for seventeen years, and he was now enjoying his retirement at the farm.

They joined Jane in the booth, and she immediately flipped open a manila folder. "At Deac's request, I've made an assessment of the farm, and these are the top three places for his new house." She gave him a quick smile, and love filled Hunter from top to bottom.

It beamed through him, because he loved his siblings, and he loved watching them interact. Of course Jane had made a map. And of course, Deacon had asked her to. And of course, Tucker frowned as he peered at the map, as if he cared where Deac built his house.

Deacon cared, though, and that was what mattered. Hunter had told him to pick anywhere he wanted, and Deacon had rolled his eyes. "Just because I own the farm doesn't mean it's mine," he'd said.

And he'd wanted everyone's input for the location of the second family home on the farm. It had never needed one until now, though Momma and Daddy hadn't moved back from Coral Canyon yet.

"This is a great spot," Tucker said, pointing to the map.

Hunter looked at it and found Tucker's pointer on a cute cartoon clipart of a cabin at the top of the meadow.

"We could put in a short road that leads to the driveway for that one," Jane said matter-of-factly. "And it's out of the way, which I think Deacon will like." She tossed him a look, but Deac wore a fine frown line between his eyes.

"We'll still have plenty of room for our family parties," Hunter said, as the picnic area and pavilion and grills stood down on the other side of the meadow. "Great shade up there."

"Yeah," Deacon said. "I like that spot."

"The others would work too," Jane said, and Hunter spotted another cabin on the other side of the red administration barn. "For this one, we'd put a road curving left where it normally only goes right. Just past that pine tree?"

"Yeah," Deacon said.

"And you'd have some privacy over there," Jane said. "Because there's nothing else. Only fields."

"Some of our best fields." Deacon raised his eyes to her, then Tuck, then Hunter. "I only need about an acre."

"You can have whatever you want," Hunter said, and he meant it. "Deacon, it's a few acres. It's not going to matter in the grand scheme of things."

"I want it to be fair," he said. "And I want you all to know I'd build a house for you on the farm if you needed it."

"But we don't need it," Tuck said.

"We like living a bit further away," Jane said.

Hunter smiled at her. "Does Cord have Clint today?"

"He's out at Gerty's," Jane said. "I'm taking them all French fries and we're having an evening play date with the new chickens Opal got."

Hunter nodded again, glad his family got along so well. He knew not every family had relationships like this, and he knew they took work to develop and maintain.

"I'd do the meadow," Tucker said. "It's close to the family farm, and the cowboy community, while still being wooded, and you'll like that, Deac."

"Yeah," Deacon said slowly. "I don't want to put in a bunch of new roads." He tapped the map over by the admin barn. "This site is out."

"I don't even see the last one," Hunter said.

"That's because...." Jane suddenly folded the map. "It's not a good one. The meadow site is the winner."

Deacon blinked, and Hunter sat back in the booth. Tucker immediately reached for the folder. "I want to see the third site."

Jane pressed her palm against the folder and glared at Tuck.

"Come on, Janey." He grinned, and she released the folder to him.

He flipped it open, and Hunter could've predicted how things would go from here. Tuck would be all nonchalant, find the third site, and make a benign comment on it. This would drive Deacon insane, and Jane would roll her eyes.

Hunter, as the oldest—and sixteen years older than Jane— usually sat back and simply enjoyed the show.

"Huh." Tuck flipped the folder closed and handed it to Deacon. "I see the potential."

Hunter chuckled and shook his head. Deacon didn't open the folder, but Ryder picked it up and opened it.

"I've got the Double Hammond," Hillie said, interrupting them, and Hunter looked up to find her sliding a plate with his hamburger and French fries on it.

"Oh, boy." Hunter reached for the fry sauce in the middle of the table as more food got passed out.

"Anything else y'all need?" Hillie grinned around at all of them, and Jane shook her head.

"Thank you, Hillie."

"Just holler," she said, and she left them alone again.

Ryder had set aside the folder, and he dunked one of his fries in a pool of ketchup. "I think remodeling the old hay barn is actually kind of genius, Aunt Jane."

Hunter's gaze flew to his sister, then the folder sitting closed on the table on the other side of his son. "The hay barn?"

"It's out of the way," Jane said, her voice pitching up. "It has a road to it already. It sits right on the border of the farm and has amazing views."

"It's decently close to the cabin community and family farm," Tuck said.

"But not too close to you and Momma and Daddy," Deacon said.

"We don't need privacy," Hunter said. "Momma and Daddy won't either."

"It might just be nice to have your place be family land," Deacon said. "Because while we'd like to think my house will be too, it's kind of like the foreman's cabin. It's business and personal."

"Sure, I'll concede that," Hunter said. "But Molly and I aren't bothered by the cowboys and cowgirls on the farm."

Deacon lifted his double bacon cheeseburger and took a big bite, his way of saying, *No, I know, but it's still something I've thought about.*

He wiped his mouth, chewed, and swallowed. "Thanks, Janey," he said. "I'll think about it, and we'll get started on the construction in a couple of weeks."

"Who did you hire?" Tucker asked.

"When are Grandma and Grandpa moving back?" Ryder asked.

Hunter looked between him and Deacon, who simply took another bite of his burger. "They're going to list the house and come back when it sells," he said.

"It's listed," Jane said. "It went on the market last Friday, but they're not expecting much."

"Summer's the best time, though," Tuck said, just before cramming three French fries into his mouth.

Hunter took a juicy bite of his barbecue-and-onion-straw burger. Deacon wiped his mouth again and said, "I'm going to have Paul Case be the general contractor. He can start at the end of the month."

He tapped the folder. "I just need to choose a location."

"Well," Hunter said. "I think any of them would work."

"My vote's the meadow," Tucker said.

"I say barn," Ryder said.

"I'm going to go with the meadow too," Jane said.

All eyes came to Hunter, though he hadn't known he'd need to cast a vote. His siblings had always looked to him to state his opinion or pick a side, and he grinned at them.

"Just to put this all on Deacon, I'm going to vote for the barn."

"Great," Deac said dryly. "Thanks so much."

"Hey, at least our lunch was free," Hunter said, and he lifted his burger to enjoy another amazing bite.

"I can't wait to see it," Tucker said. "It's going to be great for the farm."

"I agree," Jane said, and they all looked at Hunter again.

"Yes," he said. "The farm has been stagnant for a while, and this will be great. Deacon's going to modernize everything, and he needs an amazing home to do it."

thirty-eight

Tarr glanced up when the light shifted, a smile coming to his soul when he saw Briar standing there with hot pads on her hands as she held a giant pot of what he assumed to be soup.

"Are you at a good stopping point?" she asked.

Tarr surveyed the floor in front of him. He'd been doing finishing work on his house for what felt like forever, though it had only been a couple of weeks. He wasn't particularly fussy, but installing his own floors and shutters and backyard fencing would save him thousands of dollars, and Tarr didn't mind the work.

"Yeah, let me get to the end here," he said, and he moved down a plank to add another snap-in-place piece to the hard-wood-look-alike laminate he'd been installing. He wore knee pads and a mask over his mouth and nose, as he had to go outside to the back deck to cut pieces of wood, and he didn't want to inhale the sawdust.

"It looks so good, baby," she said as she walked across the front part of the house—which had already been done—to the kitchen in the back where Tarr currently worked.

He finished up the row he was on and took a measurement for the last piece he needed. He wrote it in the pocket-sized notebook he kept on the counter, then swept the mask off his face so he could kiss his lovely girlfriend.

"What'd you make?" he asked. "I didn't even realize it was dinnertime. Tuck had that open house today, and I swear I went back for another sandwich six times." He laughed, though what he said was true.

"Did he sign anyone new?" Briar asked.

"He had almost two dozen people here," Tarr said. "And I think our demos went really well, but I'm not really sure if he signed someone or not."

"How many people does he want to take on?" she asked. "He's already got four."

"Well, another buddy of ours wants to come be a rodeo manager now that he's retired from the circuit," Tarr said. "Tuck thinks he can handle six, and if Myron can too, then he's got slots for eight people."

"Wow," Briar said. "And they're all going to live here on the farm?"

"No, Tuck's given up that idea," Tarr said. "He made that very clear during today's presentation, that the trailer community where Alex and I live is not permanent and is not an option."

Tarr moved over to the sink and turned on the water. It sputtered out, because it had only been hooked up for the past couple of days. He'd been cleaning up over at the arena, because he didn't keep any supplies here at the house.

"I hope you brought bowls and silverware," he said. "I don't have anything here."

Briar blinked at him, and since she hadn't carried in a bag with any bowls or plastic spoons, Tarr took that to mean she hadn't brought anything.

"I'll have something in my car," she said, and she turned to go get it.

While she was gone, Tarr lifted the lid on the pot and found that she'd made one of his favorite concoctions—broccoli cheese soup with chicken. He could slurp this right out of the pot, but he wouldn't want to do it in front of her.

She returned triumphantly, a pair of clear plastic spoons in her hand, but Tarr eyed them dubiously.

"Where did you get those?" he asked.

"Out of my glove box," she said. "They're unused."

"Are they? How would I possibly know that?"

"Oh, my word." She stepped over to the sink and turned it on to wash the spoons. "Now they're clean. Are you satisfied?"

"I'm just saying it's kind of weird to have loose plastic utensils in your glove box."

"It's not that weird when you've eaten out of your car a lot," she said.

Tarr tilted his head at her. "You eat out of your car a lot?"

"I mean, I used to," Briar said. "I'd leave the farm and drive to get something, and then just eat it in my car—especially in the winter—because the sun comes in and it's nice and warm through the window."

Tarr grinned at her and took one of the now-clean spoons. "I suppose we're just going to eat it right out of the pot."

"I don't have any bowls in the SUV, no," Briar said with a teasing lilt in her tone. She went straight into the pot and took the first bite, getting a chunk of chicken and a floret of broccoli with the cream-based soup.

Tarr followed suit, thrilled at this super casual date that Briar had sprung on him. At the same time, they saw each other every night, and he wasn't exactly sure why she'd shown up now, when she could've just waited for him to come over, and they could've had crusty bread and real bowls and spoons.

He watched her for a moment, quickly looking away when her gaze also darted to his. "This is real good, sweetheart," he said.

"Thank you. I wasn't sure if you'd want to come over tonight," she said. "After being down on your hands and knees so much. I know that's hard work."

"Yeah, it is," he said. "But you've got a real nice couch, and Wiggins is over there, so...." He trailed off, giving her a grin, as if he liked her dog more than her.

"I've also been thinking," Briar said. "And I've texted a little bit with Kristie after the wedding. Did you know her parents didn't come?"

Tarr had known that, but only because Tucker told him. "Yeah, I guess they had a falling out a few years ago," he said. "She texted them and invited them, but they said they didn't feel comfortable."

Briar nodded, her mouth tight. "Right."

She took another bite of soup, then twirled her spoon in her fingers. "I've got to be real honest, Tarr," she said. "I'm not sure I can handle that rejection. If I text my mom and dad and they don't text me back, or they say they're not interested...."

She let the words hang there, and Tarr kept his gaze low. Though he didn't dip his spoon in for another bite, he let several seconds of silence flow between them.

"So what are you going to do?" he asked.

"I've been thinking that I'm the one who initiated the distance between us, and I've been okay with it all this time, so maybe I don't need to text them."

Tarr looked at her then, really trying to see if that's how she felt.

"A family isn't always a family just because they're related by blood," she said. "I have you and Tuck and Bobbie Jo." She waved her hand. "And all the Hammonds; they like me, and having my mom and dad here for a wedding would just be super stressful anyway."

"Is that what you're thinking about?" Tarr asked. "Having them only in your life for the wedding?"

"I haven't given much else any thought, no," she said. "And Kristie's parents weren't at her wedding, and it was beautiful and lovely, and she was really happy."

"Yeah," Tarr said. "But you're not Kristie Higgins."

"I know." Briar's voice had turned soft and small, and Tarr hated that. "It's just what I've been thinking," she said. "Because I think if they don't respond, or the response is bad, that it will set me back five years, maybe longer."

"Well, we don't want that," Tarr said, because he couldn't imagine waiting *five more years* for Briar to be ready to marry him. Heck, at this point, he was worried she may *never* be ready to marry him, and he wanted her to continue to be able to heal. If that meant she didn't have her parents in her life, then perhaps that was the right thing to do.

"Why do you think they won't text you back or want you in their life?" he asked.

"I don't know," Briar said.

But Tarr thought she did, and just like at Thanksgiving, he felt like he could push her and get a real answer. "I think you do," he said. "Why can't you just tell me?"

His words maybe came out a little aggressively, but he didn't back down, and he didn't regret the question, because Briar said, "I'm not lovable."

Tarr scoffed. "Oh, come on, Briar. That's just ridiculous."

"Maybe for you," she fired back. "But it's how I feel, Tarr. I don't—" She cut off and made an angry sound. "I'm not like you, okay? I've never had anyone love me just for me. My mom and dad loved me because of what I could do and the fame that I could bring them, and my fans loved me for my performances, and the other rodeo cowboys I dated loved me because I had curves, and they thought they could take advantage of me."

"Wiggins loves you," Tarr said.

"Wiggins is a *dog*," Briar practically shouted.

"Tucker and Bobbie Jo love you," he said.

Briar's jaw hardened.

"I'm just not sure that I can take the rejection," she said. "They let me go so easily, and I don't think they want me back in their lives."

"But you don't know that," Tarr said. "You made it hard for them to find you."

"Did I?" she asked. "How many people do you know named Briar?"

Tarr had only ever met her. "Well, I think you're totally lovable," he said.

"But I'm not," she said back, and she seemed determined to argue with him today. "And just because you feel like that doesn't make it true, and it doesn't mean that I can automatically flip a switch and feel like other people can love me."

Tarr wanted to throw his plastic spoon as far as he could and knock over the pot of soup, because Briar felt further than ever from being able to be with him long-term. Sure, they spent time together every day, and he held her and he kissed her, and they talked about their favorite TV shows and the animals on the farm and *his* dreams and goals—but not hers. Never hers.

The anger boiled in his stomach along with the soup she'd brought, and he really wished he could just go back to work and hammer out his frustrations and disappointments. She was essentially rejecting him in this moment, and Tarr honestly had no idea what he'd been doing for the past six months.

No, he thought. *The past year and a half—you've been dealing with this woman, trying to get her to see something in you that maybe doesn't exist for eighteen months, cowboy. Or maybe it does exist, but she's not ready to be with you.*

"Well," he said, "I know for a fact that you're lovable." He looked right into her eyes, finding every angry fleck and defiant edge. "Because *I'm* in love with you, Briar, and if you're not lovable, what does that make me? A fool? Hopelessly romantic? An idiot?"

He shook his head. "If you're not lovable, why do I love you?"

He reached up to swipe his hat off his head, then realized that he wasn't wearing it. "I'm the biggest moron on the planet, thinking that you can change enough to want to be with me."

"Tarr," she said.

"It's fine," he said. "It's fine."

He looked at the pot of soup and at the stupid plastic spoon in his hand. "I'm gonna take a walk, and then I'll come back and finish my floors. Thanks for the soup, Briar."

He tossed the plastic spoon onto the countertop, where it clattered, mimicking the shattering sound of his heart as he turned on his heel and started for the front door. He unstrapped the knee pads as he went, and he stalked right past Wiggins, who lay in the spot of shade on his front porch that the setting sun had started to illuminate. For the first time in Tarr's life, he didn't reach down and pat the dog and tell him how wonderful and smart and handsome he was.

He simply left his house—this site that was supposed to be a place of comfort and refuge for him—and started walking down the dirt road that led toward the highway, an empty landscape in front of him, just like he now had a blank future waiting for him too.

thirty-nine

Briar stood on Tarr's front porch and watched her dog trot down the street behind him. Wiggins caught up to her boyfriend—ex-boyfriend now?—easily and settled into an easy walk at the cowboy's side.

Tarr didn't move in an angry way, and he hadn't gotten in his truck and driven away.

Briar looked down at the kneepads she'd collected as she'd followed Tarr outside. She breathed out, everything inside her that had tightened and gotten boxed up during her conversation with Tarr now deflating.

I'm in love with you, Briar.

Tears pricked her eyes, and Briar moved to the top step and slumped to a sitting position. She looked down the road where Tarr had gone, but she couldn't see him anymore.

"What just happened?" she asked herself and the blue-blue sky surrounding her. She'd spent the afternoon making one of Tarr's favorite soups, because he'd been working so hard to finish his house. He wanted to move into it desperately, and

Briar had thought if she brought him dinner and just sat with him, he'd be able to keep working on the floor installation.

She should've known he'd question her about her decision not to try to make contact with her parents. That was what Tarr did, and Briar didn't hate it. Sometimes, his questions helped her iron flat her own thoughts and feelings, and she'd been able to find her way through the maze of them to what she should do—or not do.

"I don't want to be rejected by my own blood," she whispered.

But being rejected by Tarr was far, far worse.

He has to come back here, she thought, and part of her wanted to get behind the wheel of her SUV and just start driving. It didn't matter what direction she went in; she just needed to go.

She stayed put, because Briar didn't want to run from Tarr. He did have to come back here, and Briar wanted to be there when he did.

She wouldn't run, and Tarr had promised he wouldn't abandon her. She checked the road again, her pulse increasing in volume in her ears. He had walked away, but she told herself that everyone deserved a few minutes—or an hour, whatever—to clear their head.

Tarr had given her so much time, in so many instances, to gather her thoughts, or defer a hard conversation she didn't want to have. She could give him whatever he needed.

"He's not a fool," she said to his house. "He's hardworking, and smart, and loyal."

With her spoken words, a new door opened in Briar's heart, then her soul. "Tarr is loyal."

And not only to Tucker and Bobbie Jo, or his rodeo brothers, or the animals he cared for and trained.

Tarr had been nothing but loyal and true to Briar herself.

"I can trust him." Her voice rang with truth, and tears rushed into Briar's eyes and right down her face. She wasn't sure if she'd been holding herself back from trusting Tarr, but she'd never realized or acknowledged that she did, in fact, trust the cowboy.

"A cowboy." She scoffed, but she couldn't look away from the dirt road where Tarr had last been. Yes, she trusted a cowboy, and a former bull rider at that.

"Miracles do happen," she whispered, and she leaned over her knees and cradled her head in her arms as she closed her eyes. "Lord, I need more miracles, please."

Even if she didn't deserve them, she prayed that God would give her the words she needed to explain everything to Tarr. She prayed God could give him a forgiving heart. She begged the Lord to provide a way for her and Tarr to find their way back together.

"We could be a family together," she said. "Me and him, and then neither of us are alone, and it doesn't matter where our blood comes from."

Kristie had said something similar when Briar had talked to her about her parents not attending her wedding. She lifted her head and navigated to those texts now, needing the reassurance of them.

Honestly, Kristie said. *It was a much better wedding without them there. If they had come, it would've been so stressful, and I would've been on-edge the whole time.*

They'd chatted a little bit about that, and then Kristie had said, *I'm not sure I made the right decision by reaching out to them. They know where I am, and they can reach out to me any time they want—and they don't.*

Briar's situation wasn't exactly like Kristie's, especially since her parents didn't know where she was. They didn't have her phone number. For all they knew, she'd fled the continent and could be anywhere.

She sat there with those thoughts, the way she had in the past, trying to find how she felt about these facts.

She arrived right back where she'd been before bringing up this topic with Tarr. "I don't miss them," she whispered. "I know that's sad, but I don't. I don't want to be the Briar I was in Canada. I can't go back, and I don't want anyone from that time of my life in this chapter of it."

Her resolve to not reach out to her parents solidified, and Briar wasn't doing it out of spite or hurt. "Or preservation," she murmured. It simply felt like the right thing to do, and she knew that sometimes those things morphed and shifted as time went on. So what felt right today might change in five years, or ten, or twenty.

When Briar thought that far ahead, she saw herself on this farm, with a dog, and maybe a cat, and all of Bobbie Jo's goats.

And Tarr?

"Yes," she said as the picture came into clear focus. "Yes, Tarr is there with me. I'm with him."

She closed her eyes and let the fantasies roll through her head as if someone had made a movie of her future just for her.

Do you love him?

That question rolled through her body and soul, and Briar tried to riddle through the complicated emotions, former promises she'd made to herself, and miles of fear to find the answer.

She wasn't sure, but as Tarr's words filled her ears again— *I'm in love with you, Briar. I know you're lovable, because I love you* —Briar decided she didn't have to know the answers to every question that entered her mind.

She knew she wanted Tarr in her life long-term. She wanted

him to be her family. She didn't want to be alone anymore, and more specifically, she wanted to share every aspect of her life with none other than Tarr Olson.

Now, she just needed him to come back so she could tell him.

forty

Tarr rode in the saddle of his personal horse, a pretty black and white mare named Skunk. She cut like a champion, and while Tarr didn't use her for real cowboy activities, she'd been a loyal friend and amazing horse for roping in the rodeo as well.

She was tall and strong, and Tarr hadn't ridden her enough this winter. Now, with the fields in front of him looking so much like the Texas range where he'd grown up, Tarr could function on autopilot, letting Skunk wander where she wanted to wander.

Tarr's thoughts did the same thing, and he simply breathed in the fresh air, glad April had finally given way to May. It would likely rain a lot this month, but Tarr would take rain over snow any day of the week.

Besides, he'd be moving into his house next weekend anyway, and then the weather could do whatever it wanted. He'd have a solid roof over his head, and a functioning furnace, air conditioner, hot water heater, and full-sized appliances. The wind could blow, and the rains could lash the windows, and Tarr would put on his slicker, his cowboy hat, and get in his truck—parked in a garage.

A smile touched his face, because he'd missed having a garage more than anything else about living in a permanent structure.

Plus, he knew Tuck wanted the trailers gone from the side of the arena, and Tarr didn't want to annoy his best friend for any longer than necessary.

After all, Bobbie Jo's parents were still in the mansion, despite Tucker and Bobbie Jo's efforts to help them rent or buy somewhere else. Heck, Tuck had even offered to build them their own little cabin down on the main highway.

Tarr hadn't heard what the final decision was on that, and he made a mental note to ask Tucker—not that he usually had to ask. Tuck would text him, vent everything out, and Tarr would find a way to make everything okay.

Right now, he turned Skunk back toward the farm, the dotting of goats in the distance giving him the picture-perfect view of his small-town life. He sighed, because he couldn't be unhappy with views like this, and yet, Tarr was the most unhappy he'd ever been.

A sting ran through his bloodstream, making every vein and vessel constrict painfully. Every breath hurt his lungs, because it expanded them against his bleeding heart.

"You're so stupid," he muttered to himself. Skunk picked up the pace, probably sensing his shift in mood and not liking it. He shushed her, wishing it would calm him too. He had to be in the right frame of mind to train and work with horses, and Tarr seriously wanted to pack a bag and leave the farm for a little while.

"That's not going to work," he told himself. He'd gone and

fallen all the way in love with her, and he'd have to deal with the consequences of that.

His phone vibrated in his hoodie pocket, a garment he'd grabbed out of the barn before climbing into the saddle and going for this ride. He pulled it out and swiped on the call from Tuck. "Hey," he said, and his voice sounded somewhat normal. Guarded, maybe, but normal.

"Hey, where you at?" Tuck asked, and Tarr detected something in his friend's voice.

"Riding Skunk," he said. "Why?"

"He's out riding," Tuck said, obviously not to Tarr. "Okay, just wondering."

"You're just wondering?" Tarr's irritation spiked. "Why? It's not like I give you a minute-by-minute itinerary of my day."

"I thought you'd be at the house, laying down the floor," Tuck said. "I stopped by to bring you...." He trailed off, and Tarr really wanted him to continue. He remained quiet, though, because Tucker couldn't stand silence.

After only a moment, he sighed loudly. "Fine, I came by to bring you those gross spicy hot Doritos you like, because Bobbie Jo found them at the gas station on our way home from what could finally be 'the one' for Jim and Linda."

He paused only long enough to suck in another lungful of air. "It's a nice little condo. Anyway, we have the chips, and I don't want them in my house, so we stopped by your place. And I found a big pot of soup on your countertop, your truck in the driveway, and the house empty. I was worried."

"Aw, thanks, Tuck," Tarr said with a smile. "But I'm fine."

"Are you alone?"

"Do you think Briar would be out here riding with me?" Tarr chuckled, the sound definitely darker than he wanted Tuck to hear. He'd tried to get Briar to go horseback riding with him, and she'd declined forcefully enough for him not to ask twice. She claimed to have gotten back in the saddle a time or two, but she much preferred keeping both feet on the ground, feeding goats, and throwing a ball for Wiggins if they both got too restless.

Tarr craved the wide open sky, nothing but the rush of the breeze in the leaves in his ears, and his own wits to try to center himself and find a way through the busyness and noise of life to the path he should be on. He'd like it even more with his beautiful Briar at his side, but he quickly shook his head, cutting off the thought.

Briar wasn't his, not truly, and she probably never would be. She wanted to belong to herself more than to someone else, and Tarr would have to figure out what that meant for him.

"I mean, I don't—" Tuck cut off again. "I have you on maps, so I can keep an eye on you. When do you think you'll be back?"

"I don't know," Tarr said, the fight blowing right out of him. "I was going to try to finish the flooring in the house tonight, but I'm tired."

"It's not a big deal," Tucker said. "Another few days in the RV isn't going to matter."

Tarr tried to hear what Tuck really meant between the words. "You hate the trailers."

"Yeah, but it's a few days," Tuck said. "We've had Bobbie Jo's parents living with us for months, and I've learned that I can do anything for a few days."

Tarr smiled again. "Are they any closer to finding their own place?"

"You mean are me and Bobbie Jo any closer to finding them their own place." Tuck didn't phrase it as a question. "And yes, as a matter of fact. We went to look at a house this afternoon;

that's why we stopped by the gas station and then your place on our way home."

"Maybe you need my house more than me," Tarr said, an idea popping into his mind. "Her parents can have it, and I'll find somewhere else to stay—not the RV."

"Tarr—what?" Tucker scoffed. "Why would you do that?"

"It's summertime now," Tarr said, though the lower the sun sank in the sky, the cooler it got, definitely telling him it was not summertime. "I can rent somewhere nearby and just commute to and from the farm. Isn't that what Alex is going to do?"

"Yeah," Tucker said slowly. "But Tarr, buddy, you bought that land from me. It's yours, and not even part of the farm anymore."

"Yeah." Tarr sighed like what Tuck had said was a major wrench in his life plans. "All right, well, I'm going to go out to that meadow that Bobbie Jo keeps for the hottest part of the summer."

"Did you eat?" he asked. "That soup pot—I couldn't tell if Briar had left it for you or if you'd eaten before...."

"I'm fine," Tarr said again, giving Tucker zero details. "You've got me on maps, and I'll be back before dark."

"All right," Tuck drawled, and Tarr let him end the call. He turned Skunk toward the meadow on the northeast side of the pasture where he currently rode, not quite ready to go back yet.

He wanted to see Briar desperately, while another part of him hoped he'd never run into her again. His heart flipped over in his chest, and his stomach twisted. No, he'd be devastated if he never got to see her again. Even a glimpse of her from a distance might be enough for Tarr.

"You're delusional," he whispered to himself, and then he set her out of his mind and tried to enjoy the farm the way he wanted to, as Tarr Olson, a man who wore his emotions on his face, said too much, pushed too hard sometimes, and had just had his heart broken by a woman who'd made it very clear to him from the first moment they'd met that she might never be able to be truly his.

"Hopeless romantic," he muttered now. Yes, that was what he'd become, because he believed that God could change people. That people could change themselves. That, for him, Briar could—and would—change.

But maybe she never would.

That doesn't mean she's not worth loving.

The words sat there, and Tarr let them filter through him letter by letter, and by the time he reached the meadow, he felt calmer than he had in a couple of weeks now. Still unhappy, but somehow calm about what had happened at his house earlier.

Tarr sat up from where he lay in the longer grasses growing along the tree line, his heartbeat pumping hard against his breastbone. Hoofbeats. He'd heard them, and it didn't take him long to blink and see a pretty palomino walking toward him.

Briar rode in the saddle.

Tarr scrambled to his feet, his stomach dropping to the soles of his cowboy boots at the same time his hopes shot toward the moon.

Briar wore the same thing she'd had on at his house: jeans, a long-sleeved shirt the color of the sky, and her hair back in a ponytail. She didn't have a pot of soup, or her dog with her, though Wiggins perked up from where he'd been curled into Tarr's side.

He yawned, stretched into a play bow, and then trotted over

to greet his master. Tarr stayed right where he stood, not quite sure what to make of this situation.

"Can I join you?" Briar asked when Party Girl—the horse she rode—neared Skunk. The two equines seemed to turn canine as they stretched their necks toward one another, as if to get a good sniff of the other.

Tarr couldn't speak, so he simply gestured in a flap of his hand, as if to say, *I don't own this meadow.*

Then he settled back onto the ground, laying flat on his back and looking up into the dusky sky, the way he'd been doing before the hoofbeats had alerted him of her presence. He heard her slide out of the saddle, murmur something to Wiggins, or maybe Party Girl and Skunk, and then the grass rustling as Briar walked through it.

She made no noise as she sat only a few feet from him, and Tarr actually closed his eyes. "I was coming back to the house," he said.

"I know," she said. "You left your keys and took my dog, so I knew you'd be back at some point."

"Your dog came with me of his own volition," Tarr said, just because he didn't feel like bending to Briar in anything. "I didn't ask him to come, and I certainly didn't *take* him."

"My mistake," she whispered, and she sounded so broken that Tarr's heart squeezed and instant guilt swept through him. "Tarr, I'm really sorry."

"Me too," he said. "It's okay, Briar. Not everything works out the way we want it to, and it's okay."

She sniffled, but Tarr remained steadfastly on his back, his eyes now squinched closed. It wasn't his job to make her feel better. Heck, *she'd* caused this rift between them, and while Tarr hadn't broken up with her, he didn't see how they could stay together either.

"Just say it," he said. "You like me, *but*. We could be so good together, *but*. It's fine, Briar. I can handle it."

"I'm not going to say that," she said.

Tarr pushed himself up onto his elbow and found Briar sitting with her legs crossed, plucking at the grass in front of her. "Why'd you come out here then?"

"Your front steps are hard," she said, lifting those gorgeous blue eyes to meet his gaze. "I couldn't stand the thought of you out here by yourself, thinking…whatever you're thinking about me."

"I get to think what I want."

"Yeah, I know." She gave him a glare, then softened as she sighed. "I came out here to tell you I trust you implicitly."

Tarr blinked, his mouth falling open for a moment as if he might say something, then realized he didn't have a response to that.

"You're the first person I've trusted in years," she said. "And I know it's not the same as 'I love you,' but for me, it's pretty dang close."

Tarr sat all the way up, his pulse now bobbing in the back of his throat, that stupid hope cascading through him like water rushing over cliffs. "What are you saying?"

"I don't want to break up with you," she said, back to plucking at the grass again. Wiggins lay over by the horses, who had really struck the jackpot in the snack department this evening.

"When I imagine my life in a year, or five years, or a decade, you're there." She lifted one shoulder in a lazy shrug, almost like she couldn't get it to go any higher. "You're with me, and I'm with you, and we're—" She swallowed. "We're family, Tarr. Me and you."

Tarr wanted that more than anything.

"I don't know if there are children or not," she said. "And I don't know if we're in that house you're finishing up, or on this farm, but when I close my eyes, and I think about it, there's you. And there's me, and my mind stops there, because that's all I need."

She looked at him again, and Tarr saw the love shining in her eyes, whether she said it out loud or not. "*You're* all I need, Tarr."

He wanted her to go on, but his mouth couldn't stay straight. He grinned, bellowed a noise filled with joy, and catapulted himself at her.

"Hey," she protested as he wrapped her up in his arms, both of them falling back to the grass behind her. "Tarr, you animal."

He laughed, shifting to cradle her against his chest. "You trust me," he whispered, his lips skating dangerously close to the soft skin along her neck.

"Yes," she gasped.

"You want a future with me."

"I do."

A question he'd asked her before came into his mind. "So can you see yourself living with me in that house I'm finishing up?"

"Yes." Her voice came out like a ghost wafting through the air, unanchored to anything.

Tarr touched his mouth to her neck then, stealing a kiss in his favorite spot. "Sounds like love, sweetheart."

She didn't say anything, and Tarr kissed his way up to her ear, then across her cheekbone. He pulled back and found her eyes closed lazily as she accepted his kisses. When he didn't go on, her eyelids fluttered, and she opened her eyes and looked directly into his.

"I can't say it yet," she murmured. "Because I don't think

I've ever loved anyone, Tarr, and I need—I need a minute to figure out how it feels, so I can name it."

"You love Wiggins," he said.

"He's a dog." She gave him a smile. "You're a cowboy."

Tarr grinned down at her. "So we're not breaking up."

"No."

"And I'm not a fool."

"Well...." She laughed as he blinked and then sobered quickly. "No, Tarr. You're sweet, and amazing, and far too good for me."

"That's just not true," he said. "But I meant what I said in my cabin, though I maybe said it a little roughly."

"Yeah?" Briar's eyebrows went up. "What did you say back in the cabin?"

"I said I was in love with you." Tarr said it strongly, because he did feel it, and he did know it, and he wanted her to feel and know it too. "You are lovable, because I love you."

Tears filled her eyes, but she managed to give him a faint nod.

"And I don't care if you don't want to text your parents. I just want you to be happy," he said. "I don't want you to regret not having them at our wedding, and I would move any mountain and lasso any moon to get you what you wanted. So if you want me to text them, I will. If you want me to take you home to Calgary to get married, then that's what we'll do."

"I don't want either of those things."

"I just don't want us to not talk about things," Tarr said, running the tip of his nose down the side of her face. "I have to know what you're thinking, and I have to be able to ask you questions without you getting too frustrated with me."

"I didn't mean to do that," she said.

"I didn't mean to get so irritated and hurt either," he said. "I don't want to walk away from you."

"Taking a moment to clear your head isn't the same thing as walking away," Briar whispered. "Can I ask you a question now?"

"Sure," he said.

"If we're not breaking up, when are you going to kiss me?"

Tarr grinned at her again, chuckled, and then lowered his mouth to hers and kissed her with all the passion and love he possessed for her.

forty-one

"Are you sure we're okay?" Briar touched her lips to Tarr's again, despite the fact that his phone had vibrated against her side for the third time in as many minutes.

"Yeah, I'm great." Tarr kissed her again, sliding his mouth along her jaw and then over the delicate bones along her collar. "Tuck is going to send out a search party, though." He finally pulled away, and Briar reached up and ran her fingers through his hair.

"Tarr?"

Since she'd been outside all through sunset, her eyes had adjusted to the darkness gradually, and she could see him just fine. Of course, Tarr sort of blended into the night, and oh, how she loved that about him.

"There are so many things I love about you," she said. "How you seem to be able to say whatever's on your mind, how you're so good with horses, how you kiss me." She remained straight-faced, and he stayed quiet. "Is that the same as being *in love* with someone?"

"I don't think so, sweetheart," he said. "Because I'm fond of how Bobbie Jo loves her goats so fiercely, but I'm not *in love* with Bobbie Jo."

Briar nodded, the back of her head grinding against the hard ground. "Maybe if I list the things I love about you every day, there will come a time when I recognize that I've fallen in love with you."

Tarr rolled to her side, his fingers still twined with hers. "There's no—I don't want you to feel any pressure, my thorn-filled Briar. You'll know when you know."

"But we're good?"

"You said you envisioned your future with me, and I know you can't see your own face, but I could." He spoke softly, reverently, as if he didn't want to scare the stars away by speaking too loud. "And when you said that, I could see that you love me, so yeah. I'm good, and if you're good, then we're good."

She lay there on her back, her eyes searching the skies, as his words sank into her soul. He could see the love she held for him on her face—and that never happened. Perhaps it was a new thing about her that she hadn't discovered yet. She could hide almost all of her emotions, but apparently, not love.

A smile touched her lips, and then she rolled too, put her palm on Tarr's chest, and pushed herself up. He groaned in an over-exaggerated way, and curled into himself. "Let's go," she said. "We already have to ride back in the dark, and Tucker's going to lose his mind."

"I'll text him." Tarr stayed on his side, curled up, as he pulled out his phone. The screen lit up his face as he texted quickly, and then he sat up and got to his feet. "We can walk back," he said. "The horses will just come with us."

He bent to pick up his cowboy hat, which he reseated on his head, completing the vision of the perfect cowboy silhouette against the rising moon. "Or can you ride in the dark?"

"I used to be able to ride upside down and with my eyes closed," she said.

"Yeah, but on a trained horse," he said.

True, she thought. Stunt-riding horses trained for years, and they were as important as the girls who rode them. They had to hold steady lines, with a constant clip, never missing a step or leaning too far.

Briar had loved her stunt horses with her whole soul, and a powerful wave of nostalgia and missing flowed through her as she joined Tarr at the horses. "I can ride," she said quietly, telling him she was ready to take another step forward in her healing.

She'd already come so far, but getting back in the saddle—literally—was something she'd never really felt like she needed to do.

Until Tarr hadn't come back to his cabin, and Briar couldn't stand the thought of not talking to him for another moment. She'd gone over to the arena, assuming he'd be there, since he hadn't taken his truck.

She hadn't found him, and she'd returned to Tarr's with a heavy heart. Only a minute later, Tuck and Bobbie Jo had pulled up, a big bag of Doritos for Tarr.

Tucker had called Tarr for her, and Briar had become a master in gesturing and mouthing words, so Tuck wouldn't give away the fact that it was her asking after Tarr. He'd seemed truly surprised when she'd arrived, so she'd had one minor success today, at least.

"Tarr, baby?" She slipped her hand in his as he finished checking his horse's saddle.

"Mm?" He drew her into his arms and pressed his lips to her forehead.

"I'm really sorry about earlier," she said with every ounce of sincerity she could muster.

"You already said that."

"Yeah, but I think you forgave me too fast."

He chuckled. "Is that something someone can do?"

Frustration flared inside her, but she tamped it down. "I just want you to understand that I'm really sorry. I wasn't just saying it. I feel it throughout my whole body. I don't mean to be so snappy with you, and I don't mean to be so ineffective at communicating. I *am* working on myself, and I *will* get to the point where I can look you straight in the face and tell you I love you."

She pulled away and looked up at him. "Okay?"

"Okay." His mouth barely moved as he spoke the word. "And hey, I think you just said it." His lips curved up into a smile, and he lowered his head to kiss her. Briar stayed in that moment, standing in the darkness within the safe, comforting circle of Tarr's arms, the stroke of his mouth against hers, and his body heat combining with hers.

She wasn't sure what love felt like, but she strongly suspected it felt just—like—this.

* * *

Briar eyed the three-story office building made of off-white stone. Various business names and logos sat up near the roof, and she saw the one she'd come for.

Premier Family Counseling.

Her heartbeat stuttered in her chest, but Briar turned off her SUV and reached for her purse. She'd left the farm early today, after telling Bobbie Jo why she needed to leave. She'd driven herself here. She'd planned to get lunch for her and Tarr on the way home from their favorite gourmet hot dog joint.

She wasn't going to back out now, when all she had to do was walk inside and give a receptionist her name.

Tarr had offered to come with her to her first therapy session, but something about it felt too...intimate to her. She wanted to be able to talk freely—maybe even about him—and in the end, Briar had decided she needed to handle this appointment herself, from beginning to end.

She waited behind someone on a knee scooter, as the first floor housed a foot and ankle clinic, and then she stepped over to the elevator and pushed the button to go up. The counseling office waited for her on the third floor, and Briar pushed through the pristine glass doors easily. She approached the counter there, where a young woman probably five years her junior beamed up at her.

"Good morning," she said. "Name?"

"Briar Prescott." She pulled her purse across her body. "I had a referral from my primary care physician." She plucked the card from the front pocket of her bag in case she needed it.

"Yes, I see that...Doctor Filigree?"

"Yes," Briar said. "I have an appointment at eleven with Doctor Margrint."

"Yep." The woman looked up at her. "Have you been here before?"

Briar shook her head and pressed her lips together. This receptionist wasn't the therapist, and Briar could tell the doctor about how nervous she was once she got called back.

The receptionist leaned over and picked up a clipboard. "We have all our first-time clients fill this out." She handed Briar a pen and offered a smile.

Briar couldn't bring herself to return it. She hated paper-work, because the doctor wasn't going to look at it. She'd still make Briar say everything out loud anyway, but she hurried through it and returned the clipboard back to the receptionist before retaking a seat in the waiting room.

Her nerves ran through her unbridled, and Briar found herself biting on her fingernails. She forced her hands back to her lap, and thankfully, a woman with lovely auburn hair opened a door, looked right at her, and said, "Briar?"

She stood and went with this new woman, who had to be closer to forty than Briar was. "We're right here," the woman said. "This is Doctor Margrint's main office, as she's just finishing up with a group session in the conference area." She smiled at Briar as she moved past her, and Briar noticed she didn't come in the room after her.

Instead, the woman loitered in the doorway. "Feel free to look around. There are snacks over on the counter to your left, and drinks in the little fridge underneath there. Doctor Margrint will be right in; shouldn't be more than five or six minutes."

Briar gazed at the huge floor-to-ceiling windows in this office, and the door had nearly clicked closed before she remem-bered to say, "Thank you."

Gorgeous landscapes of the Rocky Mountains hung on the walls, and Briar gazed at them with joy singing through her soul. The doctor had a large, raw-edge wooden desk in front of the windows, but the whole left side of the office felt more like the waiting area she'd sat in with Tarr before their couples' massage.

The snacks, the ice water with sliced cucumbers in it, the mini-fridge filled with bottles of sparkling water, Gatorade, and Diet Coke.

Briar almost didn't dare to touch anything, but she admired

the gold lamps with cream shades, and the dark mahogany bookshelves that held novels instead of Doctor Margrint's textbooks.

Several seating options waited for Briar, and she chose a chaise, the way she would've at the spa. A blanket lay over the arm of it, and she slid off her shoes and covered herself with it, really sinking into the cushy furniture and sighing out her worries.

"Briar," a woman said, and Briar practically jumped out of her skin. "Oh, don't get up." A brunette strode toward her, her navy pants clearly made from high-quality fabric as they swayed around her legs like dark water.

She arrived at Briar's side and squeezed her shoulder. "I'm Doctor Margrint, and I'm so glad you found something comfortable for you."

"This is such a nice place," Briar said.

"I try to make it as inviting as possible." She moved over to the windows and pushed a button. Shades started to lower, and the lamps came on as the room dimmed. "I hope this is okay. I find the light to be so harsh near midday, and I want us to have a relaxing, calm first session."

"It's fine," Briar said. "I really have no idea what to expect. I've never been to a counselor before."

"Are you nervous?"

"Yes," she admitted. "I barely like talking to people I know." She laughed lightly, though she wasn't kidding.

Doctor Margrint smiled a real smile, and that put Briar further at ease. "So tell me why you decided to come see me."

Briar tried to find the words that would sum up the thirty-one years of her life. How did one do that in only a few sentences? Would it sound like she was making excuses? She didn't want to do that—she needed to own her own culpability for the person she was, and the life she currently lived.

"That's a big question," Briar said. "So I guess I'll just start with the most basic thing: I'd like to learn how to love myself. See, I have this amazing boyfriend who loves me and wants to marry me, and I don't think I'm lovable. So I have a hard time believing the things he says, and I want to get to a place where I can and do believe him—and that I know what it feels like to be loved, and to love another person."

Doctor Margrint didn't scoff or smile at her like she was simple. She nodded, made a note on her tablet, and looked at Briar again. "There's a lot here, so let me start with this. Do you think you can't recognize love?"

"I can for horses and dogs and friends," she said. "But romantic love?" She shook her head. "I've never experienced it, and I've actually had quite a few bad experiences, so...."

The doctor looked at her tablet again. "This says you were a professional stunt rider for years."

Briar's throat closed, though she knew she needed to go through this conversation to find closure to the stunt riding. "Yes," she said.

Just think of Tarr, she coached herself. *You're doing this for yourself, so you can be with Tarr.*

Buoyed by that thought, she opened her mouth and started telling the story of the woman she used to be...in the hopes that she could find the things still infecting who she was now and preventing her from becoming who she wanted to be.

forty-two

Tarr rounded the back of the truck and lowered the tailgate, still whistling softly. "Last load, buddy," he said to Wiggins, who'd followed him out of the cab. If only the dog could help carry in some boxes.

He grinned as he pulled a couple of bins toward him, then groaned under the weight of them as he settled them in his arms and started toward his new house.

He'd been delayed in moving in for an additional couple of weeks, but he'd moved his RV to the cement pad that ran along the side of his house and into the backyard, where he still needed grass and a fence.

"And once I get that fence in, bud, I'm going to get you a doggy friend to play with." He grinned at Wiggins, who *totally* understood what Tarr was saying.

He labored up the seven steps to his front porch, which he'd stained himself, and through the open front door. His air conditioner pumped against the rising heat of the May morning, with

June only a week away. Tarr loved summer in the Rocky Mountains, and he loved that he could stand on his back deck and see those peaks against a sunset every single evening.

Right now, the house felt like a bunch of scattered pieces that needed to be gone through, sorted, and put together. He'd pulled everything out of storage, packed up his belongings in the RV, and had purchased plenty of new items for his new home too.

"Incoming," he said, and Briar looked up from the box she was currently elbow-deep into.

"There's room on the table," she said quickly, and Tarr quick-stepped past the end of the couch and into the dining area at the back of the house. He slid the boxes onto the surface, instant relief rushing through his shoulders and back.

"Wow, that was too heavy for me."

"Someone's gone soft since his rodeo days."

Tarr found her smiling at him, and she radiated so—much —life. She lifted her hands out of the box, a pair of crystal clear glasses in her possession. "I've almost got your new dishes put away," she said. "Do you want a tour of your own house?"

"Yes, ma'am." He joined her on the other side of the island, happy to listen to the sound of her voice as she detailed where she put his bowls, plates, and plastic containers for leftovers. She had a reason for all of her placements, but Tarr didn't much care. He simply loved being with Briar, and talking to Briar, and inhaling the peachy floral scent of Briar.

She'd started counseling a little over a week ago, and she went to town three times a week to talk to a therapist. Tarr still recognized her as the blue-eyed beauty who'd snapped at him with all the strength of a crocodile, but she'd come even more alive since starting her sessions.

He hadn't asked her what she spoke with her counselor

about, choosing instead to let her lead those conversations. She'd told him about the first session, detailing how much she liked the office and the staff, and that the doctor had made her feel like she could say anything and not be judged.

"We started at the beginning," she said, and she hadn't said much else after that. Tarr himself was still learning bits and pieces about Briar and her past, though he supposed the same could be said for anyone he knew. Heck, sometimes he thought he knew himself better than he did, and something would come up and he'd have to evaluate what he wanted to do, the person he wanted to be known for, and how to proceed.

Tucker had signed two new cowboys from his open house event, one of them the reigning champion in calf roping.

"I need you to work with him, Tarr," Tucker had told him. "You'll get seventy percent of his fee, but dude, you're better than me with a rope—heck, you're better than him, after being gone from the circuit for a couple of years."

Tarr could still see the pleading in Tucker's eyes.

"He elevates our whole facility," Tuck said. "And he signed, because you're here."

"Fine," Tarr had said. "But Tucker, I'm retired."

"Sure, you are," Tuck had said easily. "You're not riding the rodeo. You won't have to go to rodeos."

"Really? As his roping coach, I won't be required to travel?" Tarr did not believe his best friend for a moment, and he met Briar's eyes as she looked up at him from a drawer in his cabinetry.

"So, what do you think?"

"I think it's all amazing," he said, wrapping one arm around her waist.

"I think you're distracted." She gestured with one open palm toward his kitchen. "Where are your plastic zipper bags?"

Tarr looked blankly down his pale blue cabinetry—which he'd painted himself, thank you very much. "Um, I'm sure they're in a drawer."

Briar scoffed. "I literally showed them to you fifteen seconds ago." She toed the drawer in front of them. "They're right there, and I asked if they'd be too low."

"They're great there," he said.

"What were you thinking about?" she asked.

"Tucker and Stetson," he said. "I need you to be really firm with me, sweetheart. I don't want to travel the circuit."

"No traveling the circuit," she said. "Got it."

"Like, throw a fit. Threaten to quit at the farm. Tie me to my bed frame. Anything. I do not want to travel with Stetson. Tuck can advise him while they're on the road. I can watch film and give advice over the phone."

Briar giggled. "I'm not going to do any of the above." She raised her eyebrows at him and turned back to the now-empty box that held the glassware. "Tie you to the bed frame. Do you hear yourself?"

He tipped his head back and laughed too. "Maybe I'll throw a fit and threaten to quit."

"I'd like to see you do that." She grinned at him and broke down the box with her bare hands. "Now, what else have you got for me to do? I promised Bobbie Jo I'd go look at some new lambs with her this afternoon."

"You're going to go look at lambs?" He surveyed the wreckage that was his house, with boxes and bins everywhere. "I'm in a crisis here, honey."

She took a step back and cocked her hip. "Throw a fit about me leaving, then. Let me see what that looks like from you, and if it's good enough, I'll stay."

"Good enough?"

"You'll need practice if you think you can throw a fit about traveling with Stetson in a convincing manner." Her eyes glittered like sapphires, and Tarr counted her as his single greatest blessing.

"I'm the luckiest man in the world, you know that?"

"Is this part of your fit?"

He smiled and shook his head. "You're my favorite person ever."

"Stop it."

"I won't," he said, taking a step closer. "When I wake up, my first thought is of you, and I love it. If I catch a glimpse of your blonde hair shining in the morning sun out in the Goatel, my whole day is made. When you let me stop by your office with lunch, and then we take an extended lunch hour, it gives me enough oomph to get through the afternoon."

"I'll show you some oomph," Briar said dryly.

He took her into his arms. "I love you, my thorny Briar." Tarr leaned closer and breathed in the scent of her skin and hair and neck. "Tell me your truth for today."

With the two of them swaying slightly, Briar wrapped her arms around his back too, and Tarr loved the way she melted into his chest, into his whole soul.

"My truth for today is that I like putting together someone else's house."

"I really appreciate you coming to help," he said.

"You're easy on the eyes," she said, and Tarr chuckled.

He still had plenty more to get out of the back of his truck from his latest trip to the storage unit, and he reluctantly stepped back. "Well, the storage unit is empty, but I still have a handful of boxes in Tuck's garage." He rotated his shoulder. "So I better get back to work."

"Before you go," Briar said, and she picked up another box

from the floor. It held new silverware, and was the last thing she'd unpack before the kitchen would be complete. She picked up a pair of scissors and knifed right into the box with them.

"I love your enthusiasm for this new house," she said, her eyes only flicking to him for a moment. Tarr leaned against the counter and tucked his hands into his pockets, enjoying this part of the day where Briar told him the things she liked about him.

No, the things she *loved* about him.

He'd told her she didn't need to do that, but her therapist had thought it a great idea too, and Briar had committed to telling him a few things—no set number—each day until she ran out of things to say.

"I love your beard right now, all trimmed up and nice." A smile came to her face as she lifted out a stack of butter knives. "I love the way you smell after you shower, and I love it when you smile at me like you're happy to see me."

"I'm always happy to see you, sweetheart."

Briar looked fully at him then, and he gave her that smile she liked. She returned it and nodded. "I love helping you put this part of your life together, and I love that you've asked me to help you with something in the future that you know is going to be difficult for you." She drew a deep breath and abandoned the silverware to face him fully.

"I'm wondering if I can ask you for the same favor."

"Go for it," he said, his pulse suddenly skipping around in a nervous jump-hop-leap pattern that made no sense.

"I know it might not make sense to you, but I'm still a little scared of...us." She gestured toward him like he was the problem, but Tarr knew her well enough now to know she didn't mean it badly. "Namely—I need to be specific."

She took another breath. "Namely, I'm scared of the proposal." She nodded and rolled her eyes. "That sounds even more ridiculous when I say it out loud, but it's the truth."

"You're worried about...me askin' you to marry me?"

"Yes," she said.

"We've talked about getting married a bunch of times now."

"Yes, we have." Briar went back to the silverware, the metallic clinking of it joining the conversation. "I can do that. I want to marry you, Tarr. I want to dance with you on our wedding night—and I want to be married in the spring-almost-summer, and I do want an evening wedding."

"Good to know," he said, because this was new information for him.

"I can think about the future here with you, and I even *dream* about it." She sighed, the sound wistful. Tarr could admit he liked hearing it, because he'd like Briar there in his house with him that night.

Tomorrow. Every day until forever ran out.

"I can see the ring on my finger. That's something else I'm working on with Doctor Margrint. Visualizing things before they happen; then I'm not afraid when they do happen." She finished putting the silverware in the white holder in the top drawer of the island and faced him again.

"But I don't know what the proposal will be like. I can't see it, and it feels scary because of that."

Tarr nodded even as disappointment cut through him. "Will I never be able to surprise you with anything?"

A line appeared between Briar's eyes as she thought about his question. "I think I'll get better and better with it," she said. "But I'm going to ask you to help me with this thing. Will you please just give me some warning about *when* it will happen?"

Tarr studied her, trying to figure out why the timing of it mattered so much. He also didn't like how she needed a *warning* to say yes to being his wife. He still had a lot to learn about Briar, and that thought comforted him.

She didn't want to get married for at least another year, and Tarr had the time both of them would need to start their life together on the best possible foundation.

"Do you need to know how? The details of it?"

"Funnily enough, no." Briar turned away from him again, tossing the mangled silverware box into another bigger one with other trash and broken down boxes. "For some reason, not knowing when it's going to happen is freaking me out."

"Well, I haven't even bought a ring yet," he said. "I thought maybe me and you could go shopping next weekend, after I'm moved in, and Bobbie Jo has her new lambs, and all of that."

Briar reached for the scissors and cut open one of the boxes he'd brought in from the storage unit. Tarr hadn't done much of anything since bringing in the bins still sitting on the dining room table, and he wished she'd stop working.

She wouldn't, and Tarr had learned that she operated better if she had something to do with her hands and eyes while she talked about things that were difficult for her.

"These are towels," she said.

"They go in the hall closet," he said. "Briar, honey, talk to me about going ring-shopping next weekend."

She looked at him then, and Tarr raised his eyebrows. "I should have the fence in by then, and I wanted to go to the animal shelter too. Since I can't pick a dog without you, you'll have to come with me, and I thought we could stop by that custom place by the Maven's."

Briar nodded. "Can we go to Maven's for lunch after?"

"Maybe dinner," he said. "It's a vacation-schedule day on the farm, and I don't want to get up any earlier than I have to." He grinned at her. "You're okay with a custom ring?"

"Yes," she whispered.

"It might take them a couple of months to make it," he said. "So there wouldn't be a proposal for at least that long."

A slip of relief ran through her expression, and Tarr tried not to take it personally. "That's okay, I think." She took a step toward him, and then another. "Is that okay with you?"

"Sweetheart, you know I want you here right now." He let her take his hand, the feminine touch of her skin against his welcome and wanted. "I'd take you to City Hall this afternoon and make you mine. You could move all your stuff in here this weekend, and we could start our family with each other tonight."

She blinked, her eyes wide and filled with vulnerability.

"You do know that, right, Briar?"

"Yes," she whispered.

"I love you," he said. "I'm not the one who needs the wedding, or the engagement, or the time. I'm happy to give you anything you want—the wedding you want, the engagement you want, the time you need. Heck, I'd tear this house down and live in the RV while I rebuilt it to your precise specifications if that's what you wanted."

Her eyes turned glassy, and she sniffled.

"I'd give you the world if I could," he whispered. "And I will do whatever I can to make sure you're happy, and cared for, and that you feel absolutely loved. Okay?"

She nodded, and in that moment in time, Tarr really thought she believed him.

He drew in a breath and hauled Briar against his chest. "You don't need to worry about a proposal until probably August or September, honey. And yes, I'll let you know beforehand, all right?"

"I love your sexy Texan drawl when you say, 'all right?'"

Tarr smiled and stepped back. "How much time do you need? Like, do I need to tell you a week out? A couple of days? What are you thinking?"

Briar laid her head against his chest and breathed in with him. "Honestly, Tarr, now that I know it's not for a couple of months, I feel—great. Maybe I don't need to know more than that."

He ran his hands up and down her back, his palm stopping on the side where she'd been injured. He covered it and pressed in. "You don't need to keep unpacking for me, honey. You've been on your feet too long."

"My back and hip are aching a little," she admitted. "And I still have to go back to the Goatel."

"Let's go," he said. "I'll give you a ride over there." He took her hand in his, and they left his house together. Soon, it would be *their* house, and Tarr tipped his head back into the near-summer sky and once again thanked the Lord for His bounteous blessings.

"I love the blue sky," he said.

"I love the scent of dirt at this time of year," she said back, continuing the game they played sometimes without him having to nudge or remind her.

That made his heart swell with love for her too. "I love your hair when it catches the sunlight."

"I love the fact that Bobbie Jo is getting more lambs."

He chuckled. "I love steak."

She rolled her eyes. "If that's your way of asking me to dinner at a nice steakhouse, then yes, I accept. If it's just you making our fun game less fun, then lame."

Tarr laughed, sending the sound up, up, up into the atmosphere. "A steakhouse date sounds awesome," he said. "I love that God put me here on this farm at the same time as you."

Briar beamed up at him, and Tarr felt like he'd just scored major victory points. "I love that, Tarr. I love that God brought you here to the farm while I was living here too."

She hadn't told him she loved him, but Tarr knew she would soon. Very, very soon.

forty-three

Briar gazed into the ring case, the diamonds all glinting back at her with such pretty faces. "I feel like this is way beyond me," she said.

"Oh, come on, sweetheart," Tarr said from a few paces down. "You've worn crowns before." He flashed her a smile, and Briar tucked it away inside her heart.

"Okay." The man who'd been helping them bustled up with a velvet-lined tray in his hand. "I've got the pink diamond, with the princess setting, in the white gold here." He slid the tray onto the glass case as Tarr joined them.

"This won't be the right size, and it's more ornate than you want, but this will give you a good idea of what the cut looks like, in that color." Grayson lifted the ring pinched between two fingers.

Briar pulled in a breath as the diamond caught the overhead light and flung it around the shop. "I really like that." She leaned into Tarr as he put his arm around her. "The pink diamond and the cut."

She did not like the extra diamonds all clustered around the large middle one, but this wasn't her custom ring.

"And the white gold is nice," Tarr said. "Since you don't like yellow gold."

Briar hadn't known that until she'd walked into this shop that she didn't want to wear anything shiny and gold on her finger. But she'd had a violent negative reaction to it, and she'd been listening to her gut and instincts more and more lately.

"How do you feel about the size of this diamond?" Grayson asked.

"It's too big," Briar said. "It makes sense on this ring, because it's like…a whole garden of gems. But I just want one diamond."

Grayson wore a dubious look. "Let me show you some of our simpler pieces, now that you know the shape of the princess cut." He stepped over to another case and asked a woman there for several pieces.

She brought them over and Briar listened as he pointed out a simple cluster of diamonds that would look nice with the pink princess center gem. She tried to imagine how they'd look and couldn't quite do it.

She pointed out her favorites, answered the questions, and an hour later, Grayson and his assistant had a digital mock-up of her potential wedding ring. It rotated in 3D on the computer screen, and Briar sighed and sat back.

"I love it," she said. "Tarr?"

He looked up from his phone, a frown sitting between his eyes. "Sorry." He stuffed his phone away and met Briar's eyes. "Tuck's already talking about me going to San Antonio 'just for a couple of weeks' to go to some training."

He blew out his breath. "It's nothing."

Briar laced her fingers through his and squeezed. "I think

this might be the ring." She nodded to the screen, glad when Tarr's expression cleared and he leaned forward to peer at it.

"Yeah, that's real nice, sweetheart."

Him and that drawl. Briar loved it, and she loved his patience with her, and she loved sitting here in this shop with him.

Then Grayson said the price, and, "We're about seven weeks out right now."

Tarr lifted up onto his left hip and pulled out his wallet without blinking, but Briar's breath had caught in her throat. "Tarr," she managed to say.

He paused in pulling out his credit card. His eyes narrowed slightly. "What's wrong?"

"He said twelve thousand dollars," she hissed. "I don't need—"

"An engagement ring isn't about need, sweetheart." Tarr smiled at her and handed Grayson his card.

"We can do three payments," he offered.

"Just do all of it," Tarr said. "And seven weeks is just fine too."

Briar swallowed hard, trying to get all the words she wanted to say to go back down. Tarr wouldn't want to argue with her in front of others, and she didn't want that either. She knew he had money, and she managed to wait until Tarr had his receipt, a tentative delivery date, and they'd left the jeweler before she couldn't hold back any longer.

"Have I ever told you that I have a...significant amount of savings?" Briar laced her arm through Tarr's and kept her attention facing forward.

"No, you haven't," Tarr said just as casually. "I mean, I assumed, what with your career and all, but no. You've not said much about it."

"I nearly lost everything," Briar said. "My last boyfriend claimed to also be a financial planner, and I think that was the first time in my life that alarms went off in my head and I actually listened to them."

Briar didn't like revisiting her past, but it wasn't nearly as painful now as it had been in the past. "I broke up with him, and I managed to get my money out of his control before he spent it, or stole it, or moved it."

She released her breath and stepped in front of Tarr. "I just have to say it."

"I wouldn't expect anything less, sweetheart."

"Twelve thousand dollars is a ridiculous amount of money for a ring."

Tarr tilted his head in that annoyingly sexy way he had. She heard him ask, "Is it?" in his gorgeous voice before he actually asked it.

She cocked her hip right there on the sidewalk, only steps from Maven's. They weren't going to eat next anyway, as Tarr hadn't realized the animal shelter was doing an adoption event that day and wouldn't be open afterward.

He'd looked up the one on the south side of the city, and they were driving there next.

"Sweetheart, it's a token of love. It endures all things, and it's a power that nothing else can compete with. It's not about the diamonds or the gold or the shape or the cut. It's about me telling you, *I love you,* every time you look at it. It's about you thinking, *he loves me so much,* every time you slip it on your finger."

Tarr reached up and swiped his cowboy hat off his head, ran his fingers through his hair, and put himself right back together. "Love needs a token, and I will pay any price to give you the one you love most, so that every time you see it or feel it on your hand, you'll know that it's a symbol or *our* love." He added a smile to his statement and pulled his keys out of his pocket. "Now, can we go get my dog?"

Briar watched him for a moment, and then another one. The emotions running through her felt heavy and light at the same time, and they sparkled with nothing but joy upon joy upon joy.

And she now knew what loving a really, really good man felt like.

"I know it's a long drive, but—"

"I'm in love with you." Briar practically shouted over him. He fell silent, and actually stepped back, his eyebrows now riding high on his forehead.

Briar swallowed, but this time it wasn't to keep words down but an attempt to steady herself so she could say what teemed beneath her tongue. Down in her chest. In her heart. Everywhere.

"I love you, Tarr Olson," she said, her voice cracking on his last name. "And I can *feel* it, and I know what it is, and it's—it's —it's *incredible*."

Tears streamed down her face, but Tarr laughed right out loud and wrapped her up in his strong cowboy arms. He spun her around until she was laughing too, and when he set her on her feet, the world stayed tilted for only a single moment.

Then she looked into Tarr's eyes, and everything became absolutely right. Her chin shook, but her resolve and her feelings remained rock solid.

"I love you," she said again.

"Yeah, you do." He kissed her, laughing at the same time, and pulled away. Then Tarr sobered, gathered her close, and pressed his cheek to hers. "I love you too, honey."

forty-four

"Look at that, baby." Gerty pointed up, though she'd been cradling West and they'd both been looking up into the dark summer sky for the past ten minutes.

The firework exploded—finally—and sheer gold sparks formed into what Gerty had grown up calling "witch's hair."

"It's the witchy one, Momma."

Gerty shifted, her sciatic nerve uncomfortable on this metal bleacher, despite the blanket and pillow Mike had brought for her. "Yeah," she said amidst the patriotic music blaring over the crowd.

Mike moved too, supporting her from behind, the way he had been all night. But they couldn't lie on the lawn the way they had in past years, and they couldn't make their annual trip to Coral Canyon to celebrate the Fourth with Mike's aunts, uncles, and cousins.

Gerty was due with her second baby in only two days, and she'd never been more uncomfortable. Another round of fireworks filled the air, this time filling the sky with red, white, and blue sparks as the song ended.

The unmistakable tightening across her belly made Gerty gasp. She automatically reached and clamped her fingers around Mike's forearm, and he leaned down. "Mike," she gasped as families around them *ooh*ed and *ahh*ed at the next round of cascading sparks.

This could not be happening. Perhaps she'd just felt the baby move.

"Are you okay?" Mike practically shouted in her ear.

Gerty released her grip on his arm and turned to look at him. His dark eyes scanned her face with the same intensity she'd seen during their most serious discussions.

"What's wrong?"

"I think I just had a contraction."

Panic ran through Mike's eyes. He blinked. It cleared. "Okay," he said, and he started getting to his feet. "Let's go."

Gerty had to move as he did, and she stumbled to her feet too. A white-hot pain shot across her stomach and around to her lower back. "Oh," she groaned, and that was definitely a contraction.

"Momma," West complained. "Why you movin'?"

The music started to crescendo, and along with it, so did the fireworks being shot into the sky.

"We have to go," Mike said loudly, and he scooped West into his arms. "Leave everything, Gerty. My parents can get it."

"They're down on the lawn," she said, her breath coming quickly.

Others in the crowd turned their way, and Mike said, "Sorry, everyone. My wife is going into labor. Can I get a path cleared?" He gripped her arm this time, and because he'd spoken in his CEO voice, people actually did what he said.

They cleared a path. In fact, one man went ahead of them, calling out, "Make way, please. This man's wife is going into labor."

"Good luck, honey," one woman said, but Gerty had gone face-blind. She pressed one hand to her belly and kept the other knotted tightly in Mike's.

They'd just reached the end of their row when another contraction hit, stronger this time, and Gerty doubled over slightly, one hand pressed to her rounded belly.

"Come on, sweetheart," he said. "We need to get to the truck." He looked up the aisle to the top of the bleachers, which they'd walked down to their seats. The parking lot sat up there too, and Gerty did some quick calculations in her head.

You can't stay here, she thought, and with that, she took the first step.

The same man helped keep the steps clear, and by the end, he was also gripping Gerty's other arm and helping her step up.

"Maybe your mom can take West," Gerty gasped when they finally reached the top.

"There's no time," Mike said. "He came so fast, Gerty. We have to go now."

She remembered how fast West had come, and people said second babies came even faster. But her water hadn't broken yet, and she set her jaw and kept putting one foot in front of the other.

She made it to the truck; Mike strapped in West while she let the stranger help her into the front passenger seat. "Thank you," she managed to say before another contraction stole her breath.

"Yes, thank you so much, Steven." Mike shook the man's hand and ran around the front of the truck.

"How do you know him, Daddy?" West asked, because Mike

seemed to know everyone. Well, at the very least, they knew him.

"We met him tonight, buddy," Mike said, shooting a glance over to Gerty. She pulled her seatbelt across her body, but Mike just put the truck in reverse and backed out of the stall.

"Maybe we'll beat the traffic out of here," he said. "Can you imagine if we got stuck in the flow of people leaving the fireworks?"

Gerty pressed her eyes closed, that awful scenario entering her mind. "And I was worried about getting snowed in with West," she said, her breath coming quickly. "I thought a summer baby would be easier."

Mike chuckled, because yes, all of Denver was celebrating the Fourth of July two days early—tonight, a Friday, when they could stay up late and sleep in tomorrow. Otherwise, they would've had their town celebration on the Fourth, and everyone would've had to go to work the next morning.

Mike had given the entire company at HMC the next two weeks off. No emails. No online meetings. No texts. "Plastic will still be here in two weeks," he'd said, and this was an initiative he'd started implementing every summer for the past few years.

All employees had paid time off for two weeks in July. The building turned into a ghost town. No one was even allowed in —not even security guards.

"Daddy, why you drivin' like that?"

Gerty grinned, because West was the ultimate backseat driver. He had to know everything too. *Who was that man, Daddy? Where are we goin', Momma? How much is a dollar? Can I get a puppy for myself like Max and Boots? I'm so good with dogs, Momma.*

"Because, buddy," Mike said. "Momma's gonna have the baby tonight."

"Finally," West said, and that got Gerty to giggle a little bit, despite the situation. "What are we gonna name this baby?"

He sounded so much like his father that Gerty opened her eyes and looked over to her husband. "What a great question."

"No, the great question is whether or not I can deliver this baby in the backseat of this truck." Mike slowed at the same time he spoke, and the next thing Gerty knew, they'd come to a complete stop behind a line of cars.

"What is this?" she asked.

"The fireworks are over," Mike said. "And this is the other side of the arena. They're out already."

Gerty blinked at the red, red, red tail lights in front of her, her panic rising like the ocean at high tide. "Mikey," she whimpered. The word turned into a moan as her belly tightened again —and her water broke.

She sucked in a breath and swung her attention to Mike. "My water just broke."

Mike gripped the steering wheel with both hands, kneading the solid surface as he stared at her. Then he looked out the windshield and said, "Call Opal Hammond."

He really needed to update his contacts to include Opal's new last name. She and Tag had been married for almost two years now, after all.

"Calling Opal Hammond," his truck said back to him.

"What are—?" Gerty yelped as Mike swung the wheel violently to the left.

"Hang on," he said. "West, buddy, hang on, okay?"

Gerty pressed one hand to the top of her baby bump—really a mountain—and reached for the handle above the door with the other. "Mike," she gasped.

"We can't wait," he said, and he laid on the horn as he went up and over the curb, the height of the truck and the width of the tires making it easily.

Other people honked back at him, but Mike obviously didn't care. Behind her, West started to cry, and Gerty twisted to reach one hand toward him. "Baby," she said, wiggling her fingers. "Westy, honey, look at Momma."

His dark, sad-scared eyes would've inspired tears in anyone, and Gerty's hormones had been all over lately. Her eyes filled with tears too, but she said, "Hold my hand. Daddy's in control, and he's going to take good care of us."

Gerty trusted her husband explicitly, and she kept her eyes on West's as Opal finally answered the phone. "What's goin' on?" she asked. "There's one more song at this concert."

"Gerty's gone into labor," Mike said as the wheels bumped over something. Gerty hoped it was something like shrubs, because any other alternative wasn't pleasant. "We're trapped in some traffic I'm trying to get us out of, and I might need that crash course in emergency delivery now."

Opal said nothing, which really spoke volumes.

"Hold on, guys," Mike said. "I have to go over another curb." He gunned the accelerator first, and the bumps this time were definitely bigger than before. It felt and sounded like the truck had just lost a bumper or a hubcap, and Gerty couldn't hold back the cry that flew from her mouth.

"Okay," Mike said. "We're fine now."

West wailed out another cry, and Gerty squeezed his hand.

"Westy, we're fine," Mike said firmly. "Hush up, now, okay? We're okay."

Gerty nodded at her little boy. "We're okay."

West nodded and sniffled as he started to calm. "Why you cryin', Momma?"

Gerty shook her head, because she didn't know. "Lots of reasons, baby."

"Where are you?" Opal asked, and Gerty released her son's hand and faced the windshield.

"We just left the rodeo arena," Mike said. "I came out the east side, went over some curbs, and I'm taking the road a bit north."

"I'm getting in the car right now," Opal said. "I'll meet you at the junction of thirty-six and Harrington."

Mike looked over to Gerty. "How far are we from that?"

Gerty shook her head, because she had no idea.

"I can see you on my map," Opal said. "I'll probably be two minutes behind you, because you're moving fast."

"My wife is in labor, and we barely made it last time," Mike clipped out.

"I'll meet you and take West," Opal said. "I'll call the hospital and let them know you're incoming."

"What if the baby comes faster than I can get her there?" Mike asked, and he looked out his side window, almost like he didn't want to face that possibility.

Gerty didn't want to, she knew that.

"Then we'll deal with it at that time," Opal said crisply. "Right now, Michael, your job is to get Gerty and West to the junction at thirty-six and Harrington."

"Okay," he said, and Opal ended the call.

Gerty didn't know what to say, and tension filled the truck as Mike raced through the darkness. Only eleven minutes later, Gerty had had six more contractions, and Mike turned into a dirt lot at the junction of Highway Thirty-Six and Harrington Avenue.

Opal's SUV already sat there, and she got out before Mike had come to a complete stop. She held her phone to her ear, and to Gerty's surprise, she approached her door instead of the back driver's one, where West's car seat sat.

"I'm going to check her," Opal said. "Give you the stats. You're four minutes out?" She tilted her head, her dark eyes in full Doctor Mode. "Eight. My word. Fine. I'm putting the phone down for a minute. Don't hang up."

She tossed the phone onto the dashboard and reached into the truck. "Gerty, how far apart are your contractions?"

"Ninety seconds," Gerty said even as another one started.

"I'm going to lower you and do a quick check." She glanced over to Mike. "Get West transferred to my car, Mikey, and come stand here next to me."

She focused on Gerty again and held up a blanket Gerty had not seen. "I'm going to cover you with this, okay?"

"Opal," Gerty whimpered. "I don't want to do this here."

"I've called an ambulance. You guys are still a half-hour from Denver General, and you have to pass through two small towns also celebrating the Fourth to get there." She wore a fierce expression and spread the blanket over Gerty's chest.

"You only have to lie there, sweetie. I'll do all the work." With that, Opal scooted the seat all the way back and started to lay it down too.

Gerty pressed her eyes closed as Opal worked, and she knew the moment her husband had returned.

"Get my phone," Opal told Mike, and he complied. "She's dilated to a nine, and I can see the baby's head. Where the devil are you?"

Tears slithered out of Gerty's eyes. *I don't want to have this baby at the junction of Highway Thirty-Six and Harrington*, she thought.

"Momma and Daddy are on their way too," Opal said.

"They'll go to the hospital to make sure you have what you need."

"I don't have the baby bag," Gerty said, trying to sit up.

"Tag called your daddy," Opal said. "He's on his way to your house to get it. He'll bring it over to the hospital too."

Pure gratitude ran through Gerty as the night air disappeared under the covering of the blanket.

"I'm going to sit you up," Opal said. "The paramedics will be here in ninety seconds, and I think you can hold off on having him until then."

Gerty had never had ninety seconds pass so slowly, and it seemed to take forever for the ambulance to arrive, even after she first heard the siren.

Two men approached with a gurney, and Opal gave them all the information she had. Gerty let herself get loaded from the passenger seat of her husband's truck to the gurney to the back of the ambulance.

Mike climbed in with her, immediately taking her hand. "We're okay," he told her, leaning over and pressing his lips to her forehead as the IV went into her wrist. "They have all the medical equipment we need."

She looked up and into her husband's eyes. "I like the name Thad the best."

He grinned at her. "And your daddy's name for the middle name?"

She nodded as another contraction rocked through her, the need to push so, so, so strong. She groaned and tried to sit up, saying, "I need to—"

"Nope," the paramedic nearest her said. "I don't want you to push yet." He put a firm hand on her shoulder. "We're almost ready, though."

Mike had to move back, and the paramedics started talking to her, asking her questions, and giving each other instructions—all while the ambulance raced toward the hospital, its siren screaming.

* * *

A couple of hours later, Gerty opened her arms for her perfectly wrapped baby boy. Love filled her from head to toe, and her face contained a smile she couldn't have erased if she tried.

"Here he is," Mike whispered. "All bathed and ready for you, Momma."

She couldn't look away from Thad's beautiful face, his perfect little nose, his wisp of light blonde hair. "He looks like me," she whispered. West had been all Mike, all Hammond, all day long.

Thad seemed to have picked up on some of her genes, and Gerty looked up at her husband. "Thank you for going with him."

She'd delivered the baby in the back of the ambulance as they'd arrived in the emergency bay. Four nurses had met them, and they'd immediately whisked the baby away, into a more temperature-controlled environment.

Gerty had sent Mike with them, while the paramedics had moved her into a room in the emergency department, where she'd delivered the afterbirth, been monitored for an hour, and then moved to the maternity department.

She'd been waiting to meet her son since, and now, she relaxed into Mike's side as he slid into the narrow hospital bed with her, curling his arm around her and Thad and securing them both against his chest.

"You're incredible, Gerty," he said.

"We almost made it," she said.

"Almost." He chuckled. "West is in bed at Opal's, and your daddy dropped off the baby bag. I sent my parents back to the farm too. They'll all come in the morning to meet him."

Gerty nodded and closed her eyes as she relaxed into Mike's safety and warmth. "Next time we have a baby, we're moving into a suite next door to the hospital and not going anywhere for the last three weeks of the pregnancy."

"Yes, we are," Mike whispered. "Yes, we absolutely are."

forty-five

Briar loved summer in Colorado. She loved the way August gave way to September too, and how golden and glorious everything became in October. She'd helped with a robust harvesting season, thanks to the agricultural specialist Tuck and Bobbie Jo had hired, and Bobbie Jo had more goats than ever.

Tuck and Myron worked with eight cowboys now, and Tarr hadn't left the farm once to help out with Stetson's training. Briar had only had to be firm with him about it once, and he'd done the same with Tucker.

The weather had started to turn colder and colder, and all the trees had lost their leaves now. Her roof had been replaced that autumn, and Briar had just had her cord of wood delivered. She was set for another winter here on the farm, and she pushed herself back and forth in the rocking chair on her front porch, her morning coffee steaming into the air.

She'd bundled herself up in her coat and hat, and she smiled as Wiggins did what Wiggins always did—sniffed around for the just-right spot to take care of his business.

She smiled at him and finished her coffee. She couldn't stay outside much longer, because she still wore her pajamas, and the fabric wasn't thick enough to keep her legs warm. "Come on, Wiggy," she called, and he came joyfully bounding back up to the porch.

They went inside together, where she shed her coat and hat while he went to get a loud, lapping drink. Briar put her coffee cup in the sink and went down the hall to brush her teeth. With that job halfway done, Wiggins started barking his fool head off, and she made a half-gargled yell at him to stop it.

The dog didn't stop, and he came running past the bathroom door, practically bellowing out his barks.

She heard the knocking on the front door this time, and she quickly finished brushing her teeth and went to answer it. "Just come in," she called, because it had to be Tarr. No one else ever came here, and they were going out to the Hammond Family Farm for Thanksgiving dinner later that day.

She pulled open the door, her irritation and the choice words she had for her boyfriend dying on her tongue when she saw Tarr there.

Not standing.

But kneeling. Down on both knees, the ring she'd picked out months and months ago shining in the space between them.

He'd told her to expect the proposal before Christmas, and to be honest, Briar had started wondering when it would happen. She didn't need to book a venue, and she had plenty of experience getting amazing outfits made, so a wedding dress wouldn't be too hard either.

She'd stuck to her decision not to reach out to her parents, and she hadn't wanted a long engagement anyway.

"You're not dressed," he said, his smile etched on his face. "We have to leave in a half-hour."

"I know." Briar leaned into the doorway, her own smile stretching across her face.

"I will throw you over my shoulder and carry you to the truck, pajamas or not," he said, echoing his threat from a year ago.

"I'm going to change," she said. "I just finished brushing my teeth."

"Well, you won't be fully dressed until you're wearing my diamond ring on your finger, and we can't go to Thanksgiving dinner until you're ready."

She smiled at him. "Oh, I see how it is."

"Good," he said. "Now, I think we've both waited for this day for long enough. I'm happier than ever, and I want you in that house. It's so lonely and big without you—and Wiggins." He grinned over to the dog who sat at his side, both of them watching Briar with the same hopeful expression on their faces.

"I love you," he said next, and the words reverberated all the way through Briar.

"I love you too," she said back, because she loved saying it, hearing it in her own voice, and *feeling* it.

"My truth for today is that I can make it through this sixty seconds, though I'm pretty nervous," he said. "Because I know you're going to say yes."

"You better just ask then."

"My thorny Briar, will you marry me?" He lifted the diamond ring a little higher, as if she hadn't seen it before now.

She let her feelings fill her over and over again, and then she said, "Yes, my dark cowboy. I'll marry you."

Briar held out her hand, and it stayed perfectly steady as he slid that wonderful symbol of love onto her finger. He kissed the knuckle above it and then the one below, deftly turning her wrist over and kissing her there too.

Tarr sure knew how to send electricity through her whole system, and she waited while he got to his feet and took her face in his hands. "I love you, honey."

Briar looked him straight in those dark eyes she loved and repeated her daily truth to herself.

I am lovable, because Tarr loves me.

And with the utmost confidence, she said, "I love you too, Tarr."

* * *

I absolutely love the faithful, healing journey Briar needed to take to be with a cowboy like Tarr, and I adore that he loved her so much that he could give her the time she needed to do it! If you are too, **please leave a review for His Eleventh Hour by scanning this code on your phone.**

You can read the first two chapters **HIS TWELFTH BLESSING** now! Just keep turning pages.

sneak peek! his twelfth blessing, chapter one:

Deacon Hammond pressed his palms into the soft dough, feeling that he'd gotten it just right. Working the honey whole-wheat dough with steady, rhythmic motion helped quiet the restless energy thrumming through his chest.

After all, he had interviews today, and Deacon couldn't think of anything he disliked more about running his family's farm. He really just wanted the wide open sky, and the good, earthy scent of cattle, and hay, and leather.

He could for-sure leave interacting with cowboys and cowgirls at the door. Gloria Whettstein and Deac's sister-in-law, Molly, still ran Pony Power, and they did all the hiring of counselors and horseback riding instructors.

But Deacon needed people to care for those horses. Feed them, water them, exercise them, clean their stalls. That all fell to him. Plus, he had hundreds of acres of alfalfa to deal with every year, and the fences that protected the fields, and the structures they needed to store that hay.

Oh, and he couldn't forget about the systems they needed to plant, water, and harvest the alfalfa. Oh, and the equipment and vehicles necessary to do all of the above too.

Yes, sometimes Deacon just needed to disappear with some bread dough for a while. And bonus, he got to eat freshly baked bread whenever he wanted it. Molly had given him the recipe and taught him how to knead until the dough "felt" a certain way.

It turned then, and Deacon scooped it up, made a neat ball by pulling the edges down and under, and slid it into the already-oiled bowl. He picked up the white tea towel with a green tractor embroidered on it—something his aunt Annie had sent him for Christmas a few months ago—and lay it over the top of the dough.

"Ninety minutes for you," he said, reaching for his phone. When he realized he was still a bit floury and wheaty, he dodged over to the kitchen sink to wash up. Then he set a timer on his phone, checked the clock, and started for the hat rack beside the front door.

He positioned his black cowboy hat on his head as he stepped outside. The morning air filled his lungs easily, though it still had a late-spring bite to it. Deacon loved it with everything inside him, and a smile settled on his face for the first time in days.

No, he had not been in love with Sariah Mitchem.

Leaving thoughts of their nearly three-month relationship right there on the doormat, Deacon strode toward the steps and down them. The generational house had a patch of lawn in front of it, but no sidewalk and no parking area. He parked around the back of the main farmhouse, and he could reach the dirt road that ran in front of his place in about six strides if he really stretched his legs.

Sometimes, he parked an ATV there while he came inside for lunch, and he could always tie up his horse in the shade when he came home too.

Just because he hadn't been in love with Sariah didn't mean their break-up didn't sting. But she'd be graduating from college in just another week or so, and she'd gotten a job in Tempe.

Arizona.

Not Colorado, and not the greater Denver area.

Deacon *owned* this farm, and he had no desire to ever leave it.

"So you'll just find someone else to take to the wedding," he muttered to himself. He'd given up on dating for a while there, but spring had a way of renewing a man's courage. He'd met Sarah at the Ivory Peaks Harvest Festival last year, and they'd danced back and forth for a few weeks before he'd finally asked her out in the middle of November.

So maybe they'd dated for a little over four months, not three.

"Hey, now you know you can go out with someone more than once." That sentence didn't exactly soothe Deacon, and his dark mood about doing interviews when the spring sunshine shone so gloriously returned.

Besides, he'd already talked to most of them over the phone. He liked to look through their applications by himself, usually at night, alone in the generational house when the farm sat still and silent.

Then, he'd line them up and pick out the ones he felt the best about. He called those people—old-fashioned, pick-up-the-phone-and-dial called them.

Deacon could text, and his generation definitely lived on their devices. He wasn't that different from other twenty-eight-year-olds, but he certainly didn't live a fast life. He didn't even want to.

No, Deacon had been born in Ivory Peaks, and the dirt here on the farm ran in his blood. Soon, he'd have his own house here too, and Deacon sighed thinking about the chore that build had become.

He'd had to fire the first contractor, though it wasn't really his fault. They'd gotten the basement dug out and the foundation poured, and then his wife had been diagnosed with cancer.

Paul had disappeared completely, and when Deacon's patience finally gave in, he'd moved on to hiring someone else. In the meantime, the foundation had cracked, and the new contractor actually thought it would be more beneficial to take it out, reinforce the dig, and re-pour the cement.

So they'd done that. Unfortunately, that hadn't happened before harvest season, and then winter had set in, and the next thing Deacon knew, it was the New Year, and his house still stood with only a skeleton wrapped in plastic.

It didn't matter anyway, he thought as he kept walking between two pastures. His parents' house in Coral Canyon hadn't sold that summer, and they'd taken it off the market for the wintertime. They'd come to Ivory Peaks and stayed out at Jane's with her, only just returning to Wyoming a couple of weeks ago to re-list the house.

They'd probably pack up as much as they could and bring it back to Coral Canyon with them when Jane had her second baby. She was due at the end of June, only a couple of months from now, and a sting of jealousy moved through Deacon.

"Life moves on," he muttered to himself. "Even when you feel like you're standing still."

He glanced left when he heard a vehicle crunching over gravel, and he found Molly's minivan kicking up dust behind it as she left to take her kids to school. She was coming up on two years since her concussion, and she'd healed completely now.

Deacon twisted, expecting to see Hunter—his oldest brother—standing on the porch. He didn't disappoint, and as Deacon watched, Hunt lifted his coffee mug to his lips and took a sip.

After another deep breath, the peace and comfort and quiet Deacon craved settled right into his soul. It pushed out the disappointment of still being single, of trying to find someone to be with for over two years now.

The mountains and country air had a way of making his nearly year-long construction project okay. In fact, he had a meeting with the HVAC subcontractor tomorrow morning, and Deacon would be in his new house probably about the time Jane brought home her baby girl.

"If there are no more delays and backorders," he grumbled to himself. Who could've predicted that building supplies would be so hard to get?

It wasn't the building supplies, though, and Deacon knew it. It was the custom cabinetry he wanted. The exact color of paint for the walls. The gorgeous stone he wanted for the front façade —that had taken forever to arrive, and then he'd had to hire a specialist to cut it.

So perhaps he'd been a little particular about the house. It was going to be his for a long time, and Deacon felt like he'd earned the right to be a little bit fussy about this one thing.

Now, with summer on the farm on the horizon, Deacon almost felt invincible.

He could make it through these interviews, no problem. He only scheduled an applicant for an interview if they could handle being cold-called out of nowhere and asked some questions.

With those thoughts grounding him further, Deacon finished the walk to the barn and entered through the back doors. He had an office here, and he used the long dining room table in the generational house as a back-up. Once he moved into his new place, he'd have a dedicated office space at home too.

His daddy and Matt, and now Mission, had all run this farm with precision and perfection, but Deacon was still struggling to find systems and methods that worked for him.

For his vision of what the Hammond Family Farm could become.

He sighed as he sat down, the air still escaping his lungs as he pulled a stack of folders toward him.

First up, Chapelle McRae, a soil scientist who claimed to have everything he needed to get a higher yield of alfalfa, a better field rotation schedule, and be able to take the farm into the future.

Inspired by the agriculturist Tuck and Bobbie Jo had hired last year, Deacon dreamed of upgraded irrigation systems and equipment, and he knew he could be doing a better job with the agricultural and land management. But he'd never gone to college, and he certainly didn't know much about soil composition, pH levels, or any of the other things Chapelle had asked him about during their miniature phone interview.

In fact, he felt like he'd failed that interview, which had been reversed on him, and he frowned at the woman's file as he flipped it open.

No picture that he could find, though she'd worked for a couple of small family farms recently. That had happened last summer, after she'd quit her job in Coral Canyon, of all places.

Deacon looked up and out the window to his right. The

morning sun glinted off the peaks of the Rocky Mountains in the distance, reminding him of his summers in Coral Canyon.

Maybe he should go there again this summer, the way he had every year growing up. Just leave the farm in the capable hands of Mission, and Molly and Hunter, and Cosette and Gloria. They did just fine without him, and perhaps a few months away would reset the things inside Deacon that needed to be reset.

If only he knew what those things were.

But his house could be finished without him, and he could return refreshed and ready to move in. Ready to move on.

To what, he didn't know. But something.

His phone buzzed, and Deacon's eyes dropped to it. His father had texted: *Good luck with the interviews today.*

Momma says to get back out there and ask someone to Tarr's wedding. It's been a few weeks since Sariah broke up with you, she says, and we both know the right woman will want the same things you want—the farm, the mountains, the scent of honey and butter and freshly cut grass.

His third text was only emojis, all faces, ranging from smiling to laughing, with the last one the one that blew a heart to the recipient.

Fine, it made Deacon smile as he let the love his parents had for him course through him. They alone knew how lonely he was, and how he'd been dating for years now, trying to find someone who did want the same things he wanted, even if was something as simple as the smell of freshly mown grass.

It's hay, Daddy, Deacon sent back, just because he could. *I like the scent of freshly cut hay.*

Fine, the scent of freshly cut hay.

A pause, and then: *Do you have anyone in mind for who you could ask?*

Deacon sighed and looked up. "No," he said, the short word carrying a hint of bitterness. Sariah had worked at the bank while she finished up school, and Deacon had picked her up there a couple of times. Perhaps someone there, or....

No, he typed out. *I've been out with everyone in Ivory Peaks, and it's hopeless. I'll just sit by you guys at the wedding.*

Tarr and Briar would be married in another three weeks, and Deacon really did want to take a date.

Maybe you could just hire someone....

That thought lingered in the back of his mind as he refocused his attention on the files. After Chapelle, he was expecting to meet with a man named Winston Roundy, who should be an amazing addition to their stable crew. The man came from Texas, and he'd worked with animals on the rodeo circuit for years. He claimed to want a slower pace of life, and he'd fallen in love with the same mountains that Deacon could admire any time he wanted.

"Deacon."

He looked up at the sound of his name and found the long-time manager of the farm, Cosette Whettstein, standing in his doorway. "Your first appointment is here." She gave him a smile and held up yet another folder.

Oh, how Deacon hated paperwork and folders.

"I put her in the conference room with all the soil samples, and I've got the field maps you requested right here."

Deacon pushed away from his desk. "Thanks, Cosette. I appreciate you getting everything ready." He took the folder from her but didn't open it as she turned and went into hall.

He followed her as she said, "She said she reviewed the preliminary reports you emailed, and she had a notebook." Cosette glanced over her shoulder, a smile painting across her face. "She said she hoped you were ready to answer some questions."

Deacon's mood worsened, and his step slowed. He really didn't want to be the one in the pressure cooker today. He was the boss, not the one looking for a job.

"Oh, and when you're finished with her, Mission said he needs you for two seconds before your next interview." Cosette gestured toward the closed conference room door, as if Deacon didn't know where it stood.

"Two seconds, sure," Deacon said, knowing that would put him behind after only the first interview. If he didn't cram them all into a single morning, it wouldn't be that big of a deal.

Apparently, he liked to torture himself, because he'd scheduled the hardest interview first and only had many more to go before lunch.

At least you'll be able to slip away and check on your bread, he thought, and then he reached for the doorknob. "Thanks, Cosette. Hold everything else unless someone's bleeding or something's on fire, okay?"

He gave her a wry smile, and she laughed lightly as he entered the conference room. He mentally recited what he could remember about Chapelle McRae as he stepped inside: Soil and Water Conservation Engineer, with specializations in sustainable agriculture and crop optimization. She'd worked on projects throughout the Mountain West, including one large-scale operation that had seen significant yield improvements after implementing her recommendations. She'd been employed by the city of Coral Canyon until—

Deacon took in the gorgeous blonde woman standing in his conference room, her head bent over the soil samples he'd had collected specifically at her request.

She reached up and tucked her wavy hair behind her ear,

and she clearly hadn't heard him, because she muttered something to herself, scratched something in her notebook, and moved down to the next sample.

Chapelle McRae, he thought. *Soil and Water Conservation Engineer, farm consultant, and Chinese-food thief.*

A smile touched his mouth, barely lifting the corners of it.

Church seat-stealer, he added to her résumé.

For the woman standing in his conference room and whom he was about to hire was none other than that woman he'd encountered while visiting his parents over a year ago, hundreds of miles north of here.

His thoughts ran rampant, from if he was dressed nicely enough for this meeting, to whether or not he'd brushed his teeth that morning before diving into bread-making.

Why does this matter? he screamed at himself as his world continued to tilt sideways.

He pulled in a breath at the raging attraction flowing through him, and Chapelle looked up. Her distinctive blue-green eyes met his dark ones, and it only took her a single beat of time to recognize him.

Something like a scoff came out of her mouth, and she settled her weight onto her back leg.

Deacon's mind shouted at him that *he* was the boss, *he* would be leading this interview, and *he* would be asking the questions here.

Too bad the only one he could think of was whether or not she still had that boyfriend.

sneak peek! his twelfth blessing, chapter two:

Chapelle McRae had been prepared for a lot of things when she walked into the Hammond Family Farm conference room that morning. She'd been prepared to discuss soil pH levels, irrigation efficiency, and crop rotation strategies. She'd been prepared to explain why her sustainable agriculture methods could increase alfalfa yields by twenty to thirty percent. She'd even been prepared to justify her consulting fees, which weren't exactly cheap.

What she hadn't been prepared for was the dark-haired, dark-eyed cowboy from Coral Canyon standing in the doorway, looking just as stunned as she felt.

Of course, she thought, her grip tightening on her pen. *Of all the farms in Colorado, I had to apply to work for the grumpy cowboy who thinks I steal everything.*

Deacon Hammond.

At least she knew the man's name now—and it wasn't Deke.

"I just have to know," she said, her mind working quickly to catch up to the situation. "Which dish was yours from The Darling Dragon?"

He blinked, his long, dark eyelashes sending a thrill through Chapelle she didn't know what to do with. If she had her way, this man would be her boss.

Not your boyfriend.

"The hot honey chicken," he said.

Chapelle nodded. "Of course."

That seemed to crack the ice between them, and Deacon glowered at her. "Let me guess—yours was the vegetable tempura."

She raised her chin, though he'd guessed right.

He actually chuckled as he entered the room fully and toed the door closed behind him with the tip of one very expensive cowboy boot. He wore jeans, a brown belt with a big buckle, and a blue tee tucked into all of the above.

His black cowboy hat shone in the overhead lights, matching the glint on those matching boots.

She watched him warily as he walked down the other side of the table, cursing herself for being so focused on the farm's impressive acreage and their willingness to invest in modernization to dig deeper into who exactly she'd be working with.

And now here he stood, filling the whole room with his broad shoulders and that same brooding expression he'd worn at church over a year ago. He'd been displeased with her then, and oh, he didn't look much happier about her presence in his space now.

His dark hair was shorter than she remembered, but those eyes…. A woman never forgot eyes like Deacon Hammond's.

"I suppose you'll have a good recommendation for Sunday services," she said, her voice catching on something in her throat. Probably her complete humiliation.

Something that might have been amusement flickered across his face. "I suppose I could tell you where to go for church," he said. "But I'll tell you the wrong time, so I can get there ahead of you and get my seat."

Chapelle's pulse kicked up a notch, her traitorous mind now imagining what it would be like to attend church with Deacon on purpose.

"Well, let's do this interview." He took a seat at the head of the table and indicated she should sit too.

She yanked out the chair in front of the soil sample she'd been examining when he'd arrived, and the force of it sent her stumbling backward for an extra step. Her face flamed hotly as she managed to step around the chair with the well-greased wheels before she fell down.

Chapelle did semi-collapse into the chair, but she hoped she made it look like she'd meant to do so. After scooting forward and adjusting her notebook and pen, she looked up.

She so hadn't made it look like she meant to be nearly knocked over by an office chair in her haste to do what her almost-boss wanted. Her thoughts scattered as the moment between them lengthened, and Deacon's gaze would not let go of hers.

She wanted to know how old this man was. Was he conducting the interviews at his father's request?

Was that why he was so salty?

No, her mind whispered among the chaos. *His parents live in Coral Canyon.*

Still, he didn't seem very old, and certainly not old enough to be in charge of this entire operation.

"So," he finally said, clearing his throat and dropping his chin. Chapelle did the same, the energy in the room buzzing like a live wire had been attached to an angry hive of bees.

"Soil science," he said. "My brother seems to think that increasing our soil...effectiveness will help the farm produce more hay."

His brother. Of course. Probably an older brother.

"Your soil is your most important asset," she said. Chapelle could talk about the most boring things for hours, and in this case, she needed to so she wouldn't blurt out anything embarrassing or inappropriate about Deacon's...other assets, all of which were far superior to the soil here on the farm.

"I have some good methods of increasing the production on farms just like this," she said while sternly telling herself to remain professional. "And I deliver results. Did you have a chance to contact the farm managers I provided?"

"Just one." His gaze didn't waver, and he didn't look at the folder he'd brought in with him. "A...." He tilted his head, as if trying to bring the name forward. "Denny Case."

Chapelle smiled as relief cascaded through her. "Yes, Mister Case is a nice guy."

"He seemed to like you."

"That's because he won the Giant Pumpkin contest last fall," she said, fondness touching her tone. "His soil was too acidic before that, but I implemented a tailored plan for his garden area."

"And what would a 'tailored plan' look like?"

Chapelle cocked her head too, sure Deacon wouldn't take her plan and somehow implement it. "It was pretty simple in the end," she said. "I did a nice mix of lime to raise the pH, a compost top-dress for organic matter, and a micronutrient bump. Once we nudged his pH toward neutral, everything else started working the way it should."

She shook her head and smiled again. "You should've seen his pumpkins. They were *huge*."

"I'm sure," Deacon said dryly. "I'm not trying to win some small-town gardening contest." His eyes sparkled with mischief, with amusement, with danger. "I have hundreds of head of cattle to feed, and we board and care for over four dozen horses here at the farm. I need to feed them."

"So you want more alfalfa per acre."

"I want more alfalfa per acre," he said. "Where would you start?"

"Baseline data," she said. "Alfalfa likes a slightly alkaline to neutral soil—think pH six-point-eight to seven-point-two. At that range, your rhizobia bacteria fix nitrogen efficiently, and your phosphorus isn't locked up."

"I'm sure my phosphorus is caged right now."

Chapelle noted the slightly sarcastic tone, and she actually appreciated it. "I'll pull a composite soil sample from each management zone, not just one bucket from the headland." She looked at the sample he'd provided, and she'd already taken a couple of notes on it.

"We'll test pH, organic matter, cation exchange capacity, base saturation—how much calcium, magnesium, potassium you've actually got on the exchange sites—plus phosphorus, sulfur, and boron."

"Boron?" He lifted an eyebrow. "That's a made-up word."

Chapelle actually laughed, because Deacon had a really nice timbre to his voice. "Boron is a chemical, Mister Hammond. It's small but mighty for alfalfa. Too little and you get poor flowering and stunted growth. Too much and you burn the stand. I can help you be precise."

She took a deep breath. "I'll also run an electrical conductivity map so we can see texture and salinity differences across the field, and I'll check compaction with a penetrometer. If the roots can't get down, yield stops at the hardpan."

Deacon folded his arms, the corner of his mouth quirking. "You've used a lot of big words."

"You're guessing every year when you plant your crops." She raised her eyebrows, clearly challenging him.

"Life is always a little bit of guesswork, isn't it?"

"Not if you want more alfalfa per acre." She flipped open her notebook and looked at her handwriting, which detailed how his soil was too light. "Once we have numbers, we build your fertility plan. Alfalfa doesn't need added nitrogen after establishment if the rhizobia are happy, but it *is* a potassium hog. We'll likely be feeding K and a bit of sulfur each cutting. If pH is low, we'll lime—calcitic or dolomitic, depending on your calcium-to-magnesium ratio. If salinity shows up, we'll talk gypsum and leaching."

Deacon considered her for a moment, then folded his arms. "I want to get out of the 'open the headgate and pray' business when it comes to irrigation."

"Ah, now you're talking my love language." Chapelle could throw his cuteness back at him, though she didn't believe for a moment that this cowboy knew how to flirt with her.

She exhaled heavily when Deacon remained stone-faced. "I'll modernize scheduling and delivery. We'll install a couple of soil-moisture probes—capacitance sensors at different depths —so you're irrigating to crop need instead of habit...or guesswork. I'll set you up with an evapo-transpiration feed for alfalfa, so you're replacing what the crop actually used. If you're staying with the pivot, we can add low-energy precision applicators and variable-rate nozzles, so the sandy spots get a little more, the heavy spots a little less. If you're in gated pipe, we'll look at surge valves to improve infiltration. Either way, we add flow meters so we know, not guess, how much water your alfalfa actually needs."

Deacon nodded slowly. "Sounds expensive."

"It's an *investment*," she said. "But the payback shows up in uniform stands, fewer drowned corners, and less wheel ruts. Plus, alfalfa hates wet feet. Short, timely sets beat long soaks every time."

He hooked a thumb toward the hay yard. "What about rotation? A good friend of mine says I push my stands too hard."

"You might be," she said. "I don't really know that, but I can develop a rotation schedule for you, after I've seen what's going on at the ground level."

Literally.

Chapelle smiled internally at her soil joke, though she knew it was a little bit on the lame side.

"Soils can be finicky with different crops," she said. "But I have a checklist: Test, amend, irrigate to demand, feed what the plant actually removes, rotate on purpose. We'll map the farm into zones, write a simple playbook for each one, and you won't be guessing when to cut, water, or replant."

Chapelle sat back, confident that she'd just landed the job. "I'll need a couple of weeks to go over everything here—your well water, take all the samples, get them tested, go over your field maps—and you can't do anything in that time. You can't plant, you can't fertilize. Then, I'll hand you a plan with numbers attached."

Deacon exhaled and got to his feet. He considered her for a moment, then extended his hand toward her. "And your rate is...? Are we talking hourly or per-acre? I'll fund everything you need to implement, of course. Lime and...boron, and all that."

"For your acreage, it's going to be a lot, Mister Hammond. You have what? Three hundred and thirty acres?"

"It's not all alfalfa," he said. "We usually just do about one-fifty planted, and we let the cattle pasture the other fields."

"How many head do you have?"

"Only about one-twenty," he said. "Cow-calf pairs. We're not at capacity."

"But you've got the horses."

"Yes," he said. "And I don't love cattle ranching. I just like farming."

Chapelle smiled at him, because he possessed a lot of charm despite his grouchy demeanor and refusal to smile. "I think for your current alfalfa block, I'd quote a flat twenty thousand for my plan, pass you the lab fees at cost, and then I'm going to need thirty-five hundred per month to be here for tuning, check-ins, and consultations."

She got to her feet and extended her hand this time. "If you prefer hourly, I'm two hundred per hour for all-season scouting, and it'll be thirty per acre with full nutrient and water management."

Darkness returned to Deacon's expression, and he ducked his head. The brim of his cowboy hat hid the top half of his face, but she heard the disgruntled way he blew out his breath.

"I want to retain you," he said.

"Sounds scandalous." Chapelle pulled her hand back, since Deacon wasn't going to shake it anyway.

He lifted his eyes and glared at her. "I'll pay for the plan, the lab costs, your thirty-five hundred per month. I can offer you a cabin here at the farm too, and all you have to do is pay your utilities and food. Gas for your car, you know, to get to church and back on Sundays."

His mouth twitched, almost curving into a smile. "And I'll try not to hover while you deal with the dirt."

"Hover all you want," she said. "It's your dirt, and you're paying me to consult. Who am I going to consult with if not you?" Her eyebrows went up. "The owner, perhaps?"

"I am the owner, ma'am." He tucked the folder under his arm. "I'll ask Cosette to write up your contract, and she'll have it ready for you to sign in the morning." He hooked his thumb toward the exit. "Do you want me to show you the accommodations? I'm hiring a bunch of new people, so you'll likely have a cabin-mate, but just one."

Based on the samples he'd already run and the reports he'd sent her, his soil pH was inconsistent across his fields, and his fields weren't retaining water or nutrients.

But oh, this cowboy had a lot of other things going for him, from the way those long eyelashes blinked slowly to the way his dark eyes drank her up as if she was the only water he'd seen in days to the power in the muscles in his chest and shoulders.

Deacon moved to stand beside her, close enough that she caught a hint of his cologne—something woodsy and clean that made her think of mountain air and leather—with just a hint of...yeast?

"Not to rush you," he said. "But I have to show you the cabins now, because then I have to get my bread in the oven and back over here for yet another interview." He spoke calmly, almost too slow, and Chapelle liked it. "If you need time to think about the job, no problem. Just let me know, and I won't put Cosette on a rush to get your contract done."

Chapelle gazed up at him, and while Colorado wasn't that much warmer than Wyoming, it was moving into summer, and it would be considerably less windy. Heck, anywhere was less windy than Wyoming.

She could work here all summer and into the fall, and she wouldn't have to have another job lined up for a few months. "I want the job," she said. "I like a good challenge."

Deacon, to her surprise, chuckled. "I'm sure you do, Miss McRae, and I hope my farm can give it to you." He tipped his hat at her. "I'll talk to Cosette, but we really do need to look at the cabins, so she'll know if she needs to put it in the contract."

Chapelle didn't have housing lined up, as it was one of the questions she currently carried in her notebook. He'd answered part of it already—the housing was included in the contract, sans utilities and food—and as long as the cabin didn't look like it would fall down in the next spring storm, she'd take it.

She'd be living on this farm, presumably mere steps from Mister Deacon Hammond himself. *You need the job, Chapelle*, she warned herself as she followed him out of the conference room.

He led the way further into the barn, then out the back exit. The scent of manure and fresh sunshine filled her nose, and Chapelle couldn't help taking a deep breath of it.

He glanced over to her. "When did you leave Wyoming?"

"Oh, last spring," she said. "I did a job in Idaho, and then one in Southern Utah, and now I'm here."

"You didn't like Coral Canyon?"

Chapelle repressed her sigh, and she searched for an answer that wouldn't reveal her gypsy soul and naturally dissatisfied demeanor. "I decided municipal work wasn't the right fit for me long-term. I prefer the challenge and variety of private consulting."

It was true, on the surface. She simply didn't mention that she'd left Coral Canyon because she'd been suffocating in that job, in that town, in the relationship with Bryson that had been slowly strangling her spirit. She didn't mention the panic attacks that had started when she realized she was only twenty-seven years old and felt like she was already trapped in a life she didn't want.

"And you're comfortable with the physical demands of this job? It's not all lab work and computer modeling. You'll be out in the fields, working with equipment, getting dirty."

Despite everything, she almost smiled. "Mister Hammond, I grew up on a farm in Idaho. I know what hard work and farming looks like, sounds like, smells like, tastes like, and I'm not afraid of it."

He looked over to her for a long moment, and Chapelle couldn't keep him from seeing all the way inside her. She had the very unsettling feeling that she'd answer any other question this man had, and she quickly faced forward lest she trip over her own feet. After all, such a thing had happened before.

They walked down a single-lane dirt road, with cabins dotting another road running perpendicular to this one. A gorgeous farmhouse stood on her right, with another, much smaller, one almost right on top of it.

"I live in the generational house," he said. "Well, I mean, for now. It's—complicated." He drew a breath and seemed to be steadying himself.

"My older brother, his wife, and family live in the farmhouse. Molly owns and operates Pony Power." Deacon nodded to their left. "It's a children's equine therapy unit, and we do horseback riding lessons too. Our kids go to their counseling sessions in those cabins, and we have another community behind the personal farm. That's where your house will be."

She nodded, enjoying the quick tour and the powerful strength in his subdued tone. "Who else are you hiring?"

"We need lots of people for farm clean-up and spring planting," he said with a sigh. "Then, I just lost a full-time cowboy, so I need to replace him, and Molly added two new counselors a couple of days ago." He cleared his throat but his stride remained even. "Listen, this is going to sound stupid, but...do you have a boyfriend?"

"I—" She clamped her lips shut, thoroughly surprised.

"It's just—you had one last time I spoke to you, and—well,

a good friend of mine is getting married in a couple of weeks—three or four, maybe—anyway." He cleared his throat, obviously nervous.

Chapelle calmed and smiled as she faced the ground. Even a dirt road here was kept beautifully.

"I need a date," he blurted out. "To the wedding." A sigh slipped between his lips. "It's just one evening," he said quietly. "Dancing, dinner, celebration. Nothing serious."

Nothing serious.

The words stung for some inexplicable reason. Chapelle had been on a strictly male-free diet, and her habit of moving from place to place, farm to farm, had really helped with that.

No, she wasn't with Bryson anymore and hadn't been for a long time. With every new job she took, and every new place she visited, she learned more about herself. Things she'd fought hard to learn, and she didn't want to compromise the job—or her self-discovery—for a handsome face, gorgeous eyes, and a sexy voice.

Despite everything, she found herself wanting to say yes.

Which was exactly why she needed to say no.

Ohhhh, what's Chapelle going to say? It's just one evening, after all... Find out in **HIS TWELFTH BLESSING**, coming soon! **Preorder by scanning this QR code with your phone.**

His First Love (Book 1): She broke up with him a decade ago. He's back in town after finishing a degree at MIT, ready to start his job at the family company. Can Hunter and Molly find their way through their pasts to build a future together?

His Second Chance (Book 2): They broke up over twenty years ago. She's lost everything when she shows up at the farm in Ivory Peaks where he works. Can Matt and Gloria heal from their pasts to find a future happily-ever-after with each other?

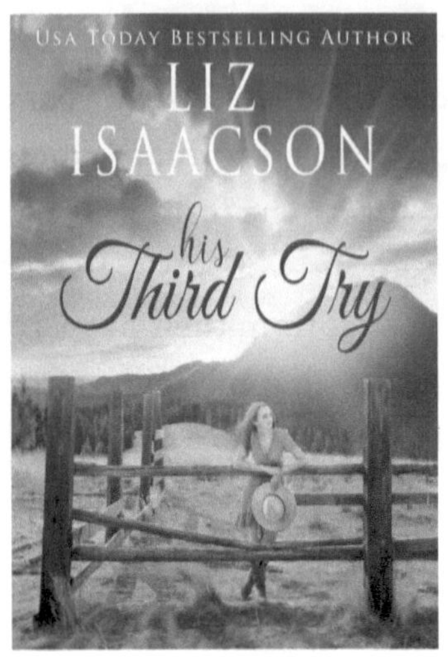

His Third Try (Book 3): He moved to Ivory Peaks with his daughter to start over after a devastating break-up. She's never had a meaningful relationship with a man, especially a cowboy. Can Boone and Cosette help each other heal enough to build a happily-ever-after...and a family?

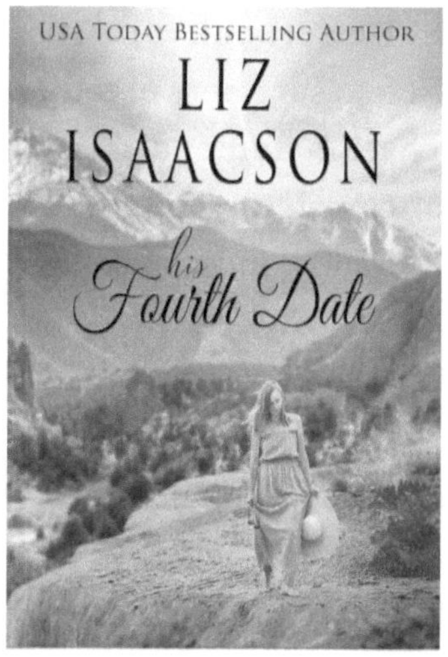

His Fourth Date (Book 4): Their relationship has been nothing but loose goats, a leaking roof, and her complete humiliation after he pays her mortgage so she won't lose her farm. Travis wants to go back in time and start over with Poppy, but he doesn't know how. Can a small town speed-dating event get their second chance off on the right foot?

His Fifth Kiss (Book 5): They once had a few summers together. Now, Michael Hammond is back in town after a devastating injury overseas. He's looking to reset and recover...not to fall in love. But with Gertrude Whettstein also back at the farm, can Gerty and Mike make their second chance romance into a happily-ever-after?

His Sixth Sweetheart (Book 6): She's had a crush on him for decades. He's finally in a place where he feels ready to date the boss's daughter. Can Cord and Jane take their relationship to the next level without getting burned?

His Seventh Stop (Book 7): He's a seasoned cowboy on a delivery mission. She's a resilient hobby farm owner braving the winter storm. Can Keith and Lindsay forge a bond in the heart of a tempest and find love in the calm that follows?

His Eighth Ride (Book 8): Tag has secretly admired Opal from afar. He even went so far as to ask her out, but the timing was all off, and now he's just awkward around his best friend's little sister. Can their unexpected reunion mend the fences between them and finally lead them to the forever love they've been waiting for?

His Ninth Promise (Book 9): At home on the Hammond Family Farm, where gypsy souls and rodeo dreams collide, Tucker's heart has been beating for Bobbie Jo. But with her heart set on a distant love and Tucker searching for something more, their paths seemed destined to cross but never converge. Can he stick it out for another ride if the promise is coming home to Bobbie Jo?

His Tenth Dance (Book 10): Mission has carried the weight of his past for a long time, and letting someone in feels like a risk. But maybe, just maybe, Kristie is worth it. When his granddad tells her about his secret crush, sparks fly between them, walls come down, and love might just get a second chance to take the lead... if Kristie and Mission are willing to take a leap of faith.

His Eleventh Hour (Book 11): Champion bull rider Tarr Olson thought getting injured and losing his rodeo career would be the biggest challenge he'd face. That was before he met his neighbor—the beautiful but ice-cold veterinarian who wants nothing to do with him.

His Twelfth Blessing (Book 12): He's a grumpy cowboy billionaire who lives for the family farm. She's a brilliant agricultural consultant who never stays in one place. Can Deacon and Chapelle find their forever home together?

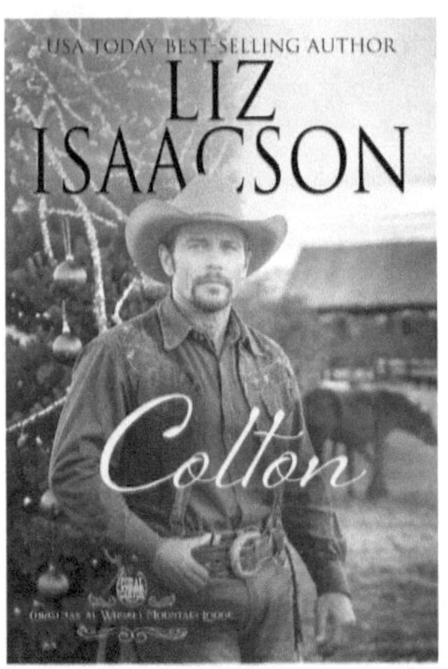

Colton (Book 1): All the maid at Whiskey Mountain Lodge wants for her birthday is a handsome cowboy billionaire. And Colton can make that wish come true—if only he hadn't escaped to Coral Canyon after being left at the altar...

Wes (Book 2): She broke up with him to date another man...who broke her heart. He's a former CEO with nothing to do who can't get her out of his head. Can Wes and Bree find a way toward happily-ever-after at Whiskey Mountain Lodge?

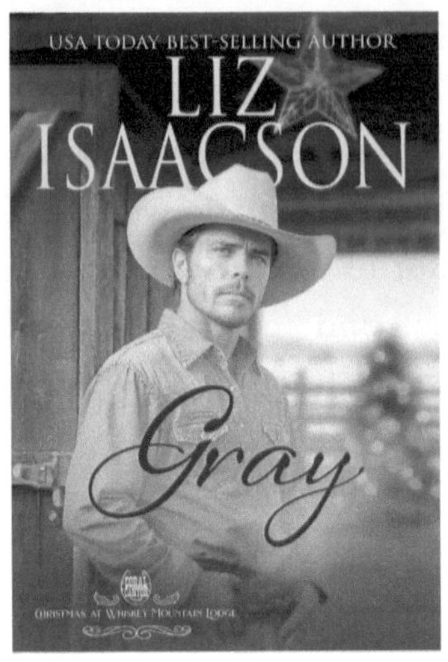

Gray (Book 3): She's best friends with the single dad cowboy's brother and has watched two friends find love with the sexy new cowboys in town. When Gray Hammond comes to Whiskey Mountain Lodge with his son, will Elise finally get her own happily-ever-after with one of the Hammond brothers?

Cy (Book 4): A cowboy billionaire beast, the woman he asks out in front of everyone, and the family traditions that softens his heart and bring Cy and Patsy together.

Ames (Book 5): A cowboy billion-aire who's rough around the edges, the woman he ghosted last Christmas, and their second chance at happily-ever-after.

Graham (Book 1): Graham Whittaker returns to Coral Canyon a few days after Christmas—after the death of his father. He takes over the energy company his dad built from the ground up and buys a high-end lodge to live in—only a mile from the home of his once-best friend, Laney McAllister. They were best friends once, but Laney's always entertained feelings for him, and spending so much time with him while they make Christmas memories puts her heart in danger of getting broken again...

Eli (Book 2): Since the death of his wife a few years ago, Eli Whittaker has been running from one job to another, unable to find somewhere for him and his son to settle. Meg Palmer is Stockton's nanny, and she comes with her boss, Eli, to the lodge, her long-time crush on the man no different in Wyoming than it was on the beach. When she confesses her feelings for him and gets nothing in return, she's crushed, embarrassed, and unsure if she can stay in Coral Canyon for Christmas. Then Eli starts to show some feelings for her too...

Andrew (Book 3): Andrew Whittaker is the public face for the Whittaker Brothers' family energy company, and with his older brother's robot about to be announced, he needs a press secretary to help him get everything ready and tour the state to make the announcements. When he's hit by a protest sign being carried by the company's biggest opponent, Rebecca Collings, he learns with a few clicks that she has the background they need. He offers her the job of press secretary when she thought she was going to be arrested, and not only because the spark between them in so hot Andrew can't see straight.

Can Becca and Andrew work together and keep their relationship a secret? Or will hearts break in this classic romance retelling reminiscent of *Two Weeks Notice*?

Beau (Book 4): Beau Whittaker has watched his brothers find love one by one, but every attempt he's made has ended in disaster. Lily Everett has been in the spotlight since childhood and has half a dozen platinum records with her two sisters. She's taking a break from the brutal music industry and hiding out in Wyoming while her ex-husband continues to cause trouble for her. When she hears of Beau Whittaker and what he offers his clients, she wants to meet him. Beau is instantly attracted to Lily, but he tried a relationship with his last client that left a scar that still hasn't healed...

Can Lily use the spirit of Christmas to discover what matters most? Will Beau open his heart to the possibility of love with someone so different from him?

Todd (Book 5): Todd Christopherson has just retired from the professional rodeo circuit and returned to his hometown of Coral Canyon. Problem is, he's got no family there anymore, no land, and no job. Not that he needs a job--he's got plenty of money from his illustrious career riding bulls.

Then Todd gets thrown during a routine horseback ride up the canyon, and his only support as he recovers physically is the beautiful Violet Everett. She's no nurse, but she does the best she can for the handsome cowboy. **Will she lose her heart to the billionaire bull rider? Can Todd trust that God led him to Coral Canyon...and Vi?**

Liam (Book 6): Rose Everett isn't sure what to do with her life now that her country music career is on hold. After all, with both of her sisters in Coral Canyon, and one about to have a baby, they're not making albums anymore.

Liam Murphy has been working for Doctors Without Borders, but he's back in the US now, and looking to start a new clinic in Coral Canyon, where he spent his summers.

When Rose wins a date with Liam in a bachelor auction, their relationship blooms and grows quickly. **Can Liam and Rose find a solution to their problems that doesn't involve one of them leaving Coral Canyon with a broken heart?**

Finn (Book 7): Her sons want her to be happy, but she's too old to be set up on a blind date...isn't she?

Amanda Whittaker has been looking for a second chance at love since the death of her husband several years ago. Finley Barber is a cowboy in every sense of the word. Born and raised on a racehorse farm in Kentucky, he's since moved to Dog Valley and started his own breeding stable for champion horses. He hasn't dated in years, and everything about Amanda makes him nervous.

Will Amanda take the leap of faith required to be with Finn? Or will he become just another boyfriend who doesn't make the cut?

Zach (Book 8): When Celia Abbott-Armstrong runs into a gorgeous cowboy at her best friend's wedding, she decides she's ready to start dating again.

But the cowboy is Zach Zuckerman, and the Zuckermans and Abbotts have been at war for generations.

Can Zach and Celia find a way to reconcile their family's differences so they can have a future together?

Tex (Book 1): He's back in town after a successful country music career. She owns a bordering farm to the family land he wants to buy...and she outbids him at the auction. Can Tex and Abigail rekindle their old flame, or will the issue of land ownership come between them?

Otis (Book 2): He's finished with his last album and looking for a soft place to fall after a devastating break-up. She runs the small town bookshop in Coral Canyon and needs a new boyfriend to get her old one out of her life for good. Can Georgia convince Otis to take another shot at real love when their first kiss was fake?

Morris (Book 3): Morris Young is just settling into his new life as the manager of Country Quad when he attends a wedding. He sees his ex-wife there—apparently Leighann is back in Coral Canyon—along with a little boy who can't be more or less than five years old... Could he be Morris's? And why is his heart hoping for that, and for a reconciliation with the woman who left him because he traveled too much?

Trace (Book 4): He's been accused of only dating celebrities. She's a simple line dance instructor in small town Coral Canyon, with a soft spot for kids...and cowboys. Trace could use some dance lessons to go along with his love lessons... Can he and Everly fall in love with the beat, or will she dance her way right out of his arms?

Blaze (Book 5): He's dark as night, a single dad, and a retired bull riding champion. With all his money, his rugged good looks, and his ability to say all the right things, Faith has no chance against Blaze Young's charms. But she's his complete opposite, and she just doesn't see how they can be together...

...so she ends things with him.

Gabe (Book 6): He's a father's rights advocate lawyer with a sweet little girl. She's fighting for her own daughter. Can Gabe and Hilde find happily-ever-after when they're at such odds with one another?

Jem (Book 7): He's still healing from his vices, and Jem has dedicated everything he has to his two kids. At least he's not mourning his divorce anymore, and in fact, he might be ready to move on. She's his former best friend, and once he breaks his wrist, his nurse. Can Sunny somehow rope this cowboy's heart?

Luke (Book 8): He swore off women when his ex told him he might not be their daughter's father. But a paternity test confirmed he is, and Luke Young has dedicated his life to his little girl and his brothers' band. There hasn't been time for a girlfriend anyway. He's tried here and there, and the women in small-town Coral Canyon are certainly interested in him.

But he's been thinking about his massage therapist for a while now. Can he ask Sterling out when all they've ever been is professional? Oh, and there's the fact that she's seen practically every inch of his body... Awkward, right?

Bryce (Book 9): Bryce Young has been broken and drifting for years. After giving up his son for adoption, he left Coral Canyon and hasn't returned...until now.

Harry (Book 10): He's a country music star who doesn't live in town. She's a Missing Persons Investigator with strong ties to her community... and she's not so sure about Harry's T-shirts... But Belle knows her heart sings whenever she sees Harry - if only that were more often.

Joey (Book 11): He's a renowned celebrity assistant, now taking over as manager for Country Quad, the legendary band of Young Brothers. She's a young cowgirl trying to find her place in life and her family. Can Joey take a leap of faith and land safely in Adam's arms? Or will small town gossip and expectations crush them both?

Boston (Book 12): He's a country music star who doesn't live in town. She's a Missing Persons Investigator with strong ties to her community... and she's not so sure about Harry's T-shirts... But Belle knows her heart sings whenever she sees Harry - if only that were more often.

about liz

Liz Isaacson writes inspirational romance, usually set in Texas, or Wyoming, or anywhere else horses and cowboys exist. She lives in Utah, where she writes full-time, takes her two dogs to the park everyday, and eats a lot of veggies while writing. Find her on her website, along with all of her pen names, at feelgood fictionbooks.com or authorelanajohnson.com.